Born and brought up in Islington, London, Susan Oudot worked in publishing for eleven years before becoming a literary agent. From there she was tempted into the world of journalism, where she worked for various newspapers and magazines, before turning freelance. *Real Women,* her first novel, was made into a highly successful BBC series. The sequel *All That I Am* is currently in production. She lives in North London with her husband and four daughters and is at work on her next novel.

Also by Susan Oudot

Virtual Love
All That I Am

Real Women

SUSAN OUDOT

POCKET
BOOKS

LONDON · SYDNEY · NEW YORK · TOKYO · SINGAPORE · TORONTO

First published in Great Britain by Simon & Schuster, 1995
This paperback edition first published by Pocket Books, 1996
An imprint of Simon & Schuster UK Ltd
A Viacom Company

Simon & Schuster UK Ltd
Africa House
64-78 Kingsway
London
WC2B 6AH

Simon & Schuster Australia
Sydney

A CIP catalogue record for this book is available from the British Library.

ISBN 0-671-85471-2

3 5 7 9 10 8 6 4

Printed and bound in Great Britain by Caledonian International Book
Manufacturing, Glasgow

For David
My inspiration
. . . my love

~ *Anna* ~

The car horn sounded again, this time with an urgency that made Anna almost spill the contents of her handbag over the hallway table.

'Keep your bloody knickers on,' she said beneath her breath, checking herself one last time in the full-length mirror.

Beep, beep.

She took a deep breath, then, satisfied that no more could be done, turned and opened the door. *Keys, bag, card, mobile-phone, she thought,* running through the usual checklist in her mind as she went down the front steps to the gate. Behind her, back in the flat, the house phone had started ringing. She turned, then, conscious of Mandy waiting in the car, hurried on, leaving it to the answerphone.

'About time,' Mandy said, leaning out of the driver's window of her white Escort XR3i. 'I said we'd be there by nine, and it's ten-to now.'

Anna raised her eyebrows, surprised. She'd never thought of her friend as the sportscar type; Mandy had always seemed more of a Cortina or Cavalier person.

'They'll be late,' she said as she climbed in to the passenger seat. 'They always are.'

'Maybe,' Mandy said, pulling away abruptly before Anna could get her seat belt fastened. 'But I said we'd be there by nine.'

Anna clicked in the belt then sat back, trying to look calmer than she felt. She'd never felt safe with Mandy's driving. 'Nice car,' she offered. 'Is it new?'

'It's Pete's new toy. He bought it two weeks back. I wanted him to get one of those Shoguns — you know, the ones that look like scaled-down Range Rovers, but he thought this'd be more practical. Practical, my arse. Personally, I reckon he's going through his mid-life crisis prematurely. But then he's always been a bit premature,' and she let out a breathy laugh.

Anna enjoyed the joke at Pete's expense. She had never understood what Mandy had seen in her husband. He was a total slob — the kind you'd cross the MI to avoid. If ever there was a bungalow, it was Pete: nothing up top and, according to Mandy, not a lot down below either!

Ahead the lights turned red. For one brief, awful moment Anna thought they were going to go straight across, then, with a jerk, they pulled up.

'Well?' Mandy asked, pushing her glasses up her nose as she turned to face her, a wide grin suddenly splitting her features.

'Well what?'

'Well? What d'you reckon to all this?'

Anna laughed, confused. 'All what?'

Mandy turned away, studying the lights. 'You know . . . about Susie. She meets this guy, falls in love and

4

. . . well, it's all a bit sudden, ain't it? I was just wondering . . .'

'What?'

'If there was a reason for the rush.'

'Like what? Good luck to her, I say. We're none of us getting any younger . . .'

'Thanks for reminding me!'

'What I mean is, once you get past thirty-five most men you meet are either ugly, married, divorced with problems, or gay. Believe me! If this one's an exception then *I'd* have rushed him up the aisle a bit bloody quick, too!'

'Yeah, I know all that,' Mandy said. 'But that's not what I meant.'

The lights changed and they pulled away, Mandy leaning over the wheel as if steering her way around Brands Hatch. Anna held on tightly to the glove compartment with one hand.

'I wondered if she was up the duff . . .'

'Susie's *pregnant*?' Anna asked uncertainly.

'Well, she could be. She's *very* fertile, as we all know.'

'But you don't *know* that she is?' Anna persisted, wanting confirmation.

'No. But it could be one explanation. I mean, we ain't even met this guy!'

'Maybe. Then again, they could just be head over heels in love. Some people *are* you know,' and the minute the words left her lips she regretted them, despising herself for allowing Mandy to bring out the bitch in her.

But Mandy seemed not to notice. 'I know,' she said, a broad smile on her face. 'And I do like a good wedding, don't you? Great excuse to wear a hat and have a piss-up!'

Anna blew out a long breath, wondering, not for the first time, what her work colleagues would have made of her friends. Most of the journalists she worked with were from comfortable middle-class backgrounds, their insight into the working-class psyche gleaned from episodes of *EastEnders* and *Coronation Street*. She had come a long way since they'd been schoolgirls together.

God, we are getting old, she thought. *Time's running out.* She shivered, then looked back at Mandy, realising she had said something to her.

'Pardon?'

'I was talking about presents,' Mandy said patiently, as if talking to a child. 'I just wondered what you'd bought her. Pete was all for off-loading the awful vase his mum bought us last Christmas. You know what he's like – he's so tight it's a wonder his arse don't squeak! But I said no. After all, she is one of my oldest friends. Twenty-six years we've known each other. Twenty-six years! It's bloody amazing when you come to think of it.'

Anna groaned softly. Inside, she barely felt twenty-eight, let alone thirty-eight; in fact, if the truth be told she felt much the same as she had when she was eighteen – just as unsure of herself, just as insecure . . . just as *young*. Except that back then she had felt hopeful, optimistic; life was different now.

As Mandy reminisced, Anna could picture the five friends – her, Mandy, Susie, Janet and Karen – as old ladies, their zimmer-frames parked in the corner of the restaurant while they sipped brandy and coke and talked of their operations. It was a ghastly thought.

6

'. . . so in the end I bought her a decanter. John Lewis do some lovely ones these days. Real crystal.'

Christ, Anna thought, *the only use Susie would have for a decanter was if the batteries for her vibrator ran out.*

'It's strange she hasn't married before,' she said, changing the subject. 'I mean, she's had enough men after her.'

'She had more sense,' Mandy said with feeling. 'Besides, half of them were married already. But you know what she always says . . .'

Anna joined in with her as she said it.

'. . . no one misses a slice from a cut loaf!'

The two girls laughed, suddenly – and for the first time that evening – together in the old way.

Mandy glanced at her. 'But what about you? I thought for a while you'd be sending out the invitations yourself. We'd got it planned how we'd all jet over to the States for it!'

Anna looked down. 'We were friends, that's all. When I first went over to edit the magazine I knew nobody except a few freelance writers I'd used when I was working from London. I was a stranger there and he kept me company now and then. That's all there was to it.'

Mandy shrugged. 'If you say so. It's just that I thought . . .'

She broke off abruptly and slammed her foot down on the brake. The car squealed to a halt. Anna felt herself thrown forward, then back again.

'Sorry,' Mandy said. 'I almost overshot. Get me talking and I just forget what I'm doing.'

Anna let her breath out, relieved. 'That's okay,' she said. 'We didn't hit anything.'

Mandy laughed, then, taking off her glasses, reached down and undid her belt. 'Well, if we did, it didn't cry out!'

The street was busy as tourists and Londoners made their way along, enjoying the window displays or looking for an evening's entertainment. The sign over the restaurant doorway was an incongruous mix of palm trees and Manhattan skyscrapers, the two words 'Up West' pulsing orange, green and red in the fake neon sky.

Anna caught her reflection in the glass door as they approached and stopped a moment. With practised ease she scrunched handfuls of her long auburn hair to give it some life, ran slender, manicured fingers down her sides to unwrinkle the body-hugging black dress beneath her tailored black jacket, and rolled her thin lips in on each other to redistribute the glistening red lipstick.

Beside her she saw Mandy's reflection looking at her, her green, cat-like eyes peering out through the fine wisps of her fringe.

By comparison Mandy's image appeared distinctly conservative as she unfastened the buttons on her cream-coloured jacket to reveal the scooped neckline of a black lycra t-shirt.

'Come on, you old tart,' Mandy said affectionately, gently nudging her friend in the ribs. 'You fit?'

Anna nodded, then, taking a deep breath, followed Mandy inside.

Almost immediately she heard shrieks of laughter from the far side of the room, and focusing her gaze saw the smiling faces of her friends, arms waving in the air to attract her attention.

'Can I help you?'

She turned, to find herself staring directly into the eyes of a young waiter; tall, early twenties with that dark, handsome look that suggested he was destined for something much better. *Probably another aspiring actor*, Anna thought cynically.

'It's okay,' she said, feeling the faint stirrings of interest. 'We're with them . . . I'm afraid.' She pointed to the corner table. Four laughing faces beamed across at her, their voices calling out raucously above the general buzz. Anna ignored their pointed looks and gave the young man a friendly smile. 'Thanks anyway . . .'

'It's okay. Enjoy your meal.'

She turned, met Mandy's knowing eyes. 'You've scored there, girl,' she whispered, leaning close.

In answer, Anna dug her elbow into her ribs and began to make her way across the room.

Up West was typical of the kind of place her friends liked to frequent. There was a large, black-lacquered bar with strips of green and red neon running around its rim and a list of cocktails with outrageously sexual names prominently displayed. The walls were glass with a stylised Manhattan skyline etched in black, potted plants – tiny palms, their long leaves brown-edged and fraying – scattered at intervals along the walls. Being a Thursday night the place was comfortably full, though far from over-crowded. As she followed Mandy's tall, dark figure, edging between the square tables with their bright pink cloths, she felt a strong sense of déjà vu, as if she'd done this a thousand times, something that the music – too low to disturb the flow of conversation, too bland to disturb the conscious listener – seemed to confirm.

9

'You're early,' she said, embracing first one and then another, making her way round the table until she got to Susie. 'I thought we'd be the first ones here.'

'Nah . . .' Susie answered, beaming up at her, a vision in white, her bust, as ever, prominently displayed. 'Gerry borrowed the van. He gave us all a lift.'

'The van?' Anna stared at her horrified, then leaned closer, sniffing the air around them. 'You mean the vegetable van?'

Susie laughed. 'Nah, silly. The sports club van. You can get a whole rugby team in there.' She paused, put a brightly-painted red fingernail to her lips. 'Now *that's* a thought, eh?'

There was a great roar of laughter from all round. It was reputed that Susie had once slept with ten of her then boyfriend's football team — twelve if you counted both substitutes. It would have been all thirteen, but the goalie had been gay. Whether it was true or not — and she suspected, like many of the stories about Susie, it was somewhere in-between — it always came to mind whenever she heard those statistics about how many men were gay. One in four, some said. One in eight, others claimed. But Susie *knew*: it was one in thirteen. Anna giggled, partly ashamed of herself. In her first two months in New York she had met many unattached males and they *all* seemed to be gay when it came down to it.

She sat down next to Karen, Mandy falling in beside her, and reached across the table for an empty glass.

'Can I fill that for you?'

She turned, looking up. It was him again. All round the table the girls were watching her, momentarily quiet, waiting to see what she'd say, how she'd react.

'Yes . . . please,' she said, smiling back at him, brazening it out; enjoying the way he leaned across her to take the bottle, noting for the first time the cologne he wore.

'Thanks,' she said, taking the glass and lifting it to him in a toast. He nodded and turned away, as if he had merely been doing his job, but from around the table came an 'oooh' of encouragement.

'You've struck lucky there,' Janet said, leaning across the table towards her. 'Play your cards right and you could be washing the dishes with him later on.'

'A lot later if you're *really* lucky!'

'Well,' Anna said with a sigh, ignoring their comments and resting her elbows on the table. 'How is everybody? You're looking terrific, Susie, love obviously suits you.'

Susie beamed across the table at her. 'Yeah, I'm really happy,' she said. 'He's good for me. Takes care of me, which is a nice change.'

'It certainly is,' said Lyndsay. Susie's sister was three years her senior and had always been the more sensible of the two, her advocacy of unadventurous conformity irritating the life out of the ever-adventurous Susie. Not only that, but Lyndsay looked much older too, her short, sensible crop perfectly befitting her station as wife and mother of two.

Susie threw her sister a glance that said 'Not tonight. Don't rattle me tonight.'

'What about you?' she said quickly. 'You're looking great, Anna. Your hair looks brilliant. Makes you look ten years younger.'

'Thank God for that,' laughed Anna. 'Actually, I'm going grey.'

'Go on. I can't see any,' said Susie, peering across at her, her own blonde locks sweeping the table as she leaned forward.

'That's because I've put a rinse on it. I couldn't leave it — there's loads of it.'

'Huh,' scoffed Janet, running a hand through her salt and pepper bob. 'You wait till your fanny hair turns grey as well . . .'

The girls shrieked with laughter.

'You're joking,' said Mandy.

'I'm not. Completely grey.'

'Why don't you put some colour on it?'

'Oh yeah, I can just see myself turning up at the salon and asking for a cut, a blow dry and a fanny rinse!'

Again there were howls of laughter. Anna listened to the conversation with a mixture of fascination and embarrassment. In many ways she envied her friends' easy openness; in another she cringed at their bluntness, their loud coarseness.

'Who are you talking about?' she asked, missing the details of the latest topic.

'Linda Gifford . . .'

Anna stared back at Susie blankly.

'You know, year below us at school. Married the bloke who ran the Two Brewers.'

Anna still didn't know who she was talking about, but nodded, marvelling as she did at Susie's recollection of someone she'd barely known more than twenty years ago.

'Apparently she was carrying on with the fella who was building their extension and her old man caught 'em at it.'

'I'm not surprised,' Karen said drily. 'She's been carrying on with half the men in the borough. Brickies, chippies, hod-carriers . . . the whiff of a building site's like an aphrodisiac to her! Not only that, but when they ran that pub they reckoned she pulled as many blokes as her old man pulled pints, and right under his nose.'

'According to Pete his brother had a fling with her,' Mandy added, leaning in towards them all conspiratorially. 'Which only goes to prove that she'll shag anything!'

There were squeals of delight. A glass went over and was ignored.

'In fact,' Mandy added, warming to her theme, 'he told Pete that she'd had so many dicks up her that fucking her was like waving a stick about in the Albert Hall!'

Anna almost choked on her wine as the table erupted with helpless laughter.

'Talking of dicks,' Susie announced, taking her cue, 'have you seen what Lyndsay's bought me?' and rummaging through her bag she produced a video.

'Let's 'ave a look,' said Mandy, reaching across and grabbing hold of the case. 'Dicks,' she read with a beam of delight. 'I like the title. But what the hell is it?'

'It's a film showing lots of different men's what-nots.'

'I thought she might recognise one or two of them,' quipped her sister.

'Bitch! Mind you, I might need to resort to looking at videos of it now I'm becoming a respectable married lady.'

Anna was aware that almost everyone from the surrounding tables was tuned in to their conversation, amused by the ribald humour and repartee. It was always the case when she went out with them, but if the other girls were aware of that interest they didn't show it nor appear to care. It was as if they were alone in the restaurant.

'Come on, tell all,' Mandy said, interested. 'Who is this man who's making an honest woman of you?'

'Yes,' Anna chipped in, 'and where can I get one?'

'He's gorgeous,' said Janet. 'Go on, Susie, show them the photos. She's got some pictures of him. He's just like Kevin Costner in *The Bodyguard*, but with slightly longer hair.'

Susie reached down for her handbag. 'Hang on, I'll show you . . .'

'Where did you meet him?' Anna asked, resting her chin on her hand.

'Through a friend. A bloke called Simon Paxman. Actually, he's gonna be the best man. You don't know him.'

'What does he do, Suse?' Mandy chipped in.

'He's a . . .'

'Don't tell us. Not another grease monkey!'

Susie had always had a soft spot for mechanics.

'He's a business man, actually,' Susie replied in her poshest accent, pushing her nose into the air.

'Oooh, very nice,' Mandy said. 'What kind of business?'

'Buying and selling,' she said, and then laughed. 'I know it makes a change for me to go out with a bloke who actually wears a shirt for work!'

'You met him, Lyndse?' Mandy asked, leaning across the table.

'Yeah,' Susie interrupted, glancing at her sister. 'She

came round for a nose when he came to meet the parents.'

The other girls laughed, imagining the scene.

'What's his family like?' Anna asked, amused by the whole business. It was, after all, so unlike Susie.

Susie rolled her eyes. 'Well, put it this way. I'm probably not their ideal daughter-in-law, but I ain't 'ad to tamper with the gin bottle.'

They all laughed, knowing she was referring to a story involving her cousin, Lucy, who so loathed her in-laws she took revenge on them whenever they visited by spitting in their gin-and-tonics before handing them over with a smile.

Just then the waiter appeared. 'Are you ready to order, ladies?'

Susie stopped searching and put the bag down beside her chair. 'I'll show you later.'

'Well?' the waiter asked, staring at Susie expectantly. 'What would you like?'

There was a moment's hesitation, a mischievous little flicker in Susie's eyes. Her mouth opened . . .

'Married woman,' Karen said hurriedly, anticipating her response.

Susie laughed, then reached across to lay her hand over her friend's. 'Not yet I bloody well ain't!'

Karen leaned across the ruins of her meal and shook her head exaggeratedly as she interrupted Susie's latest anecdote.

'Oh, come on! Tell us the truth! Even *she* wouldn't do *that*, surely?'

'But she *did*, I tell you!' Susie insisted, looking to the

others for support. 'She even made me stand guard at the door!'

'No . . .' Janet was staring at her, mouth open in astonishment.

'I swear by my old dad's testicles!' Susie said, making Anna spit her wine back into the glass. 'It's absolutely true. Maggie told the air steward that she'd lost one of her contact lenses down the pan and as soon as she got him in there, she slammed the door shut, pinned him against the wall and dropped her drawers!'

'No . . .' Janet said again, doing her best impression of a beached mud skipper. 'And he did the business?'

Susie sat back, nodding. 'From the sounds coming out of that cubicle, I reckon they must have been going at it like a pair of steam-pistons. The old girl waiting behind me in the queue couldn't make it out!'

'So what did you say?' Mandy asked, her chin rested on her hand as she beamed across at Susie.

'Well, what *could* I say? "Turbulence", I told her.'

'Tur . . .' There was a roar of laughter.

'Anyway,' Susie said, winking at them all, enjoying, as ever, being the very centre of attention. 'So Maggie emerges afterwards, cool as a cucumber, and says to me, "All yours, my dear". And you know what? She didn't have a single hair out of place. She looked just as immaculate coming out as she'd looked going in.' Susie nodded emphatically. 'Style, I call it. Real style!'

'And the steward?' Anna asked, looking past the flickering candle into her friend's face.

Susie laughed. 'You know what?'

'What?' Karen asked, anxious to know, it seemed, despite her earlier scepticism.

16

'Well . . . two minutes pass, then three, and he still ain't come out and I'm beginning to think that maybe Maggie's done for him . . . you know, what with us being five miles up an' all that, and I'm just starting to get really worried when one of the stewardesses comes up and, squeezing past me, raps sharply on the door.

'"Andy?" she says, "there's a whole row of people out here asking for you." Well, there's a deep groan from inside and then the guy pokes his head round the door. "Are you all right?" she asks and he shakes his head. "What is it?" she asks, beginning to get a bit concerned. Well . . . he can't really say that he's just been jumped on by an eighteen-year-old nymphomaniac, can he? So he invents something about being taken ill.'

Susie reached for her glass, took a large swig, then continued.

'By this stage, two more stewardesses have turned up. They stand there a bit, discussing what to do, then one of them turns to me and asks me very politely if I'm waiting to go in. Well, what can I say? I look her in the eyes and say, "No thanks, love. He's no bleedin' good to me now!"'

Anna sat back slightly, listening to the laughter roll from their table, wondering — not for the first time that night — just how much was true and how much exaggeration. Not that she didn't believe Susie was capable of half the things she claimed to have done — and seen — it was just that she sometimes found it hard to believe that you could have so colourful a sex life and still come out of it a survivor.

She sat back, stretching her legs under the table. The food had been rich and filling and she was feeling just the teeniest bit drunk. Not *drunk*-drunk — not falling-over-and-making-a-damn-fool-of-yourself drunk — but certainly well on the way to being tipsy.

'So what's Maggie doing now?' she asked, feeling languid and relaxed.

'Six kids,' Susie said, then nodded. 'No lie. She met this Irish guy, Kevin, and set up home with him. Last time I saw her she'd bloated out to about twenty stone.'

'Kids do that to you,' Mandy said authoritatively.

'We *are* talking about the same girl,' Anna said, unable to believe what she was hearing. 'Maggie O'Dowell? Five-foot four and slim as a pin?'

'That's the one,' Susie said, checking three bottles before she found one with some wine in. 'Only now she's five-foot four and fat as a pig!'

'Christ!' Karen said, shaking her head. 'Fancy having sex with someone who's twenty stone!'

'Lots to hold on to,' Mandy threw in, giggling.

'Well, her hubbie don't mind,' Susie said. 'He's a bit of a fat git himself. The Go-Lightlies, we call them!'

'Just imagine it,' Karen said, sitting back and shaking her head, and for a moment they all did just that, giggles rippling around the table.

'They say it's the fourth one loses you your figure,' Mandy said. 'After that, well, you ain't got a cat in hell's chance. The muscles are shot, your pelvic floor's up the spout . . .'

'Well, I think they ought to be sterilised,' Karen said, making a face. 'Six kids! It's disgusting!'

'At it like rabbits,' Mandy agreed.

'Two-ton rabbits,' Susie added, at which they all burst

out laughing again. All except Janet, who sat there staring down at her hands.

'I just think they're lucky,' she said quietly. 'I mean, six. It's not fair, is it?'

'Hey,' Karen said, reaching across to squeeze her shoulder. 'Look, I didn't mean . . .'

Janet looked up at her and smiled. 'I know. It's just . . . well, it's just so bloody frustrating at times. You see all these people walking round who've got kids and don't want them − don't give a shit about them − and then there's people like me and Steve . . .'

She fell silent. Around the table the others looked at each other, sharing the guilt, regretting their moment of insensitivity. Janet's childlessness was like a disease that no-one wanted to mention, a taboo behind which they hid. It was Lyndsay who changed the subject.

'Have you heard what happened to that Gary Hammond?'

'What, that big ginger geezer Mandy's brother used to go to school with?'

Lyndsay nodded. 'That's the one. I always thought he was a bit of a creep. Used to help out with the boy scouts. You know the sort. Anyway, seems he got himself a job in a children's home. Local, like. Kids who'd run away from home or been in trouble with the police. Anyway . . . the police get a call one night and they go round there and find the bastard in bed with two of the poor little sods. Boys. Twelve and nine they were.'

'Poor little mites,' Mandy said, her face all sympathy.

'Yeah. Anyway . . . it seems he'd been buggering all the young boys who went through there.'

'He ought to be bloody castrated!' Janet said, her face

hard, uncompromising. 'I'd do it myself, give me half a chance! But you know what'll happen? They'll give the guy some social worker, I bet, some whining arsehole of a woman who'll be full of sympathy and middle-class bullshit. You know, one of those spinster types. And she'll molly-coddle him and try to *understand* him . . .'

'And he'll get eight years and'll serve five after parole,' Lyndsay added bitterly. 'There's no bleedin' justice, is there?'

'Well, I'd lock him in a room with the parents and let them get on with it,' Susie said. 'It'd soon teach cunts like that to keep their hands to themselves.'

'But isn't that the problem?' Anna said, surprised by the anger, the venom with which her friends pursued the subject. 'I mean . . . the fact that the boys' parents didn't care to start with? If they'd cared . . .'

But Susie hadn't heard her. 'I mean, I don't give a toss what people get up to in the privacy of their own homes. Dogs, donkeys, who gives a shit? But kids . . . Nah, there's some things you just don't do.'

'I'd draw the line at donkeys, myself,' Karen said mischievously.

'You don't mind dogs, then?' Susie retorted, raising an eyebrow.

'I've known a few,' Karen said, warming to the game.

'Gettin' personal now, are we?'

Karen laughed, then touched her tongue to her teeth. 'You serious about that? I mean, about what people get up to.'

'Sure!' Susie said lightly. 'You only get one shot at life, so you might as well enjoy yourself while

20

you can. This ain't the rehearsal, girls, this is the show!'

'Better not let your Joe hear you say that,' Mandy said, 'or he'll have you locked up in a chastity belt.'

'I should be so lucky.'

Anna, watching the exchange, smiled inwardly, conscious of how quickly their faces had changed, from laughter to anger and back to laughter; of how superficial and yet how deep these friends of hers were. In the circles she'd come to frequent these past ten years people never behaved like this. They had opinions, sure – there wasn't a single thing they didn't have an *opinion* on – but feelings, deep-rooted convictions, *those* they were sadly lacking in. It was like the people she'd been born among were more real, more *alive*.

She felt them to be an odd collection of women to have remained friends so long; even during their schooldays it had seemed a strange alliance. Anna remembered the day they'd met – none of them more than eleven – on that first, terrifying day at secondary school. One by one their names had been called from the register and they had stood up so that everyone could see who they were. She had eyed each one, peering through the heavy fringe she had habitually hidden behind at the time, each so similar to the last – dressed as they were in the school uniform of dark green gymslip, white blouse and tie – yet at the same time so distinctly themselves.

It was strange the details she remembered. Anna smiled as she recalled Susie introducing herself to the class, her arms folded self-consciously across her chest to try to hide the fact that her dress gaped as it stretched across her developing bust. Only later did she learn that it was a hand-me-down from her older but much slimmer sister. Perhaps it was even that — that small sign of vulnerability — that had attracted her to Susie. Whatever, they had quickly become firm friends.

But Susie wasn't the only one wearing hand-me-downs that day. As Mandy had stood up that first time, Anna had noticed that under her slip she wore a shirt that buttoned up on the wrong side — on the boy's side — and when, later, she bent down to pick up a pen she'd dropped, the shirt tail could be seen hanging down almost to the hem of her dress. The shirt, she'd told Anna years later, had been her cousin, Philip's, and her mum hadn't thought to lop off the bottom. But for Mandy the effect had been traumatic, for in those first few days of fear and insecurity she had been deeply ashamed of appearing different from the rest.

Vulnerability again, Anna thought, recognising a pattern in it after all.

As for Karen, well, they had taken to each other instantly and, having sat beside each other on that first day, they had continued to do so for the next five years, inseparable companions until they reached the more relaxed atmosphere of the sixth form.

Only Janet had been an acquired taste, her tongue on occasions as sharp as a razor. She had been Susie's friend more than hers at first, but then a single incident had warmed Anna to her.

A small, mousy girl in their class had let slip her undying passion for Cliff Richard and had confessed that she couldn't get undressed in her room at night because of all the photographs of Cliff looking down at her. This revelation had made her the butt of numerous cruel jokes and much teasing from a number of girls in the year above. Most of the girl's so-called friends had turned a blind eye, not wanting to be picked upon themselves, but eventually it was Janet who had marched into the bigger girls' classroom and had it out with them face to face, threatening to do unprintable things to them after school if they didn't desist. After that, there had been no more bullying of the girl.

That moment, and many others across the years, had revealed the true qualities of her friends — their courage, their sense of fairness, their basic decency, and above all their sense of fun.

Anna sighed, glad suddenly that she was back here among the girls. Glad that she had kept in touch all these years.

'I wrote an article not so long ago about people's sex lives,' Anna confessed. 'It was a real eye-opener.'

'Really?' Intrigued, Karen rested an arm on the table and turned sideways to face Anna. 'What kind of thing was in it?'

Susie was beaming. 'Was it all kinky stuff?'

There was nothing more fascinating, it seemed, than what other folks got up to between the sheets.

'Not really. In fact, the one thing that came out of it was that nothing should be considered kinky if the people taking part consent to it. But I did come across a couple of oddballs . . .'

'Like who?'

'Well, there was some guy who could only get it up if there was a full moon and he could roll around — outside, thankfully — in cow shit!'

Howls of laughter engulfed the table.

'You're pulling our legs!' Mandy accused. 'Cow shit!'

'No. I promise you. And there was a girl I interviewed who could only ever climax if she had this one particular fantasy. In it she'd be standing on the football terraces at Old Trafford, sheltering under an umbrella with three friends. Anyway, it's a full house, packed out, and they're standing there, the rain pouring down, engrossed in the game, when a football fan comes up behind her and carefully lifts up her skirt. All the while she's concentrating on the game. Gently he pulls down her knickers and gives her one from behind, and just as she's about to reach orgasm Eric Cantona goes streaking up the pitch heading for goal. 'Ooh, ahh, Cantona! Ooh, ahh, Cantona!' she screams as she comes, her whole body slumping with relief as good old Eric scores again. And then the bloke pulls up her knickers, smooths her skirt back into place and disappears into the crowd again, without her ever having seen his face.'

Anna sat back, smiling at the looks on their faces.

Janet grimaced. 'If I was her husband I'd find it a bit bloody off-putting having her shout "Go, Eric, go!" every time she got a bit excited, especially if my name was Roger or something.'

'That's not it,' Anna said matter-of-factly, enjoying the shock value of this particular story. 'She needed the fantasy to help her masturbate. It seems she preferred it to having sex with her husband.'

'I can understand that,' Mandy said flatly.

'I'm just amazed that people actually talk to you about that kind of thing,' Karen said, interrupting her, suddenly serious. 'After all, you're a complete stranger.'

'But that's exactly why they *can* talk to me. It's much

harder to tell somebody you're close to something that you might be a little ashamed of. You'd be worried that they'd sit in judgement of you, or look down on you or something. As it was, I knew I'd probably never see that girl again — and so did she — so it really didn't matter what she told me. In fact, it was probably therapeutic for her.'

'Doctor Anna,' Susie said mischievously. 'I can just see it. You should do it professionally. There's good money in it.'

Anna laughed, then sat forward, meaning to say something more, but Susie had already launched into a story, her voice rising as she became more animated, performing for her audience.

'That reminds me of a bloke I went with once. Turned out he could only get going if the woman swore at him while they were 'aving it off. He kept saying, "Talk dirty to me, talk dirty" and do you know, I couldn't think of a single fuckin' thing to say. He might just as well have been talking to a nun. My mind went completely blank. And the more I thought about it the funnier it all seemed. I just wanted to laugh.'

'So what *did* you do?' asked Karen.

'Well, we were getting nowhere and his John Thomas was beginning to wilt like last week's lettuce, so I forced myself to dredge up a few well-worn obscenities — you know, fuck and bugger and the like — and he finally did the business.'

'Sounds wonderful!' Lyndsay said, her voice heavily ironical. 'Why didn't you just tell him to piss off?'

Susie stared thoughtfully at her nails. 'Dunno, really. Didn't like to, I suppose. I should've done. He was such an arsehole. Do you know what he said when I asked him if he had a condom?' She looked around the table. 'He said, "Not me, babe, I only ride bareback!" Can you believe that? Only ride bareback! What a tosspot!'

The girls nodded their heads in agreement.

'Mike was like that when we first got married,' Janet said, referring to her ex. 'He used to say that wearing a johnnie was like having a shower with your raincoat on.' She made a face. 'He moaned about it for years. Never stopped going on about it. If only we'd known we needn't have bothered, we could've saved a bloody fortune on rubbers! It's quite funny really.' But neither she nor the others laughed.

'Do you ever see or hear from him?' Karen asked.

'No. I speak to his sister now and again; I always did get on well with her. Seems he's living down in Kent somewhere with the woman and their kid.'

She looked up and smiled at her friends, determined to reject their pity. After all, that look seemed to say, she had no need of it, not now she had Steve. Her life was worth something again. Now, at least, there was hope.

Anna listened in embarrassed silence. Even after all this time she felt Janet's humiliation as something tangible. When Mike left her she had blamed herself, of course; she'd even found excuses for him; had somehow made herself understand his deception, his selfishness. Her barrenness had taunted her like a cruel playmate, forcing her to accept his betrayal, to see it as somehow *inevitable*. Anna and the others had been more of a mind to string Mike up by his balls until the over-active little fuckers turned black and dropped off. It had got to the stage where there was an unspoken agreement among them not to discuss what had happened. They couldn't bear the way she defended him, the way she *understood*. That somehow seemed a betrayal of *them* — of their female solidarity.

Mandy leaned close to Anna, her breath warm as she whispered in her ear.

'Penny for 'em.'

'I was just thinking, that's all.'

'About what?'

'About sex, and kids, and life. The usual stuff.'

Mandy's eyes studied Anna's face thoughtfully a moment, then she nodded. 'It hits you at our age, don't it? I mean, you start getting all moody about stuff that didn't occur to us when we were young.'

'Like what?'

'Like ... well, like what we were talking about earlier. About kids. You know, I found myself looking at you when you were talking just now and thinking, Anna Nichols, you don't know just how lucky you are. Having a career and no kids to get in your way. I mean, they muck up your sex life, ruin your figure, tie you down for the best part of twenty years and then they bugger off! If I had my time again . . .'

'You'd do just the same, probably.'

'Probably,' Mandy agreed, flashing a smile. 'But not with Pete.' She was quiet a moment, her eyes troubled, then. 'You know, sometimes I find myself wishing I'd been born a twin. Then one of me could have had the kids while the other was out gallivanting round the world.'

'The trouble with that,' Anna said, 'is that it'd probably be you who got stuck at home. And maybe it'd just be worse, knowing that your twin was having all the fun. Maybe you'd just have the jealousy to cope with as well as everything else.'

Mandy stared at her, then laughed. 'You know, I'd never thought of that. Jealous of myself.' For a moment she seemed amused by the idea, then her face changed again and she looked down at the table. 'It's just that it gets to me sometimes. A lot of the time, to be honest. And then . . . well, I just find myself really resenting them.'

'You don't mean that,' Anna said, reaching out to cover her friend's hand with her own.

Mandy looked up, meeting her eyes.

'It's not that I don't love them. It's just . . . well, sometimes I feel that life's passed me by. Take you, for instance. You were lucky, I reckon. Right from the start you knew just what you wanted. You weren't anyone's fool, were you? Nah. You knew what you wanted and you went for it. And blokes . . . well,' she laughed. 'I used to envy you, you know that? I mean, you never fell for any of that Mills and Boon crap – you got a good job, travelled, had the freedom to do what you wanted when you wanted. And me . . . what the hell did I get?'

'Peter-fucking-Evans,' Susie answered from across the table, making them all – Mandy included – laugh.

'Mister Unimaginative,' Mandy said, nodding, talking to the whole table suddenly. 'You know what his idea of foreplay is?'

Susie, suddenly interested, shook her head. 'Nah. Tell us.'

'Well, Pete's idea of foreplay is to ask me if I fancy sex just before he climbs on top!'

'At least he's interested,' Lyndsay said, a degree of resignation in her voice. 'The only reason both my kids

28

are born in September is 'cos Derek thinks sex is reserved for birthdays and Christmas!'

'Never mind, Lyndse. Santa'll soon be coming down your chimney!' Susie said, erupting into laughter, enjoying having a joke at her sister's expense.

'None of them are much good when it comes down to it,' Karen said, a hint of bitterness in her voice. 'Thick as they come and selfish with it.'

'I dunno,' Janet said. 'There are a few nice guys around.'

'Around where?' Lyndsay said. 'Around the corner?'

Susie tapped the side of her glass with her knife as if calling a meeting to order. 'Now just hang on a minute. Personally, I *like* men.'

'Sure,' said Lyndsay caustically, 'two at a time, usually.'

Susie narrowed her eyes and glared at her sister, then, smiling, looked to the rest of them. 'I mean, for all their faults, they're all we 'ave, bless 'em. Without them . . . well, I just can't see myself living on my own the rest of my life. You know, I was in Sainsbury's the other week, standing at the checkout, and I was watching this bloke in front unload his little basket onto the conveyer belt. He 'ad some of them little tins of beans and some of those meals for one, and then he got out all of these little see-through bags of veg, one after another, all neatly tied — one carrot, one courgette, one parsnip, one leek. I just stood there thinkin' to myself, "You sad bastard". Nah, there's no way I fancy being an old-age spinster.'

'Depends just how desperate you are,' Karen said.

'Desperate for Dan,' Janet chipped in, but no one laughed.

Susie rounded on Karen. 'So this new guy of yours, this Chris, he's a bastard, too, is he?'

Karen stared back at her. 'I didn't mean . . .'

'Well, what did you mean? I'm getting bloody married in two days' time. If I didn't believe Joe was the one – if I didn't think I had a chance this time out, well . . . well, I'd fuckin' shoot myself!'

Karen stared at her a moment then relented. 'Maybe,' she said. 'It's just . . .' She looked up again and smiled. 'Maybe, eh? I hope so, anyway, for your sake.'

'Ta,' Susie said, reconciled, whatever anger she'd momentarily felt drained from her. 'I tell you one thing about him, though.'

All five of them leaned in toward her, responding to her sudden, conspiratorial manner. 'What?'

'We have the best sex I've ever had in my life, and I mean the *very best*!'

Two hours had passed. Seven empty bottles cluttered the centre of the table. As Anna searched in her handbag for a pen to write down Susie's new address, the young waiter brought another four bottles – one red, three white. As he set them down he looked across at her and, with a broad smile, winked, then got to work uncorking two of the bottles.

She looked down, embarrassed but also rather excited by his attentions. She wasn't sure quite what she felt about him. Flattered, certainly – he had to be a good ten years younger than her at the very least, but she knew that some young men liked that. It made them feel . . .mature. Not that she'd met that many who actually *were* mature. She glanced at him, noticed how he would

30

look to her now and then, then turned her attention back to Susie.

'What was that again?'

Susie repeated the address for her.

'It's not far from where I'm working,' she said, putting the pen and the slip of paper back into her handbag. 'I'll have to pop round one evening.'

'Should I fill your glass?'

She turned, surprised. He was at her shoulder, leaning over her, the smell of his cologne stronger than before.

'Sure . . .' she answered, trying to put on an air of casual disinterest. 'The chardonnay . . .'

'I know,' he said softly, leaning almost to her ear. She watched the pale, clear liquid splash into the glass, conscious all the while of him there, breathing softly at her shoulder, and felt a small nervous thrill run down her spine.

'Thanks,' she said, her voice almost failing her. But he wasn't done.

'Here,' he said, and handed her a small slip of paper.

She sat there, the slip held tightly in her closed fist, the eyes of the girls on her.

'Well?' said Susie finally, once he was out of earshot. 'Ain't you going to read what it says?'

They watched expectantly but Anna's fist remained clenched around it.

'You know, it reminds me of something I heard,' Janet said, her voice already slurred, 'about that Carol Stover, used to work in Wetherby's, the Chemists.'

'What, down the market?'

'That's the one. Anyway . . . it seems that she was put on the counter that sold the condoms. Well, some girls'd

31

be a bit shy, maybe ask to be put somewhere else, but not her. She made the most of it.'

Susie leaned closer. 'What'd'ya mean? She nicked 'em?'

Janet shook her head, leaned even closer into the middle of the table. 'No. Nothing so straightforward. What the cheeky cow used to do was write her telephone number on the boxes before she gave them out. Any bloke she fancied, she'd give him her number. Apparently it worked a treat until one day some woman came in and clocked her one. Seems her husband wasn't even aware that she'd written on the box. When he got home his wife wouldn't believe he wasn't up to something. Got her the sack.'

'Serves her right, too,' Susie said, straightening up.

'Just 'cause you didn't think of it,' Lyndsay said, raising her wine in a toast, an acid smile on her lips.

Anna looked down, opened her hand, stared at what was written there.

'Well?' Mandy said, trying to peek between her fingers. 'What's it say? Does he want a bonk, or what?'

'*Mandy*!' Anna said, turning, shocked by her friend's bluntness.

Mandy shrugged. 'Sorry. But you know what they're like, these young 'uns.'

Anna stared at her a moment, then laughed. 'Here.'

Mandy looked at the piece of paper, then held it out for the others to see.

Susie took it from her, then read it out loud: 'I finish at midnight. Would you come out with me?'

There were oohs around the table.

'Well, what d'you reckon?' Karen asked, looking at Anna. 'Are you going to go?'

Anna looked down, her voice suddenly small. 'I think . . . I think I need to go to the loo.'

There were ironic cheers, yet as she made to get up, Mandy leaned close and whispered in her ear. 'You okay?'

She stood, looking down at her old friend. 'Sure. I'm fine.'

The fluorescent strip above the mirror flickered fitfully, as if it was on its last legs, and there was a sickly scent about the place that was vaguely nauseous, even so Anna stood there, staring down into the grey marble sink, reluctant to go through and join her friends again.

She dabbed at her eyes, angry with herself for being so stupid. The drink had made her more than usually sentimental, and when that song had come on it was enough to start her off. As she looked up and studied her reflection in the mirror she willed herself to remember the first time she'd heard it, torturing herself with the memory. New York. Fifteen months ago . . .

She was flattered when Guy Porcaro, the publisher of Fifty State Magazines had called and asked her to fly over. Flattered but not really serious about taking the job he was offering. After all, she was a London girl, always had been, and her work, her flat, her friends — they were all here. Oh, it was nice to be 'in the frame' for a top-flight job, but she wasn't *serious* about taking it. Or so she'd told her friends. 'It'll be a good lark,' she'd said; 'a few days in New York in a posh hotel and all expenses paid, what could be better?' But when she'd got there things were very, very different. It wasn't just the sleek black limousine they'd had waiting for her at JFK airport, nor was it that first, memorable glimpse of the Manhattan skyline as they drove along the Expressway, it was the place itself. It was everything she'd ever imagined and more. She had been seduced. There was no other word for it. The glamour of New York had grabbed her.

Guy had met her in the massive marble and glass foyer of the company's building on Times Square and taken her up a full twenty-eight floors to his penthouse office where they'd chatted for an hour or so before he'd introduced her to the rest of the board. It was standing there, looking out through the full-length window wall at the magnificence of New York – at the challenge that those vast straight lines of skyscrapers represented in her mind – that she'd decided, long before Guy spelt out the terms they were offering.

Her own magazine. Hers to design and shape and launch onto the stands. How could she have turned it down? She'd done it before, of course, back in England, which was why they'd headhunted her, but this was different. The market was ten, maybe twelve times the size of that back home, and – if the board was to be believed – she would have full editorial control.

She'd have been mad not to say yes. Two weeks later she was back with just a suitcase and a copy of the contract Guy had had Fed'Ex'd to her overnight.

One hundred and twenty thousand dollars a year, plus car and expenses. She had simply laughed when she'd read the figure. Laughed because who was she after all? Just plain old Anna Nichols, born in Islington and educated in a Secondary Modern. What right had she to be taking fashionable jobs in New York and riding in the back of massive limos like some latter-day movie star?

She remembered what she'd done, that first day back there, even before she went to look at apartments. She had gone out and bought four postcards and, sitting in a coffee bar on 34th and Madison, had written to each of them — her oldest friends — telling them where she was. Telling them — because she didn't quite believe it herself — that for her the fairy-tale had come true.

They had put her up at the Algonquin, a small but luxurious hotel two minutes walk from Times Square, while she looked for her own apartment. At first she'd seen nothing she liked, then, coming back from a meeting 'up-state', she'd found a place on Fifth Avenue, a fifteenth-floor apartment looking out across Central Park towards the Upper West Side and the Hudson. Putting up a year's rent in advance, she had moved in at once.

That first month was just a haze in the memory. Looking back, she didn't know how she had managed to fit it all in. Seeing and hiring staff, getting costings, dealing with accountants and distribution managers, not to talk of the nights she'd spent in her apartment, a jug of coffee at her elbow as she worked through portfolio after portfolio, trying to find the specific look she wanted for the magazine. As she'd said at the time, she had survived on air and pure adrenaline and had felt like Queen of the City. Queen of all New York!

By the end of the month she had something resembling the staff of a magazine assembled on the sixteenth floor of Fifty State's own skyscraper. All that remained was for her to get out a dummy for the publishers.

It was then it had happened.

She could remember the precise moment. She'd just come out of a meeting with her fashion editor and was staring out the window towards the twin shapes of the World Trade Centre when her art director, Jeanne, had knocked and popped her head around the door.

'We've a problem. The guy we hired to do the shoot tomorrow has just cried off.'

'Well get someone else. Work down the list.'

'I have. They're all booked. Earliest we could re-schedule would be Thursday.'

'Shit! I could do without this. Jack Nicholson's just cancelled the interview, so I'm left without my major lead, the PR for Ford has phoned to say that they'll pull the car out of the competition if we don't increase the size of the picture on the cover, and now it looks like I won't have a fucking fashion spread! She looked at Jeanne. 'He just phoned?'

Jeanne nodded. 'You want me to call up the agency and cancel?'

'What, and pay some brainless bimbo two thousand bucks for sitting on her arse at home? No way!'

She stabbed at the numbers angrily, then sat back, waiting as the phone rang at the other end.

'Some fucking nerve. Call themselves professionals . . .'

She took her hand away. 'Hello. Is that Callum O'Neil? . . . Good, well this is Anna Nichols. Yeah, *that* Anna Nichols . . . *Sorry*? What good is *sorry*? Four thousand dollars, that's what it's going to cost us, not to talk of the inconvenience. Not that you'd give a flying shit about inconveniencing us! But what I want to know, Mister, is this — what does it feel like to commit professional suicide? . . . Your *mother*? What the hell has this to do with your mother?'

Yes, she remembered the moment. Remembered how frail and tired his voice had sounded on the other end of the line, how she had felt when he'd repeated the words she hadn't properly heard first time round.

'*My mother's dead. She died this morning. I'm sorry if my assistant didn't make it clear but . . . well, it's been chaos here. I . . .*'

She put her hand over the receiver and looked across, her voice subdued. 'Cancel the session, Jeanne. Re-arrange it when you can.' Then, taking a deep breath, she uncovered the receiver again. 'Look, I'm sorry. I didn't know . . . Of course. I understand. I . . . Sure. I guess you've a lot to arrange. I . . . Yes, bye.'

She had sat there for a long time afterwards, staring at her hands, angry with herself; angry because she'd let the job take her over to the exclusion of everything else.

Queen of New York, huh? Queen Bitch, more like. Then, noting down the address onto a piece of paper, she went through to her secretary and ordered flowers.

It was a week before she'd heard from him again. She had been about to go out to lunch when the call came through.

'Who is it?' she'd asked.

'It's Callum O'Neil. I just wanted to say thank you for the flowers. It was a kind thought.'

'It was the least I could do. I felt . . .'

'You were angry. *Boy* were you angry.'

She laughed. 'I was, wasn't I?'

'Sure. And you had a right to be. I let you down.'

'No. You were right. If it had been my mother . . .'

'Even so, I feel bad about it. I'd like to make it up to you somehow.'

'Is this a come-on?'

His laughter was warm, generous. 'It wasn't meant to be, but . . .'

'But what?'

'You've a nice voice.'

'So have you.'

'So? Dinner?'

She swivelled in her chair and looked out across the city towards where she knew his studio was. 'When?'

'Tonight?'

'I can't.'

'Boyfriend?'

'No.'

'So when?'

She opened her diary, flicked through. 'Friday night? Eight o'clock?'

'Fine. Where?'

'How about . . .' She tried to remember the name of the restaurant she had been to that first week — the really nice Italian one in Soho.

'How about Amanci's?' he said.

That was it! The very place she'd been trying to think of.

'Are you a mind reader, Mr O'Neil?'

'No. But I *can* juggle.'

She laughed, then, more calmly than she felt she said. 'Okay. Eight o'clock Friday, then. At Amanci's. I'll meet you in the bar.'

'That's great. But how will I recognise you?'

She was flustered a moment, wondering what she could wear — whether she ought to dress up for the occasion or be more casual — then realised it was much simpler than that. She put on her best business voice. 'I'll fax you details, Mr O'Neil. Okay?'

'Well, it's *different*.'

'And you?'

'Me?' He laughed, a warm, wild-Irish laugh that she liked instantly. 'Why, I'll be wearing a red rose, Ms Nichols. What else?'

She had been late — and not just five minutes late but a full hour and ten minutes. He was there, however, red rose and all, getting up from his stool as she came through the bronze panelled doors, his hand extended as he walked towards her, looking — and the resemblance was striking — like a young Kris Kristofferson, the black t-shirt beneath his white casual suit emphasising the similarity.

'Well now, Ms Nichols,' he said, taking her hand firmly, his green eyes smiling at her. 'I'm delighted to make your acquaintance finally.'

'Anna, please. Look, I'm so sorry. Really I am. Did you get the message? The meeting just went on and on and . . .'

He shook his head, amused. 'It doesn't matter. Really it doesn't. You're here, I'm here, the night is young and . . .' He smiled mischievously, then turned, indicating the bar. 'Anyway, let me buy you a drink. You look like you could do with one.'

'A Jack Daniels,' she answered, letting him lead her to the vacant stool beside his own.

'You always drink that stuff?' he asked, signalling to the barman.

'No,' she admitted. 'But when in Rome . . .'

He looked back at her. 'You been to Rome?'

She shook her head.

'Nor me.' He laughed. 'Been to London, though. Nice place. Stayed in Kensington. Hotel off the Brompton Road. I forget the name.'

He ordered drinks, then turned to her again. 'Oh, and I liked the fax. Who took the photograph? Anybody I'd know?'

She laughed, starting to relax. 'Just a friend. In London. I'm glad you didn't send me one.'

'Really?' He raised an eyebrow. 'Why's that?'

'Because it would have spoiled the surprise.'

'Surprise?' He looked for a moment as if he didn't know what she meant, then he laughed and, taking the glasses the barman had just brought, gave one to her and raised his own in a toast.

'What shall we drink to?'

'How about rude editors and Irish charm?' she teased.

'Sounds like a great combination! To the beginning of a beautiful friendship!'

She raised her glass, chinked it against his own. 'And to Fifty State Magazines, without whom . . .'

In a dimly-lit corner of Amanci's they sat facing each other, deep in conversation. They had already eaten and a second bottle of wine rested in the ice bucket beside Callum's elbow as he leaned toward her, his manner easy and relaxed, his strong, Irish-American features clearly etched in the candle light.

'So . . .' he said, in that lovely mid-west drawl of his, 'you still haven't told me why you decided to come to New York.'

'An offer I couldn't refuse.'

'The job?'

Anna nodded. 'It seemed like a good deal – my own magazine, more money than I could spend, a new challenge. Besides, there was nothing to keep me in London.'

'Glad you came?'

'Yes,' she said, a coyness about her as she looked up from her hands. 'Yes, I am.'

'And what about your folks, your friends . . . don't you miss them?'

She shrugged. 'I don't really miss my parents. I mean, I didn't see that much of them even when I lived round the corner from them. But I do miss my friends. Or would, if I wasn't working quite so hard,' she added, making light of it.

'Brothers or sisters?'

She shook her head. 'An only child, I'm afraid. Used to getting my own way, I guess. And you? I bet you've dozens.'

'Nope.' He sat back slightly, then reached for his glass, draining the Burgundy in a single gulp. 'Not now, anyhow.'

He was quiet a moment, then looked up again, meeting Anna's puzzled eyes. 'My brother was killed in 'Nam.'

'Oh God . . . I'm so sorry.'

'It's okay, you didn't know.' His smile was warm, friendly, and Anna's momentary embarrassment quickly faded. 'I guess you could say we're pretty much in the same boat. Only children. Loners.'

'Your father . . .' she ventured. 'Is he still alive?'

'Guess so,' he said, filling her glass, then seeing to his own.

'Don't you know?'

'Nope.'

She waited a moment, intrigued but sensing his discomfort. 'Don't you want to know?' she asked finally, in spite of herself.

Callum sat back, his whole manner suddenly thoughtful, as if this was a different, much older man suddenly. Anna, watching him intensely, noticed once again the shape of his hands, large yet strangely delicate, as he cupped the wine glass between them.

'My father and I don't speak. He's never forgiven me for turning my back on the Marines – it was his life, you see, and his father's before him – even though his own son was killed.'

Callum swallowed, then shook his head, a look of incomprehension briefly in his face. 'You know, he never ever cried. Not once. Never shed a single damn tear . . .'

Anna reached across the table and lay her hand on his.

He looked up, waiting to catch her eye, but Anna, embarrassed suddenly by this act of familiarity, stared resolutely at her hand, immobilised by indecision, by her very Englishness, it seemed.

Callum's thumb moved gently beneath her palm to stroke the side of her hand.

'So you became a photographer instead,' she said,

easing her hand away, hoping he'd not feel it was a rejection.

He sat back slightly, suddenly more businesslike, the moment of openness past, it seemed. 'I left Chicago the day I was eighteen. Packed my bags and came out east. For a time I lived off hand-outs from my Mom, then I got a break – got me a job as a photographer's assistant.'

'But wasn't your father proud when you finally made it?'

He laughed bitterly then shook his head, a deep, abiding pain at the back of his eyes. 'Maybe if I'd have been a pimp he'd have accepted it a bit more easily. He'd have understood that, after all – it would have been a *man's* job. But for a son of his to take up a wuss profession like photography was the ultimate act of betrayal as far as he was concerned.'

'And your Mum?' she asked, surprised but also moved by this glimpse of what lay behind that mask of omni-competence he wore.

His smile this time was warm, genuine, with a touch of wistfulness in it. 'Oh, Mom was proud of me, sure enough. Especially when my by-line began to appear in the magazines and she could show all her friends. But Dad refused to have me come near the house, and with John dead there was nothing to keep them together. In the end they got a divorce.'

'I'm sorry,' she said. 'Really I am.' But it seemed a totally inadequate response.

'It's okay,' he said, then emptied his glass once again. 'It was a long time ago. I'm over it now.' And, without meeting her gaze, he looked away, across the crowded restaurant, signalling to the waiter to bring the check.

43

They got a yellow cab back to her place, and as they headed through the rain-soaked streets, the pavements sweating like rivers of coal under the neon lights, her mind raced ahead. Should she invite him in? And if so, what should she say? Should she sleep with him? She knew she wanted to, but the dilemma was whether or not she should. Anna silently chastised herself. It was crazy that she still felt the need to protect her reputation as a 'nice girl' at her age, but some things you never shook off, or so it seemed.

As they stepped from the cab he slipped his jacket around her shoulders to protect her from the rain. She looked up at him and smiled, feeling a little foolish.

'Would you like to come up?' she said, looking not at him but away, her eyes focusing vaguely on the gusts of steam that issued from the manhole in the middle of the near-deserted street. 'For a drink,' she added hastily.

He gave a short, amused laugh. 'I think I've had enough for one night,' he said. 'Perhaps another time?'

Anna looked up into his face and smiled, suddenly feeling very vulnerable. Damn it! Why did she ask him in? She should've just said, 'Thanks for a great evening,' given him a peck on the cheek and walked inside. Instead she heard herself say: 'That would be nice. I'd like that.'

Oh shit, she thought. *It sounds like I'm desperate*.

'What I mean is,' she said, 'that would be nice.'

'Yes . . . it would,' he answered, smiling down into her face.

'Here,' she said, taking the jacket from her shoulders and handing it to him. 'Thanks.'

He slipped it over a shoulder and, with his other hand,

reached up to catch a raindrop that had fallen on her face. The touch of it was warm and intimate and stirred something in her.

'Goodnight, Anna,' he said simply and bent down to kiss her warmly on the lips, then turned and walked off into the night, or what was left of it.

She lay across her bed, her clothes and shoes discarded in a heap by the door. The sound of the rain lashing against the window was strangely comforting. Unable to sleep, Anna allowed herself to relive the evening. She closed her eyes, wanting to recapture the image of the man, to see his face and hear his voice again. Over and over she replayed their conversations, recalling a certain look, a laugh, smiling to herself at the memory of it. And inside her she knew that something had happened; that things had somehow changed. She knew that this man had triggered something in her that she hadn't felt for a long, long time – a desire, a longing. She'd never felt quite like this about any man. Was it simply lust? She didn't know. One thing *was* certain, however – she wanted to find out.

Anna busied herself with work that weekend, angry with herself that she hadn't even thought to give Callum her home phone number. She had his, of course, but it was out of the question that she should make the first move. Nice girls didn't do that kind of thing.

By Sunday lunchtime, unable to concentrate, she donned her trainers and a tracksuit and took to the streets, telling herself that the exercise would do her good; would shake off this pathetic moping.

Without admitting it to herself, she headed in the direction of Callum's studio. Approaching it, she slowed, her heart pounding in her chest — whether from exertion of excitement she couldn't tell. Like a besotted schoolgirl she jogged past the brownstone building where he lived, hoping — for what? A glimpse of him? To bump into him? Whatever it was she was hoping for, she knew it was ridiculous.

It reminded her of the time, years before, when she, Mandy and Janet had taken a fancy to three boys working in the local butcher's shop. They would stand for hours staring through the window at them across trays of blood-soaked offal and weekend joints, hoping for some small sign of acknowledgement; dreaming, perhaps, of a quick snog behind the counter. They had kidded themselves that they didn't look at all obvious standing there every day; that it didn't seem at all odd that these three teenagers should take such interest in the hanging strings of sausages and skinned rabbits.

After the butcher boys there was an infatuation with a boy who lived in Janet's flats. He played in a group at the weekend and in their adolescent eyes was a fully fledged celebrity. Every evening one or other of them would sit on the stone staircase leading down to the landing, literally having their arse frozen off, and as they heard his door open and close along the way, would trip down the stairs so casually and bump into him. They would chat and flirt and if the boy knew they were laying an ambush he would never let on. Once he had given Anna a lift home on his scooter. She'd felt like a million dollars, holding on to his waist, nuzzling in to his neck, the smell of Brut filling her nostrils, intoxicating her. It had been

Heaven. That was, until she'd seen her mother's face as they pulled up outside the house. Her heart sinking, she had tried to hurry him away before he could witness the inevitable confrontation, but she knew he had heard her mother shout to her — 'Anna! Where's your brace?' — as she went down the path to her front door. Blushing like a beetroot she had retrieved the wire conundrum from her pocket and, picking off the pieces of fluff that had become attached to it, pushed it back into her mouth.

Abashed and humiliated, she had turned to watch him disappear around the bend in the road, a puff of exhaust in his wake.

Walking back across the bustling sprawl of New York City she laughed aloud at the recollection, then, sobered, wondered if she would someday laugh at today's escapade.

'Okay, Jeanne, we'll go with this one,' Anna said, drawing a square around the transparency. 'And let's try it cropped right down and also with the neck and shoulders left in. Great!' and she handed the set of pictures back across the desk.

Her art director stood there smiling down at her.

'Was there something else?'

'I was just wondering how your date went with Callum O'Neil?' Jeanne said, a broad grin splitting her features.

'My date?'

'Joel said he saw you two at Amanci's a few nights back.'

'Oh, yeah . . . Well, it wasn't a date exactly. I just thought I should apologise for being such a bitch about his mother. Remember?'

'Yeah, well, whatever. How was it? You do know that every woman in this place is half in love with him, don't you?'

Anna laughed out loud, imagining how he'd react to that news. 'So that's why we use him so much!' Then, seeing that Jeanne was still watching her, she smiled. 'Actually, it was very nice.'

'Nice! God, how English! There was a time I'd have sold my mother for a date with Callum O'Neil!'

'Your mother?'

'Damn sure!' Jeanne said, a twinkle in her eye. 'My grandmother too!'

'But not any more?'

'No way. I've already worked through that particular obsession with my therapist. I sure as hell ain't gonna pay sixty bucks an hour to go over that ground again!'

Anna laughed. She still wasn't used to the way everyone constantly referred to their shrink – those that weren't on Prozac, that was! What was wrong with the good old English way of buttoning up your emotions! As far as she was concerned, a little bit of repression was a good thing. Especially in company.

'Anyway,' Jeanne said, 'I'll check out his version of events later on.'

'Later on?' Anna sat back, suddenly tense, wrong-footed by the thought that Jeanne would be talking to Callum before she'd had a chance to talk to him again.

'Sure. He's doing the Arabian Nights fashion shoot for us today. Remember?'

Anna hadn't remembered. The shoot had been fixed up more than a month ago, long before she'd met him, before she'd had a reason to retain such details.

She tried to seem casual. 'So where's the session?'

'At his studio, of course.' Jeanne smiled, enjoying her boss's discomfort. 'You want the address?'

Anna laughed. 'I *have* the address. I was just . . . interested, that's all.'

'Interested . . .' Jeanne's smile broadened, then. 'Any-thing else?'

Anna shook her head.

'Okay, then, I'd better run. Before the boss starts checking up on me!'

Anna closed the door quietly behind her then stood unnoticed at the back of the studio. On the way there she had rehearsed a casual reply to Callum's inevitable question — Why was she there? But standing there, her heart pounding in her chest, her mouth dry, she felt that she would never utter a coherent sentence again.

Jeanne looked across and saw her. She went to call out, but Anna quickly held a finger up to her lips.

The model — all luscious hair and cheekbones — sat elegantly on a brocade chaise-longue, swathes of richly textured fabric draped behind her. The hairdresser, make-up artist and stylist fussed around her while Callum stood behind the camera, waiting.

'Okay, everybody ready?' he said patiently, signalling for them to clear the set. Then he looked down through the camera and began.

Anna watched him as he worked — setting up the shot, taking a polaroid, repositioning a piece of fabric, the fold of a skirt, shooting the film, encouraging, praising, shooting again.

It was three rolls of film later and the end of the

session before Callum realised she was there. She wasn't sure how he'd react; whether he'd be embarrassed by her visit, or maybe even angry.

'Hi,' he said, walking across to her, 'this *is* a nice surprise.'

'Hi,' she said shyly. 'I had to come over and check out the new stylist. We haven't used her before.'

'Ah,' he said, as if he understood, then smiled again. 'Anyway, it's good to see you.'

'And you,' she said, starting to relax.

'I enjoyed myself the other night.'

'Me too,' she said, conscious of Jeanne staring at them from across the room.

Callum glanced across at her, then looked back at Anna. 'Look, are you busy this evening?'

'This evening? Well, I . . .'

'It's just that I'm free and . . . well, I wondered whether you'd like to go out.'

'On a date, you mean?' she said, her voice teasing now.

'Sure.'

She smiled. 'I'd love to.'

His smile was strange, relieved, almost as if he'd expected her to say no. 'That's great. I mean, that's really great. I'll pick you up at eight. From your place. Okay?'

'Okay,' she said, beaming now, unable to stop herself. 'Eight o'clock. Tonight.' Then, knowing she'd say something to spoil it all if she stayed a moment longer, she turned and, with a wink to Jeanne, left.

In the lift up he kissed her for the first time, a long,

50

lingering kiss. As the lift jolted to a halt at the fifteenth floor, he looked down at her, his eyes so green, so beautiful she could feel her body responding. Without speaking he took her hand and led her out onto the deep pile carpet of the landing.

She smiled nervously and nodded toward one of the doors, then reached into her bag for the keys, her heart pounding in her chest.

Closing the door behind them, she flicked the wall switch. A pair of lights in the open-plan living room yawned into life, their subdued glow casting the shadows of miniature palm trees onto the walls and ceiling.

His hand gently brushed her back, sending a shiver through her. She turned, facing him.

'Can I get you a drink?'

The words were barely audible. It seemed almost wrong to speak.

He reached down and took her hand again, then shook his head.

'Anything?'

Callum brought her hand up to his lips and gently kissed it, his eyes on hers the whole time. 'I want to make love to you.'

The words surged through her like an electric current, jolting her, filling her with a feverish excitement. She trembled, her legs close to giving, and stepped closer, wanting to feel his body against hers. Gently she touched his face, running her fingers slowly across the stubble on his cheek until they lightly brushed his lips, his breath warm as they parted to kiss her fingertips.

He drew her closer still, one hand pressed into the small of her back, the other brushing her neck, then tilting her chin up to meet his face in a long slow kiss.

His lips still on hers, he let his jacket fall to the floor. Staring up into his face, she ran her fingers over his chest, tracing the contours of his muscles, then pulled his t-shirt up over his head.

She shivered, fascinated by him. He felt so good. His body was so firm and tanned, the dark hair on his chest running down past the buckle of his leather belt, his arms so strong and beautifully formed.

She wanted him. This time there was no doubt. Each touch made her body ache with longing, yet at the same time she wanted to prolong the agony, to wallow in this delicious torment, this bliss of anticipation.

His hands were on her back now, unzipping her dress, his eyes piercing, his face suddenly serious and intense as he watched the shoestring straps slip from her shoulders.

Her dress fell to the floor.

Through the dark lace of her bra, her nipples stood hard and erect as though reaching out for his touch. With practised ease, he pulled at the hook, releasing her breasts, then cupped them in his hands, bending close to kiss and tease them until she thought she would come with the pure pleasure of it. Then he lifted her up and as he moved his head back she gasped, but his eyes held a sudden urgency.

'Where's the bedroom?'

'In there.' She nodded towards the door behind him.

He smiled and then leaned into her again, kissing her face, her breast, then turned and carried her through into the darkness, the hard muscularity of him making her ache with desire.

He lowered her gently onto the bed, then moved back away from her. She waited, for one terrible moment thinking he'd had second thoughts.

'Callum?'

He answered her with a kiss. Then his hands were caressing her again. She reached out to touch him, then giggled, realising he was naked.

'What's so funny, girl?'

'Nothing . . .' She drew a long, shivering breath. *Nothing at all. Everything was just perfect*. And, wrapping her arms about him, she pulled him onto her, kissing him passionately, her skin inflamed by his touch.

She had woken just before dawn and gone to the window, standing there naked, looking out across Central Park. Silently he had joined her, embracing her from behind, kissing her neck and shoulder.

'Hi,' she said, leaning into him, comforted by the warmth of his naked body.

'Hi. You always up so early?' He yawned, nuzzling into her hair, breathing in deeply to fill his nostrils with the scent of her.

'I couldn't sleep.'

'You need something to relax you.'

Anna giggled. 'What do you have in mind?'

'I thought you English girls were supposed to be all prim and proper,' he said, amused by her response.

'You still think that, after last night?'

His laugh was warm. 'Okay. I stand corrected. But I was thinking more about a nice deep bath, a little massage, maybe, and then my own personal remedy for insomnia . . .'

'Mmm, sounds perfect,' Anna said, turning to face him, gently teasing the dark hairs curled across his chest. 'I could get used to this.'

'I sure hope so.'

During the weeks that followed they had spent every free moment together, although with his commitments and her workload it often meant meeting up in bed at midnight. And always they would make love, the passion of a new romance so intense, so consuming, that Anna felt herself being carried along without even thinking about where it might lead.

She soon decided that she couldn't cope with staying at Callum's studio; it drove her mad not having her things around her in the morning, never having the right clothes to wear. He was so much more adaptable, so much more used to moving around with only a toothbrush in his bag, and pretty soon he was leaving that in her bathroom along with his dental floss and razor. Piles of his t-shirts formed like termite hills around her bedroom until the daily help received instructions to put them through the wash and fold them away in a drawer in the bedroom. Without a conscious decision having been made Callum had moved in.

Not that that was a problem. Anna adored having him to come back to; loved the feeling of travelling home knowing he'd be there for her. Above all she delighted in the unfashionable feeling of belonging to someone.

The safety net was Callum's studio. While he had that they both knew they were only playing at living together

– that there was always somewhere else for him to go if things went wrong. The pressures of living together – of knowing that there was no other option – were removed, while their pleasure in each other's company seemed to grow with each passing week. He didn't *have* to be there with her, he *wanted* to.

They had spent hours walking round New York City. He had taken her to her first baseball game, to exhibitions and to Broadway shows. He had introduced her to his friends and taken her to parties, but the best and happiest times had been when there were just the two of them – curled up on a sofa watching TV or walking hand in hand through Central Park. And then there were the unexpected surprises.

Anna was due to present a package to the magazine's prospective advertisers. That week before the crucial Monday morning meeting had been a long, hard slog: pulling together the crumbs of an idea so that it worked as a feature, getting the pictures, the tone of the headlines and the selling strap just right, nurturing and harnessing the magazine's talent to work with a schedule. By the Friday evening, however, it was done and the team could relax. Anna had felt elated, yet when she'd phoned Callum to tell him, he'd seemed distracted, unaffected by her excitement, and for the first time she felt an acute disappointment in him. But that had lasted less than an hour, for as she stepped from the First State building he was waiting for her, a hired limo at the kerb.

'What's this?' she'd asked as he ushered her into the back and ordered the chauffeur to drive on.

'A little surprise,' he said, settling back into the

plush interior next to her. 'You've worked hard, Anna. I thought you deserved a break.'

'A break?'

He leaned forward, and, opening a hatch in the interior wall of the limo, revealed a small drinks cabinet. He turned to her, offering a Jack Daniels with ice, then chinked her glass with his own. 'How does the Grand Bahamas sound?'

She stared at him, amazed. 'It sounds . . . wonderful.'

That evening, standing beside him on the balcony of their room in the Xanadu Hotel, looking out across the moonlit bay, the sound of Caribbean music drifting up to them from the lively bar on the far side of the yacht marina, she realised that she wanted this man; wanted to be with him for the rest of her life; to grow old with him. She had shivered and drawn him close to kiss him tenderly, and afterwards, when they made love, it was somehow different, as if yet another barrier had gone down between them.

That weekend had been idyllic. He had hired a jeep to tour the island, stopping at white sand bays to swim with her, or to shop in the market place. They had spent long hours relaxing in palm-shaded bars, their faces pressed close in conversation, needing no one but each other for company.

Idyllic, but soon she was back. Back to New York and to reality.

The meeting with the advertisers had gone well. They seemed to like the package she had put together, and as she watched the video presentation she had felt more proud than nervous.

The pages of the magazine had danced with life, the combination of quality photography and graphics giving the product a classy image that looked both interesting and attractive. It was the kind of thing she'd read herself . . . and she considered that a compliment.

Anna sat at her desk, her chin resting on one hand as she looked intently at the papers spread out before her. A half-eaten sandwich lay discarded at her elbow and a glass of mineral water fizzed in the glass in her other hand.

Jeanne popped her head round the door. 'Got a minute?'

'You bet,' she said, looking up. 'Anything rather than do these budgets,' and she slammed the folder shut. 'What've you got?'

Jeanne lay before her three alternative dummy covers for the first issue. This was the exciting bit; the work she enjoyed best of all. The decision making. She was the one who sowed the seeds, was the inspiration behind it all, and ultimately she was the one who had the final word. It was scary sometimes, but she loved the thrill of it all, the power it gave her, the certainty she felt in this aspect of her life.

Anna looked at each in turn. 'What do you think?' she said, not lifting her eyes from the images before her.

'I like this one,' Jeanne said, pointing to the one in the middle.

'You would!' she said, laughing good humouredly. 'I've never known an art director yet who liked to have words on a cover if they could help it! No, seriously, I agree that that's the best image, but I want you to use these graphics,' she said, pointing to the layout on the right, 'and make these alter-ations.'

She scribbled a blue pencil across the clea · film, Jeanne looking down at her with admiration. She li ked an editor who could make a decision.

'Let me see the revised version at tn : meeting this afternoon.'

'Great!' Jeanne gathered up the l youts and made to go, but Anna shook her head and nodded to the chair opposite. 'Come and talk to me for a bit.'

The intercom buzzed on Anna's desk. She pressed a button and her secretary's voice came through the speaker.

'Anna, it's Dr Levis on the phone. Says it's personal.'

'Dr who? Oh, yeah, put him through,' she flicked the button. 'Medical insurance,' she said to Jeanne before picking up the telephone receiver.

'Hello? Dr Levis? Yes, this is Anna Nichols. There's nothing wrong is there?' Her tone was confident, joking. Sun-tanned from her romantic weekend, she had never felt or looked better.

'Pardon? What did you say? I'm *what*?' All of the bounciness was suddenly gone from her voice. She spoke flatly now; a horrible certainty descended on her. 'You're sure? No, no . . . of course. I understand. Three o'clock. Fine. I'll be there.'

She placed the receiver down and sat back in shocked silence.

Jeanne was staring at her, worried. 'Anna? Are you okay?'

Anna's hand still rested on the telephone. Her other hand reached for the glass of water. She took a mouthful of the lukewarm drink then looked at her friend with glazed eyes. The colour had drained completely from her face.

'I'm pregnant.'

'Shit! How?'

She made to answer flippantly, then shook her head. 'I don't know. I thought it was safe. I thought . . . Oh god.'

'So what are you gonna do?'

'I don't know. I have to see the doctor this afternoon to see how far along I am.'

'Didn't you realise?' Jeanne said incredulously. She had been pregnant twice and she'd known straight away both times.

'My periods have been odd ever since I got here. I put it down to stress and change of location. I didn't think . . .'

'Do you want it? I presume it's Callum's.'

Anna looked down, close suddenly to tears, realising the enormity of it. 'How *can* I? I've only just started here. I've got a magazine to get up and keep running and . . . well, shit, Jeanne . . . why now? Why fucking now?'

'What are you doing in here, honey?'

The grey mist of morning hung around the building as Anna opened her eyes. It felt as though she had only just gone to sleep.

'What time is it?' she asked, ignoring his question.

'Seven o'clock. Hey, but when did you decide we had to have separate rooms?' he said, laughing, as he lifted her feet from the sofa so that he could sit down, caressing her toes as he lay them on his knees.

'I couldn't sleep. Didn't want to wake you.'

'What's the problem?'

'I guess it's the launch.' She sat up, stretched her arms. 'I'm probably just a bit stressed out, that's all.'

'Anything I can help with?'

She looked away, feeling guilty for not telling him the truth. 'No. I'll work it out. But thanks.' She turned her head slightly, attempting a smile, but couldn't quite meet his eyes. She looked away again, staring at the window.

He kissed her toes gently, lifted her legs from his lap and stood up. 'I'll get you some coffee.'

'No, I . . .'

'Orange juice?'

'No. Thanks.'

'You really should, you know. You need to get some vitamins . . .'

She screamed at him. 'I said no-bloody-thanks! Why can't you just leave me be? I'm not a bloody baby!'

He stared back at her, shocked, a deep hurt in his eyes.

She glanced at him, the silence like a veil of ice between them, then looked down again.

'I'm pregnant, Callum.'

She couldn't look at him; couldn't trust herself to witness his reaction. It was a classic 'no-win situation'. If he said that was great she'd feel a bitch for killing the child, whereas if he said 'Hey, I'm outta here' then it would show he didn't love her.

She groaned, desperate to be anywhere – *anywhere* – but there at that moment.

Her voice sounded cold and toneless in the grey-lit room.

'I'm booked in to have a termination this afternoon. Jeanne said she'd come with me. She's an old hand, it seems.'

She heard herself laugh; a bitter, disappointed laughter. And all the while Callum stood there looking down at her, unable to speak, unable to believe what he was hearing.

'Say something,' she said, dreading the silence more than any words. 'Please say something. Anything!'

His voice was different somehow; smaller than usual – defeated. 'Say what? You've told me what's happening. You've just booked yourself into a clinic to have an abortion like it's a dental checkup or something, and I'm supposed to have a view on it?'

Her voice was small, frightened. 'Yes.'

'You announce you're about to kill our baby . . .' He stopped, a small uncertainty in his eyes. 'I presume it *is* mine . . .'

'You bastard!'

'Yeah, sure, *I'm* the villain now. *You* decide to kill *our* baby – without even consulting me, and . . . well, Christ Almighty, woman! What am I supposed to feel? Jesus, Anna! Jeanne and the whole fucking office probably knew before I did, isn't that the truth?'

'That's not fair. I needed someone to talk to . . .'

'Then talk to me, for Christ's sake! Talk to me.'

He dropped down next to her on the sofa. She didn't want to look at him; didn't want to see the pain in his eyes. She couldn't allow herself to think how much she loved him.

'It's not the right time, Callum. We've only known each other three months. A baby would spoil everything, can't you see that? It's so . . . *impractical*. And there's the launch . . .'

'Oh, let's not forget the fucking launch now!' he said sarcastically, his voice getting louder again. He stood up, then turned away from her, pacing the room. 'I mean, God forbid that a mere thing like a baby should get in the way of your precious fucking magazine. Yeah, it's probably best to kill the fucker. Poor little bastard'd never get to see his mummy anyway, would he?'

'Callum! Don't . . . *please* . . .' The hurt was unbearable. She was trembling now, the tears flowing freely down her cheeks. But he wasn't even looking at her. He was just hunched into himself, all of his hurt held in.

'Don't what? Tell you the truth? Well, let me make it clear. If you go ahead with this you'll be taking a life. Killing *our* baby.' He stopped and looked at her, anger flaring in his eyes. 'You understand *that* clear enough?'

Anna hugged her knees and buried her face.

'Anna?' he said, his voice softer, calmer now; 'Do you love me?'

'Yes,' she answered, her voice a whisper.

'Then don't do this. If you love me don't go ahead with this . . . this awful thing.'

'If you love me don't ask me not to.'

Looking up at him through tear-filled eyes, Anna willed him to hold her, to comfort her, to tell her he did love her, did want her baby, that he also understood why she had to do it her way.

But she could see from his face that the pain was too raw, the love too fragile, and understanding only something she could hope for in the future. Without saying a word he turned and walked through to the

62

bedroom, emerging minutes later in t-shirt, jeans and trainers, his hair still dishevelled from sleep, his jacket slung across his shoulder.

'Callum!' she cried as he made for the door without as much as a sidelong glance.

'Callum! Please!' but the door had already slammed behind him.

Wincing at every jolt and bump in the road, Anna leaned against Jeanne in the back of the cab, her head resting against her friend's shoulder. The faint smell of expensive perfume and the feel of soft cashmere against her cheek was comforting, wrapping her in a warm embrace.

'Nearly home,' Jeanne said reassuringly, as though to a child. 'You okay?'

'Fine,' Anna said, her reply falsely cheerful. 'Do you think we should try him again on the mobile?'

'You only phoned ten minutes back at the clinic. He's probably out on a shoot. Call from the apartment. We're nearly there.'

The sky outside was a fitting grey, drizzle dancing around the streets, blowing a fine mist across the windows of the cab. Anna sank deeper into the seat, feeling safe, cocooned in this place, cut off from the real world outside.

She closed her eyes, a sudden weariness engulfing her. Over and over again she had replayed the conversation, seen him looking at her, accusing her. Even as she lay on the trolley in the clinic, waiting to go into theatre, she could still hear his voice. '*If you love me don't go ahead with this . . .*' The tears had welled up in her eyes – burning, choking tears – until the nurse had asked if she was all right. She had nodded and tried to smile. She knew she was doing the right thing, and she knew he'd come to realise it too given a little time. At the same time she hated him for not being there.

Drowsy with drugs she convinced herself she could feel the child inside her, as though it had grown to fill her. She had placed her palm against her abdomen, stroking it over and over again, wanting somehow to touch it, to cause herself pain, torturing herself for wanting to kill Callum's baby. And as her hand moved back and forth in rhythmic motion the tears rolled silently down her face and onto the pillow beneath.

The cab pulled up outside the apartment block. With the smell of a good tip in his nostrils, the Asian driver walked round to the passenger seat to let them out.

Anna eased her feet out onto the sidewalk and turned to look back at her friend.

'I'm fine Jeanne. You don't have to come up.'

'Course I do. I have to make sure you're okay.'

'Look, I'm fine,' she said, smiling weakly. 'I'd . . . like to be alone for a while.'

Jeanne nodded and took hold of her hand. 'If you need me, just give me a call – day or night. Promise?'

Anna nodded. 'You're a real star, Jeanne . . .'

'Hey, get outta here . . .' she said and kissed Anna's cheek as she climbed out onto the pavement.

Closing the apartment door behind her, Anna turned to look at the room. It was exactly as she'd left it that morning – the pillow still on the sofa, tissues screwed in balls on the floor. Leaning back against the door she closed her eyes, feeling weary from the memory of it all.

It had been a long day, but her real dread was that it wasn't over yet.

Lying on the bed in the recovery room she had fantasised about Callum waiting for her when she came home. In the dream he had bought her a bunch of flowers – lilies, her favourite – and had held her, crying, begging her forgiveness for being such a shit.

She took a long breath, then opened her eyes again. The room looked drab and lifeless in the half-light. Wiping a hand across her eyes, she dropped her handbag and coat to the floor then walked across to the telephone.

The answering machine was flashing. She sat on the sofa then pulled it into her lap. There were four messages. Eagerly she pressed rewind, urging the machine to speak to her, to put her out of this misery.

The machine clicked, then the messages began, ringing out around the twilit room, filling it with alien voices; voices she did not want to hear. As the machine clicked off, she pushed it aside, then let her head fall onto the cushion, feeling an overwhelming sense of despair. Through misted eyes she looked down the length of her body at the gentle swell of her abdomen, tilting her hips forward. Slowly she ran her hands across it, back and forth, back and forth.

'I'm sorry,' she whimpered. 'I'm sorry.' Over and over she said it – to her baby, no longer there, to Callum, and to herself – until, completely exhausted, she fell into an uneasy sleep.

When Anna finally woke the room was in darkness, only the distant lights of the West Side visible through the window. She lay curled on the sofa, her shoes still on her feet, her face tight from dried tears. She clicked on the table lamp and looked at her watch. It was two a.m. She reached down and drew the answering machine to her again, switching it to rewind, listening once more for the message she knew wasn't there.

Her mouth was dry. Slowly, wearily, she walked across to the fridge and poured herself some juice.

'*Have some orange juice . . . you need to get some vitamins . . .*'

She could hear his voice in her head, saying the words in his slightly nasal tone and for that split second felt her longing for him turn to hatred. She cursed him for punishing her in this way. Why wasn't he here, comforting her?

She went back and, composing herself, punched his number on the phone. On the fourth ring his machine activated and his voice sounded in her ear.

'Bastard!' she screamed, throwing it down, the disconnected signal droning up at her. 'You heartless fucking bastard!'

She couldn't take any more. Her body ached now with an overwhelming tiredness.

She bent down and picked up the phone, settling it back on the table, then got up and walked across to the bedroom. Standing there, staring into the darkness of the room, she could remember that first time — the way he had carried her through, her legs wrapped about him, his lips on her breast. The thought of it tormented her. Why wasn't he here? Why?

She flicked on the light switch and looked, her eyes drawn immediately to the keys laying on the bedside table. They were his keys — the keys to her apartment.

She went across and stood there, staring down at them, imagining him standing there, wrestling with the key ring, then dropping them onto the table as though it meant nothing to him; as though she meant nothing.

Slowly, each movement an effort now, she went to the drawer where he kept his clothes. Empty! She turned, looking across to the dressing table. His aftershave was gone, and the two matching ivory figures he had placed there.

She sat down heavily on the bed. Gone. He'd taken everything.

The aftermath of that terrible night swam in the depths of her memory. All weekend she had sat by the telephone waiting for Callum to ring, rehearsing over and over again the conversation they would have when he finally called. There was never any doubt in her mind that he would . . . eventually; when he'd had time to consider her viewpoint, to see her side of things. But the call never came and her messages remained unanswered.

Jeanne came by to check on her, oozing sympathy and cheerful optimism in turns, and on her part Anna was grateful for the company while resenting the intrusion into her private grief.

On Monday morning she reached the office later than usual. Was it her imagination or were people looking at her strangely? Did they all know that she'd had an abortion? Were they all sitting there secretly in judgement on her? She'd told her secretary that she was having more tests for her medical insurance, but the girl could easily have listened in to the call from Dr Levis. That or Jeanne had opened her mouth.

Anna sank into her chair, staring blankly at the piles of paperwork and layouts on the desk in front of her. She clicked on the computer and looked at the screen, flicking through from one piece of copy to the next, absorbing nothing.

Through the smoked glass door she could see a queue of people forming outside her office, awaiting an audience, requiring a decision from her. She buzzed her secretary.

'Anna?'

'Who needs to see me?'

There was a brief hesitation, then. 'Lucy needs you to approve the Check Mate fashion layout, Rosie wants to discuss the Doing Europe copy with you, Mike urgently needs to talk to you about space in the second issue, and Jeanne's got the covers you asked to see.'

'Okay. Ask Jeanne to come in and tell everyone else we'll buzz them when I'm free.'

'Will do!'

Outside she heard murmurings as the message was relayed and figures dispersed to the open-plan office. Jeanne tapped on the glass, then popped her head round the door.

'Okay to come in?'

'Sure,' Anna replied. 'What've you got?'

Jeanne placed a revised cover layout in front of her boss and waited for her reaction. Anna stared at it a moment, then looked up and smiled. 'That's fine,' she said, pushing it back across the desk.

'You're sure? You don't want these screamers any bigger, or this flash changed?' she queried, unused to Anna's instant agreement.

'Do you want an argument or do you want to get on with it?'

'No. That's great. I'll push it through.'

Anna looked down at the papers on her desk and began rummaging through. After a moment she looked up again, realising Jeanne was still there.

'Was there something else?'

Without waiting to be asked, Jeanne sat down and leaned across the desk towards her.

'It's Callum. My secretary took a call from him first thing. It seems he's cancelling the two sessions he was booked to do for us. Said he wouldn't be around for a while – that he's going off to Eastern Europe to work on a book project or something.'

Anna said nothing. Her mouth had dried up and nausea fluttered around the pit of her stomach, welling up inside her. She stared across the table, unseeing.

Jeanne reached across and took her hand, squeezing her fingers between her own. 'I'm so sorry, Anna. Maybe he just needs some time. You know how it is . . .'

'It's okay,' she answered, the words threatening to choke her. Tears clung unsteadily to Anna's eyelashes and she willed them not to fall. 'I'm all right,' she whispered and squeezed Jeanne's hand before relinquishing it.

Not wanting to meet her friend's eyes – afraid, perhaps, of the sympathy, the *pity*, she would find there – she turned back to the computer screen, scrolling through the pages as if looking for something.

Anna waited, holding her breath, willing Jeanne to be gone. As she closed the door behind her, Anna slumped in the chair, a sound escaping her that was barely human, coming up from deep within her – the sound of the raw, inescapable pain that was consuming her.

*   *   *

In the days and weeks that followed Anna's only salvation was her work. It gave her somewhere to go, something to do between the tormenting hours of the night. Memory was a torturer, punishing her unrelentingly, forcing her to confess, to say that she'd been wrong. Over and over she played out the scenes, like an over-familiar video on permanent rewind, each time reading more and more into what had been said between them, though the words themselves never changed and the ending was always the same.

Barely a month after the abortion she was hauled up before the Board. They had noticed a change in her; felt she had become distracted; heard she'd got personal problems. The latest issue? Well, it didn't really work, did it? Didn't have the spark, the freshness of the first. Put bluntly, they weren't happy with how things were going. They wanted to see the flatplans for the next three issues by the end of the week.

She knew they were right. She knew she hadn't given of her best those past four weeks. In fact, if the truth were told, she had been going through the motions, and everyone knew it. Even so, things could be saved. She could turn them round.

With not inconsiderable effort she knuckled down to work on the next few issues, drawing on all her old instincts. Friday was four days away. She could do it! But on the Wednesday she got another call — from Guy Porcaro himself — summoning her to the Penthouse. There, without ceremony, she was handed a cheque and told her services were no longer required.

In a daze Anna wandered from the lift into the Ladies' Room, where she promptly vomited all over the floor. She stood there, staring down at the contents as they swam before her.

'Oh shit! Shit, shit, shit, shit, *shit*!' she screamed.

She had gone straight to her office, told her secretary to gather everyone together in the Conference Room, then had announced to them all that she was leaving. There had been tears and bewilderment, hugs and anger – the full spectrum of emotions – before Anna had departed, determined to hang on to her own self control. But deep inside she felt herself crumbling like a sandcastle about to be hit by an incoming wave.

Jeanne had run after her, had travelled down in the lift and held her hands as they stood in the reception hall in front of the revolving doors.

'What now?' she asked.

'I don't know,' she confessed. 'Back to England, I guess.'

'No. You've got to stay, Anna. Find something else.'

'I don't think so, Jeanne. There's nothing for me here now.'

'But . . .'

'Nothing. It's over.' Anna wiped a hand across her eye then reached up to wipe away a tear from her friend's cheek. 'I'll let you know where I'm living just as soon as I find a place. Keep in touch?'

Jeanne nodded.

'And thanks, Jeanne. You've been a real friend.'

They hugged each other, Anna savouring the warmth and comfort of their closeness, then she turned and walked through the revolving doors without looking back.

*   *   *

Anna sat there in the darkness of the executive cabin, staring sightlessly at the seat-back screen, the headset playing some bland classical piece she didn't recognise. Below her – some thirty thousand feet below – lay the vast, untenanted tracts of Greenland. Home, she was going home, not, as she'd anticipated when she'd first set out, in triumph, but in defeat. Home, to lick her wounds and see old friends and try – God knew she intended to try – to put the past behind her.

After a thoughtless moment she focused on the seat in front of her, staring at the two bickering figures on the tiny screen, unable to make out what they were saying. *And does it really matter?* she asked herself, a sense of glacial distance descending on her as she watched the silent but angry exchange between the two. *Does anything matter any more?*

She felt a profound sense of listlessness, a world weariness that seemed to permeate every single atom of her being. 'Things will get better,' Jeanne had said as she held her and kissed her goodbye at the airport. 'I promise you they will. Just hang on in there, okay? And any time you need to talk, you just phone me, *okay?*'

But she knew she wouldn't phone, no matter how bad things got. That part of her life was done with. All she wanted now was to forget . . . *As if she could. As if each moment wasn't part now of some slow, unending process of self-torment.*

She sighed, then looked up, removing the headset, realising the stewardess had been speaking to her.

'Pardon?'

The young stewardess leaned close, neat as a pin, her

perfume under-stated, her accent a clipped and perfect English. 'Are you all right?'

Anna considered a moment, then smiled bleakly and shook her head. 'No. But I'll survive.'

'Would you like another drink?'

She made to refuse, then changed her mind. 'Okay. A Jack Daniels . . . No . . . A gin and tonic, please.'

'A double?'

She laughed. 'If I must.'

'It's just what the doctor ordered.'

The stewardess disappeared, returning a moment later with two ice-filled glass cups, two miniatures and four small bottles of tonic.

'There,' she said, the smile returning, 'that should keep you going for a bit.'

Eventually she emerged into the Arrivals Hall.

'Anna, Anna! Over here!'

Karen's face held that familiar, reassuring smile Anna knew so well. Promptly she burst into tears.

Anna stood at the tall sash window looking out across the tree-lined square of terraced, Georgian houses. Clouds moved quickly overhead, casting fleeting shadows across buildings and pavement. A fringe of honeysuckle hung above the window, its sweet, intoxicating fragrance filling the afternoon air. For a moment she closed her eyes and breathed deeply, drinking it in, filling herself with a momentary pleasure.

Pushing up the bottom half of the window, she perched outside on the small, iron balcony, looking out across the beautiful, central gardens, its colourful borders neat and calm. Down below the bright blue removal van shook as its engine spluttered into life. A short, wiry man in his fifties, cap pushed back on his head, slammed the tailgate shut, waved up at her, then climbed up into the van next to his mate. Anna watched it rattle up the street and around the corner out of sight.

All done, she thought, the sunlight and a sense of satisfaction making her feel languid, almost cat-like. Swivelling round, she ducked beneath the sash and stepped back into the room. For a moment she paused, looking about her. Furniture and packing cases stood in disarray in the elegant surroundings. The high ceiling of the room, its ornate cornices and marble fireplace demanded order and calm. Smiling to herself, she went through to the kitchen to make herself tea, fetishistically touching walls and lintels as she went, thinking all the while, *This is mine*.

She had fallen in love with the flat the minute she had seen it. She knew she had to move back to Islington, to the security of those places and people she knew so well. The clutch of Upper Street estate agents had thrown up a wide range of options, but the instant she had set foot inside the bright, elegant hallway of this house she had felt at home. It was a lot grander than the flat she'd had before going to the States, but her pay-off from Fifty State had enabled her to invest in something more extravagant than she'd been used to. It was, she kept telling herself, her consolation.

Returning to London had been a weird experience. Those first few weeks she'd stayed in a rented flat in Bloomsbury. From there she'd phoned friends in the business, asking them to put the word about that she was back and open to offers. It had proved to be a sobering few days. Some contacts didn't bother to return her calls, others evaded her.

'I'm sorry, she's in a meeting right now. Can I help?'

How often had she had her own secretaries use that line to put off an unwelcome caller? But being on the receiving end of it really pissed her off. Even so, she played the game, crossing that name off her list and phoning the next.

After four days she'd begun to despair, suspecting that someone from Fifty State had got to her contacts first, but then things began to come good and by that first weekend she had enough freelance work to keep her busy for a month. It wasn't exactly what she'd wanted – with her track record she'd hoped she might walk straight into an editorial position on one of the lower circulation magazines – but it would do. For a while.

Besides, she wasn't sure, after her failure in New York, whether she *could* just go straight back into that kind of job. Even running one of the smaller magazines was quite demanding. And just then she wasn't certain she wanted it. Or so she rationalised. Anyway, it had given her time to go flat-hunting, and if she'd not had the time then she'd never have found this, and if she'd never found this . . .

She stopped, looking about her, the pleasure she'd been feeling draining from her. The phone was ringing in the other room.

For a moment she stood there, listening to it ring, torturing herself, imagining it was Callum, phoning her to say hello and to congratulate her. Then, forcing herself out of the trance, she went across and switched on the kettle.

Stop it, she told herself. *It isn't him. If he cared, he'd have phoned long before now.* But as the ringing stopped and the answerphone clicked on, she found herself tense, straining to hear whose voice it was.

My mother, she thought, a surge of disappointment washing over her. For a moment . . .

When will it stop? she asked herself, biting her lip, the tears beginning to well in her eyes. *When will it bloody stop hurting?*

But no answer came. Only the click of the answerphone as it switched itself off, followed an instant later by the click of the kettle as it came to the boil.

Anna rested her hands on the washbasin and moved her face closer to the mirror. The glare from the harsh fluorescent light overhead rendered her familiar features almost alien as she stared critically at her reflection, aware of the small lines appearing in the skin around her eyes. Laughter lines, Callum had called them.

She dabbed at the smudged mascara beneath her lashes, applied another layer of lipstick, and stood back to inspect herself in the kinder, full-length mirror on the back of the door. She still had a good body – her tits hadn't dropped like Mandy's, but then her friend had breast-fed two kids. Anna turned sideways and ran a hand over her stomach. She should be eight months pregnant now – not a day went by when she wasn't aware of it – and the flatness of her abdomen seemed somehow sickening to her, a cruel reminder of her self-chosen barrenness.

Stepping through the doorway into the restaurant, music and noise filled the air, bringing her back to reality with a jolt. Sitting at the bar, just a few yards away, his neck-tie loosened and his shirt hanging outside his black trousers, the young waiter sat casually talking to the barman. As his companion nodded, acknowledging her, the young man turned towards Anna. She wondered if they had been talking about her, joking at her expense, perhaps, but there was no sign of it in the young waiter's face. A bottle of Bud in one hand, he self-consciously swept a bang of dark hair back from his face, revealing the youthfulness of his features.

'Well? Is it an offer you can refuse?' he said, smiling.

Anna laughed at his easy manner. It was attractive. 'I'm flattered, but . . .'

'Flattered? Why flattered?'

She looked down, embarrassed at being questioned like this. 'Look, it's difficult.'

'Why?' he persisted.

'It just is. It's my best friend's hen night and we're going on somewhere.'

'Can I call you, then?'

'I don't think so.'

'Please. Just for a drink.' He smiled again.

'I'll call you,' she said. 'Give me your number.'

He pulled a serviette from the counter and wrote on it.

'James,' she read, smiling back at him.

'It sounds nice when you say it.'

Anna laughed loudly. 'You're original, I'll give you that,' she said, teasing him. 'My name's . . .'

'Anna. I know.' And for a moment his eyes held hers before she looked away, across at her table.

'Look, I've got to go. My friends are almost ready to leave.'

'Now that we're on first-name terms, how about a kiss before you go?' And, without waiting for an answer, he reached out and took hold of her hand, gently pulling her towards him. He reached up, a hand softly caressing her cheek as he guided her face towards his own, their lips meeting in a tender kiss, his mouth warm and surprisingly sweet on her own.

As he released her from the embrace, Anna stood there, torn between embarrassment and arousal. She could *feel* her nipples hardening beneath her dress and knew that he could see it too. Amused and pleased by his effect on her he was confident enough to rest his hand on her thigh without fear of rejection.

'Are you sure you won't change your mind?' he said, his fingers moving down to stroke her leg through her sheer silk stockings.

'Perfectly sure,' she said, removing his hand and smacking it playfully.

He smiled and shrugged. 'Later? Maybe after you've "gone on". You could phone me. Say you're coming over. I wouldn't mind *you* waking me up.'

She felt a strange ripple of desire pass through her at the thought, but shook her head, then walked across the restaurant to rejoin the others, smiling back at him over her shoulder.

'You old tart,' Mandy said affectionately. 'Fancy snogging in a public place at your age!'

Anna simply laughed and nudged her playfully.

'Well, he wouldn't have to ask *me* twice,' said Susie.

'Hannibal Lektor wouldn't have to ask *you* twice,' responded Lyndsay predictably.

'Well, he wouldn't bloody bother to ask you once, Miss Iron Knickers!' her sister retorted.

The rest of the girls, sensing that the inevitable family argument was about to ensue, made noises about paying the bill, reaching in their handbags for wallets and chequebooks.

'So where are we off to now?' Karen asked, hoping against hope that someone would say 'Home'.

'A great place,' said Mandy enthusiastically. 'Me and Susie were there a couple of months back. You'll love it!'

'Oh, Christ! Where is it?' asked Janet, knowingly.

'Nah . . . you'll love it!' agreed Susie. 'You will!'

'What is it?' repeated Anna, an awful certainty descending on her.

'It's a place that specialises in hen nights,' Susie answered, her eyes widening as they moved from one friend to the other. 'You know,' she continued conspiratorially, 'one of those male strip joints.'

'Oh, Susie! No!' Karen wailed, appalled at the thought of it.

'Oh don't be such a stick-in-the-mud. It's my hen night for Christ's bleedin' sake. You'll love it. I promise.' And she looked to Mandy for support. Mandy, half drunk already, nodded enthusiastically.

'God, you two are *so* tacky,' laughed Anna. 'C'mon, you lot. Let's go,' and she prodded Mandy to lead the file through the jumble of tables towards the door.

'You won't be disappointed,' Mandy called over her shoulder. 'The bloke me and Susie saw was hung like a bag of satsumas!'

'Mandy!' Anna cringed, aware of people listening to

70

their conversation on all sides. She gently pushed her friend on. But Susie had warmed to the subject now. 'Yeah. When he came and waved it about in front of me it was so big it blocked out the spotlights.'

'Christ! What did you do?' asked Lyndsay despite herself.

'I said "No thanks, I'm a vegetarian; that fat old tart over there ordered the mixed grill!" and pointed to some roly-poly bird with glasses who was wetting her knickers with excitement.'

'So what happened then?' Lyndsay asked, stopping by the door, all pretence of indifference gone from her. 'Did he go over to her?'

'Yeah! Course he did. Must have seen she was a walkover.'

'And?' Janet said.

'Well . . .' Susie looked about her. People were watching from all the tables now, listening. 'He took her hand and pulled her up onto the stage with him, got her to rub baby oil into his wodger and then – can you believe this? – he undid her blouse, got out her 42 double Ds and rubbed it between them. We were under the table we were laughing so much!'

And she shrieked at the memory of it as she led the way out to the pavement in search of taxis.

Susie led the way through the entrance lobby into the bar, where she promptly took orders for drinks. The large, square room was dark and predictably sleazy with little attempt at refinement. The wooden tables and chairs that were dotted around the outside of the room were empty, while a number of men in leather bomber jackets and white t-shirts stood drinking nearby, eyeing the various groups of women as they passed through to the back room for the evening's entertainment.

'Like vultures, ain't they?' Susie whispered, leaning in close to Anna as she handed her her drink.

'I don't know,' Anna answered her. 'Vultures are generally better looking than that!'

Susie giggled then looked across at Mandy. 'We fit, then, Mand?'

Inside, tables lined the walls on three sides, forming a kind of stage area in the middle. At the far end a black curtain covered the wall through which, it was anticipated, Fabulous Frank would soon appear.

Clutching her vodka and tonic, Susie led the way to their reserved table just inside the room.

'I'm not sitting on the outside,' said Karen as she eased her way past the others to a chair in the corner.

'Nor me,' said Anna, as she slid into the seat beside her.

'Christ Almighty!' Susie laughed. 'Anyone would think it bit!'

'We'll leave that to you to find out, thanks,' Lyndsay said, moving in next to Anna.

The others sat with their backs to the stage, facing their friends, sipping their drinks and giggling as the room began to fill. Then they turned as the lights went down and a solitary spotlight focused on the centre of the black curtain. Slowly the music – a piece of Elvis Anna didn't recognise – increased in volume, heightening their expectation.

All of a sudden a figure burst through the curtain into the spotlight. Shrieks rang out from all sides, mixed with an almost hysterical laughter, as a tall man wrapped in a black cloak flapped his way round the stage like a great hairy bat.

As he strutted around, swinging his cloak this way and that, coloured lights began to pulse around the room, the music growing louder and louder, drowning out the noise from the crowd.

Karen sat in the corner with her hand splayed across her eyes, peering through the gaps between her fingers as if she was watching a horror movie. Beside her, Anna and Lyndsay, huddled together in helpless laughter, slid further under the table each time Frank headed in their direction, while opposite them Susie and Mandy sat on either side of Janet, clapping and cheering, egging Frankie on.

Surveying the scene, Anna realised that this would be great meat and drink for a feature, then laughed to herself at the rather inappropriate metaphor, storing it as a possible headline for the piece. It was totally amazing how a roomful of women – wives and mothers, most of them – could be thrown into such a frenzy by someone as totally unimpressive as Fabulous Frank, someone they might give only a quick second glance to if they passed him, fully-clothed, in the street. It was not her cup of tea at all. Nor Karen's by the look on her face.

As the tempo slowed, allowing Frankie to sway provocatively in front of a cowering member of the audience, beckoning her to undo the ties of his cloak with her teeth, Anna winced for the poor woman, ashamed and embarrassed to be a part of it.

Unrobed, Frank looked just like a boxer, his fake tan glistening in the spotlight. He danced around the floor, moving his lithe, well-muscled body to the music's rhythm, the tiny black G-string he wore leaving little to the imagination. Victims were plucked from the audience and held close, their bodies moulded to his as he fondled them in an intimate embrace, stroking and squeezing their breasts as he poked his tongue down a cleavage or into a willing mouth.

Susie's turn on stage was the one inevitability of the evening. Requiring little persuasion, she allowed herself to be led out into the centre of the room where she divested Frank of the last item of his clothing. Taking hold of her hands, he slid them up and down his body until he brought them to rest on either side of the thin, black string. Susie pulled at the threads, releasing the scanty garment. It lay in a pathetic mole hill on the floor, Frankie's old feller standing proud and erect in its place.

Erupting with laughter, Susie kissed her forefinger and tapped the end of his penis before returning to her seat to rapturous applause as Frank disappeared through the billowing curtain.

'Oh my God . . . how *could* you?' Karen shrieked.

'Ah, it's only a bit of fun!' Susie answered her, brushing away tears of laughter and trying not to smudge her mascara.

'And those women whose boobs he had out! Could you believe it!' Janet added.

'Yeah, but d'you notice how it's always the fat, ugly ones he does it to – they're probably really chuffed!' said Mandy, a touch defensive about Frankie, who, after all, had been her discovery.

'And to think he gets paid as well! I know dozens of

blokes who'd do this job for nothing!' said Janet in total disbelief. 'In fact, I know one or two who'd *pay* to have his job!'

'Yeah, but are they as well endowed?' asked Susie. 'I thought it was gonna pop up and hit me in the eye when his little knickers fell to the ground!'

'Well, your eyes ain't far from where it'd usually be heading,' Lyndsay quipped.

'Just because you think a good blow job is inflating the balloons at a kiddie's party!' Susie responded.

'I've never understood that,' Janet chipped in.

'Understood what?' Susie asked.

'Why it's called a blow job. After all . . .'

'I always thought fellatio was a bit of a mouthful . . .'

'I always thought he was an Italian!'

And again they were crying with laughter.

'Right,' Mandy said, getting up from her seat. 'Shall I get in another round before the next show? What's everyone having? Karen?'

'I'm fine,' Karen answered, lifting her half-filled glass. 'In fact, I'm not sure I'm gonna last the course. I'm so whacked. Would you mind if I sloped off in a minute, Suse?'

'Oh, Karen . . . d'you 'ave to?' Then, seeing the look on her friend's face, Susie realised there was no point making a fuss. 'Course I don't mind. As long as you're there Saturday.'

'Wild horses wouldn't keep me away,' she said, getting up from her seat with an almost indecent eagerness.

'Or donkeys,' Susie quipped, standing to embrace her friend as she made her rounds, kissing and hugging everyone in turn.

As she disappeared out the door, Mandy turned and looked about her. 'Poor Karen. Not really her scene, was it?'

'No. I thought she'd die when he came and waved it at us.' Lyndsay drained the remains of her glass and handed it to Mandy.

'Has anybody actually seen this bloke of hers?' Mandy said, gathering up the remaining glasses and making a mental list of what everyone was drinking.

'He's a teacher, like Karen,' Anna offered. 'Least, I thought she said he works at a comprehensive.'

'She keeps him pretty much under wraps, don't she?' Mandy went on.

'Too bloody right!' Susie chipped in. 'I was beginning to think she'd invented him, you know? Still, we should get to meet him at the wedding on Saturday. She said she'd bring him.'

'That'll be a novelty,' Janet said. 'I don't think I've ever met one of Karen's boyfriends.'

'Well, let's face it,' Susie answered, leaning into her drunkenly, 'she never had that many. I mean, she never had one at school, did she? Remember that time we fixed her up with nutty Garry Lloyd that time?'

The girls nodded, their giggles anticipating the familiar story.

'The dirty git managed to slide his willy out of his trousers while they were snogging. He meant to bring her hand down onto it, all secret, like, then someone went and turned the lights on. Karen looked down, saw it and ran out of the room shrieking.'

'That's right,' Janet added, when the laughter had died down. 'I was in the kitchen when she came out. She was hysterical. Shouting about how he'd pushed this big, purple, veiny thing into her hand. You'd have thought it was a horror movie!'

'I think "big" was something of an exaggeration,' Susie said with a feigned seriousness.

'You'd know, of course,' Lyndsay responded.

'Only because he had such tiny hands,' Susie answered, and the two collapsed onto the table, laughing.

Anna turned, looking about the place, for that one brief moment distanced from her friends. She had listened in silence, her smile fixed in place as the stories she'd heard a hundred times before were related once again, as comforting to them as an oft-told fairy-tale to a young child.

At tables all around the hall groups of women were leaning in close to each other, drinking, laughing, sharing their most intimate secrets. Or so it seemed.

She looked back as Susie leaned forward again. 'Do you remember that bloke she got off with when we went camping?' She shrieked with laughter. 'God, when he poked his head through the tent flap the next morning I thought a horse had escaped from the next field! I'd never seen such an ugly bastard!'

'Poor Karen,' Janet said, wiping tears away from the corners of her eyes. 'It wouldn't have been so bad but they spent so much time snogging, his stubble brought her face out in a rash. It was all red and blotchy for days!'

'Yeah,' Susie chipped in, 'and when she got home her dad wanted to know what was wrong with her and marched her off to the doctor's. He reckoned she 'ad an allergy.'

'The only allergy she had was to pricks like that one,'

Mandy declared, reaching for her drink. 'She couldn't get rid of the fucker, could she?'

'She hasn't had much luck with blokes, has she?' Janet said. 'Then again, who has?'

'Well I certainly ain't,' Susie answered. 'Not until recently, that is.'

'Lucky cow!' Janet said, mock-bitchily, then stood and straightened her skirt, looking about her for the Ladies.

'It's through there,' Susie said, nodding towards the door that led through to the bar.

'Well, let's face it, Suse,' Lyndsay said, as both Mandy and Janet moved out from their seats, 'you've been round the block more times than Sally Gunnell! At your age you need to be settling down.'

Anna saw how Susie looked at her sister and smiled insincerely. Though Lyndsay was quite right – Susie'd had enough adventures for them all in her time! – she clearly resented how Lyndsay always made a thing of it. More than once when they'd been out together, Susie had confessed how much it pissed her off that her sister had always seemed to get things right while she always made a hash of things. But now things had changed. Now Susie had found Mr Right. A man she could trust. A man she wanted to be with for the rest of her life. That thought made Anna both happy and sad at the same time – happy for her friend, who deserved a bit of good luck after all the bad, and sad for herself, that the one time she too could have had the same she had made a mess of it.

She sighed, then looked around, just as Mandy and Janet returned.

'Move your bums!' Mandy said, setting the tray down

in the middle of the table. "'Ere,' she said, 'I've just seen the stripper. In the bar.'

'Has he put his knickers back on yet?' Anna joked, the thought of him standing among all those macho males in the altogether bringing a smile to her lips: she could just imagine them puffing out their chests and rearranging their tackle.

'I'm not sure,' Mandy answered, beginning to hand out the drinks. 'He had his cloak on, more's the pity. You want me to go back and ask him?'

'You do what you like!' Susie answered her. 'Personally I prefer salami to chipolata!'

'Talking of which,' Mandy said, taking her seat again, 'did I tell you about the party the other week at Barry's?'

Barry was her husband Pete's brother, and was only marginally brighter than his younger sibling. For Anna it was a constant source of embarrassment that she had experienced her first orgasm while snogging him at a party when she was fifteen.

'How is the little charmer?' she asked sarcastically.

'Oh, you know,' Mandy said, reaching for her double vodka and lemonade. 'Anyway . . . I'm sitting in the back garden with him and his mate Colin, you know, the guy who owns all those shops, and Barry starts holding forth on his favourite subject . . .'

'Don't tell me,' Susie said. 'Let me guess. The philosophy of . . .'

'What?' Mandy said, frowning. 'Nah. *Sex*. He's always talking about it.'

'Nah . . .' Susie, Janet and Lyndsay said as one.

'Yeah . . . well, he's wittering on about how he'd like

88

to go in for some wife-swapping, how he's not fussy, when Pete comes strolling towards us. So Barry leans forward. "'Ere, Pete!" he bellows up the garden, "tell me honestly, would you fuck Elaine?"'

'Elaine?' Lyndsay asked.

'You know, his wife. The traffic warden. Well, seeing me sitting there he's not about to say a dickie bird, is he? But quick as a flash, Colin, next to me, says, "Well I fuckin' well would. Dress her up in a pair of baby dolls, black stockings and her warden's hat — fucking great! Tell you what, Barry, we'll come over for the weekend. You supply the baby dolls and I'll bring the Viking helmet and leathers for my old lady!"'

'He didn't . . .'

'He did,' Mandy said, turning to Janet. 'And you know what? I don't think either of them was joking. Can you imagine! A fucking Viking helmet!'

The second mention of the Viking helmet was too much for Janet. She laughed so suddenly that she farted — very loudly — and toppled over on her chair, ending up in a heap on the floor.

Laughing hysterically, tears streaming from their eyes now, the others pulled her to her feet. And not before time, for as Janet regained her seat, muttering something about being as 'pissed as a fart', the lights began to dim and the music started up again. The second stripper was about to come on.

'This one's the best,' Mandy said confidentially, leaning towards Anna and covering her hand with her own. 'His name's Gorgeous George. He's an ex weight-lifter, so they say. A big black guy. He's lovely. All smothered in oil.'

'Oil?' Anna said, more for something to say than because she wanted to know.

'That's right,' Mandy said. 'And if you're really lucky he hands the bottle around and you can rub it in. Wherever — and I mean *wherever* — you fancy.'

Anna smiled. 'And if I don't fancy?'

'Then pass the bottle over to me!'

Suddenly, to a fanfare of trumpets, George stepped through the curtain in all his gorgeous, glittering glory, his pectorals bulging, his perfect white teeth revealed in a ferocious smile.

Oh God! Anna thought, staring at him goggle-eyed, the thought — the very idea — of George singling out her with his bottle of baby oil, sending her into a bout of nervous embarrassment. *Not me*, she prayed, beginning to sink beneath the table once again. *Please God, not me!*

Home . . .she almost went home. Then, sitting there in the back of the taxi, the empty, brightly-lit shop-fronts of Tottenham Court Road flashing by outside, she decided that she'd had enough of waiting for *that* phone call.

Anna took the trim little mobile from her bag, then pressed the power button. By the yellow-green illumination of the screen she quickly pressed out the number the young waiter had written on the serviette for her.

After the second ring she almost switched the phone off. It was after three. He'd be asleep. He . . .

'Hello?'

He sounded groggy, as if he'd just woken. She swallowed, her finger hovering over the button, then spoke. 'It's me. Anna. From the restaurant. I . . .'

90

He was suddenly more alert. 'Anna? Black hair? Beautiful?'

She smiled at that, not really caring whether it was sincere or simple flattery. 'I was thinking . . .'

'Are you coming over?'

Again she hesitated, then, her voice much smaller. 'If you want me to.'

'If I . . .' He laughed; a soft, sexy, deeply attractive laugh that she hadn't noticed before. Then again, perhaps he hadn't laughed in the restaurant. 'Where are you?' he asked.

She stared out the window. 'Right now I'm in the back of a cab heading east along the Euston Road.'

'Great. I'm not far off. You know Richmond Avenue? It's in the Barnsbury area.'

What am I doing? she thought. *What in God's name am I doing?* Then, steeling herself, she answered him. 'I know it.'

'Okay. Well, I'm at number one twenty-six. Top flat. It's . . .' Again that laugh. 'Well, you'll see, huh? Ten minutes, okay? And Anna?'

'Yes?'

'Did I tell you what lovely eyes you have?'

Bullshit, she thought. But it was pleasant bullshit. The kind a woman liked to hear. 'Ten minutes,' she said, then pressed the power button again, switching it off.

She sat back, getting her breath, wondering suddenly just how much the middle-aged taxi driver had heard, then, smiling — suddenly absurdly pleased with herself — she leaned forward and tapped on the glass.

'Change of plan,' she said. 'Can you drop me at Richmond Avenue. Number one twenty-six.'

'Whatever you say, love,' he answered, steeling a glance of her in his mirror. 'A lady's prerogative, or so my old woman says.'

Anna laughed amiably. 'You must see all kinds of things,' she said, feeling suddenly chatty, the thought of what lay ahead — the adventure of it — making her discard her usual inhibitions.

The taxi driver laughed. 'You don't know the 'arf of it, doll. You get all sorts when you do this job. Toms. Gays. You name it, it's been sat back there where you are, love. And some of 'em just don't care!'

'Go on,' she said, intrigued.

'Only last week, for instance. I picked up this toff — pin-stripe, brolley, rolled copy of The Times, the lot — just off Leadenhall Market. You know, down in the City. I was about to drive off when he opened the door and whistled — yeah, whistled, like a barrow boy. A moment later a young tart, a secretary, I guess — you know the sort, made up like a dog's dinner — jumps in beside 'im, bold as brass and slams the door behind 'er. "Where to?" I says. "Euston", he says, and proceeds to sit 'er on 'is lap, one leg either side of 'im. Well, I try to concentrate on me driving, like. I mean, it's none of my business, right? But for the next ten minutes they go at it hammer-and-tongs in the back, her tongue down his throat, his John Thomas up there where the sun don't shine. Me? I act as if I don't know what's going on. Whenever we stop at a red, I sit there, like Simon Templar, and if anyone tries to get my attention, I give 'em the wink.

'Anyway. We get to Euston and the guy jumps out, as spruce as he got in, and hands me a tenner. A moment later the girl gets out, brushing herself down, like a cat who's just had a full bowl of cream, as well she might! I count out the change — two twenty, it was — and hands it to 'im, expecting maybe he'll say "No, keep it." But he takes it, hands me back the twenty pence and, bold as brass, says "Have a nice day." So . . . they're about to walk away when I leans out and, waving the cloth I use to keep me windscreen clean, shouts at 'em, "Hey, Miss! You forgot your knickers!" And you know what? The silly tart only lifted her dress to check!'

Anna chuckled. It was as if the evening had made her immune to such tales. Indeed, she was about to repeat one of Susie's stories when he pulled the taxi over to the side and stopped.

'Here we are, love. Number one twenty six.' He turned, looking at her. 'Boyfriend?'

She laughed. 'Sort of.'

'You seem a nice girl.'

'I *am* a nice girl.'

She took out her purse and looked at him. He was watching her strangely. 'Anyway,' he said, 'why ain't you married? A nice girl like you? Still young. Attractive. All your own teeth!'

At any other time she'd have told him to piss off and mind his own business, but for once his question touched a chord in her.

'Haven't found anyone rich enough,' she joked.

'That's just bollocks!' he said. 'What you really mean is you ain't found Mr Perfect. But let me tell you, love, the truth is he don't exist. The trouble is all you women fill your 'eads with this romantic fiction crap! All it does is make us all fucking miserable, 'cos us blokes just can't measure up to it. All *we* want is a pint or two most evenings, our footie on a Saturday, a good sex life, and our dinner on the table when we get 'ome. I mean, it ain't much to ask for from life, now, is it?'

She laughed, astonished by him. 'It sounds to me like you're just nostalgic for the days before women's lib.'

'Women's lib? Don't give me women's fuckin' lib! I've never met a woman yet – unless she was a raving les – who didn't, in her 'eart of 'earts, want just three things.'

Anna, who only moments before, had found herself amazed by the apparent depths of the man's old-fashioned chauvinistic ignorance, now sat forward, intrigued.

'Three things?'

'Yeah.' He ticked them off on his fingers. 'A nice home, a husband who didn't knock 'er around, and babies.'

She put her bag on her shoulder then reached for the door handle. 'I . . . I've got to go.'

'Your change,' he said, offering it to her.

She smiled. 'Keep it. I mean, I don't want you waving your shammy at me as I go up the path, do I?'

He laughed. 'Thanks. Oh . . . and one last thing.'

Anna had opened the door and stepped out. She clunked it shut then turned, facing him again, seeing him properly for the first time. He was fifty-five if he was a day, balding and ugly as sin. 'Yes?'

He beckoned her towards him, then, in a whisper, said. 'Just remember . . . there's nothing a man likes better than a woman who puts on her lipstick *before* she gives him a blow-job!'

And with that he roared off, giving her a double-beep as he turned the corner. She stood there briefly, half in shock, then turned, facing the big, square, semi-detached house, a pair of stone sphinxes standing guard on either side of the steps leading up to the front door. There was a single light on in the top flat.

She pushed the gate open and walked quickly down the path, the heels of her shoes clicking loudly — too loudly, it seemed — on the tiles. Reaching up she went to press the top bell, but even as she did the door opened.

'James?'

'What kept you?' he said, then reached out and took her hand, drawing her into the shadows of the hallway.

'I . . .'

But he didn't want an answer. He drew her close and kissed her — a kiss like that first kiss in the restaurant, but longer, and this time he held her close, unafraid that she would draw away, his whole body pressed against her.

She drew back from him, aroused, astonished by what she was feeling, seeing, in the half-light from outside, that he was smiling at her. She smiled back.

'Did you have a good time?' he asked quietly.

She nodded.

'I didn't think you'd come.'

'No. I . . .'

'You didn't intend to, did you?'

She hesitated, then shook her head, conscious that he still held her hands, conscious of the sweet warmth of that contact and of the way her heart was pounding in her chest, like a schoolgirl's.

'So why did you?'

In answer she pushed her mouth against his once more, kissing him more aggressively this time, her hands moving round his body to feel the shape of his back, his sides.

When they broke from the kiss it was his turn to look surprised.

'My mother warned me about women like you!'

'Did she?'

He nodded, a smile coming to his lips. 'And my father warned me not to miss out on them!'

She hit him playfully, liking him suddenly, this stranger, this . . . well, this *forward* young man.

'Are we going to stand here all night?' she asked.

He stared past her and shrugged. 'You got a better idea?'

She nodded, then turned and closed the door. *This isn't me*, she thought as she turned him and pushed him towards the stairs. *I'm a nice girl. The kind who marries, gets a nice home and has babies.* But the truth was she wanted him. Wanted to know what he looked like naked. What he smelled like when she was making love to him and how his face changed at that crucial moment of passionate release. She wanted to know what turned him on, what kind of things aroused him.

Is it just me? she wondered as she pushed him up the stairs, her hands playfully touching his back, teasing him. *Or are we all like this? Wanting . . . forever wanting what we think we can't have?*

No answer came.

On the top landing, outside his door, he turned and took her in his arms again. She kissed him, willingly, eagerly, surrendering to the darkness and the moment, and this time when his hands lay on her thighs she did not push them away but pulled him closer. As his fingers brushed the soft, naked line of skin beneath her knickers, she sighed, then gave a throaty laugh.

'Let's go inside.'

'But . . .'

'Inside!' she repeated, insistent, emphasising the word by pushing him hard.

'Okay,' he said, putting his hands up in mock surrender. 'I get the message.'

'Good,' she said, pulling him to her and kissing him again. 'Because I've been thinking about this all evening.'

It was no less than the truth. For all her introspection, for all the crazy, hectic things that had happened 'Up West', she had not stopped thinking about him all night. But thinking something and admitting it — uttering it — were different things. In the light from the landing window she could see how his face had changed, how it was suddenly more serious.

'Why *did* you come?'

She stared at him, wondering what to say. Because she was lonely? Because she was desperate? Or was it something else? Was it a running away from something? Whatever, behind his question she sensed something unexpected.

'Do you try it on often, then, and get turned down?'

She expected a lie — a denial — but to her surprise he laughed and nodded.

'Yeah. All the time. It's like . . . practice. You know. Exercising those old primal instincts.'

'And sometimes you get lucky, right?'

'Sometimes . . .' he stopped, staring at her, then shook his head. 'Look, this is weird, you know? Earlier, before you called, I was thinking about you. About the way you moved, about your hair, your eyes. I . . . well, it's not usually like that. But there was something about you.'

She laughed softly. 'It's a song.'

'Pardon?'

'Something about you. You know. Level 42.'

He shrugged, too young, it seemed, to remember it. Not only that, but it was as if she'd interrupted him at the wrong moment. He looked down, disappointment in his face.

'Well?' she said, taking his hands again. 'Are you going to take me inside or not?'

'I . . .'

Suddenly he seemed very different from the brash, arrogant young man she had met at the restaurant. Suddenly, inexplicably, he seemed vulnerable, a little boy almost.

He turned from her and pushed the door open, then stood back to let her pass.

She stepped inside, into this stranger's rooms, looking about her as he turned on one of the mounted wall-lamps.

It was nice. Far nicer — and far tidier — than she'd expected. It was a big room, comfortably decorated, with a plush beige carpet and a long, brown leather sofa to one side. The shelving, to her left, was what she'd heard described as 'Japanese techno black', complete with high-tech stereo, a reel-to-reel, TV and huge speakers. Books — hundreds of them, filled the rest of the space. Strangely, it suggested a degree of affluence, yet he was a waiter.

She looked across at him. He was tidying, conscious, it seemed, of her critical eyes. That too was strange.

'Do you share?'

He shook his head, then, straightening one last cushion, looked up at her. 'Would you like some coffee?'

Green eyes, she thought, surprised that she'd not remembered.

'I want to go to bed,' she said. 'Don't you?'

'I . . .' He laughed, suddenly embarrassed. 'I'm not usually like this. I . . .'

She went across and held him, kissing him again, trying to rekindle the fire she'd felt in him earlier, and slowly he responded.

She put her mouth to his ear, gently stroking it with her tongue, then whispered softly into its shell. 'Undress me, James.'

It felt strange, almost as if someone else – Susie, perhaps – had taken her over, yet she knew this was herself. The wine – the very context of the evening – had freed her to be like this. That and her vulnerability.

She felt his hands undo the zip of her dress, felt it fall away.

Surrender, she thought. When it comes right down to it, we all surrender to the darkness in us.

His mouth sought her own again, his kisses sweet and delicious, and then he was kissing her exposed breasts, his teeth nibbling at them, making her groan and trace her hands down his sides until they rested at the top of his thighs, her thumbs slowly stroking up and down the swollen shape of his penis.

As he broke from the kiss, his eyes, looking into hers, were bright with desire, the pupils large. His voice was a husky whisper. 'You want to go through?'

She shivered, then gave the slightest nod.

'Come, then,' he said, moving back from her, leading her by the hands, his eyes holding hers all the while.

And then they were lying there, facing each other on the bed, naked in the shadows of the room, his fingers stroking her breasts and inner thighs, caressing her intimately, while hers gently cupped and stroked his balls, the long shaft of his penis. And all the while their mouths met in small, delicious kisses that heightened their mutual desire, until she could bear it no more and drew him up on to her.

Though her hands on his buttocks urged him to enter her, to have her and to fuck her, he hesitated.

'Are you . . .'

'It's okay,' she said, her eyes pleading with him, her need suddenly urgent. 'Please . . .'

She lifted her face to his and kissed him once again, a long, intimate kiss as her fingers stroked and smoothed his sides, then found his penis again, leading it slowly into her.

She watched his face in the half light from outside; saw how her own need was mirrored in it as he began to fuck her, that oldest of rhythms, encoded in the bone and muscle of the species, taking them both over, feverish and frantic, separating them from their normal thinking selves until, in the hot, sweaty darkness, they both spasmed and cried out, the moment both a release and an agony.

Afterward she lay there, breathless, the sweat cooling on her and James beside her, and felt a sense of wonder that the evening had ended in this manner; that she had taken so strange, so huge a step away from her normal self.

A nice girl. Well, even nice girls did things like that. *And Callum*? She blew out a silent breath. Callum was gone. He'd left, walked out on her, just when she'd needed him most. And all this time she'd blamed herself. And maybe she *had* been wrong, maybe she *should* have had the child — God knows she wanted one now — but that didn't excuse him walking out on her. It didn't excuse him giving up on her. Nothing excused that. For a long while she hadn't understood that; she had lived in abeyance, waiting for him to call and forgive her, and take her back. But now that was over. Finally she'd stopped waiting. From here on she would begin to live her life again.

Fun. What was wrong with having a little fun?

She turned her head, looking at the man who lay beside her. James was watching her, his eyes, as once before, strangely thoughtful. Seeing that, she smiled and saw her smile returned.

He reached out and placed his hand gently on her stomach; a curiously intimate gesture — more intimate, it seemed, than all that had gone before, for that had been simple fucking.

She shivered, moved suddenly by the desire to know more about this man who lay beside her in the darkness. She placed her hand over his and lifted it to her breast.

'What are you thinking?' she said quietly.

'Oh . . .' His fingers gently caressed the yet-sensitive bud of her nipple. 'I guess I was wondering who you are. Why you came.'

She laughed softly. 'Because you asked.'

His fingers fell still. 'I don't mean that. It's . . .'

He lifted himself up onto one elbow, looking down at

her. Taking his hand from her breast, he drew the hair away from her face, tracing her features.

'You're beautiful, you know that, Anna.'

She smiled. 'And you're young.'

He laughed; it was not a boastful, cocky laugh, but pleasant, almost self-conscious. 'Not *too* young, I hope,' he said, bending to plant a gentle kiss on her nose. Again it was strangely intimate – the kind of thing a lover might do. She shivered and briefly looked away.

'What is it?'

She looked back at him and smiled. 'It's nothing. It's just that it's so strange.'

'This?' He shrugged. 'What's so strange about this?' Then, relenting, he nodded. 'I know what you mean. You peel away the clothes and it's like you peel away all sorts of other layers, too. When we're like this – when we're naked – it's like we're suddenly constrained by the need to be honest with each other – to strip away all the pettiness and the untruths.'

She stared at him a moment, surprised not only by his words, but by the intelligence – the thoughtfulness – she glimpsed behind them.

'What do you do?' she asked, curious suddenly to know.

'I wait.'

'For what?'

His laughter this time was warm and unrestrained. He sat up. 'You know, I really like you, Anna. There's something . . .'

'*Mature* about me?'

He put a hand on her knee, gently kneading and

caressing the skin beneath it with his thumb. 'Does that worry you?'

'Doesn't it you?'

'I don't know. I haven't really thought about it. But I guess not. I mean, I don't think I'd have made a pass at you . . .'

'Honest?'

'Honest.'

For a moment she closed her eyes, cat-like, letting herself be drawn into the soft touch of his fingers against her flesh. Wasn't that enough? But she knew the answer. If it were enough – if it had *ever* been enough – then she'd have been more like Susie and the others. But it wasn't. It was never enough. So maybe the taxi driver was right. Maybe she was too much of a perfectionist. Maybe she ought to ask less of life. And maybe she couldn't. Maybe she was fated to be as she was.

She opened her eyes and smiled at him. 'So what *do* you do? When you're not waiting, that is.'

'I study.'

'*Really*? Like . . . what?'

'Like . . .' His hesitation, mimicking her own, amused her. 'I'm studying to be an architect.'

'An architect?' Her surprise was unfeigned. 'Really?'

'Like . . . *really*.' He raised an eyebrow. 'Why, what did you think? Did you think you were just fucking some young waiter?'

His comment caught her unprepared. What *had* she thought? Indeed, it all kept coming back to that. Why had she come? Just to fuck him? Or had she sensed something else?

'I . . . I liked fucking you.'

'But?'

But I wanted more, she answered in her thoughts. *That's my trouble — I* always *want more.*

'So?' he said, moving closer, until his face lay by her face, his body right up against her body. 'Shall we try something else? Shall we try and make love this time?'

She got home just after seven, smiling to herself as she put the key in the lock, tired but astonished by the night's events. She had left a note beside him on the bed and then gone, slipping away silently, walking along the empty avenue as the dawn came up, across the unusually traffic-free junction at Liverpool Road and into her own square, its stillness in the early morning light delighting her.

Stepping inside, she put her bag down on the hallway table, then looked at herself in the glass, strangely, absurdly pleased with herself. Younger . . . There was no doubt about it — that Cheshire-cat smile made her look younger, despite the fact she'd had no sleep.

And what would her friends have made of that? Old stick-in-the-mud, cautious Anna, having such adventures? Well, she didn't intend telling them, because . . . well, because they wouldn't understand; because they'd think it purely a physical thing.

For a moment she closed her eyes, remembering. Fucking . . . No, that hadn't been fucking, not that last time — that had been something else. Something more.

She shuddered, simply thinking about it; about how sweet, how loving he had been to her.

Anna nodded to her reflection, looking deep into her eyes the way he had as he had entered her. Yes, there was no doubting it. It had begun again. Against all the odds and in the most inauspicious of circumstances, she had found someone.

She walked through into the living room, unable to keep the smile from her face, imagining him waking to find her note.

James, it read. *Thank you for the sweetest of evenings. I've things to do, but I'll call you later, before you go to work. Love Anna.*

She looked about her as if seeing it all anew, then, from habit, went across and pressed the rewind button on the answerphone, plumping down into the armchair to listen.

There was a click, a small delay, and then the taped recording ran. At once she was sitting bolt-upright, alert, her heart pounding.

'Anna? It's me, Callum . . .'

~ Mandy ~

'Afternoon,' Jonathan Ball said sarcastically, opening the door and letting her pass. 'You're late.'

'Sorry,' Mandy said, pulling off her coat and looking about her for somewhere to hang it. Even though their three-month affair had been solely conducted in properties such as this — ones that Jonathan was supposed to be selling through the estate agency — she still wasn't used to being in other peoples homes uninvited. 'I had to collect the car,' she said.

She let the coat fall onto the floor then turned, looking at him.

He was looking out into the street. 'So where've you parked?'

'I had to leave it with Pete,' she said, her hands reaching up to rest on his shoulders.

Guiding her inside he pushed the door closed, then turned, facing her.

'God,' she said, 'you look awful.'

He laughed, straightening his tie. 'Sorry. I had a heavy night with some of the lads. Besides, you look a bit frazzled yourself.'

'Frazzled? Thanks a bunch. You sure know how to charm a girl!'

He reached out and pulled her towards him, his hands cupping her buttocks, holding her tightly against him until she could feel the swell of his groin against her own. 'I charm *you*, don't I?'

He kissed her; a soft, sensuous kiss, while his hands gently stroked her back, moving with almost painful slowness from the neck right down to the base of her spine.

'Christ, I've missed you,' she whispered hoarsely, as he drew her down onto the floor, right there in the hallway. 'Have you missed me?'

''Course I have,' he said, unzipping himself with a haste that was almost indecent. 'I nearly sprained a wrist thinking of you.'

She laughed coarsely, picturing it. 'What was I doing . . . you know, when you were thinking of me?'

He let his trousers fall down over his knees and straddled her awkwardly as she lifted herself towards him, her skin tingling with desire, her nipples painfully stiff. With little finesse he pushed her dress up around her waist, revealing her nakedness above the blackness of her stocking tops. Again, the brutality of it made her catch her breath.

'Just this . . .' he answered, glancing at her briefly, a dancing smile on his lips. Then, with an abruptness that was typical, he was inside her, his hot warmth filling her, making her cry out.

'Oh God, oh Jesus Christ!'

'You're a bad girl,' he said, grunting, thrusting down into her again and again. 'A *bad* girl.'

*　　*　　*

She lay there in blissful disarray, her dress rucked up as he'd left it, as she listened to him walking about overhead, seeing him vividly in her mind, his clipboard in his left hand, his silver fountain pen in the other as he noted down the details of the property. She smiled and closed her eyes.

For twenty years her life had revolved around her family, and that had been okay. It was what she'd always wanted — a home, kids. But now the boys were older, independent, and it was just her and Pete . . .

She shivered, thinking about it. There was an emptiness, a loneliness now that the boys no longer needed her, the feeling had come upon her unexpectedly, overwhelming her, filling her with a sense of having served her purpose. For months she had moped about the house, knowing that there was nothing to look forward to — that this was the beginning of the end — and that glimpse into her future had filled her with horror.

For a day or two she had even toyed with the idea of ending it all. It was more of a morbid fantasy really; imagining her friends mourning her, her kids realising how much they would miss her now she was gone, the kind of flowers people would send. She'd always hated chrysanthemums — she hoped nobody would send chrysanthemums. She'd never actually do it, of course. Besides, there was too much life in her, an unfulfilled longing to experience something more: there just *had* to be something more. Yes, she remembered sitting there in her kitchen, realising for the first time just how much of herself had been denied all those years. And with it had come a desire to know what it was like to be with another man, to feel someone other than Pete inside her.

III

To know that someone else wanted her, desired her . . . even loved her, perhaps.

It was when she had decided to put their house on the market, to find something smaller, that she'd met Jonathan. From that moment on she knew her life would never be the same. He had lit a spark in her, bringing her back to life.

By the end of the first month of their affair Mandy had lost count of how many strange tables, floors and beds she had made love on. Having the keys to numerous houses, Jonathan never had a problem finding somewhere to take her. At last she had discovered what it was like to make passionate love and she couldn't get enough of it.

'Mandy?'

She stirred herself and opened her eyes. He was standing at the foot of the stairs, staring at her. He had put the clipboard down and was toying nervously with his tie.

'Why don't you join me?'

He hesitated, then shook his head. 'I can't, I . . .'

'Come on,' she said, leaning up on one elbow. 'Let's 'ave seconds.'

He looked away. 'Look, you know I'd like to, but . . . well, I've got a lot on today.'

She stared at him, astonished. In all the time she'd known him, she'd never known him refuse seconds. The second time was what made it for her. The first time was always for him − a quick, explosive fuck − but seconds, that was when she got *her* pleasure. A long, slow . . . She shivered with anticipation of it.

'Jonathan?'

He glanced at her, then away again. 'I can't. Honestly, Mandy.'

She stood up slowly, her eyes never leaving his, pulled her dress up over her head and let it fall to the floor. Now she was naked apart from her stockings. She saw how his eyes took her in and then looked away. He wanted her. She *knew* he wanted her.

She went across and took his hand, moving it to her mouth and gently playing her tongue upon his fingers, pulling each one between her lips in turn. Holding his eyes she took up his other hand and placed it on her breast, the nipple stiff beneath his touch.

'Come on,' she whispered huskily, leaning into him, aroused by the rough feel of his suit cloth against her naked skin. 'Fifteen minutes. You can spare me fifteen minutes, surely?'

She reached down, her hand tracing the line of his groin until it rested on his crotch. *There*, she knew it! If he didn't want to fuck her ragged then she was Mary Whitehouse.

She kissed his neck while she stroked him, hearing him moan softly, then, knowing he was hers to do with as she would, she eased down the zip of his trousers and reached inside, freeing his stiffly erect penis.

'Ten minutes?' she whispered.

'No ...' he protested weakly. 'I've got to go. Really ...'

But he wasn't going anywhere. She had his cock in her hand and he was as likely to leave now as Colonel Gaddafi was to ring on the bell and ask if she wanted to buy any cheap dusters or dishcloths for charity.

'Upstairs,' she said. 'Let's go upstairs,' and taking him

by the hand she led him step by step up the narrow stairway, feeling his eyes on her as she went, excited by the power she felt at that moment.

Deep inside she felt a surge of triumph. *If Pete could see me now*, she thought and smiled.

But Pete wasn't here. Only her . . . and Jonathan.

She lay there afterwards, his body half across hers, and let her eyes wander about the room. It was a nice room, prettily decorated with lots of pink and white flowers and flouncy blinds – the way she'd have had her own bedroom if it hadn't been for Pete. He wasn't really the frilly type, and in any case he couldn't see the point in spending good money on poncing up a room you only slept in. Poor Pete! He was definitely at the end of the queue when imagination was being dished out. Not like Jonathan – his was wild! Before she'd met him Mandy had thought lovemaking was laying on your back with your eyes closed for two minutes, maximum, working out what you needed to get out of the freezer for tomorrow night's dinner. But that had all changed.

Mandy let out a contented sigh.

Jonathan traced a finger lightly across her breasts, teasing her.

'I really must go.'

'Are you sure?' she whispered, gently nibbling his ear.

'God, you're insatiable, woman,' he laughed, then kissed her quickly and got up, standing beside the bed.

'Just making up for lost time.'

'I'm glad I could be of service, madam,' he said, beaming down at her.

She felt her breath catch, looking at him. 'You can service me any time.'

He threw a pillow at her in mock disgust, then gathered his clothes from about the room. And as she watched him dress she thought how beautiful he was. She had always fantasised about a tall, dark, handsome lover, and now she had one, only with Jonathan it was better than she had ever imagined. Unimaginably better.

As he pushed his fingers through his hair, she slipped out of bed and picked his tie up from the floor. Looping it playfully around his neck, she pulled his face down to her own, kissing him softly on the lips.

'When can I see you again?' she asked, crossing one end of the silk fabric over the other.

'I'm not sure.' He looked away guiltily, busying himself with the button on his cuff. 'I have to go away for a couple of weeks. Business.'

She gave a laugh of disbelief. 'Business? But you're an estate agent! Your business is here.'

He glanced at her, the slightest colour in his cheeks. 'We're thinking of going into foreign properties. Retirement stuff, you know, in Spain. I have to go out there to set things up.'

She felt a vague anger stir in her. 'When did you know about this?'

'Two days ago.'

'You bloody liar. You've known for weeks, 'aven't you? You knew and you didn't have the bottle to tell me.'

'I swear,' he said, raising his hands, as if she were about to hit him. 'Don't you think I'd have told you sooner if I'd known?'

'You could've told me on the phone.'

He huffed, exasperated. 'And then you wouldn't have come today, would you?'

She let the ends of the tie fall from her fingers and looked away from him petulantly.

'Look, Mandy, I'd have told you if I'd known, honest I would, but it wasn't certain. Not 'til the other day.' He reached up and took her by the shoulders, kissing the back of her neck. 'You know how I feel about you.'

'You could do something,' she said quietly.

He drew his head back, looking at her openly now. 'What?'

She turned, her eyes searching his a moment, and then she said it, the words almost a whisper. 'You could take me with you.'

He laughed, then shook his head. 'Mandy! Be realistic. You're *married*.'

'I *know* I'm bloody married!' She felt a small lump in her throat; suddenly she wasn't angry any more; suddenly she was very close to tears. 'You don't have to remind me that I'm bloody married!'

He gave a heavy sigh. 'Look . . . you know I'd take you with me if it were possible, but . . .' He shrugged. 'I'll miss you. You know I will.' And as he spoke his fingers brushed gently over her breasts and down her sides, hesitating briefly at the top of her legs, caressing her with the lightness of a butterfly, moving slowly, teasingly across the swell of her pubis, the touch so soft, so arousing that Mandy closed her eyes, her body aching from inside.

'You bastard,' she moaned, the words barely audible as his fingers parted her. 'You bloody bastard . . .'

*   *   *

In the beauty salon Mandy sat alone in the cubicle, relishing the surroundings. Soft pastel curtains hung on wooden rings along two sides, with pale, pine panelling covering two more; the paraphernalia of pampering and self-indulgence — bottles and jars, brushes and tissues, creams and lotions — lining the shelves of one of them. Mandy kicked her shoes and stockings under the bed and swung her legs up on top of it, lying against the raised back-rest, her body relaxed for the first time that day. Leaning forward she turned at the waist and adjusted the angle so that when she lay down she was almost horizontal, then closed her eyes.

She had got home some time after three, completely sozzled, somehow managing to be up again at seven so she could collect Pete's car from the West End, where she'd abandoned it the night before. By the time they'd left the restaurant she had been four sheets to the wind and in no fit state to drive, and the session at the strip joint had just about finished her off. Her abiding recollection was of limbo dancing under the crotch of some magnificent black stallion, his legs astride her like two pillars of gleaming ebony, his lunch dangling above her head like an invading eel.

The audience had cheered wildly as the two of them gyrated around one another, the sound of stamping feet vibrating across the dance floor like a herd of marauding wildebeest.

Mandy cringed at the recollection and squeezed her eyes tighter shut as though to erase the memory.

The last time she'd been there — with Susie a couple of months before — the evening had ended very differently, with the police being called in. Some inadequate moron, jealous of one of the dancer's rather generous attributes, had picked a fight with him out in the bar. Friends on both sides had bundled in, almost wrecking the place as chairs, tables and glasses went flying around the room. One of the Sunday papers had got hold of the story and ran it under the heading 'Big Dong Ding-dong'. That really tickled Mandy and she gave a little chuckle.

No, last night had been entirely good humoured, and once Anna and Karen had left they had felt free to enjoy themselves, no longer inhibited by their friends' unspoken disapproval.

We had a good laugh, she thought, grinning at the memory. *A bloody good laugh*.

The sound of curtain rings clacking together interrupted her thoughts. She opened her eyes with a start. A tall, slim blonde with a flawless complexion and manicured nails stepped through the curtains and into the cubicle, her button-through white coat denoting her professional status. She smiled across at Mandy before turning to close the curtain behind her.

'Hello, and how are you? Haven't seen you here in ages.' The words rose and fell as though she were singing, the last word of each sentence drawn out, clung on to.

'Fine, thanks. I've been busy.' She looked down the length of her body at her bare legs. 'They definitely need doing, though.'

The girl reached down and ran a cool hand up and down Mandy's shin, the short, coarse hair bristling beneath her touch. She shook her head and tutted her disapproval.

Mandy fidgeted uncomfortably, the thick, green paper

towel covering the bed sticking to her skin and tearing beneath her weight.

'I've shaved them,' she apologised.

'Mmm.' The girl ran her hand up and down the leg once more and smiled up at Mandy. 'Naughty girl!'

'Are they long enough d'you reckon?'

'Just about.' The girl patted Mandy's knee and turned to stir the wax, melting in a metal container on the side, the smell of heated camomile filling the air, reminding her of Germolene ointment on a grazed knee. 'We'll just give it a couple more minutes, all right?' she said, the echo of that final word lingering in the air, following her through the curtains as she disappeared from sight.

Mandy looked down at her body with a critical eye. Her dress was pulled up around her waist, below which only scanty black knickers relieved her nakedness. She ran a hand across her abdomen. Beneath her touch the ridges and indentations bore testimony to the lives she had carried within her, the children she had borne. She hated to think of Jonathan seeing those stretch marks; they belonged to another life, another Mandy; a woman whose sexuality had been dormant, unawakened. She smiled to herself at the thought, remembering how they'd met.

The idea of selling the house was just a seed in Mandy's mind, and one she'd not yet attempted to plant in Pete's. Browsing through the window displays in the cluster of Upper Street estate agents had been motivated by little more than idle curiosity. She had been fantasy shopping for the house of her dreams. They had bought their own house at a generous discount under the Council's 'Right to Buy' scheme, and now the area had been bought up by the monied middle classes and, she was informed, she lived in a 'desirable village' and that her house was a 'villa', so they stood to make a handsome profit if they sold up and went for something smaller once the boys had gone. When the time came, that, if nothing else, would convince Pete that moving was a good idea.

Self-conciously she pushed open the heavy glass door to one of the offices, the besuited young men and women briefly looking up at her before returning to their work.

'Can I help you?'

She turned to see a man – late thirties she guessed – smiling across at her.

'I . . .I wondered if you had a list of properties.'

'Of course.' He walked over to a smoky glass-topped table near the door, picked up a sheaf of cream-coloured paper and handed it to her. 'Are you looking for a house or flat?'

'A house.'

'How big?' he said, returning to his seat and gesturing for her to take the seat across from him. He reached into a drawer, took our a white index card, then took his pen from his jacket pocket.

'Quite small. Two bedrooms, I s'pose.'

'Any area in particular?' he asked, ticking a box.

'Not sure, really. I've only just started looking. I just wanted to get an idea of what was around – you know, prices and stuff.' She was conscious of wasting his time and moved to the edge of her seat.

'And how much can you go to?' he said, undeterred.

'Er, I'm not sure.'

'Is your own property on the market yet?'

She shook her head.

'Well, perhaps you'd like us to value it for you? I could pop round tomorrow if you like,' and he flipped open the desk diary laying in front of him. 'Say, about eleven?'

Mandy nodded. 'Eleven sounds fine.'

'I'll just take down some details,' he said, smiling across at her. Mandy eased back on the seat, enjoying his attention. 'Oh, and here's my card.'

'Jonathan Ball,' she said, reading aloud the fine italic print before placing the card in her handbag. 'My name's Mandy Evans.'

That had been the start of it all. He came round as arranged, measured up the rooms, wrote down some details, and then they'd chatted over coffee, parting after an hour on first name terms. And when he phoned the following day to ask if she would like to view a property he thought would interest her, she felt excited at the prospect of seeing him again.

They went through the motions of looking at the house – a small terraced property on Matilda Street – inspecting each room, admiring the original features, lamenting the north-facing garden; playing the game. In the kitchen he had brushed past her in the doorway with no apology for the physical contact, and in the hallway he'd caught her by the arm as she tripped on a rug, his hand resting there a moment longer than necessary. They had chatted, become familiar.

When he phoned later that day asking if she would like to see another property the following morning, she knew instinctively that there was more to it. She agreed of course, only later realising the implications. But by then the need to see him again had become all-consuming; the thought of it both terrifying and exciting.

As soon as Pete and the boys left the house she started getting herself ready, opting for a little Nicole Farhi number she'd bought, knocked off, from a mate of Susie's, finished off with fake Chanel earrings and a liberal splash of Coco eau de toilette. And even she had to admit she looked pretty tasty.

At the house he was already waiting for her, standing in the doorway as she pulled up in the car. She could feel the tension between them as she walked past him into the hallway. They didn't speak as he led the way around the ground floor rooms, and then up the stairs towards the bedrooms. The curtains in the master bedroom had been pulled across, the heavy damask drapes falling in luxurious folds onto bare wooden floorboards. Jonathan switched on the bedside lamp, throwing a warm glow around the walls and ceiling. The large brass bed with its antique, white coverlet, dominated the room. Mandy walked slowly around the far side of the bed, her hand caressing the smooth, cold metal as she went. She looked across at Jonathan standing on the opposite side and their eyes met for the first time, each acknowledging the inevitability of what was about to happen.

He knelt on the bed and held out his hand towards her. She reached across, allowing herself to be eased onto the bed, feeling detached, as though it were somebody else here with this stranger, as though she were an actor with a script and soon somebody would shout 'Cut!'.

But there was nobody to intervene. There were just

the two of them, and as he undressed her she wanted to release herself up to him. She knew he wanted her and she wanted to please him. But even as her body responded to his touch her mind swam in a confusion of guilt and fear, her head filled with images of Pete, the boys, her mother, her love handles. Even as they kissed, his mouth warm and moist over her own, she felt somehow detached, worrying about the next move, consumed by uncertainty. He undid the buttons of her dress and ran a finger across her breast to trace the outline of her bra along the rise of her cleavage, her nipples hardening to his touch. Sliding a hand beneath the cream lace he gently cupped her breast until she moaned with pleasure, her inhibitions dissolving with each stroke, each caress. Slowly he undressed her, his hands never ceasing to caress and tease her, his eyes reassuring her all the while.

Encouraged by him, she helped him off with his tie and shirt and then his trousers. As he kicked off his pants she stared at him, fascinated by the sight of his nakedness, her eyes drinking in the sight of his taut, well-muscled body, his long, stiff cock. He stepped towards her and, placing his hands on her naked shoulders, slowly pushed her down onto her back, smiling now, enjoying his power over her. He climbed onto her, the feel of his warm nakedness against her own taking her breath. For a moment he lay there, his hands teasing her, his hot mouth nibbling at her neck and face, making her shiver with pleasure; then, suddenly, urgently it seemed, he parted her legs, forcing them apart with his knees. She cried out, thinking he was about to take her, but he hesitated then bent down over her, kissing her neck, her breasts, her stomach, before finally he reached down and, parting her with thumb and forefinger, guided his penis up inside her.

She gasped, almost coming on the spot. She felt such a need suddenly, such an awful, overwhelming need to be had by him.

The look of him, the feel and smell of him – everything was so strange, so excitingly strange and different. And as he began to fuck her, her cries of pleasure sounded alien even to her own ears. She pushed back up at him urgently, her legs wrapped about him, her hands grasping his buttocks tightly, forcing him down into her, all inhibitions gone from her suddenly, replaced by a burning need. Then, all too soon, he came, his body stiffening, spasming against hers as he forced his seed into her, sending tiny explosions of pleasure rippling through her.

'Don't stop,' she pleaded quietly in his ear, caressing his buttocks tenderly as he began to relax against her. 'Please . . . *please* . . .'

Slowly, very slowly, he began to move again, his body grinding sensuously against her own, in synch with it, it seemed, as if he could anticipate every movement of her muscles. His hands stroked her breasts and thighs, his fingers teasing her nipples then tripping lightly across her stomach to trace the moist length of her sex, each touch of his making her moan with delight. And all the while his beautiful face was above hers, smiling down at her, encouraging and watching her as she worked herself to a frenzy against him.

Having sex with Pete after that first time with Jonathan

124

had been tortuous. She wondered sometimes how she could still allow him to make love to her – though the notion of it having anything to do with love always evoked a wry smile. If she could have brought herself to discuss things with him she might even have suggested that he use a prostitute, but then she would have worried about infection.

Standing in the doorway to the living room that evening, she observed him for some while before he even realised she was there. The way his body slumped in the armchair had an air of sadness about it, so that she almost felt sorry for him. Sensing her there suddenly he turned, then grunted dismissively, his attention returning immediately to the TV screen in front of him. The re-run of an old *Cagney and Lacey* episode playing out before him with comforting familiarity.

'I'm off to bed. You want anything before I go?'

'No, I'll be up in a minute,' he said, never taking his eyes from the screen.

Mandy's heart sank. After all these years she had learned to read the signals.

Upstairs she lay in the cold bed, her nightdress encasing her like a shroud. The darkened room echoed with the ticking of the clock on the table beside her. As the door opened her body instinctively stiffened and she closed her eyes, feigning sleep.

Mandy listened with loathing to the sounds of his clothes being removed – the jangling of the change in his pocket as his jeans hit the floor, the rustling of his shirt as he lifted it over his head – and clenched her teeth in anticipation.

A rush of cold air washed over her as he lifted the

duvet from the bed, then she felt the heat of his body as it moulded to the contours of her own. His hand, rough and hard, was hateful against the warm softness of her skin.

'Get the nightdress off.'

She sat up, staring straight ahead, their eyes never meeting. Quickly, clinically, Mandy lifted the nightdress up over her head, then threw it to the floor.

His lovemaking was crude, uncaring, and Mandy was only thankful that it was at least quick. Afterwards, as she lay curled up at the edge of the bed, her faced turned away from him, tears of pain overwhelmed her and fell silently down her face onto the pillow, until, finally, she was swept away in sleep, an image of Jonathan's face in her mind.

The curtains were pulled aside as the young beautician came smiling into the cubicle. Mandy's eyes slowly opened, as though heavy with sleep.

'Should be ready now,' the girl said, walking across to the container of wax and stirring its contents with a wooden spatula. She took some moist tissue from a plastic box and wiped it down the length of Mandy's legs, removing the greasy residue, then placed some thin tissues around the edge of her panties to protect them from the wax.

'Okay, off we go!' she said and smiled at her client before taking up the spatula and spreading the warm wax in strips down her shin, each one laid thinly in one swift, expert movement, like someone icing a cake. She moved rapidly down each leg, removing the wax section by section, placing a sheet of thick kitchen paper over it and pulling hard. Mandy thought nothing of the pain; she was used to it. *You wouldn't catch a bloke doing this*, she thought, wincing as a strip of wax was pulled from the soft skin along the inside of her thigh. *But then, maybe they've got more sense.*

Gritting her teeth as hairs were removed along her bikini line – not that she'd had the nerve to wear one of those for years – she heard Susie's voice, loud and familiar, wafting in from the reception area. She smiled to herself at her friend's easy manner.

'Hi, Mand. They said you was in here.' Susie stood in the corner of the cubicle, a bunch of curtain in each hand.

The young beautician looked round at her and smiled. 'All done! Come through to cubicle six for your facial when you're ready,' she said to Mandy, easing past Susie into the corridor.

Mandy turned over onto her back, easing her dress down over her bottom.

'Aw my gawd, you look like shit!' exclaimed Susie, coming into the cubicle and closing the curtains behind her.

'Thanks, I love you too!'

'Sorry, but you do look a bit rough,' she said, smiling. 'But it was a great night wasn't it? What about that black geezer!' And they both roared with laughter at the memory of the evening's antics.

Susie sat down on the end of the bed while Mandy pulled on her stockings.

'Since when have you been wearing those?' Susie nodded towards her friend's legs.

'I only wear them now and again, for a change. Only stay ups though; I couldn't be doing with suspenders and all that pallaver.'

'Talking of suspenders, what do you think of this?' She reached down to the carrier bag at her feet and pulled out a white basque, heavy with lace and satin trim, four suspenders dangling from its bottom. 'And I've got these ultra sheer stockings to go with it. Christian Dior. Cost me a bleedin' fortune!' she said, holding up the packet for Mandy to see. 'Joe'll love it!'

'You wanna watch he don't slide off you with that lot on!'

'I don't s'pose I'll 'ave them on for long anyway.' She nudged Mandy in the ribs and they giggled like teenagers.

'Here, we'd better go through and get our faces done, then we might 'ave time for a quick drink up the Crown. I've gotta go and get the flowers later on. Me mum and auntie Babs are doing the buttonholes tonight. Christ alone knows if I've remembered everything.'

'Something's bound to go wrong. It always does.'

'Thanks a bunch, Mand. It must be being so bleedin' cheerful that keeps you going! Come on, let's go and get a face pack put on you. That way you'll 'ave to keep your mouth shut.'

The girls sat side by side on reclining chairs, the stillness of the room and the subdued lighting relaxing them. The cool dampness of the small, round pads seeped into the delicate skin around their eyes, in stark contrast to the heat from the steam machines pumping hot moisture down onto their upturned faces.

Perspiration clung to their skin. Reaching up, Mandy caught a rivulet of sweat as it ran down the side of her ear and onto her neck.

'Blimey! How much longer we got to be under these?' she said, spluttering as the hot air filled her mouth.

'About another five minutes I reckon. Then they'll come back and squeeze all our spots and blackheads.'

'Charming!'

'I can't believe you ain't 'ad a facial before.'

'Well if I don't come out of this one looking like Michelle Pfeiffer I don't s'pose I'll 'ave another.'

'You only get the facial for fifteen quid. Miracles cost an extra thirty!'

'Oh don't make me laugh,' Mandy said trying to steady her jaw. 'It makes me eye pads wobble about.'

Susie placed a steadying finger on each of her own eye pads as she too shook with laughter. 'Talking about wobbling about, what about that fat bird with the stripper last night. What a sight! With a chest like that she'd never be short of something to eat her dinner off.'

'Poor cow! I felt a bit sorry for her, actually. She probably thought he fancied her.'

'Fancied her! You've gotta be joking! The only bloke who'd fancy that would be carrying a white stick, and even then I reckon she'd have a better chance with his Alsatian!'

Mandy held onto her pads as her facial muscles twitched. 'Aah, don't! Still,' she added, looking on the bright side, 'it was probably the biggest thrill she's 'ad all year.'

'Yeah, it was big all right!'

And as they both gave way to laughter Mandy's eyepads slid down onto her cheeks. 'Fucking things!' she said, pushing them back into place.

'Did you pick up the car all right?' Susie wiped the sweat from her upper lip and scratched around her nostrils with a finely manicured finger.

'Yeah. It nearly killed me getting up, but Pete 'ad to 'ave it for work 'cos the van's gone in for a service and he's on a job over in South London today. I knew he'd go off alarming if I asked him to pick it up and I wasn't feeling up to a row.'

'Is he coming to the wedding?'

'Says he is. Mind, I'd just as soon come on me own.'

'Never mind, sit him with Barry and let 'em bore each other to death.'

'Oh no, Suse. You 'aven't invited his bleedin' brother 'ave you?'

'Only to the evening. I 'ad to didn't I.'

'Why?'

'Well, he is an ex . . .'

'So you're inviting half the borough, are you?'

'Ha ha. Very funny. Besides, I bumped into him up Camden Passage the other week, and he asked if he could come. I couldn't very well say no.'

'Why not?' Mandy bristled. 'He's got the cheek of the devil that one!'

'Well . . . anyway, he'll be company for Pete.' Susie scratched the side of her neck as a droplet of sweat trickled down from her chin. 'The boys coming?'

'I've told them they can, but they're probably out

with their mates. They'd only complain about the old farts' music anyway.'

'Ah, bless 'em.' Susie had a soft spot for Mandy's kids, especially her youngest, Luke. When Mandy had asked her to be his godparent she'd had a little cry. The others had made jokes about the irony of Susie teaching Luke a moral code but she'd laughed it off, never confessing to anyone but Mandy just how moved she'd really been.

'What are you doing about the music? Is it a disco?'

Susie sniffed. 'Well I've tried to cater for everybody. I know the old man'll want to get up and sing so I've got a piano in the hall and I've warned me Uncle Bill that I'll need him to play. And then I've booked a disco so that the rest of the time we can have a bop. I've told the bloke to make sure he's got a lot of old stuff, Motown and that.'

'Great! It's ages since I had a dance.'

It was one of the things Mandy regretted about getting older. When they were younger she and the girls had gone dancing several times a week, spending hours on the dancefloor, soaking up the noise, losing themselves in the music. Being chatted up had always been something of a by-product; if it happened and he wasn't too ugly, fine; if it didn't and they had a good dance, great!

'I just hope me dad don't go over the top. You know what he's like.'

Mandy laughed at the memory of Susie's dad at Lyndsay's wedding giving it his best Frank Sinatra, belting out 'New York, New York' with such enthusiasm that he fell head first off the stage onto two elderly ladies who'd been admiring his high kicks from the dance floor.

'What does Joe make of him?'

Susie laughed. 'He's only met him a couple of times and Mum made sure he was off the sauce, so Joe ain't seen him in all his glory.'

'What about your mum? What does she think of Joe?'

'She thinks he's lovely.' Susie laughed out loud recollecting their first meeting, pushing her eyepads back into place as they slid out of position. 'The first time they met he came round for Sunday dinner. He brought her a bunch of flowers and paid her all the right compliments, even though she's a bloody awful cook; he always knows the right thing to say, does Joe. A real bloody charmer!'

'I can't wait to meet him. Here, when you get back from your honeymoon, we'll 'ave to get together, go out for a meal or something.'

'Yeah, that'd be lovely, Mand. I think you'll like him. He's just . . . well, so *nice*.'

'He sounds it. I remember you phoning me up when he proposed . . .'

Susie gave a sudden laugh as she recalled the box being delivered, remembering how she'd unwrapped it and the silver heart-shaped helium balloon had gently emerged, rising to the ceiling, the words 'Marry Me' printed in pink on one side and blue on the other.

'Yeah . . .' Susie said, feeling weepy at the memory. 'I kept checking the name and address on the box just to make sure they hadn't made a mistake.'

'Ahh, that's so sweet.'

'Yeah,' Susie sighed. 'And if he's had to work late or

something, he comes home with some flowers or a nice bottle of wine for me.'

'Yeah, just like Pete,' Mandy said flatly and the two of them burst out laughing.

There was a couple of minutes' silence before Mandy spoke. 'So. What's left to do? You got your dress ready an' all that?'

'Mmm,' Susie answered, licking away the sweat on her top lip. 'I'm quite well organised, actually. The caterers and music are sorted. Joe's done the cars, and I picked up the dresses and shoes and all the rest of the stuff yesterday . . .'

'Can't wait to see them. What colour's Karen's and the little 'uns?'

'Wait for it! Red!'

'Red!'

'Yeah, well, I didn't wanna stick Karen in some insipid pastel colour. I mean, she's no spring chicken is she? Not for a sort of bridesmaid, anyway. Nah, I thought something a bit dark and sexy'd do the trick. You know, a bit like that Paula Yates 'ad on when she got married.'

'Blimey! And what colour's yours? Don't tell me. Let me guess. Black!'

'Nah, don't be daft. Cream. Very sophisticated. I got it in 'arrods.'

'Really?'

'Yeah. I tried Harvey Nick's and a couple of them wedding shops, but 'arrods 'ad the best selection. Mind you, it cost me a bleedin' arm and a leg.'

'You should've hired one, Suse. After all, it's only for the day.'

'Nah. I wanted me own,' she said, pushing her eyepads back into place. 'Mind you, I might flog it to one of them hire shops afterwards to get some of me money back. Or should I say, some of Joe's money back.'

'Joe paid for it?'

'Yeah, well he 'ad to. I couldn't manage it all, and you know my old man – short arms and deep pockets – so I ain't had no money from him. Nah, Joe said to me, he said "Whatever you want to do for this wedding, you go ahead and do it". I expect he's 'ad a bit of help from his dad. They look like they've got a bob or two.'

'Well,' Mandy said, rubbing a finger across the drops of sweat clinging to her nostrils, 'I reckon you've come up trumps with that one, Suse.'

'Yeah,' Susie said whimsically; 'it's all happened so fast sometimes I think I must be dreaming.'

Mandy reached out blindly for her friend's arm and squeezed it gently above the wrist. 'I'm really happy for you, Suse.'

'I know you are.' She curled up her fingers until she felt Mandy's hand beneath them. 'I really think he's the one for me, you know, Mand? I've finally found a good 'un,' and she let out a deep sigh. 'It's taken bleedin' long enough, mind!'

Mandy gave a little sniff and pushed the eyepads down onto her sockets. 'Don't be so maudlin; you'll 'ave me blubbing in a minute.'

Susie laughed fondly at her sentimentality and changed the subject. 'Here, what do you reckon about Anna last night?'

'That guy in the restaurant wouldn't have had to ask

me out twice I can tell you. Anna must be mad. It's not like she's seeing anybody, is it?'

'Has she talked to you about what happened in America?'

'Nah, not really. Mind you, I think it was more serious than she's letting on. Maybe she wanted a kid and he didn't; you know how broody she's been lately. It's always the thing that frightens them off. I don't s'pose Americans are any different.'

'Janet phoned earlier,' Susie said, changing the subject. 'Wanted to know if I needed any help.'

'Ain't she at work today?'

Janet had worked for the building society since she left school and even an acute hangover wasn't likely to keep her at home.

'Yeah, but she's got a new arrangement where she only works till three on Fridays. She's meeting me at the florist's later on with her car, to help me home with the buttonholes.'

'Do you know if she's had any luck with the hospital? Only I don't like to ask in case it upsets her.' Mandy found it hard to discuss Janet's infertility with her; she felt guilty at having two kids of her own and not appearing grateful enough.

'She's waiting to hear if they'll let her 'ave some more tests. I think she's hoping they'll let them 'ave this IV-whatsit treatment,' Susie said, stretching herself in the chair.

'IVF. I know someone who had that four times and it didn't work . . .'

'Yeah, but she's gotta try ain't she. I think she'll go mad if she don't.'

'What about Steve? What does he reckon?'

Janet's boyfriend was universally popular amongst her friends, and Susie was particularly fond of him. 'Ah, bless 'im. He's a real diamond, that one. Steve'd do anything to make her happy and there's not many around like that!'

'You can say that again!' Mandy agreed. 'Here talk about making women happy, you'll never guess what I heard in the hairdresser's the other day? You know that bloke Brian who's married to Maureen Hales. You know, the one who's got a kid with her and one with his girlfriend . . .'

'Janie Smith . . .'

'Yeah, Janie. Well, apparently, he had a bust up with Maureen, and Janie's heard about it and is waiting at home to welcome him with open arms, thinking he's gonna move in with her. Anyway, when he don't turn up she decides to go round his house and 'ave it out with him in front of his old lady. Well, Janie comes as a complete surprise to poor old Maureen – you could have knocked her over with a featherlight – but it turns out that she's kicked him out 'cos she discovered he was 'aving an affair with someone else . . .'

'You mean, not Janie?' Susie said, trying to follow the plot.

'No. Seems there's this other bird who lives a couple of streets away and he's just had a baby with her, an' all! Can you believe it!'

'What a bastard!'

'Yeah, hard to credit, ain't it?'

'I can't believe the wife didn't know. Especially when there were two of them. He must 'ave some bleedin' energy, that's all I can say — either that or a bloody big dick!'

'He won't have a dick at all if Janie's brothers catch up with him!' Mandy said, and the two women laughed; the situation seemed so farcical there was an air of unreality about it.

'Serve him right, dirty little bugger.'

The door opened. 'Sounds interesting. Who are we talking about?' The young, blonde-haired beautician laughed and walked towards them.

'Nobody you'd know,' Susie replied, afraid that she might know *exactly* who they were talking about. 'Here, are we finished with this thing?' She removed her eyepads, blinking up at the girl as she stood above her adjusting the position of the steam machine.

The girl looked at her watch. 'A couple more minutes,' she said pulling two fresh pads from the box on the trolley and placing them over Susie's eyes, turning to replace Mandy's before disappearing through the door.

'Karen bringing this new bloke of hers to the wedding?' Mandy asked, averting her face from the jet of steam.

'I don't think he's that new; she's just kept him a bit quiet, that's all. I think she's bringing him to the evening; she said something about him being busy during the day. What is it he does?'

'Anna says he's a teacher,' Mandy said. 'Karen met him at a conference, or something. Can you imagine if they had kids — both of 'em being teachers — they'd be right little brainboxes.' Mandy had always blamed Pete's genes for the fact that her own children hadn't done better at school. Some day they'd isolate the 'thicko' gene and when they looked at it under a microscope it'd have Pete's face on it.

'That's jumping the gun a bit,' Susie answered. 'Mind, it must be serious 'cos at least we're being allowed to meet this one. His name's Chris I think she said.'

'Oh well, you never know, maybe we'll 'ave another wedding to go to before too long.' In spite of her own situation Mandy remained a hopeless romantic. 'You know, I just *love* a good wedding . . .'

Susie planted her handbag on the top of the bar and turned to Mandy.

'So what're you 'aving?'

'No. It's my shout.'

'Don't be daft,' Susie said, reaching out to stop Mandy from getting out her purse. 'You paid for the last two rounds last night!'

'Did I? Christ! That explains it!'

'Explains what?'

Mandy put her hand on Susie's arm and giggled. 'When I looked in my purse this morning it was empty! I thought I must've given the cab driver a bleedin' big tip.'

'He should be so lucky! Nah . . .' Susie said, 'it was the double brandies that cleaned you out!'

'And what better way to blow the housekeeping!'

They leaned into each other, laughing, as the young barman came across.

'Drinks, ladies, or you had enough already?'

'I ain't 'ad anything yet,' Susie said, turning to him, smiling, instinctively pushing out her breasts. 'Mine's a vodka and tonic.'

'And for you?' He spoke to Mandy but his eyes remained on Susie.

Mandy glared at him. 'A vodka and lemonade. And don't forget the ice.'

He put his hands up defensively. 'Okay, okay!'

As he turned away, Susie looked to Mandy. 'Just the one, okay?'

Mandy winked. 'Just the one.'

Giggling, they waited for their drinks. While Susie paid, Mandy made her way across to an empty, round-topped table in the corner next to the bar billiards. Susie joined her there a moment later, easing down into her seat with a sigh.

'Hair of the dog.' She raised her glass in a toast before taking a large gulp of the cool, clear liquid.

Mandy looked about her at the cut glass windows, the heavy brocade drapes and the wood and glass partitions that surrounded the bar, and laughed. 'You know, it's ages since I came in here. Last time was Doug and Lucy's fifth anniversary.'

'Christ! That was donkey's years back! You remember that?'

'How could I forget? I was sitting between them when they started fighting. Soaked I was.'

'Not as soaked as they got, though!'

Mandy laughed. 'Nah. They went for it in a big way, didn't they? I don't think there was a full glass within reach when those two had finished! No wonder the landlord barred them for life!'

'I thought that was a bit unfair, myself. I mean, it was just a harmless bit of fun. And they paid for it all, didn't they?'

'Only after one of the barmen got Doug in an armlock.'

'Yeah . . . but he would've. I know Doug. He's harmless, really.'

'Legless, mainly!'

'Yeah . . .' Susie laughed. 'He tried it on with me once, you know? Put his hand down the back of me skirt at a Christening.'

'What, in the church?'

'Nah,' Susie spat her drink back into her glass, laughing at the very suggestion, ''Course not. At the do afterwards. Cheeky little bugger sidled up to me at the buffet and whispered in me ear. Said he'd got something he wanted to show me.'

Mandy leaned toward her mate, fascinated. 'And?'

'So I told him to meet me upstairs in five minutes.'

'You didn't!'

'I did.' Susie picked up her drink, holding it before her face and staring at it as she spoke, as if it were a crystal ball. 'Anyway, I nipped upstairs and into the bathroom. Three minutes later he joins me there, just as I'm putting on a fresh coat of lipstick. "Okay," I says, facing him, me back to the sink, "What is it you want to show me?" So, bold as brass, he unzips his flies and pops out his old John Thomas for my inspection. Course, by this time it's beginning to fill out a bit. Bleedin' great big thing it is as well. A real jumbo sausage job.'

'Really?'

'Yeah. And I'm thinkin' to myself, poor ol' Lucy, she probably didn't know whether to climb on top of it or stick it in a bap.'

'And?' Mandy said, her eyes wide with curiosity. 'Come on. Get on with it.'

Susie laughed. 'Anyway, I look at it a second or two then says to him, "Fuck me, Dougie-boy, you must be joking. You'll remove me appendix with that thing. You ain't bleedin' human!" "I'm human," he says, "Feel", trying to put it in me hand. "Above the waist you might be," I answer him, doing a quick body-swerve round him and out into the hall. And you know what? The silly bugger only tried to come after me, cock in hand. Didn't half make a fool of himself, standing at the top of the stairs with his trousers round his knees. Talk about the blood rushing to your head!'

Mandy screeched with laughter, drawing looks from all around the pub. Quietening down, she leaned toward Susie again. 'That must be horrible. Luce is a good mate of yours, ain't she?'

'Was.' Susie gave a thoughtful laugh. 'Mind you, they all try it on some time or other. All the married men.'

'*All* of them?'

'Well, not all. Your Pete   '

Mandy took a large swig of her drink. 'You can 'ave him, Suse!'

'No, ta. You're welcome, me dear.'

'Thanks a bunch. I was hoping you'd take him off my hands.'

Susie was suddenly sympathetic. She leaned toward her friend and covered her free hand with her own. 'That bad, eh?'

'Nah. Much worse.'

The two giggled, then took sips from their drinks, smiling at each other all the while.

'You know, it's really great,' Mandy said.

'What?'

'Being together again. All of us. I'd almost forgotten. Last night . . . well, it all came back to me. What fun it all was, and how much I've missed all that.'

'It's been a while, ain't it?' Susie said, sitting back and taking a leisurely sip from her glass. 'Last time was just before Anna went to the States. What . . . a year back?'

'More than that,' Mandy corrected her. 'Time really flies, don't it?'

Susie nodded, then, putting her drink down, tapped the table with her right forefinger. 'It's a shame we didn't get to go out and visit her. I've always wanted to go to America.'

'I don't know if they're ready for you, Suse!'

'Yeah, but you see, being the retiring, sensitive type like Anna don't get you nowhere. Me, I've always believed in taking the bull by the horn.'

'Horns, don't you mean?'

'You mean what you like girl, I know what I'm talking about. Take those three at the bar.'

Mandy looked. She hadn't even noticed them come in, and *she* was facing the bar. 'Yeah?'

Susie leaned closer, lowering her voice. 'See the fat one without the neck. His name's Geoff. Market trader. Fruit and veg. The one next to him — with the neat moustache and the checked shirt — is Malcolm. I don't know quite what he does for a living, but it ain't straight, whatever it is. The other one — in the Arsenal shirt, drinking the brown ale — is called Ben. He runs the video shop on the corner. You know, the one we passed.'

Mandy nodded, then looked back at Susie. 'So?'

'So you tell me this – which one's gay, which one has a crush on me, and which of them had it off with me in the loo last New Year's Eve?'

'Nah!' Mandy put her hand over her mouth. 'In the loo? In here?'

Susie nodded, then drew a cross with her finger over her left tit. 'Girl Guide's honour. Go on, then. Take a guess. Gay first.'

Mandy took a sip for inspiration, then glanced across at the bar again, hoping they wouldn't notice she was looking.

'The guy with the moustache,' she said quietly.

'Wrong. Try for the one with the crush.'

'Geoff?'

'Wrong. Third category.'

'Men's or women's?'

'What?'

'I just want to know. Did you do it in the Gents or in the Ladies?'

Susie grinned from ear to ear. 'Have a guess.'

'What is this, bleedin' animal, vegetable or mineral?'

'Animal,' Susie said, and chuckled.

'In the Ladies,' Mandy said after a moment's thought.

Susie nodded. 'Right. Now guess which one did the dirty.'

Mandy sat back, amazed. 'You mean you *really* did? With one of those three, in the ladies' loo, *here*?'

Again Susie nodded. 'As I said, bull by the horn. So?'

Mandy shrugged. She had no idea. 'Ben?'

Susie, who had been taking a sip, spat it back. 'Don't make me laugh. Ben's as bent as a nine bob bit! Can't you see that? Nah, guess you can't.' She smiled and covered Mandy's hand again. 'I guess that's the difference between us, Mand. Being married, you've never had to suss it out, whereas with me it's just been one bloke after another. A bit like buses, really.'

'I didn't know the 69 ran through Islington.'

'Cheeky cow!'

Mandy drained her glass and set it down with a clink, then looked at her friend thoughtfully. 'How many boyfriends d'you reckon you've had, then, Suse?'

'Boyfriends or men?'

'What's the difference?'

'A lot! Like the shag in the loo. That was fun. A one-off. I was half-cut and I fancied the guy. But no way would I go out with him. For a start he's married with three kids.'

'Would that stop you?'

Susie stared at Mandy indignantly. ''Course it would! I might like a bit of fun, but I'm not totally irresponsible.'

'So? How many?'

'Well, let's put it this way, it's more than the Virgin Mary and less than the Grand Old Duke of York.'

'No, seriously . . .'

'I dunno . . .a couple of hundred maybe.'

Mandy's mind reeled. She couldn't imagine it. Why, two seemed exotic enough to her.

'How about you?'

'Me?' Mandy laughed and looked down, going red at the neck.

'Is Pete really the only bloke you've ever slept with?'

Mandy hesitated a moment. ''Fraid so. Well . . .'

'Bloody hell!' Susie interrupted. 'Don't you ever wonder what it would be like with someone else?'

'Yeah, course I do. Don't you ever worry you're gonna catch something?'

'No, not really. Well, I 'aven't yet, touch wood,' and she tapped the table with her fingers. 'Well, not unless you count the warts.'

'Warts!'

'Yeah, genital warts. Had to have the little buggers burnt off.'

'Yuk!' Mandy crossed her legs and reached for her glass, draining the last drops. 'Fancy another?'

Susie nodded and drained her glass, but when Mandy went to get up, she pushed her down. 'My shout,' she said, getting up. 'You can get number three!'

'Number three? But . . .'

'Don't argue, Mand. Go with the flow.'

'Like you, you mean?'

Susie nodded and went to turn away, but Mandy grabbed her arm, pulling her back.

'So . . . which one *was* it?'

Susie leaned down to her, the smell of her perfume stronger now. 'You watch. The one who puts his hand on me bum.'

'That'll be him?'

'Nah. That's the one who fancies me. Mister One-Night-Stand is the one who'll nod to me politely, like we've met in a bus queue.'

Mandy laughed. 'You're joking?'

'Nah. He always does. 'Specially if his wife's in here with him.'

And with that she turned away.

Mandy watched. Sure enough, as Susie squeezed between them to get to the bar, the three men stopped

talking, turning their attention to her. One of them —
Malcolm — put his hand almost proprietorially on her
backside. Beside him, Ben smiled and uttered pleasantries. Geoff, however, nodded to her awkwardly,
shyly almost.

Geoff! Mandy thought, gobsmacked that she'd got it so
wrong, and unable for the life of her to picture Susie and
him getting down to the business in the Ladies. He was
so . . . so *unattractive*.

Mind you, no more unattractive than Pete, and she had
slept with him often enough.

For a moment, she watched them, mildly envious of
Susie's ability to socialise so easily with men, to win them
round. She had always found it hard. Always. Even when
they were back at school together.

Her mouth curled into a smile as she remembered
how they were back then; how simple everything had
seemed . . .

Susie had changed quite a lot since they were teenagers,
although she'd always been popular, in spite of having
a bit of a weight problem back then.

Mandy smiled to herself recalling the fun they'd had,
the way that everything had been 'just for a laugh'.
They'd considered themselves pretty grown up by the
time they were sixteen — after all, they'd been going
to pubs for years — and she remembered how excited
they'd been by the prospect of their first holiday away
together.

Mandy couldn't remember the last time she'd been
away anywhere, and out of the five of them only

Susie had ever stayed in a holiday camp. When she'd asked her mum if she could go away with her mates to Minehead she'd had to explain where it was; the woman had barely been further than Margate herself, and then it was usually a spur-of-the moment outing on a Saturday night if the old man had had a good day on the gee gees.

As they drove through the holiday camp before pulling up in the coach at the reception block, Mandy remembered feeling excited despite the less than impressive surroundings. In the brochure everything had looked bright and cheerful and the Redcoats were all handsome. In reality she found herself in a compound more reminiscent of the concentration camps she'd seen in old war films.

Velcome to Stalag Seventeen. You vill enjoy yourselves!

Outside, a large expanse of green ran along the front of the reception block. Two young Redcoats were shouting encouragement to a group of children pulling in opposite directions on a tug-o-war rope. From time to time screeches of delight would ring out as a line of youngsters fell to the floor, tumbling over each other as their opponents punched the air and yelled victoriously.

At either end of the green ran a strip of tarmac, leading to a sprawling mass of two-storey buildings. Row upon row of chalets ran in vertical lines as far as the eye could see, one atop another, the upper chalets accessed by a wooden staircase rising up through the middle of the block onto a balcony running the length of the building. Closer inspection would have revealed peeling paint and ill-fitting door and window frames, but the girls barely noticed the shabbiness. Within minutes of settling in their chalet they had unpacked their clothes, rearranged the beds and were lying across the divans, poring over the week's entertainments programme, excited by the prospect of total freedom from parental control.

'Here's one for you, Suse!' Mandy shrieked, looking to her mate. 'Monday night. Miss Chubby, Charming and Cheerful Competition!' She rolled onto her back and roared with laughter.

'Aw, piss off!' Susie snatched the programme from Mandy's hand. 'Mind you, it says the winner gets a £5 gift voucher.'

'A fiver and she's anybody's!' Karen teased.

'All right Miss Iron Knickers!' came the swift response.

But the idea of picking up some winnings excited new interest and the others leaned closer to Susie, giving the matter some serious attention.

'There's a Miss Hot Pants Competition,' Karen exclaimed, pointing to an entry in the programme, 'and a Knobbly Knees – that's one for you Jan . . .or should I say Olive Oyl!' and there was an explosion of laughter.

'Very funny,' Janet said good humouredly, snatching the programme from the bed. 'Mind, we could always stick you in for the Glamorous Granny Competition. Who knows, you might even pull a glamorous grandad!'

'I'm not *that* desperate,' Karen said and gave Janet a gentle push, making her roll off the bed and onto the floor to the delight of the rest of them.

'Hey! Look at this! Mastermind! We could put Anna in for that! You get ten quid if you win and it says here that you and your family get to come back at the end of the season for the grand finals. That'd be brill!'

'Who says I'd bring you lot! Anyway, I don't s'pose I'd

win. Nah, if we run out of money we could always put Susie on the game.'

'Cheeky mare! Here, not that I'd get the chance. Did you hear that geezer in reception going on about security patrols?' The others shook their heads. 'They only 'ave blokes with bleedin' guard dogs patrolling after the midnight curfew . . .'

'You're joking! They'd better not be Alsatians. I hate Alsatians.' Janet had been attacked by one as a child. Not only that, but the subsequent embarrassment of her mother angrily revealing the dog's teeth marks on Janet's bare backside to the dog's owner had heightened her hatred of the beasts.

'Well, that's what I heard.' Susie raised herself up from the bed and knelt on the edge. 'Right!' she said, looking at her watch. 'Who fancies a drink? Bagsy I'm first in the bath . . .'

By the time the five of them were ready to go out more than two hours had passed. Clothes, neatly folded when they'd arrived, now lay strewn across the beds, while bottles of eau-de-toilette, pan stick, false eyelashes, eyeliner, and bags spilling make-up and other assorted bottles and jars, littered the room's white formica surfaces.

They started out the evening at the Empire Bar on the far side of the camp, where they were chatted up by a couple of boys; right wallies, complete with crew cuts and fledgling beer guts. The only thing Mandy could find to admire about them was their front; she'd never have had the balls to try and chat her and her mates up if she were a bloke. Not if she was that fat and ugly, anyway. Then again, in their case it was probably a case of no sense, no feeling . . .

They finally got lucky at the Daytona Disco and by the end of the night they had paired off, losing one another in the huge and crowded room. The one that fancied Mandy wasn't bad, though it was difficult to tell what someone really looked like until you were up close – it was so dark in there, the air so thick with cigarette smoke. It wasn't until they were on the dance floor, in fact, that she realised just how round his face was; the lank brown hair hanging down below his shoulders had narrowed its appearance. But she liked the way he had a habit of pushing it back away from his eyes, the way his thin, flowery shirt clung to him, showing every contour of his body, the flimsy fabric barely concealing his lean muscularity.

They didn't talk much. She caught him looking at her once or twice and had looked away, self-conscious, embarrassed by the attention. When a slow song came on half the dancers cleared away, moving back to the edge of the dance floor. She'd allowed him to take hold of her and pull her close. It was during the second smoochy number that he tried his luck. They moved well, their bodies pressed together. Almost imperceptibly his hands moved down from her hips onto her backside, a palm splayed across each buttock, his fingertips gently kneading her. She reached down and pulled his hands back up, returning them to her waist. No words were spoken. Gradually he moved them down again, the pressure on her buttocks pushing her into him so that she could feel his shape. This time she made no attempt to reproach him; she could feel his penis harden against her stomach and the thought of it excited her. Slowly his hand moved up her body, his thumb caressing the side of her breast through the white cheesecloth fabric of her blouse, edging further and further with each stroke until he was within a hair's breadth of her hardened nipple.

The song ended and they stood there a moment, reluctant to let go of each other, hoping for another slow number, their adolescent bodies aching for the other's touch, but the next one was too lively.

'Come on,' he said, taking Mandy's hand and leading her from the dance floor.

She looked round for her friends but they had already left. She'd last seen Susie dancing, some bloke's tongue spring cleaning her tonsils, while she had left the others by the bar. Now they were nowhere to be seen. She turned back to him and smiled. 'You wanna walk me home?'

They'd had a snog on the way back, down a dark alleyway between two blocks of chalets. They hadn't done anything – no actual sex, or anything – but he had turned her on. He was a good kisser and she liked it when he'd touched her, stroking her breast through her blouse, cupping her buttocks and pulling her into him, running his hand up her thigh and resting it between her legs, moving his fingers back and forth along the seam of her crotch. She could feel the excitement engulfing her and it would have been easy to let him carry on, to go all the way, yet as his hand reached up to unzip her jeans she gently eased it away, never flinching from his kiss. His hand moved slowly up inside her shirt, cupping her breast, feeling her hardened nipple through the cotton fabric of her bra. Again she pulled his hand away, all the while kissing his moist lips, pushing her tongue deeper into his mouth. He tried the zip again, but she took hold of his hand and eased it away.

Abruptly he pulled away from her, laying back against the cold brick wall.

'What's the matter?' she said, her breathing heavy.

'I think you're a bit of a prick teaser, that's what!' His face was stern as he threw the accusation across at her. '*And* I bet you're still a virgin.'

Mandy didn't answer. She hung her head, looking down at the ground. Her body was still tingling with arousal, aching for his touch, but she couldn't move, couldn't even look at him, and gradually feelings of shame and guilt overwhelmed any urges she had had.

There was a moment's silence before he finally spoke.

'C'mon. I'll walk you back.'

He moved away from the wall and started down the alley towards the lights.

The passion was gone, the moment passed. She had wanted it to be special somehow, to be exciting and yet at the same time . . . *nice*. All she wanted to do now was to get back to her friends.

Karen and Anna were already there, clutching their plastic cups of vodka and orange juice. They giggled drunkenly as Mandy walked through the door.

'Well?' A broad grin split Karen's features.

'Well what?' Mandy pushed the door closed, kicked off her shoes and lay flat out on the bed, looking up at the ceiling.

'Did you go with him?'

Mandy laughed, then rolled onto her side, resting on one elbow. 'Pour us a drink, Kar.'

'You lucky cow! He was the only half-human one out of the lot!' Anna said, reaching unsteadily across to take the bottle from the window ledge.

'Yeah, well, you've either got it or you ain't. What happened to you two, then?' Mandy sat up, dangling her legs over the side of the bed, and took a large gulp of the warm, colourless liquid, spluttering as it hit the back of her throat.

'Well, after you and Susie went off to dance with those two blokes, the cocky one . . .'

'What, the one with the bastard haircut? You went with *him*?'

'Nah, Janet got off with him. That left me and Karen with the booby prizes.'

Mandy exploded with laughter, spraying drink across the room. She wiped her mouth on the cotton bedcover and looked from one to the other. 'Who got the little one? He was quite sweet in a way.'

'If you like gnomes.'

Anna and Mandy screeched and fell across the bed as Karen went on.

'Did you clock those bleedin' ears! In the end I said to him, "Well, sunshine, they'll know exactly who to call on if the FA Cup ever goes missing, won't they?"'

'Aw Karen, you didn't? Poor little sod!'

'Well, he got on my bloody nerves, the way he kept putting his arm around my shoulder . . .'

'Oh, no, not the arm round the shoulder routine,' Mandy teased as she and Anna clung to each other in helpless laughter.

'Yeah, well, it wouldn't have been so bad if he hadn't had to get out a stepladder first!'

She flopped down on top of the two of them, spilling her drink across the crumpled sheets. 'Every time I looked at him his face was in line with my tits, his little head bobbing up and down as though he was trying to land it in between me boobs . . .'

'He'd have needed an oxygen supply.'

'Yes, well, Anna, we can't all look like Twiggy!'

'Now, now girls.' Mandy wriggled from beneath her friends and reached for the vodka bottle, pouring three more drinks.

All three sat up along the edge of the bed, Karen pouring a splash of orange juice into each cup and a bit more on the floor.

'What was wrong with yours, Anna?'

'You mean apart from being an ugly little fucker?'

Mandy burst out laughing, barely able to squeeze out her response, her voice a squeak, tears threatening to run down her face. 'Yeah,' she sniffed loudly, 'apart from that.'

'He kept farting.'

All three were hysterical now, lying in a heap on the bed as they howled.

'I wouldn't have minded if they were short, sharp, crisp ones but they were real killers . . . you know, the silent-but-deadly kind. I had to keep putting my hand across my mouth and nose and making out I had a cough.'

'You're too polite,' Mandy said reaching for the vodka. 'You should've said, "Look 'ere you ugly bastard, if you don't stick a cork up your arse I'm gonna shove a lighted match up there and you'll go rocketing off to fucking kingdom come!"'

'Yeah,' Anna said, attempting to sound serious. 'That's just what I should have said. Thanks, Mand, I'll remember that next time.'

'Next time you get the smelly one, you mean?' Mandy said, nudging her in the ribs, then collapsing once again with helpless laughter.

'Aw, piss off.' Anna fell across her on the bed, their empty cups falling to the floor.

Above their heads came three loud bangs and the ceiling shook with the vibrations.

'What was that?' Karen looked up, her voice hushed suddenly.

'Some cheeky sod's complaining about the noise.' Mandy was used to this kind of thing at home. 'Bugger off!' she yelled at the faceless complainant as she looked around the room for a means of retaliation. Then, snatching up a shoe from the floor, she jumped on the bed and swiped it across the ceiling, barely making contact.

A knock at the door stopped her in her tracks. Mandy stepped down from the bed to answer it, expecting to see either Susie or Janet standing there. Instead, she was faced with a short, square-shaped man sporting the red uniform blazer, the material straining across the expanse of his considerable chest and pulling at each buttonhole as it met its mate. He was distinctly lacking both in neck and hair, and carried such a demeanour of ferocity as to be a perfect match for the dog sitting at his feet.

'Keep the noise down,' he grunted. It was not a request.

'Has somebody complained?'

He looked past Mandy for the owner of the voice, his eyes fixing on Anna, sitting on the bed, her back resting against the wall.

His face relaxed a little. 'They don't have to. I could hear your racket from the end of the block.'

Mandy turned away from him and looked round at the girls, winking before turning back to face him. 'We're really sorry,' she said soothingly. 'We'll try to behave.'

'Good,' he said, his face breaking into a crooked smile now. ''Cos if you don't I'll have to come back and smack your bums.'

Mandy turned round to face the girls and all three erupted into laughter, the sounds of their hysteria ringing out as he wished them goodnight and walked off down the path, the door slamming shut after him.

'Did you hear that?' Karen said incredulously. 'Cheeky bugger!'

'Christ, he was built like a brick shithouse.' Anna stuck out her own modest chest in impersonation.

'Yeah, out of season he probably rents his dick out as a draft excluder.'

'Man-dee!' Karen sometimes marvelled at what came out of her friend's mouth.

'Well, the bloody size of him!'

There was a series of sharp knocks at the door.

'Oh, shit, he's back!' Anna screeched and jumped on the bed pulling the covers up over her head. Karen jumped in beside her leaving Mandy at the door. Cautiously she pulled aside the scrap of thin cotton curtain hanging at the window, pulled it closed again and opened the door.

'Quick! Hurry up! There's a bleedin' great dog out here!' and Janet pushed past her into the room, flopping down onto an empty bed, her flowing crêpe blouse falling across it in a blissful disarray.

Mandy closed the door and walked across to join her. 'Well? How d'you get on?'

Janet's smile spread from ear to ear. 'Yeah, all right,'

she said, pushing her long dark hair away from her face. 'He's really quite sweet.'

'Did you go with him?' Karen peeped out from beneath the bedcover.

The smile was still there.

'Lucky old you,' said Anna, emerging beside Karen. 'You didn't go all the way did you?'

''Course not. Although he did try it on . . .'

'They all do!' Mandy passed around a fresh set of plastic cups and distributed the remainder of the vodka. The orange juice was finished.

Janet turned on to her side and propped herself up on one elbow, the plastic cup held to her lips. 'Susie not back yet?'

'What do you think? Though Christ knows who she's with. I saw her blow out that bloke she was dancing with. He was a mate of the one you went off with, wasn't he Mand? What's-his-name . . .'

'Pete.'

'Yeah, Pete.'

'Good morning, campers!'

Mandy slowly roused herself from sleep, tugging at covers to untangle the heap of bodies and clothes. They had slept where they'd fallen the night before. Overcome by tiredness and spent with the effects of the vodka they had finally passed out, fully-clothed.

The sun shone in through the curtains filling the room with unwelcome light and emphasising the spartan drabness of it. Mandy gently eased her hair out from under Anna's head and pulled an arm out from beneath Janet, propping herself up on one elbow. She peered across the room through the slit of one eye; the other remaining tightly shut.

'Where the hell did *that* come from?'

Karen slowly dropped her legs over the side of the bottom bunk, rubbed at her eyes and, without looking, pointed in the direction of the tannoy hanging from the ceiling.

Mandy rolled her lips in on one another trying to create some moisture. 'Christ Almighty! My mouth's like Ali Baba's arsehole! Is there any orange juice left?'

'No. Hang on I'll get you some water.'

Karen made to get up, bumping her head on the top bunk. 'Oh, shit!'

'Oh, please, don't make me laugh. My head's killing me.' Mandy gently massaged her temple.

'I wasn't trying to make you laugh. That bleedin' hurt!' She walked over to the sink and filled two cups with water, passing one across to Mandy who took two long gulps before sticking her fingers into the cup and flicking water at her two sleeping companions.

'Come on, you lazy cows! Rise and shine!'

Anna and Janet lashed out, sending what remained in the cup flying across the bed, soaking into the mangled bedcover.

'What time did Sleeping Beauty come in?' Mandy nodded towards the top bunk where Susie lay in just her bra and knickers, dead to the world.

'I let her in about three,' Karen said. 'Didn't you hear that soddin' dog barking? The bleedin' animal took one look at Susie and chased after her. Scared the shit out of her.' And she started laughing, thinking of a drunken Susie being pursued by the guard dog.

'Christ, I could murder a cup of tea,' Mandy said. 'Shall we try and get this lot up and go and get some breakfast?' She made to get out of bed when a knock came at the door.

'Who the hell's that?' she said, jumping back in and pulling the covers up around her neck. 'You get it Kar, you're decent.'

Karen pulled her jacket on over her t-shirt and opened the door a few inches.

'Susie there?' a deep gravelly voice floated in from outside, gaining the attention of the three girls on the bed. Karen held the door open a little wider and a face poked around the edge, peering into the warm, airless room.

'Who are you?' Anna said, rubbing her eyes and sitting up a little higher, the flimsy headboard creaking beneath the weight as the three girls leaned against it.

'Name's Phil. Met Susie in the disco last night. She in?' He grinned broadly revealing a set of enormous, yellowing teeth. His beady eyes sat like two gobstoppers in his long, thin face, brown, frizzy hair surrounding it like a halo of dead moss.

The girls looked from one to another, grinning broadly, then one by one they started calling Susie's name until the volume was such that even in her state she could ignore it no longer and, bleary-eyed, peeped over the bed rail.

'What's the matter?' she croaked.

'Someone to see you,' said Karen smiling up at her, nodding towards the open door.

Susie peered across, did a double-take and buried her head under the bedclothes as her friends erupted into laughter.

The bewildered visitor stood there, unsure of what to

do, not getting the joke, until finally Karen ushered him out onto the path explaining that Susie wasn't very good in the mornings and suggesting he call back later.

Back inside laughter rang out shrill and loud and she leaned against the closed door. 'Well, that one takes the biscuit, Suse. Who the hell is he?'

'The Tombstone Kid by the look of him!' Mandy chipped in. 'I've never seen such an ugly fucker!' And she wiped a tear away from her eye, smearing mascara across the back of her hand.

'I have to say, Suse,' Anna said, winking at the others, 'Ol' Tombstone there made my one last night look like David Cassidy.'

'And those eyes!' Janet was laughing so hard the words were squeezed out in high-pitched squeals. 'He looked like a cross between Marty Feldman and Trigger!'

'I can't wait to hear what you got up to with that one, Suse.' Karen said, offering up a glass of water. 'Here, drink this.'

As Susie sheepishly emerged from the bedclothes the laughter subsided as they awaited details of the encounter. But as she sat up and the covers fell from her, the girls became hysterical, hugging each other as they laughed uncontrollably.

'What? What's the matter?' There was an edge to Susie's voice now. No-one liked being on the outside of a joke.

Karen walked over to where cosmetics were spread across a small table, picked up a mirror and handed it to Susie. The room quietened as the others waited for her response.

'Oh, my God!' she screamed. Dead bang centre in the

middle of her neck was a huge purple love bite, impressive not only in its size but in its apparent symmetry. Susie touched it, rubbing it over and over again as though doing so would wear it away. 'Oh, shit!' she said. 'What the bleedin' hell am I going to do with *this*?'

Attempting a degree of seriousness Karen suggested covering it with a strip of Elastoplast, at which all but Susie erupted into helpless laughter once again.

'What I want to know,' Mandy began, trying to string the words together, 'is whether he had his choppers in or out when he did it?'

'He had his teeth in but his chopper out!' Anna said, the thin wooden struts supporting the headboard creaking as she, Mandy and Janet shook with laughter.

'Can you imagine it!' A look of distaste came across Karen's face as she did exactly that. 'I bet it was all purple and veiny . . .'

'Like Garry Hall's!' Mandy screamed, and the others joined in the joke, the volume rising as they laughed hysterically, remembering the incident she was referring to.

'Ha bloody ha,' Karen picked up a pillow and threw it at Mandy. 'Very funny.'

As the week wore on their days fell into a pattern of sleeping 'til mid-day, going to the bar for lunch, hanging out there all afternoon, then going back to the chalet at about five to get ready for a heavy evening in the ballroom, before moving onto the disco.

That week they became well-known faces in the camp and were on first-name terms with most of the male Red-coats. They were just the kind of campers the organisers loved: they were good for a laugh and entered heart and soul into the spirit of things. Like when Susie went in for the 'Miss Chubby, Charming and Cheerful' contest.

She'd drawn the second biggest cheer of the evening, only missing out on the title because the judges felt sorry for the poor old biddy who went on after her. Each contestant was asked a series of banal questions and then told to do a head-over-heels in front of the ballroom's packed house. Susie performed a neat tumble in spite of her size, her green suede hot pants rolling across the floor like an enormous cabbage. The poor old girl who went on next — a voluminous floral frock hanging on her broad, wobbly frame as she sailed to the middle of the dance floor — squatted sumo-fashion on the mat and, spurred on by cheers from the audience, proceeded to launch herself into a forward roll. Her two fat hairy legs lingered in the air like a pair of upturned barrage balloons before slamming to the ground, her dress round her waist now, revealing a vast pair of pink, passion-killing pantaloons on an arse the size of the Antarctic. As if this humiliation wasn't enough, as she struggled to her feet she realised that her wig had slipped from her head and lay at her heels like a dead squirrel. The place was in uproar. She couldn't lose!

And there had been no shortage of boys hanging around them. They realised after that first night that the place was one big shagging shop and decided they'd be better off sticking together as a group.

It wasn't until the day before they were leaving that Mandy saw Pete again. She'd gone back to the chalet alone to fetch some suntan cream, and while she sat on the edge of the bed rifling through the toiletries bag, she glanced up and saw him walk past the open door. Poking her head round the doorframe she watched him turn up the staircase leading to the floor above, and heard him shout to somebody to wait for him in the snooker room; he'd only be a minute.

Mandy slipped back into the chalet and closed the door. She ran the few strides to the bathroom and quickly brushed her teeth and then her hair before applying a liberal spray of perfume across her neck and up her skirt. Tube of sun cream in hand she moved back by the door and lay in wait, her heart pumping in her chest and blood pulsing through her head, throbbing at her temples. After a few moments she caught sight of him through the side window and as casually as she was able she opened the door, stepped out onto the path and literally bumped into him, dropping the tube of cream at their feet.

He apologised and bent down to pick it up, before realising who it was he was talking to.

'Hello again.'

He looked up with a start, recognising her voice, and gave a brief, embarrassed smile of acknowledgement, slowly rising to his feet.

'Thanks,' she said, taking the cream from his hand.

They stood there, the moment heavy with silence. Mandy struggled to find something to say. 'I ain't seen you around,' she said.

'Nah,' he said, looking about him, avoiding her eyes, pushing his hands deep into the pockets of his jeans. 'Ain't seen you neither.' He looked past her into the empty chalet. 'Where're your mates?'

'They're out on the green, sunbathing,' and she held up the tube, shaking it from side to side. 'How about yours?'

'Snooker.' He looked about him, as though observing the place for the first time, avoiding her eyes.

'What you been up to?'

'Not much.' There was a pause. 'We've 'ad a giggle though.'

'Yeah, so've we.' They each gave a brief laugh.

A moment's silence followed. Mandy could feel the colour rising up her neck to her face as she struggled for something to say.

'Don't s'pose you fancy a drink?' he said finally.

'Yeah, if you like,' she said, relieved. She turned to reach for the handle and pulled the door closed behind her. 'I'll just let the girls know.'

He nodded and they walked off towards the green, slightly awkward, slightly out of step, but together.

The sound of a glass breaking brought Mandy back from her reverie and she suddenly became conscious of the voices of the two old guys at the table next to theirs. Facing each other across their pints of Fullers ESB they were extolling the virtues of David Jack and other old Arsenal heroes.

'He was a great player, that David Jack. What about that goal he scored against Newcastle. Just before the War, it was. About nineteen thirty-four . . .'

'Yeah, I know the one you mean . . .'

'The third . . .'

'Bleedin' brilliant! Even the Newcastle fans applauded it. Hit the back of the net like a torpedo!'

'And Alex James . . .'

'Wee Alex . . .'

'Best fuckin' left winger we ever 'ad.'

'Yeah. Mind, we used to get a hundred goals a season back then. And look at the goalscorers we had! Bastin, Drake . . . Players these days ain't good enough to tie their laces!'

And so they went on.

Football. She'd never understood men's fascination for the game; that's all it was after all, just a game. Juvenile, it seemed. As if they'd been frozen in time as little boys, perpetually enthusiastic about twenty-two grown men running around a field chasing a leather bladder. Pete was just the same. The only time he came alive these days was when Sky were showing a Tottenham game and the Spurs got a goal. Not that *that* happened all that often!

A bit like sex really. Not that she was complaining. The less that happened the better, as far as she and Pete were concerned. Especially now.

She gave a little shiver.

Mandy looked across. Susie was still standing at the bar, talking with the three blokes, flirting, a full glass in each hand. Just past her, at a table in a corner, sat a couple. Mandy watched them a moment, fascinated.

The man was much older than the woman. The roundness of his face was accentuated by his combed-back greasy black hair. Mandy guessed he was in his mid-sixties. He wore a red v-neck jumper over a plain white shirt, open at the neck. His brown slacks had an almost military crease and his matching brown shoes were polished 'til they gleamed. The woman was a blonde – dyed blonde, the natural black of her hair showing at the roots – and she was a good twenty years younger than him, but she had a worn look about her. She was dressed neatly, almost fashionably. That said, she was no oil painting. Even so, he smiled at her tenderly, as if they were teenagers, and as Mandy watched, she lit a cigarette for him and placed it in his mouth.

In a way it was sad; pathetic almost. Her younger self might even have laughed at it, but right then she didn't feel like laughing. Quite the opposite in fact. Something about that tiny gesture moved her.

What's wrong with it? she asked herself. *What's wrong with the two of them getting a little happiness from each other's company? A little love, that's all we ask for. A little love. And who cares how we get it?*

She looked down, then picked up a beer mat and stared at it. 'Mr Harry' it read.

'And Tom and Dick . . .' Susie said, setting the drinks down and sliding back in beside her. 'Penny for 'em.'

'I was just thinking,' Mandy said. 'About happiness.'

'Aw, crikey, that sounds a bit heavy, Mand. All I can tell you is that it comes in lots of different packages, and in all shapes and sizes.'

'Sounds like you're back on your favourite subject!'

Susie smiled. 'Sex? No, not really. I don't think sex brings you happiness as such.' Susie fished in her handbag and removed a packet of cigarettes. 'Oh, don't get me wrong, sex can be bloody brilliant, but let's face it, most the time it's not all it's cracked up to be. In fact Lyndsay says she'd rather have a bar of chocolate than sex any day — it lasts longer and it's a lot more satisfying!' She put the cigarette to her lips, then lit it, smiling as she did.

'I thought you'd given up.'

'I 'ave. This is social.'

Mandy stared at her friend, then laughed. ''Aven't you got *any* willpower?'

'Not a lot. Enough to keep me out of trouble. Not enough to keep me from 'aving fun.'

Mandy giggled. It sounded a good balance from where she sat. But it was one she'd never managed to achieve herself. She gave a heavy sigh and took a large swig from her glass.

'What's the matter?' Susie asked, leaning in and looking at her.

'Oh, I dunno.' Mandy met her friend's eyes. 'It's just . . . well, I envy you, Suse. The way you do what you want. I wish . . . well, for instance, I wish I could have done what you did. You know . . . taken some guy out the back and just . . .'

'Just what?' Susie said, her eyes gleaming.

Mandy nudged her. 'Leave off. You know what I mean.'

Susie sat back, took another long draw from her cigarette, then gestured with her head toward the bar. 'It's easy, really. You just 'ave to let go. And you 'ave not to mind.'

'Not to mind?'

'Yeah. What people think.' Susie placed her glass on the table and wrapped her hands around it, looking down into the clear liquid. 'I know what people say about me, what they call me.'

'But . . .'

'It's okay, Mand. Really. Because I don't give a shit. Slapper, slag, easy lay — I've heard it all. And you know what makes me laugh? Deep down I know that most of the women are probably like you and would like to do just what I do, but they 'aven't got the guts.'

'But don't you 'ave to feel something for the guy?'

'Nah, not really.' Her eyes remained fixed on the glass. 'I guess I get off on the fact that they want me. Gives me a buzz.' There was a moment's silence before Susie looked up at Mandy and smiled. 'Anyway, they've all been just a load of cock until now.'

'Joe?'

'Joe.' Even as she said his name her face softened, her lips resting in a satisfied smile.

Mandy felt a tear swell beneath her eyelid.

'We did 'ave some laughs with blokes when we were younger though, didn't we?' Mandy leaned into Susie, laughing aloud at her recollections.

There was a moment's pause before Susie spoke.

'I hated it.'

'What do you mean, you hated it?' The incredulity in Mandy's voice made it shrill. 'You were always the life and soul! Always making people laugh!'

'Yeah, that was me, the joker, the entertainer. Of course I was popular. But when you lot were off with boyfriends I was 'aving to make do with the bloke who didn't mind having the fat one. I was always the one tagging along or going with some creep so that I wouldn't be left out.'

'You *weren't* fat!'

Susie looked at her and gave a broad grin, the momentary hurt gone from her eyes. 'Yes I bloody well was. And I hated it. I hated every bloody minute of it. It was different for the rest of you.'

But Mandy was shaking her head. 'I didn't realise.'

'Nah, none of you did.' Susie's mouth twitched into a brief crooked smile and she quickly looked away from Mandy.

'What's your definition of a good lover, Mand?' Susie asked suddenly, staring ahead at the three guys propping up the bar and drawing on her cigarette.

'I'm hardly the best person to ask, now am I?' she said, thinking for a moment. 'Someone who doesn't wear his socks in bed or fart under the duvet?'

'Close,' Susie replied, laughing. 'Someone who holds you after you've had sex.'

Mandy couldn't remember Susie being like this before; but then she'd never been on the verge of marriage before. 'All right. But how can you tell what a bloke's going to be like?'

Susie stubbed out the cigarette then downed the drink in one. 'Truth is you can't, most of the time. The ones who look like real hunks are often the worst lovers – too busy thinking about themselves I s'pose. Whereas someone a bit less attractive – you know, the ones you think ain't got it in 'em – can often surprise you, and in more ways than one!' She nudged Mandy in the ribs and they both smiled.

'What was he like, then?' Mandy said, nodding toward the bar. 'That Geoff.'

Susie looked across at the bar and nodded. 'Like a ferret on a pogo stick.'

Mandy spat her drink into her glass, choking on the bit she'd swallowed. 'Oh, well,' she spluttered, wiping her mouth on the back of her hand, 'each to their own. I'm sure Mrs Ferret's very happy with him. Depends what you want, I s'pose.'

'Well I know what I want now.' Susie looked at Mandy and gave a broad grin. 'I want to 'ave a baby.'

Mandy stared at her friend, mouth open. 'You mean?'

'Nah. I'm not pregnant, if that's what you mean. But I would like to 'ave one. Or a couple if I can. You know, before I get too old. Someone to look after me in me old age.'

Mandy smiled. 'That's nice. I mean, it'd suit you, Suse.'

'Well,' she said, pushing her breasts up with her hands. 'I might as well give it a go now me assets 'ave started to sag.'

'You don't know what sagging is! You wait till you're pregnant! Your tits rest on your stomach, your stomach hangs over your fanny and you go nine months without a clear view of your feet! And then there's your pelvic floor! Once that goes you pee yourself everytime you sneeze . . .'

'I can't wait!' Susie said in mock distaste.

'It's bloody brilliant! I tell you, there's nothing like the way a baby looks at you. Complete adoration. It's just a bleedin' shame they 'ave to grow up!' Mandy gave a loud sniff. 'Hark at me, I'm going all broody.'

'Not too late for you to have another one, Mand,' Susie teased.

'Nah, not with Pete. If it was . . .'

'What?'

Mandy looked at her for a split second. 'Aw, nothing. Mind the bags,' she said sliding them along the bench beside Susie, 'I've gotta go to the loo.'

Mandy made her way across, smiling sheepishly at a young man coming out of the gents. As she stepped inside

170

the Ladies she looked about her briefly, trying to imagine Susie in one of the cubicles with that Geoff. Had they done it standing up? Or had she sat down with him on top of her? Or the other way about? She tried to picture it, then shook her head. Best not, she told herself; even so, a vague picture of two knees and a hairy arse kept coming into her head. Beyond that she couldn't imagine. For some reason she kept seeing his pudgy neck. She shuddered, then chose the end cubicle, yawning as she closed and locked the door then sat down, easing her knickers over her knees. Drunk as Susie had been, what on earth had possessed her to go with him? There was obviously no attraction there.

When she got back, one of the three guys from the bar — Malcolm, in the checked shirt — was standing at the table talking to Susie, his hands resting on the table as he leaned down to whisper in her ear. Seeing Mandy, he stood up and, with a wink at Susie, departed. Mandy watched him disappear through the swing doors.

'I'm starting to feel sorry for that bloke of yours,' Mandy said, sitting down next to her.

'There's no harm in it,' Susie answered, taking her lipstick from her bag and reapplying it. 'It's not as if I mean to take him up on his offer.'

'His offer?'

Susie leaned close and whispered.

'He didn't!'

'He *did*!'

'The saucy bugger!'

And the two fell against each other, laughing.

'The nerve!' Mandy said, once she was calm again. 'Men!'

'Thank God for them,' Susie said, raising her glass in a toast.

Mandy stared at her thoughtfully a moment, then asked what was in her head. 'Do you think you can give it up?'

'Give it up?'

'You know, blokes.'

'Hope so. I'm gonna try, anyway.' Then, grinning. 'Yeah. He's the one. I'm sure of it. If I can't be faithful to him, I don't think I could with anyone. Anyway, what more could I want?'

'Oh, I dunno. I s'pose most of us spend half our time thinking the grass must be greener somewhere else.'

'Yeah, well, not me! I reckon my grass is pretty bloody green already.'

Mandy gave a short laugh, thinking how her own lawn was looking pretty bloody dead, as though it had been pissed on by every stray cat in the neighbourhood. 'What about Joe? What's his history?'

'Oh, he's shopped around a bit, had a few long-term relationships. Mind you, not that I think I'm the last turkey on the shelf,' she added quickly. 'I just think he wasn't ready before. But now he is. Now that he's nearly forty.'

'Is he? When?'

'When we're away. I told him we should get married on his birthday but he didn't want to. He didn't want a party for it or nothing like that. Said we'd just 'ave a quiet drink — just the two of us — when we're on the honeymoon.'

'Yeah, well, I can see his point,' Mandy sighed. 'There's not a lot to celebrate about becoming middle-aged. Reckon

172

I'll creep away to a health farm for a couple of days when it's my turn.'

'Aw, Mand, you can't do that. You gotta 'ave a bit of a do, ain't you? You gotta celebrate.'

Mandy laughed at her friend's eternally sunny disposition, thinking to herself that if only they could bottle it they could hand it out as a tonic on the National Health.

'So, how long ago *were* these relationships?' she said, looking at Susie over her glass as she lifted it to her lips.

'Eh? Oh, Joe's, you mean? The last was a couple of years ago. They were engaged and everything.'

'So what happened?'

Susie shrugged. 'Just grew apart, he says. Reckons that neither of them was really ready for marriage.'

Mandy was about to say, 'Who is?' but managed to bite her tongue.

'And now he is?'

'So he says. Anyway,' Susie added as an afterthought, 'it's too bleedin' late now!'

Mandy kept her mouth shut.

'Aw, bloody hell, Mand,' Susie went on, following through the thought process, 'what if he stood me up at the church?'

Mandy reached out and hugged her friend. 'Don't be daft. He don't sound the type. Besides, I reckon he knows a good thing when he sees it. You should be thinking that *he's* the lucky one to 'ave you, not the other way round. Everything's gonna be just fine, Suse, really it is.'

Susie kissed her on the cheek. 'I know.' She looked to their empty glasses and winked. 'One more for the road?'

Mandy hesitated. 'I really ought to be going, Suse. I've got to do me Sainsbury's shop.'

'Go on. Just a quick one. I've got to be off myself. I've still got bits and bobs to do.'

'Aw, go on then. But just a quick one.'

'Great!' Susie stood, sliding round the table, her cropped top revealing a band of pale skin above the narrow leather belt at her waist, her skirt so tight across her backside you could see the outline of her knickers beneath it. Not that she could give a damn, and Mandy shook her head and smiled with a mixture of affection and admiration.

Mandy looked up at the grey sky with foreboding as she placed the carrier bags at her feet and joined the bus queue. She'd often thought that if she had a pound for every bag of shopping she'd lugged home over the years she'd be rich enough to take herself off on a world cruise.

She pulled her coat about her to keep out the wind. The first specks of rain spat at her face and Mandy peered into the distance for a sign of the bus, or in the forlorn hope of grabbing a cab.

Suddenly she felt a hand on her shoulder. 'Mandy? It is Mandy isn't it?'

The unexpected touch made her jump. She turned quickly to see a face she knew immediately – familiar to her despite an absence of almost twenty years. For a few seconds no words would come, no automatic response, no pleasantries, and then finally, still not quite believing that he was actually there, she said his name.

'Nick?'

The eyes were unmistakable, clear and blue in spite of the passing years, and the face – although a little rugged – was handsome still, and distinctive in its unseasonal tan.

174

For a moment they simply looked at each other.

'What are *you* doing here?' she said, her face breaking into the smile he'd always loved. 'I thought you were in Australia!'

'I'm only here for a bit. The old girl's not too good so I thought I'd better come over and buck her up, get her back on her feet.'

'Oh, I'm sorry to hear that,' she said, meaning it. She had always got on well with Nick's mum; it was her parents who had disapproved of him, unnerved by his spirit, his straightforward, no-bullshit approach to life.

'You look just the same,' he said, smiling at her, making her blush.

'I should hope so, too,' she said, laughing. 'I've just spent a fortune at the beauty salon trying to make myself look twenty years younger. Susie's gettin' married tomorrow. You remember Susie.'

He laughed, never taking his eyes from hers. 'How could I forget her! And you're still married, I hear,' he said, pushing a hand through his blond-streaked hair, damp with the rain.

She gave him a questioning look.

'My mum,' he said. 'She's better than a newspaper.' And they both laughed.

'Yeah,' she replied. 'How about you?'

'Divorced. Couple of years back.'

'I'm sorry. Kids?'

'Nah. Yours must be pretty grown up by now, though?'

'Sixteen and eighteen. Christ! It makes me feel old when I say it out loud.'

'Yeah, well, none of us are getting any younger, but I'm not ready for the knacker's yard yet. How about you?'

She hadn't been aware of the bus arriving, but as people pushed past her she automatically scooped up her bags. Looking up at him, caught in limbo between wanting to stay and wanting to go, she was held by his eyes.

'It's my bus. I have to go.'

'Do you?' he said in the old way. He'd always tried to make her question everything, to face up to things. 'I've got a car. It's only round the corner, by the old Aggie.'

'It's the Business Design Centre now,' she corrected in a feigned posh accent.

He smiled. 'I could give you a lift, if you like. We could talk.'

'I'd better not,' she said, without wanting to think about the reasons why.

'Same old Mandy,' he smiled, not accusing her, although she felt it. 'At least call me. We could have a natter about old times,' and he scribbled down his number onto a scrap of paper, thrusting it into her coat pocket as she moved toward the bus.

As the doors closed, cutting them off from each other, she felt a strange relief, yet as the bus pulled away she saw him through the misted windows and felt the blood rush to her head as though she had been lifted into the air, turned upside down and shaken. Sitting there on the top deck of the bus her mind went back, remembering the last time she had seen him.

It had been twenty years ago and her mum had been calling up the stairs as she stood in the hallway holding the front door ajar.

'Man-dee! You're wanted!' She left the door slightly

open and walked up the stairs, leaving the caller waiting on the doorstep. Moments later Mandy came down, shouting her farewells back up the staircase.

'And don't be late!' her mum yelled down at her.

'Yeah, yeah, yeah.' The kitchen door slammed somewhere on the floor above and Mandy smiled as she opened the front door to see Nick standing there waiting for her.

'Hi!' she said simply, standing in the doorway. She was wearing the new outfit she'd bought that day with the money she'd earned from her Saturday job in the baker's. Bleached Levi's clung to her hips and thighs, a tight, black t-shirt showing every curve of her slender body. Her long, dark hair was parted in the middle, framing her face. Eyes encircled with black kohl peered out at him.

'Hi!' he said coming over to kiss her on the lips. 'You look great!'

Mandy smiled, delighting in his appreciation of her. Nick looked past her into the darkened hallway and gently guided her inside.

'What do you think you're doing?' she said with mock indignation, giggling as he quietly pushed the door closed behind them.

'Thought we could have a snog before we go.'

'Oh did you?' She giggled and put her hands around the back of his neck, pulling herself up to kiss him on the lips, her tongue exploring his mouth, the taste of him sweet and warm.

They spoke in hushed tones to avoid discovery, their adolescent lovetalk whispered into delicate young ears.

'I'd tell you how much I love you, but we'd better get to this party,' he said, nibbling the soft skin on her neck, the smell of patchouli filling his nostrils, enhancing his pleasure.

'I love you,' she said, her look serious, intense.

'And I love you,' he answered, staring intently into her eyes.

'Promise I'll be the first,' he said, his hands gently caressing her as he moved them down her body, hooking his thumbs over the leather belt at her waist.

'I don't s'pose you'll care once you get to university,' she said, her tone suddenly confrontational, her young eyes full of fear and doubt.

'Why do you have to do it?' he said, pulling away from her.

'What?'

'You know damn well! You do it every time.'

'Do what?'

'Bring up my going off to college. You push it between us, make it an issue. You're determined it'll change things between us.'

'Well, won't it?'

'Why should it? I'll come home every other weekend, and then there are the holidays. And you can come and visit if you want.'

'Oh, yeah, great! I'll just tag along behind while you hang around with your posh new college friends.'

He threw his hands up in exasperation. 'I can't win, can I?'

'Well if you don't like it you can always go out with one of the dolly birds from college. I don't s'pose *they'll* be virgins.'

He sighed heavily. 'I don't want a dolly bird, Mandy, I want you!'

'So you say.'

'You're unbelievable! You're fucking unbelievable!' And he turned and walked out onto the front steps, looking across at the park, its trees silhouetted against the darkening sky. Shaking his head, he called back to her over his shoulder. 'If we're going to this party we'd better go.'

She hesitated, then joined him on the pavement, sulking as they walked off, in step but a million miles apart it seemed, their bodies not touching, the silence between them like a solid wall of glass a thousand miles high.

They could hear the noise as they turned into Susie's street, Sweet's 'Wig Wham Bam' blaring through opened windows, filling the night.

'Christ, I hope we haven't got to listen to this crap all night!' Nick said under his breath as Mandy knocked at the door, the look she threw him one of real disdain.

Once inside Mandy felt relieved to be in a crowd and mingled easily amongst her friends, the drink calming and relaxing her. Nick sat in a corner nursing a can of lager and made no effort to hide his boredom, only moving to replenish his drink or sort through the collection of records scattered around the stereo.

The crowd was mostly made up of friends or people Mandy knew by sight — hangers-on who'd been in the pub with Susie and the others and had caught the whiff of a party. The room was in virtual darkness, the only relief coming from a shaft of light through the kitchen door, where bodies manoeuvred around each other to pour drinks or raid cupboards for food. In the darkness bodies moved to the rhythm of the music, stamping heavy feet into the brown and orange floral carpet, the sounds of Slade, Clapton and Bowie ringing out, and, inevitably, Alice Cooper and the anthemic 'School's Out'.

'What's the matter with Nick?' Anna danced alongside Mandy, facing her as they moved to the music.

'He's a pain in the bleedin' arse!' Mandy threw him a look and he glared back at her.

Anna looked over her shoulder at the dejected figure slumped in the armchair and gave him a brief smile. 'He looks really pissed off,' she said turning back to Mandy. 'Did you have a row?'

'You could say that.' She glanced across at him once more, but this time his face was hidden from her by some girl. Perched on the arm of his chair, her body obscured him, and she'd wrapped her legs round onto the seat of the chair so that his eyes were in line with her knees. 'Just look at him!' she hissed. 'He'll be just the same when he's at university!'

Anna looked round to witness the sin for herself. 'Oh, Mand, you can't blame him. That Lisa's a right little slut!'

'You would stick up for him!' All the time she spoke her eyes flicked towards Nick, tormenting herself with the jealousy that had been eating away at her ever since he'd told her of his plan to go away to college.

'Don't tell me you're not looking forward to all those fellas at university; going to all those parties,' she said, turning her aggression toward Anna as though she ought to shoulder some of the blame; as though she and Nick had colluded to make her suffer like this.

'Yeah, of course I am! But *I* don't have a boyfriend. Nick fancies you like mad. You know he does!'

180

'Really looks like it, don't it?' she said dismissively, moving across the carpet so that she could catch his eye and let him know what she thought of him.

The song ended and Anna and Mandy stood facing each other waiting for another to begin. The sound of a needle being pulled across vinyl shot through the speakers and Anna winced, and then suddenly, abruptly, Johnny Nash's gentle voice filled the room.

'I can see clearly now the rain has gone. I can see all obstacles in my way . . .'

Predictably the room began to clear as everybody headed for the kitchen, off in search of a drink while the smoochy stuff was on. Anna and Mandy were about to do the same when two blokes came over and asked them to dance: Anna had noticed them earlier and quite fancied the tall one with the long, blond hair who now had hold of Mandy's arm.

With a familiarity that was immediately acceptable on the dance floor, the guy put his arms around Mandy's waist and held her close. She placed a hand on each of his shoulders and instinctively her hips swayed to the music's beat, moving from side to side with the rhythm. She could feel the swell of her partner's penis, growing harder as they moved against each other, his hands on the small of her back now, forcing her breasts against his chest.

She was conscious of Nick's eyes on them, but still she allowed her body to mould to this stranger's, to tease him and provoke him, even though her mind was somewhere else, *with* someone else. The song ended and the guy bent down to kiss her on the lips, to take what he now considered to be his. She turned her face so that his lips brushed her cheek and in one swift, adept movement she

181

managed to pull away on the pretence that she needed to visit the loo.

It was then she'd turned to catch Nick's eye, to confront him, to say 'What's good for the goose . . .' But he had gone. And she had never seen him again. She had waited for the call but it never came and when, finally, she forced herself to admit that she'd been in the wrong and phoned him, she discovered it was too late. He had decided to go off to university early and get some work in Brighton before term started.

Twenty years ago, that had been. Twenty years . . .

She sighed, then, seeing that it was almost her stop, gathered up her shopping and made her way down the stairs.

Twenty years . . .

Promise I'll be the first, he said, his thumbs hooked in her belt as he stood facing her, frozen there forever in that hallway of her memory. But he hadn't been the first. They had never made love.

M andy reached up to pull the living room curtains against the damp night. Outside the roads were black and filmy, the fine rain clinging to the surface like sweat, the misty reflection of street lamps peering out of the blackness.

Across the road a young couple pulled up in their car. The woman got out and lifted her baby from the rear seat, kissing it on the forehead before pulling up its hood against the wind. Her husband was unloading shopping from the boot, turning now and then to make silly faces at the youngster, clearly delighting in the child's laughter.

Together they walked up the path towards the house, touching and hugging one another as they went.

Mandy felt the lump in her throat as she swallowed and her shoulders rose and fell as a sigh welled up from deep inside her. She stared into the blackness and glimpsed her image in the window, peering harder as though trying to capture the whole picture. And as she looked she could see herself clearly, a young girl of seventeen, and was overcome by a feeling of utter despair. Inside she still felt young, still saw herself as that same unsophisticated teenager, and she longed to be back there once more; not here, enduring, surviving.

The sound of the front door closing jolted her into action and she quickly pulled the curtains.

'That you?' she called.

'Who d'you think it was?'

She couldn't be bothered to respond, his indifference washing over her as if it were the air itself. She walked out into the hallway, where he stood with his back to her, hanging up his jacket. How she hated that back, the shape of that head, the horrid curly hair where he'd had it permed to disguise his growing baldness.

'What's for tea?' he said, his back still turned.

'Sausage and mash. Won't be long,' she replied, like a bored waitress in a cheap café, passing him on her way to the kitchen.

While he sat in the living room reading the evening paper, Mandy stood at the stove, playing with the sausages as they sizzled in the pan, the potatoes boiling in the saucepan next to them. Fat spat up at her from the frying pan, burning her across the cheek, and in revenge she stabbed at one of them with her knife, cursing at it, the taste of sweet revenge curling her lip into a satisfied smile. She looked down at the shrunken sausage, burst open down its middle, thought of her husband and stabbed it again savagely, splitting it in two.

'What time's this do tomorrow?' he shouted through to her as he flicked the remote control onto Teletext, searching for the racing results.

'Two thirty at the church!' she shouted back.

'That's a bleedin' laugh for a start! Church! And I bet she's marrying in white. Bleedin' hypocrite!'

'Just give it a rest will you! You don't wanna come then don't fucking well come!'

'I'll be there, don't you worry,' he said. 'What present d'you get her?'

'Just a set of glasses from the market.' If she'd felt in a combative mood she'd have told him about the expensive crystal decanter, but right now she couldn't see the point.

There was silence a moment, then. 'My suit clean?'

'Which one?'

'The Armani. The brown one.'

'S'pose so. I don't wear it, do I?'

She took the pan from the stove and tipped the sausages out onto the serving plate, then reached for the potatoes.

'Your dinner's ready!' she shouted. Then, beneath her breath, 'and I hope it fucking well chokes you!'

They ate the meal in total silence; the *Evening Standard* spread across one side of the table, her copy of *House & Garden* open on the other, Mandy leaning on one elbow, flicking through the pages.

Finished, Pete pushed his plate away, then stood,

folding one half of the paper over onto the other and pushing it under his arm.

'I'm going out.'

She looked up at him then back to her magazine without uttering a word.

'Where are the boys?'

'Out! Football or something.' Her eyes remained on the page.

'I'm dropping Brian's tools back to him and then shooting up the pub for a bit, okay?'

'Yeah, fine,' she said, her tone one of total disinterest.

Mandy's eyes followed him as he left the room, a rush of cold air swirling around her legs as the front door closed behind him. Her body slumped with relief, but she was left with familiar feelings of remorse for despising him so much and showing it so obviously. She reached for her mug of coffee, wrapping her hands around it, gaining comfort from its warmth, then shook her head.

It hadn't always been this way. In the beginning she felt sure she must have loved Pete.

After meeting him at the holiday camp they'd gone out together for a while; it turned out they knew some of the same people and lived quite near to each other in the same part of North London, but they split up when Mandy met Nick. When that relationship ended she had turned inward. She hadn't wanted to see anybody or go anywhere. She had been unable to cope with the loss, wanting nothing more than to wallow in the pain of self pity. Finally, her friends had persuaded her to go to a party with them. That was where she met up with Pete again. He was so keen, so attentive, she'd been unable to refuse when he'd asked her to go out with him again. She had felt wanted.

After the wedding, they'd lived with his mum and dad for six months, but Mandy had always felt like an unwelcome visitor. Living in that house, she wasn't allowed to be a real wife to Pete, to do all the things a wife expected – and wanted – to do. His mum did everything for him bar wipe his arse. Pete's meal would be on the table waiting for him when he arrived home from work; she could be watching a favourite TV show but he only had to snap his fingers and she'd jump up and iron him a shirt or press his jeans, with a crease so sharp it could cut a loaf of bread. Nothing was too much trouble for her Petey. Every time Mandy offered she was told to sit down, take it easy – forever on the outside of things.

Mandy would come up with excuses to take them off to their room just to have some time together – laying across Pete's single bed listening to music, or watching TV on the little black-and-white set they'd picked up second-hand, content just to be alone together. Mandy recalled the frustration of making love in that house, stifling their cries as they reached orgasm for fear that Pete's mum might hear them, or that his brother, Barry, was listening through the paper-thin wall. Pete would press his face against her neck as he came and she would smile contentedly as the sounds of his pleasure reverberated through her skin, moist with sweat.

She could remember the Sunday mornings spent standing on the touchline of a muddy football pitch over Hackney Marshes watching a bunch of gone-to-seed twenty-somethings live out their fantasy of becoming the next Georgie Best. After the game they'd go off to their local with the rest of the team, their wives and girlfriends, having afters along with the other regulars, drinking well into the afternoon — the women talking amongst themselves while the blokes gathered at the bar.

When they finally got their own place, a four-room council flat on the top floor of an old redbrick block, she was so happy. During the week they kept busy — either he'd be off at football training or up the pub playing darts, or else she'd be at keep fit — often meeting up in the pub later or back home at bedtime. But on Friday nights she would stop off at Sainsbury's on her way back from work, do her weekly shop, buying them something special for their tea, and walk home looking forward to a night in together by the telly. When she buzzed him on the entry phone he'd come downstairs and help her carry the bags up the eight flights to their little flat.

Sometimes, even now, she would close her eyes and imagine they were back there, curled up together on that first little settee they'd had, all lumpy and worn. He'd be reading the paper — always from the back — and she'd have her nose in a magazine or book, happy in their silent closeness. Or, occasionally, the familiar smell of toast and coffee would fill her nostrils reminding her of those lazy Saturday mornings, lingering in bed or pottering about the flat. It was that smell that reminded her of how content they'd been.

It was difficult to pinpoint exactly when things had gone wrong between them. The kids hadn't helped matters, that was for sure. When she'd told him she was pregnant she'd felt so special and he'd been so sweet towards her, so considerate. She could remember lying in bed with his body shadowing her own as he nuzzled into her back and neck, his arm folded round her, his rough hand gently stroking her belly, swollen with the growing baby inside her, marvelling at the miracle they had created. He never said, but she knew he was proud, knew that at that moment he had loved her.

But neither of them had been prepared for the reality of parenthood. Within two years of getting married they found themselves in a cramped flat with a screaming baby and not enough money, and the novelty of the baby soon wore thin as far as Pete was concerned. He started going up the pub more, coming home late, expecting the baby to be asleep and Mandy waiting for him to make love to her. If the baby was asleep then invariably Mandy was too; exhausted by the constant demands of a young child, she would sometimes daydream, not of wild sex but of simply going to bed and having more rest. And if she was still awake she would be preoccupied with the baby, the weight of Pete's resentment bearing down on her the minute he walked through the door.

As she thought back over their years together she realised there had been moments in their relationship that had signalled its decline. Like when they had stopped kissing. She'd had a throat infection and hadn't wanted to pass on the germs. Or so she'd said. They never kissed again after that, not even when they made love. Somehow the act seemed too intimate. And when she tried to remember the last time they had really talked to each other, she couldn't. She felt sure they must have at the beginning, but in truth they had only ever exchanged words, or had 'conversations', been polite to each other. Now they couldn't even manage that. They had nothing to say. At least, not to each other.

Mandy held her head in her hands and closed her eyes, a feeling of total despair overwhelming her. The tightness in her chest and throat threatened to choke her. What a mess! What a hopeless mess! For Pete she just felt sadness now. For Jonathan she felt desire, certainly, but was there anything more than that? Was there anything beyond the sex, beyond the excitement and sweet revenge of deceit? She wiped a hand across her eyes and pushed it into the pocket of her coat hanging on the back of her chair. Lying the crumpled piece of paper on the table, Mandy smoothed it with her fist, the numbers written on it blurring before her tear-filled eyes.

And then there was Nick. She didn't want to think about what she might feel for Nick.

The front door slammed. There were heavy footsteps in the hallway.

'Maa-um? You seen my denim shirt?'

Mandy wiped her hands on the dishcloth then went to the kitchen door and shouted up the stairs at her eldest's, Jason's, retreating back.

She quickly wiped her eyes and sniffed hard. 'In your room! Hanging on the back of the door!'

She listened to the clump-clump-clump of his heavy footsteps, the momentary silence, then the clump-clump-clump as he went down to the landing bathroom.

'You want tea?' she yelled. 'I've got some sausages here!'

'Nah!' came the answer. 'Going out. Back late.'

The bathroom door slammed. She heard the lock click shut.

Ten words, she thought, going back to the sink to

finish off the washing up. It was a lot more than she usually got from him. Like his father, Jason was a grunter.

Mandy stood there, rehearsing a typical exchange.

She faced right. 'Had a good day, love?'

She turned, facing left, screwing up her face, then shrugged and grunted.

She turned back, herself again, smiling sweetly. 'Read anything interesting in the newspaper, sweetheart?'

She turned, putting on an imbecilic expression of incomprehension. Another grunt.

So it was, day in day out. No wonder she'd lost the art of conversation. Not that she'd really ever had it. Not like Anna, for instance. Only with the girls could she talk. Only then could she really let go and say what she was thinking.

The front door slammed again. This time it was Luke. The gangly, long-haired sixteen-year-old came out into the kitchen, threw his sports bag into the corner by the washing-machine, then made a direct bee-line for the fridge.

'Couldn't you wait and have your tea?' she said, swatting at him with the dischcloth.

'Can't,' he said, taking a whole packet of chocolate digestives from the shelf. 'Going out.'

'Where you been?' she asked, wanting to talk, wanting, just this once to keep him there a moment.

'Football training,' he said, smiling and kissing her forehead. 'Gotta go out again in a minute. Just gonna change me top.'

She stared at his retreating back, then called out to him.

'A bloomin' hotel, that's what this is! Whatever happened to the art of conversation?'

'It died!' Luke shouted back at her from halfway up the stairs. 'Arnold Schwarzenegger nuked it!'

'Too fucking true,' she said quietly to herself. Not that it had ever thrived in their household; not with Pete about. A fine example he'd been to his sons. Monosyllabic wasn't the word for it! Mind you, they managed to get more out of him than she did, even if it was only football talk or golfing hints and lately, much to her dismay, the exchange of horseracing tips between Jason and his father.

She rested her hands either side of the sink, staring out the window into the back garden, thinking of Jonathan again — of his body and of what he'd done to her that morning. The mere thought of it made her tingle, made her go wet down there. He certainly knew how to please her. In fact it had crossed her mind more than once that if she'd made love to somebody like him before she'd met Pete things might have turned out differently.

For a time she stood there in a trance, remembering again.

'Maa-um?'

She turned as Jason clomped into the room, his shirt unbuttoned, stinking of expensive after-shave.

'Can you lend us a tenner?'

'What the hell have you done to your hair?' she asked, staring at his slicked-back hair which was thick with designer grease.

'Aw, mum, get off!' he said, flicking away her hand as she reached across to touch it.

191

'Well, you look like a bloody spiv! Like Dustin Hoffman in *The Godfather*!'

'Aw, leave off.' He began to button up his shirt, which hung long and baggy over his jeans.

'And don't you be too late!'

'I am eighteen you know. You were married at my age.'

'Yeah, don't remind me,' she said, relenting a little. 'Well, you mind yourself, okay?'

She took a ten-pound note from the tin on the side and handed it to him. He took it, winked at her and was gone. She counted. At seven the front door slammed.

Girls . . .

One of these days he'd bring one home. As much as she loved him she couldn't help but feel sorry for the poor cow, whoever she was. Jason was certainly a chip off the old block!

She looked about her. *My domain*, she thought; *ruler of all I survey . . . dishwasher, cooker, microwave, washing-machine and fridge.*

Well, maybe not the fridge. Luke gave a fairly good impression of owning *that*.

And when the boys were gone?

She shook her head in an attempt to shatter the image in her mind – her and Pete, alone together in this house. Till death us do part . . .

'Give me a fucking gun,' she said quietly; 'I'll end it now.'

'What, mum?'

She turned. Luke was standing there, watching her from the doorway.

'I was just thinking of all the wonderful times me and

your dad've got to look forward to once you two have flown the nest.'

'I ain't gone yet,' he said, coming across to hug her, the oversize jumper he wore over his equally baggy shirt making him look suddenly larger.

'Nah,' she said, snuggling up to him, liking his bigness, the non-sexual closeness of his embrace. 'It's just that it all goes so fast.'

She squeezed him, making him wince.

'What's the matter?' she asked.

'Nothing,' he said, moving away, touching his stomach queasily. 'Just a bit of belly ache, that's all. I gotta go.'

She smiled at him. 'I keep telling you not to eat so quickly. Okay. Now take care. And don't be late.'

'In by eleven,' he said, as he disappeared through the kitchen door.

The front door slammed.

She sighed, then walked through into the living room, watching from the window as Luke half walked, half ran down the road.

Five minutes maximum. That's all they were there for. And when they got back it'd be straight up to their rooms, the doors slammed shut and that would be that. Same in the morning. A quick trip down to the loo to pee, a hurried bowl of cornflakes and out. And so the days went by. And the years . . .

Pete was no doubt on his second pint by now. She could just see him, staring into the glass before he took a sip, as if he could tell whether a pint was a good one or not. As if he really cared.

She made to laugh, but it came out as a kind of sigh. Oh God, what was she going to do? What the fuck was she going to do? Because the thought of carrying on like this for another thirty years was more than she could bear. Thirty minutes with Pete was bad enough, but thirty years!

She turned and went back through into the kitchen and put the kettle on.

'Looks like it's just me, then,' she said, going to the fridge and pulling a Lean Cuisine from the freezer. 'On me tod.'

She had been sitting there barely fifteen minutes when the doorbell rang.

Probably one of the boys, she thought, pushing aside the ruins of her meal and getting up. *They'll forget their heads one of these days*!

She opened the front door, starting to smile, but it quickly vanished from her face.

'What do *you* want?'

It was Pete's brother, Barry. He placed a hand proprietorially on the doorpost and put his face close to hers, smiling. 'Wanted a word.'

'Pete's not in.'

'I know. It's you I've come to see.'

'I'm busy.' She went to close the door, but he pushed past her.

'Just popped by for a little chat, that's all.'

She didn't like the sound of that. They didn't have the kind of relationship where he just popped round for a little chat. She couldn't stand him and he knew it; in fact, they'd barely exchanged a civil word in years.

She closed the door and squeezed past him. 'In the kitchen,' she said. 'But make it quick. I'm busy.'

'I've noticed,' he said. Then, matter-of-factly. 'Pete gone up the boozer, has he?'

'Yeah, as usual. You'll catch him if you hurry.' She turned, planting her back against the washing-machine. 'So what is it? You in trouble? Need money, or something?'

'Or something,' he said, and gave her a strange look.

'You'd better speak to Pete,' she said, troubled by that look but not knowing why.

'Maybe I will.'

She frowned. There was something odd about this. 'Look,' she said, 'just what *do* you want?'

He came across and put his hands on her hips. 'I'll have you for a start.'

She shrugged him off and pushed past him, beginning to get angry. 'You've got a fucking nerve!'

'Me?' He laughed. 'I'm not the one who's been screwing around.'

She had her back to him as he said it. Slowly, her stomach tense, her whole body suddenly cold, she turned to face him. 'What do you mean?'

His eyes were smiling nastily, mocking her, enjoying her discomfort. 'I've seen your car about a lot lately. You've been putting yourself about a bit. Been to lots of empty houses . . .'

He was grinning now, showing his imperfect teeth. She stared at him — at his receding hairline, his beer paunch, his bad skin — taking in what he'd said. He knew. If he'd seen her car, he would have seen Jonathan's parked next to hers. Maybe he'd even seen them together. Even so, she set her jaw, trying to brazen it out.

'I don't know what you mean.'

'No?' He stepped close again, putting his hands on her shoulders. 'You think Pete would believe that?'

She swallowed. 'So what d'you want?'

His hands moved down, onto her breasts. 'I want what the estate agent's getting.'

She met his eyes, such revulsion for him at that moment, such anger and hatred, she wondered how he couldn't see it. But he was like Pete in that. All self. He was barely aware of *her*, standing there in front of him. No. She was just a piece of meat — something to be used.

Her anger gave her strength. Making no attempt to remove his groping hands, she smiled.

'Okay . . . but show me what you've got. I want to see.'

His triumphant grin was horrible, obscene. He thought he had her. Smugly, taking his right hand from her breast, he reached down and unzipped himself.

'Let me feel it,' she said, the nausea she felt at that moment almost overwhelming her, making her want to scream.

'That's a good girl,' he said. 'I knew you'd see it my way.'

She steeled herself. Looking into his eyes, she took his penis in her hand and smiled.

'Happy?' she asked.

'I will be,' he answered, grinning at her, his penis growing noticeably in her palm.

No you fucking won't, she thought and, focusing all her disgust, all of her hatred of him into one single motion, she pulled hard on his cock.

He screamed, his face convulsing. 'Oh, shit! Oh, Jesus-fucking-Christ, woman! What've you done to me?'

She stepped back, watching him as he lay there on the kitchen floor, his face screwed up in agony, his body foetal-like as he clutched his flaccid willy with both hands.

'Happy *now*?' she said, a cold fury keeping her from feeling any sympathy for him.

'You bitch! You fucking cow! You've *broken* it!'

'Serves you fucking right!' she said, bending over him. 'You nasty little bastard! Your brother's wife! Your fucking brother's wife! What kind of animal are you?'

He whimpered, backing away from her on his knees, his eyes revealing what she had always instinctively known about him: he was a spineless, worthless little shit. Beside him, Pete was a paragon of virtue.

'You can tell Pete what you fucking like,' she said, pushing her face into his aggressively, 'but remember . . . if you mouth off to him, I'll tell him what you've just tried. And your old lady too. And once she finds out you won't just have your pudding pulled, you'll have your balls chopped off and stuffed in your big, filthy gob.'

She straightened up, laughing scathingly down at him. 'You think I'd screw you? I'd sooner have three-in-a-bed with Rod Hull and Emu than fuck you, you pathetic little arsehole!'

He backed further away, his eyes fearful now, certain she was a madwoman.

'Mandy, I . . .'

'You're a slimeball, you know that? You treat your wife like shit and your kids like they don't exist. You're fat, you're balding and your cock . . .' She shook her head and laughed, crooking her little finger. 'If your cock was a chipolata, I'd take it back and ask for a refund.'

He pulled himself up in the doorway and, crouched, both hands holding his injured manhood, backed away down the hallway.

'Oh, and in case you're wondering, the guy I meet . . . he's fucking amazing. Three, four hours . . . it's nothing to him. And he's big. You know? Where it counts.'

It meant nothing to her how big Jonathan was, but she knew that Barry, like most men, had a thing about size. It hit him where he hurt.

Again she leaned close, beginning to enjoy herself. 'You think I'd even think of letting you get anywhere near me? *You*?'

She put such emphasis on the last word that he tucked his head in like a boxer trying to avoid a blow. And suddenly, absurdly, she felt like giggling. She looked aside, trying not to laugh.

'Does it hurt?'

'Hurt?' His eyes rolled. 'Shit . . . you almost pulled it off!'

And now she did laugh. Now the tension drained from her and she was laughing openly at him; her scorn falling like cleansing rain, beating down on him, *destroying* him.

He crawled away, a dog, backing away from its owner, its tail between its legs.

'Just piss off out of it!' she said. 'Go on, piss off!'

The phone was ringing. She heard it, but it was as if it was at a distance. All she could see was Barry, on his knees, his injured cock in his hands, his eyes pained and fearful. After a while the ringing stopped.

'Now clear off,' she said, suddenly tired of it all. Of Barry and Pete and the whole damn charade. 'Can't you just piss off out of it and leave me alone?'

He nodded, then, turning away, went to the door and, opening it, stepped out, limping away.

Mandy stared at the door a while, then, a feeling of emptiness invading her, slumped onto the floor.

'Fuck him!' she said, suddenly tearful. 'Why did he have to spoil it all?'

Mandy went upstairs and sat on her bed, staring sightlessly at the white laminate wardrobe, her eyes red from crying. Outside the window, the rainclouds had cleared, revealing a bright full moon, its light filling the room with shadows.

After a while she shuddered and put her hand up to her face, wiping it across her cheeks. 'What a day,' she murmured. 'What a bleedin' day!'

She reached over, meaning to turn on the bedside lamp, then froze, hearing a banging on the door downstairs.

He's back! she thought, knowing it was too early for the boys. *The bastard's come back!*

The thought scared her. What if he got violent? After all, she'd given him quite a blow to his male ego, and Barry Evans wasn't the type to take that from a mere woman. He'd want to get his own back somehow, and he was the kind of rat who didn't give a monkey's how he did it.

Thank Christ the lights are off, she thought, creeping across to the window and trying to peek out over the window sill. But she couldn't see anything over the trellis and she didn't want to stand up and look out in case he saw her. Who knew what he might do? Break the door down, maybe, or smash a window.

Mandy returned to the bed and sat there, chewing her nails nervously, her heart going fifteen to the dozen. The banging came again, louder, more urgent this time.

'Mandy? You in there? Mandy!'

She jerked round, then gave a little whimper. It was him! It was Barry!

'Shit!' she said quietly, looking about her, wondering where she could hide. Her eyes settled on the phone.

The police! she thought. *I'll phone the police!*

Silence, an awful, ominous silence, followed.

Pull yourself together, girl. He wouldn't dare. Pete'd kill him.

Even so, she sat there, tensed like a coiled spring, listening for the smallest sound — for the tinkle of glass or the splintering of wood. But there was nothing. Then, unmistakably, came the sound of footsteps going back down the stone steps, the noise of the gate swinging shut.

She let out a long breath, then lay back, trembling, on the bed.

The ringing phone jolted her from sleep. She hadn't even been conscious of dozing off, but now the room was dark. She groped for the phone and lifted the receiver, steeling herself, ready to give him a mouthful, but the voice on the other end was soft, definitely female.

'Mandy? Is that you?'

For a moment she didn't recognise it. 'Who's that?' she asked, sitting up and reaching for the lamp switch.

'It's me! Karen!'

As the lamp came on, flooding the room with its soft, pearled glow, Mandy felt close to tears once more. The sound of that friendly voice was like a lifeline.

'Oh, Kar!' she said. 'Thank Christ it's you!'

Karen's voice was suddenly all concern. 'You okay, Mand? You don't sound too good.'

She shivered, then, unexpectedly, burst into tears again. 'Oh, it's been awful, Kar! Really awful! I thought you were him! I really did! He was banging on the door, yellin' at me! I thought he was goin' to kill me!'

'Hold up, slow down a bit. What's been happening? You say Pete's been trying to kill you?'

Mandy snorted. 'No. Not Pete.'

'Then who are you talking about? Not the boys?'

'Nah . . .'

'Now calm down. You want to talk about it?'

Mandy took a long, shuddering breath, then, pulling herself up and leaning her back against the headboard, she wrapped the duvet about her legs. 'It's a long story . . .'

'Yeah, well, I'm listening. Blow your nose and tell your Auntie Karen all about it.'

Mandy showered, then sat before the dressing-table mirror, studying herself as she put on her make-up, a new determination firing her.

She'd had enough. Of Pete, of Barry, of all of them. Even, at that moment, of Jonathan. Oh, the sex was good. The sex was fucking fantastic, but what would they have once the initial excitement wore off? What would they have in common then?

'Bugger all,' she answered herself, then pouted, applying a thick coat of glossy carmine lipstick to finish off.

She had made up her mind. She was going to have it out with Pete tonight, when he got back from the pub. She was going to face him out and tell him it was over. The Big E. Finito. Done with.

Mandy took a shuddering breath. The very thought of it scared her, sent a cold shiver through her, but she was determined now. If she didn't do it tonight, she knew she'd be here forever. And forever was too long. You only had one life . . . Nick had taught her that.

Briefly she thought of the note in the pocket of her coat. It had been good to see Nick again, to see his face after all these years.

She stared at her image in the mirror once again, turning her head from side to side, casting a critical eye over her features, then nodded to herself. Susie was right, you know. She *was* looking better than she'd looked for years. Game for it! as Susie might have said.

All her life she'd played it safe. All her life she'd let her fears dominate her desires, and what had it got her?

Pete Evans. Pete-fucking-Evans!

'Shit!' she said, feeling suddenly very bitter. It was just so unfair. So bloody unfair!

And the boys? a tiny voice inside her head reminded her. *What'll the boys think if you throw their dad out?*

'They can think what they fucking like,' she told her reflection, pushing her chin out defiantly. 'They're old enough, after all. They'll cope.'

That's if they even noticed he was gone. And even if they did, was she going to let that stop her now? No. She was damned if she would!

Mandy looked down at the ring on the second finger of her left hand; a simple band of gold. On a whim she began to try to remove it.

'Fuck it!' she said after a moment. The knuckle was too big, too swollen. She couldn't get the ring past it, try as she would.

202

Soap. She could get some soap . . .

She stood, then sat again, calming herself. *No hurry,* she told herself. *One step at a time, eh, girl?*

Yet it annoyed her that she couldn't get it off. Now that the idea had seized her, she wanted to act on it at once.

She let out a long, exasperated breath, then stood. Shaking off the towel she began to dress. As she was buttoning her skirt the phone rang. She froze, staring at it, wondering for a moment if it was Barry again, then she remembered Karen's advice.

Don't let him get to you, Mand. That's what he wants. If he thinks you're scared of him, he's got you. You gotta make him think you don't give a toss. You gotta make him scared of you. Act tough, and whatever you do, don't let him get the upper hand!

She straightened her skirt then stepped across, picking up the phone aggressively.

'Yes?'

At first she didn't catch it. All she knew was that it was Pete, and what the hell was Pete doing phoning her? He was still in the pub, surely?

'What? Say that again?'

'You gotta come, Mand. It's Luke. He's been taken ill.'

Ill? No . . . it wasn't possible. Why, she'd seen Luke not two hours back and he'd been fine then. No. This was some kind of practical joke. Pete's mates must have put him up to it.

'Where are you?' she asked, beginning to get angry with him. 'You still in the pub?'

But his voice when he answered her was urgent, worried. 'Look, you gotta come. He's really bad. Peritonitis, they reckon!'

Peritonitis! That single word brought home the reality of it to her. At once she was coldly alert, remembering the pain he'd mentioned to her in the kitchen.

'Where is he? Where've they taken him?'

'The Royal Free. I'm there now. Look where the hell 'ave you been? I've been trying to get hold of you for bleedin' ages. I sent Barry round, but he said you wasn't in.'

She shivered. So *that's* what he had wanted . . .

'I'll be right there,' she said. 'I'll get a mini-cab. I'll . . .' She swallowed, suddenly very, very frightened. 'Tell him I'm coming, Pete. Tell him I'm on my way!'

'Just get 'ere. All right?'

The phone went dead. Slowly she set the receiver down.

Luke . . . She swallowed again, her throat dry, her hands trembling. Then, picking up her coat and handbag, she switched off the light and went outside, hurrying down the stairs.

– *Susie* –

It had all been Janet's idea. A friend of hers had done it the summer before and had had a great time. Left to Susie, however, they'd never even have got to Paddington to catch the train, but Janet had arranged it all. As ever.

Sitting in the downstairs bar of The Swinging Sporran on Essex Road, 'Tiger Feet' blaring from the pub jukebox, Janet dug deep into the massive hold-all she called a handbag and pulled out the thick file of letters and brochures she had written off for.

'So where d'you want to go?' Janet asked, spreading out a tourist map of the West Country and turning it to face Susie.

They'd had this conversation before, of course, on several occasions, but now they had to decide and there was a slight tone of impatience in Janet's voice. She'd put in a lot of time getting this far, making phone calls on the sly from the office where she was temping as a junior, just to get a bit of pocket money. After wasting a year doing CSE retakes, Susie had called it a day and gone to work in a shoe shop as a stop-gap, determined not to suffer a summer of hot, sweaty feet.

'I don't care,' Susie said, 'so long as it's not some dead place full of old fogeys.'

'And you want somewhere with a nice beach.'

'Yeah . . .'

Janet sat back and sighed. 'You do realise that the only time we're likely to get to see the beach is at night. It's not a holiday. We're meant to be working.'

'Yeah, but we might get lucky, eh? You know, get a place that gives us a couple of hours off in the afternoon.'

Janet laughed. Susie's eternal optimism cheered her. 'Okay. Then let me give you a few options.'

'*Options*, eh?' Susie said, putting on a posh voice. 'Tell you what . . . let's get in a couple more drinks first.'

Janet frowned at her then relented. 'Okay, you old lush. Here . . .' She reached for her handbag, but Susie, who was getting up, waved her off. 'Nah. I'll get them.'

'You're flush suddenly.'

'Yeah, well, it's this bloke I've been seeing. Insists on paying for everything. And who am I to argue?'

Janet stared at her, curious. It was the first she'd heard of it. 'Who's this then? Rothschild?'

'Roth-who? Nah . . . he's a garage mechanic.'

'Anyone I know?'

'Not in the biblical sense.'

They both giggled. Straightening up Susie smoothed a hand across her backside, her long skirt unfolding as it dropped around her calves, then waddled over to the bar on her stacked heels. Janet watched her a moment, then, chuckling to herself, began to sort through the pile, pulling out the six which had particularly caught her eye.

By the time Susie returned with the drinks, she had already made her mind up.

'Well?' she said, accepting the glass from Susie then clinking it against hers. 'Who is he?'

Susie took a large swig from her glass then leaned closer, whispering a name in Janet's ear.

'Nah . . .'

'As God's my witness.'

'Since when did you become a Catholic?'

Susie crossed herself and looked heavenward. 'Forgive me Father, for I have sinned . . .'

Janet spat her drink back into her glass, then wiped her mouth. 'Lucky old you, is all I can say. Is it serious?'

Susie shrugged. 'I don't s'pose so.'

Janet grinned, relieved. 'Okay. So where *are* we going?'

'What are the . . . *options*?'

Janet handed across the brochures.

For a time Susie was silent, looking through them, then she looked up, tapping one of the brochures with a purple fingernail. 'This is it! This one here!'

Janet smiled. 'Okay. I'll phone them, shall I?'

But as she went to get up, Susie reached out and pushed her down again. 'Hang on!'

Janet sat back, exasperated. 'What now?'

Susie shrugged uncomfortably. 'Let's just run through it again. What we've gotta do, an' all that.'

Janet shook her head. 'You can make a bed, can't you?'

'Yeah.'

'And you know how to work a hoover and a washing-machine.'

Susie nodded. 'I've been doin' all that kind of stuff since I was five!'

'Well, that's the long and the short of it, really. Only you'll be doing it for other people. Tidying rooms, making beds, helping to serve the breakfast and the evening meal.'

'An' that's it?'

'Yeah. What d'you think they want you to do? Tuck the bleedin' punters in at night?'

Susie sat back, a wry grin on her face. 'Could be a bit of a laugh.' And then suddenly struck by an afterthought, she asked, 'D'you reckon we'll 'ave to wear a uniform? You know, a little maid's outfit.'

'Bloody hell! I hope not. I reckon they're a bit bloody kinky, them.' Janet wrinkled up her nose, her face contorted into a look of total disgust.

'They only get you in them to give the blokes a cheap thrill,' Susie said knowingly. 'D'you remember old Bates?' Both girls shrieked with laughter, recalling the owner of a hardware shop where they had both worked as Saturday girls when they were fifteen. 'The way he used to tell us we had to wear dresses for work and then would stand at the bottom of the ladder looking up our frocks when we 'ad to get something from the top shelf.'

Janet nodded her head. 'Bloody perv!'

'Mind you,' said Susie, ever sympathetic, 'you can't really blame him with a wife like his.'

'Don't make excuses for him! He was just a dirty old sod and that's all there is to it.'

Susie raised her glass to her lips and took a mouthful of the warm lager, wiping a hand across her mouth as she placed it on the table before her. 'Did I tell you he touched me up once?' she said.

'No!' Janet was incredulous. 'When? Where was I?' How could Susie have kept this to herself for three years?

'You weren't there that week, you were ill or something. It was after closing. He'd locked up and there was just the two of us left. I was about to get me coat on and he called me from that little storeroom he 'ad in the basement − d'you remember − asked me to come and give him a hand.'

Janet burst out laughing. 'I bet he did.'

'It wasn't funny,' Susie said seriously. 'Anyway, I goes down there − I only 'ad that cardigan dress on over me tights − and he asks me to go in that little cubby hole bit at the back and get some of the boxes. Only, when I gets there he's standing right behind me, made me jump, and when I turned round to get past him he made a grab for me boobs, pushing me back against the wall . . .'

'Shit! What did you do?'

'I didn't know what to do. I think I was in shock. I dropped the boxes − there was stuff everywhere. Anyway he fumbles about a bit and then pushes his hand up me skirt, trying to get inside me tights.'

'You should've kneed him in the balls. Dirty bastard!'

'I know, but it all 'appened so quick. All I can really remember is that his breath stank of tuna fish . . .'

'Yuk!'

'Anyway, thank God, the next thing we 'eard was his wife calling him from upstairs in the shop. You should've seen his face!' And for the first time in recounting the story, Susie laughed at the memory. 'He looked like someone had come and stuffed a pair of electric tongs up his arse.'

'She would've if she'd caught him. Given him a perm where the sun don't shine!'

Susie nodded her head. 'He was so petrified his stiffy disappeared in a flash! He spat some kind of threat in my face about not telling anyone or else I'd be sorry, and he flew up those stairs like a fart up a drainpipe. You should've 'eard him up there being all smarmy. Little arsehole. Anyway, I did meself up, ran upstairs, grabbed me coat and I was off.'

'Why didn't you tell me?'

Susie shrugged, reaching for her glass. 'Felt a bit funny about it, I s'pose,' she said, giving the briefest of smiles.

Janet placed a hand over hers, squeezing it gently. 'But what I want to know is,' she said quietly, 'did he 'ave a big one?'

The two of them burst out laughing, clinging to each other as they rocked from side to side. As they calmed, Janet got up again. 'Well?' she said, looking down at Susie. 'What about this summer job? Are you game for it or what?'

'Go on,' Susie said, grinning. 'It'll be a laugh.'

'Yeah . . .' Janet stared at her friend a moment, unsure quite what she was letting herself in for, then, taking some change from her purse, went across to the payphone in the corner to dial the hotel.

Newquay in mid-April was unexpectedly cold and blowy. The day was overcast and as the two girls stepped from the train things looked ominous. Lugging their heavy suitcases over to the ticket barrier, they looked at each other and grimaced.

'It don't look like the fuckin' Riviera to me,' Susie whispered, as she searched for her ticket.

'That's just brochure talk,' Janet whispered back. 'But the night life s'posed to be great. Best in the West Country.'

'It better be!' Susie murmured, locating her ticket and giving the aged porter on the barrier her sweetest smile. 'Or I'll be on the first train 'ome!'

'Chin up,' Janet said, handing over her ticket, then pushing through after Susie. 'You know what they say.'

Susie turned, looking at her friend. 'Nah. What *do* they say?'

'Every cloud . . .' Janet stopped, then set her suitcase down. 'Oh, shit!'

Outside the weather had broken. The rain had started to fall with a vengeance.

'Talking of clouds . . .' Susie looked to Janet and laughed. 'Look, it makes no odds, Jan. We'll get a taxi. It'll save carting these about. Besides, it can't rain the whole fuckin' time, can it?'

As if to answer her, a thunderclap sounded overhead. A moment later there was a lightning flash.

'Welcome to bleedin' Cornwall,' Janet said gloomily. Then, as if catching Susie's mood, she began to laugh.

They were still laughing as they climbed into the back of the taxi — a rather flash-looking Chevrolet with red leather upholstery — their laughter momentarily drowning out the sound of the rain beating down steadily on the roof.

'You're a cheery pair,' the young driver said, climbing

into the car, having put their suitcases in the boot. His soft, lilting Cornish accent seemed the perfect match for his long, black curly hair. 'You here on your hols?'

Susie nudged her friend hard, then answered him. 'Nah. We're here to work.'

'Is that so?' He half turned, leaning one arm on the back of his seat and smiling at Susie, making no attempt even to start the car. 'Where's that, then?'

'The Smuggler's Inn,' Janet answered. 'Just outside town on the Padstow Road.'

'Oh, I know it,' he said, with a languidness that prevented it from seeming in the least bit rude. 'Nice place. Jack Tregerthen owns it.'

'You know him?' Susie asked, pushing her hair back from her face.

'Oh, I know everyone,' he answered, with a fulsome grin, making no attempt to avert his eyes from Susie's ample bust. 'Jack's a nice man. And his missus. You'll get on well with them.'

Susie leaned towards him. 'I guess you get to know everybody in your job.'

'That's right,' he answered, sweeping his hair back with one hand. 'You want to know what's going on in this town, you just ask Trev Penhannon.'

'That's you is it?' Janet asked, just a little pissed off that she was being left out of this conversation.

'That's me,' he said, as if unaware of the edge in her voice. 'Here,' he reached across and took a printed card from the glove compartment and handed it to Susie. 'You need me, you phone that number, day or night.'

'I bet,' Janet said under her breath. Then, louder:

'D'you think we could get going, before the rain rusts away the roof?'

He turned, smiling at her, all charm, so that she dropped her eyes, embarrassed now by his attention.

'The Smuggler's, at the double . . .'

And, turning round, he switched on the engine and was away in a single movement, throwing the two girls back into the well-padded seat.

Susie looked to Janet and grinned, flashing the card at her before she slipped it into her cleavage, causing them both to bite their lips as they stifled their giggles.

'This your first time?' he asked, as he spun the wheel one handed to negotiate a roundabout, looking at Susie in his rearview mirror.

'Nah,' Susie answered, winking at Janet mischievously. 'I've been in a taxi lots of times!'

And, all three of them laughing, they hurtled along the rain-swept seafront.

The Smuggler's was a big old coaching inn with black wooden beams and a cobbled courtyard round the back where the coaches used to stop. As they passed under the arch and juddered across the yard, both girls peered out through the misted windows, trying to make out if the place resembled in any way the picture in the brochure.

It was still pouring down, and while Trev the driver got their cases, they dashed across to the shelter of the open back door, where, beside an oven big enough to cook for the giant in a fairy story, Ivy Tregerthen was standing, her long black hair tied back, an apron about her ample girth, a huge beam of a smile on her pleasant, rosy-cheeked face.

'So there you are, me dears,' she said, putting an arm out to each of them and giving them a motherly hug. 'Good journey?'

The warmth of the welcome was unexpected and Susie could see how embarrassed Janet was by it. Her family weren't the huggy, cuddly sort. Nor were her own, when it came down to it, but she enjoyed the physical contact — didn't feel embarrassed by it the way Janet did.

'Lovely,' she said, beaming back at the woman as she released them. 'There's some beautiful countryside.'

Yes, and bloody lots of it, she thought, remembering how bored she'd been after the novelty of looking out at all those open fields had passed. She didn't know how country folk could stand it. Perhaps that was why they had so many pubs.

'Jack — my husband — he's helping John, our barman, sort the cellar out right now, but he'll be up in a bit to see you. But let's get you settled in first, eh? Then we can have a cup of tea and a nice chat.' She looked from one to the other and smiled again. 'So which of you is Janet?'

'That's me,' Janet offered awkwardly. 'I spoke with Mr Tregerthen.'

'Ah,' she nodded then looked to Susie. 'So you must be Susan.'

'Susie,' she corrected her. 'Least, that's what everyone calls me.'

'Then Susie it is.' The smile was genuinely affectionate. Ivy looked past her to the yard. 'Look . . . here's Trevor with your bags.'

'Thanks, Trev,' Susie said, taking her case.

'Don't forget, day or night,' he answered, grinning broadly so that a gold tooth revealed itself at the corner of his mouth. Then, with a definite lightness to his walk, he went back to his car and, with the same abruptness reversed it in a tight circle and, without seeming to stop at all, swung out through the gate.

'Nice lad, our Trev,' Ivy said, staring thoughtfully out through the rain-streaked window, 'but a bit of a ladies' man.'

'I'd never have guessed,' Janet said.

Ivy laughed. 'Well, follow me, girls. I've put you up the top at the back. It's nice and quiet up there and you'll be right next door to each other.'

Susie looked to Janet and smiled. Then, lifting their cases, they followed Ivy through the glass-fronted kitchen door, along a narrow, sloping corridor that smelled of beer and old cooking, and up an even more narrow staircase, which seemed to turn and turn and turn, a tiny casement window at each bend.

'Christ!' Janet whispered, halfway up, 'it's like climbing the bloody Eiffel Tower!'

Susie giggled, then nudged her to keep up with Ivy, who could be heard a turn ahead of them, wheezing gently as she kept up a steady pace.

The inn was old. Everywhere they looked they could see signs of that. The wallpaper seemed varnished onto the walls, the woodwork painted over fifty times or more. Everything creaked when you trod on it or touched it, and there was a general underlying smell of mustiness and age. But all in all it was not unpleasant. For the first time since she'd set foot on the train, Susie allowed herself to feel excited. This was an adventure, a genuine adventure.

Their rooms really were 'up the top at the back'. In fact, they were in a little garret that stuck up above the rest of the inn and was reached by the narrowest stairway yet, so that both girls had to pull their cases after them, there was so little room.

'I hope I don't put on any more weight,' Susie quipped to Janet keeping her voice low so Ivy wouldn't hear. 'I'll never get out of my room!'

They emerged onto a small landing from which three doors led off. Overhead the rain drummed constantly on the roof. Ivy was standing in the first doorway, smiling. Behind her was a room which an estate agent might have described as 'compact' but which was in truth the smallest either girl had ever seen without it being called a cupboard. Janet's was little bigger, but it did at least have *some* floor space. The third room was a bathroom, if you could call a broom cupboard with a hip-bath and a wall-mounted ascot heater a proper bathroom. There was no sign of a loo.

'There's a loo on the next floor down,' Ivy said, reading their thoughts, 'but there's something under your bed if you're caught short in the night. I'll leave you to settle in then. Come down when you're ready. I'll make some tea and scones and we can have a chat, eh, girls?'

'Thanks, Mrs Tregerthen,' both girls called to her.

'Ivy,' she called back up the stairs. 'You must call me Ivy.'

Janet was humming to herself as Susie came into her room. She'd unpacked and was putting the last of her things into the drawers of an ancient-looking dresser.

'Jee-sus-fuckin'-Christ, Jan. You still humming that song?'

All the way down on the train Janet had been humming

the same song to herself — 'Seasons In the Sun' — like some demented jukebox.

'Well, I like it,' Janet said, poking her tongue out.

'I wouldn't mind, only it's pissed down ever since we got here.'

Janet shrugged, then smiled. 'It'll get better. The rooms are okay, ain't they?'

'The view's nice. You can see right over the harbour. But it's like a bleedin' shoe-box! There's no room to swing a mouse, let alone a moggy!'

'Well, you won't be in it much, eh? Only to sleep.'

'Yeah, well, I can't see us smuggling many blokes up here, can you?'

'Not any fat ones!'

'Nah.' Susie giggled. 'Besides, they'd need a fucking oxygen mask, what with those stairs. I thought I'd die, carrying me case up.'

'It's good for you,' Janet said, closing the drawer. She stood, facing her friend. 'It'll keep your weight down.'

'I can think of better ways to keep me weight down.'

'Like Trev the Rev, you mean?'

Susie made a face. 'He can start my engine up any day!'

'Dirty mare,' Janet said laughing. 'And trust you to get off with the first person you meet in Cornwall!'

'He wasn't the first. There was the ticket collector . . .'

'Yeah, but he was eighty if he was a day!'

'Yeah, but kinda sweet I thought.'

They giggled.

'Well?' Janet asked after a moment. 'What d'you reckon?'

'What, about ol' Poldark?'

'No, you silly moo. About this place.'

'S'all right, I guess.'

'And Ivy?'

'She seems nice. Straight. Let's hope her old man's the same, eh?'

Jack Tregerthen turned out to be even more of a sweetie than his wife. From the first he treated them like his own daughters. As for John the barman — John the Jug, as Susie later re-christened him, due to his habit of sitting with his 'jug' of ale after closing — he took one look at Susie and was instantly besotted, taking every opportunity he could over those first few weeks simply to stand and watch her. But it was Trev Penhannon who made the first move.

The work was hard but undemanding and both of them had quickly settled into the routine of the inn. But it was only toward the end of the second week that either of them felt they had enough energy in reserve to 'do the town'. It was then that Trev made his appearance.

Susie was up in her room, a towel wrapped about her, having squeezed herself into the tiny hip bath, when she heard a creak on the stairs leading up to the landing.

'Jan? That you?'

'No,' Trev answered, standing in the doorway, looking in, one hand resting on the doorframe, his eyes looking appreciatively at her bare shoulders.

'Oh, fuck . . .' she said, looking round for her dressing gown. And even as she did the towel fell off her.

'Here,' he said, handing it to her, suddenly there beside her in that tiny space beside the bed.

'You've got a bloody nerve,' she said, half laughing,

conscious suddenly that she hadn't quite finished that diet she'd begun back in February.

'Have I?' he said, his eyes twinkling at her.

She didn't fancy him particularly. They'd flirted whenever he'd called by for a drink or dropped off a passenger, in a jokey sort of way, but Susie hadn't given him much thought otherwise. But the idea of being alone with him, naked in her room, was having a strangely aphrodisiac effect on her.

Slowly, knowing he'd had a good look at her, she fastened the towel again, then turned, looking up into his face.

'So what do you want?'

'I was wondering . . .' he laughed softly, conscious that she was teasing him, then reached out, placing a warm hand on her wet and naked shoulder. 'I was wondering if you wanted . . .'

'Yeah?' she asked, tilting her head slightly, invitingly.

But he didn't finish. Drawing her toward him, he kissed her. And this time, as the towel fell away, he didn't bother to pick it up.

Breaking from the kiss, she looked up at him again and gave a little shudder. Her nipples were hard now, and she saw how his eyes were drawn to them.

'I think you'd better shut the door,' he said, smiling. 'That's if you want me to stay.'

Susie stood there, confused. She felt trapped and wasn't sure how to get out of this one; the part of her that had no desire to escape struggling to overcome the feelings of guilt that she should want to be here with this man, like this.

'You do want me to stay, don't you?' he whispered into her ear, nibbling the delicate skin, his warm breath on her neck sending shivers through her body.

'You do like me, don't you, Trev?' she said, leaning back, trying to see his face.

''Course I do, my little beauty,' he said, smiling down at her.

She made to speak again but he put a finger gently to her lips. 'Just shut the door and come to bed.'

Hearing footsteps on the stairs, Susie reached out and pushed the door closed, before falling onto the soft mattress.

'I've never slept with a Cornishman,' she said, pulling the covers back and slipping in beneath the sheets, moving back against the cold, white-washed wall.

'Well, I'll do my best not to let the county down,' he said. Then, pulling his shirt off over his head, he began to unbuckle his jeans.

'God, you should have seen him,' she'd told Janet later that night. 'Must be all those pasties. Like a fuckin' steamhammer he was. It's a bleedin' wonder we didn't go through the floor!'

'I know,' Janet said. 'I could hear you through the wall. The bloody noise you two made, it's a wonder half the inn didn't complain.'

'You were next door?' Susie burst out laughing.

'It's not funny,' Janet said. 'It's bad enough Trev the Rev slavering over you all the time without me having to listen to the blow by blow action . . . complete with running commentary.'

Susie giggled. 'Yeah, he don't 'alf talk, don't he?'

'I thought you said he was a romantic? Sounds like a common and garden bleedin' pervert to me!'

'You're only jealous.'

'True.'

'Well . . . why don't you ask John the Jug up here. We could make it a foursome.'

'Janet and John, ha ha . . .'

Susie stared at her, then put a hand to her mouth. 'Christ! I hadn't thought!' And she burst out laughing again. 'Just think, Jan . . . you could write a book about it. Janet and John have a shag. It'd be a best seller.'

'Yeah, I can see it now . . . they'd have it in all the schools. Aah says Janet. Janet says aah. Ooh says John. John says ooh. Janet and John go aah and ooh.'

And off they went again, collapsing into each others' arms they were laughing so much. They were still laughing when Ivy poked her head around the door.

'You all right, girls?' she asked, smiling.

'We're fine, Ivy,' Susie said, getting up and wiping the tears from her cheeks. 'I was just about to turn in.'

'That's good,' Ivy said maternally, 'only Jack was thinking of starting a bit earlier tomorrow. We've got the heating people coming in, you see.'

'Yeah?'

'Seems Jack noticed a bit of a noise earlier on — sounded like a banging in the pipes — so he's got them in . . . just to check it out, mind. No point taking risks, is there?'

Janet looked down, stifling a giggle, but Susie looked back at Mrs Tregerthen with a straight face. 'I'll set the alarm for six. That okay?'

'Lovely,' and with that she was gone.

Susie turned, looking to Janet, both standing with their

hand clamped over their mouth as they listened to Ivy's retreating footsteps on the staircase.

'So,' Janet said, when they'd finally calmed. 'You gonna see Radiator Boy again?'

Susie gave an unlady-like snort. 'Well I can tell you this much — there was nothin' wrong with *his* pipework!'

'Suse!' Janet grimaced. 'Do you have to reduce *everything* to the same level?'

'You moany cow,' Susie answered, giving her a playful push. 'Anyway, it's only 'cos you're frustrated. What if I ask Trev if he's got a mate?'

'He'll probably be fat with spots.'

'What if I specify: no fat geezers with acne?'

Janet shrugged. 'I dunno.'

'Well, maybe we can get him to take us to a disco. We could go tomorrow — it's always lively on a Saturday night, and we ain't been out on a Saturday night, oh . . . well, for a fortnight at least!'

Janet laughed. 'All right. We'll get all dolled up, eh? Show the local yokels how it's done, North London-style, eh?'

'Atta girl!' Susie got up and went to the door.

'And Suse . . .'

'Yeah?'

'Be careful, eh?'

Susie smiled back at her friend and winked. 'I know what I'm doing.'

Trouble was, she didn't. After that first time, she'd seen Trev regularly — most evenings, in fact — and whilst it had remained casual on her part, he had got more and more possessive as the weeks went by. She liked being with him, certainly, but all the time she was with him it seemed somehow . . . well, *unreal*. Like this was a fantasy while her real life was back in London waiting to be continued.

One night, particularly, remained vivid in her memory. It was after midnight and he had driven her down the coast to a bay they'd visited on several occasions. There, on the dunes beside the sea, they had made love beneath the full circle of the moon.

As he'd rolled from her, spent from his exertions, she stared up at the sky. It had been so great. He had a way of making her feel really good about herself. Thinking of how he'd pampered her, she laughed softly.

'What is it?' he'd asked after a moment.

'Just this,' she said, sitting up slightly and leaning on an elbow to look at him. 'It's lovely. Being here. Being fucked by you on a sandy beach. It's . . . well, it's just like in a book.'

He stared at her a moment, then looked away. 'I wish you wouldn't say that.'

'Say what?' She stared at him, puzzled. 'What, that it's lovely?'

'No. That word.'

She shook her head, not understanding.

'You know . . .'

'What? *Fucked*?'

She saw how he almost winced and felt a tiny shiver go through her.

'What's wrong with it?' she asked after a moment. 'It's nice.' She reached out and covered his hand with her own. 'At least, it is with you.'

Suddenly she felt self-conscious again.

'What's the matter?' she asked, after the silence had gone on just a little too long. 'Don't you want to see me any more? Is that it?'

He laughed and looked to her, his dark eyes more serious than she had ever seen them. 'No. That's not it. I . . . look, I can't stop thinking about you, Susie. When I'm not with you I can't wait to see you again. Every time. I think . . .' He stopped and looked down, in some strange kind of anguish. 'I think I love you.'

The words surprised her. 'Nah . . .' she said, feeling a little tremor of fear deep down inside her; trying not to feel anything back in case she got hurt. 'You just think you do, that's all.'

She got up onto her knees, then reached out and turned his face, so that he was forced to look at her. 'Look, Trev, you'll meet someone else, some nice Cornish girl, and you'll settle down and have lots of little Cornish babies. All dark hair and brown eyes. But not me. I'm just here for the summer. Don't get me wrong. I like you, and I like you . . . making love to me. But I don't wanna marry you. Okay? I just thought we'd 'ave a bit of fun together and I'd go back home.'

He closed his eyes, then shook his head. 'You don't understand . . .'

'That's where you're wrong, Trev. I *do* understand. It's you who've got it wrong. You think this is love. It ain't. It's just fucking. It's nice, but it ain't love. Not real love. You're just . . . well, you'd see. You'd get bored with me soon enough if you 'ad me ring on your finger.'

He opened his eyes and looked at her defiantly. 'You're wrong.'

'Yeah?'

'Yeah . . .'

But after that things hadn't been the same between them and after a couple more evenings the thing had died out. He had wanted more than she could offer; more than her physical, sexual self. He had wanted *her*. And back then that had been too much.

She had cried when he'd stopped coming round to see her. She hadn't told anyone that. Not even Janet. No. She'd shed a few tears, then wiped her face and got on with things. Just as she always did. Because it hadn't been meant to be serious. It was supposed to be a laugh.

After that she made sure she only had one-night stands, meeting guys in pubs and discos in town and making no promises to see any of them again. And for most of them that was fine. But simply having known Trev – having had someone want her that much – had changed her. Had left a tiny scar in her psyche, alongside all those others she'd already suffered in her short life.

And then things changed again. As June phased into July and the hot days of the summer arrived, Jack offered her an evening job serving behind the downstairs bar. Though it meant giving up her evenings out, she jumped at the chance, especially as it would mean working alongside Janet, who had taken on the food bar weeks before.

'Hello, stranger,' Janet welcomed her, as she came into the bar that first night. It wasn't strictly true, as they spent most of their days in close proximity, but there'd been a growing distance between them after the incident with Trev, and Susie felt warmed by the smile her old friend gave her. Going over to her, she gave her a hug.

'I'm sorry, Jan. I . . .'

'Forget it,' Janet answered. 'You just watch yourself with John, okay?'

'John says ooh,' she answered, and winked.

'Yes,' Janet said, leaning close and whispering, 'and Janet says mind your arse when you bend down to get a glass. That bugger's not as tame as he looks!'

Despite the odd melancholy twinge — usually brought on by the sight of Trev moping about in his car in the street outside — the final eight weeks of their stay at the Smuggler's was a hoot, a laugh, a real giggle. Why, Janet even found herself a boyfriend. But that was a little later.

With Susie behind the front bar business quickly picked up until you couldn't get near the counter at night without fighting your way through a mob of young locals, among them a few of Susie's more recent conquests who, to her surprise, thought her not the 'slag' she had come to expect from the average North London Male, but a good lass with a 'heart of pure tin'. She'd thought this an insult at first, until someone had told her that as tin was more important to the locality than gold or silver, it was a real compliment. That had pleased her.

Susie herself had developed a lovely tan from odd half hours snatched in the yard. That had cost her dearly once when a neighbour's dog had got in while she was fast asleep in the chair and ate all of the barbecue meat that was laid out on the table in the kitchen. That was the only time she saw Jack even close to angry, but it hadn't lasted long — not when Ivy had reminded him that she'd doubled his takings at the bar single-handed.

*   *   *

Mid-August saw Susie embark on another of her more memorable 'little adventures' as she called them. A young couple — bookish and churchy-looking — had come into the restaurant for lunch and had decided to stay on for a few nights. Showing them their room, Susie had noticed how the guy kept staring at her, looking away when his wife turned to thank Susie for her help. That night the wife had sat in a corner of the quieter back bar, a pair of heavy reading glasses perched on her nose, immersed in a library book while her husband went out for a walk.

The next morning, at breakfast, he'd dropped a spoon on the floor, then, as she bent down to pick it up from beside his foot, he'd reached down also, slipping a piece of paper into her hand. As she straightened up, she'd smiled at him thinking he'd given her a tip, and it wasn't till she got back to the kitchen that she realised exactly what it was. Throughout the day she would pull the note from the pocket of her apron, unable to decide what to do about it.

Watching him as he sat in the bar that evening Susie found it hard to believe that he had actually written it. For an hour or more he sat there, nursing a half of the local steam bitter, without so much as acknowledging her, while his wife sat almost motionless beside him, engrossed in her book. Finally, downing the remainder of his beer in one, he got up and, muttering something to his wife, went out of the side door.

Leaving things to John, Susie hurried round the back, slowing as she came out into the yard. He was there, waiting, just like he'd said he'd be. Hurrying across, she smiled at him then, taking his hand, led him into the shadows of the old garage.

'I really shouldn't be here . . .' he began.

'Well, why are you, then?' Susie teased, gently stroking the palm of his hand with her finger. 'It was *your* idea.'

'I kept thinking about you last night,' he said, by way of explanation and looking faintly embarrassed.

'Really? That must've been nice for you,' she said, smiling, enjoying his discomfort.

'Can I kiss you?' he said, laying his palm along the side of her face, tilting her chin so that she looked up at him. Susie gave no spoken answer but as his face moved towards hers she parted her lips to meet his.

His hands were all over her then, pushing inside her blouse, fumbling with the zip of her jeans, and as his excitement grew the noise he made almost made her choke with laughter. After a moment or two, she drew back.

'Come on,' she said, leading him across to Jack's workbench, his penis standing up stiff and long in the half light from the end window. 'I know what you need, and it ain't a long walk!'

She let go of his hand a moment to shrug off her jeans, then leaned back against the bench. 'Well?' she asked, drawing him closer once more. 'This is what you're after, ain't it?'

He'd needed no more asking. In the twinkle of an eye he was going at her like he'd been doing it all his life, pushing her so hard against the bench that she had two broad red marks across her bum for the rest of the day.

He came with a noise like a sheep giving up the ghost. Again she almost burst out laughing. Sex was ludicrous sometimes. Such a furtive and undignified affair.

For the next two days he'd tried to hide from her, and when she'd served them at table, he had almost buried his head in his lap trying to avoid meeting her eyes. She'd told Janet everything, of course, and they'd had a giggle about it, but Janet also looked at her sometimes as if she wasn't quite sure of her sanity.

'I know what I'm doing,' she'd say.

'Oh yeah?' Janet would answer.

'It don't mean nothing.'

'Well then, why do it?'

Susie shrugged as if to say, *Well, why not?*

'You'll end up catching something,' Janet persisted.

'I'm a bleedin' barmaid, not a fisherman!'

'You know what I mean.'

'Well, you ain't gonna catch a cold, the way you carry on. You make the Virgin Mary look like a good time gal!'

That one had hurt. But they soon made up again. They always did. Without Janet there, Susie would never have stayed. Janet anchored her. If she ever got in trouble, she knew, Janet would bail her out. She always had done.

Like the time they'd missed the last bus home from the disco and, without sufficient money to get a cab, decided to hitch a lift. Susie had been as drunk as a skunk and barely able to walk when they were stopped by the police, who told them off for hitching and then took pity on them, offering them a ride home. Unfortunately Susie had taken them literally and in the back seat of the car had collapsed over the young copper's lap and as she lay there had fumbled with his flies and grabbed hold of his cock. Janet, looking on in horror from the other side of the startled young policeman, had hurriedly slapped her hand, and almost without thinking had taken hold of it and slipped it back inside his trousers. Then, cool

231

as a cucumber, she'd said; 'You have to forgive her, she must've thought you were an old friend.'

No more had been said, but they had had a good giggle for the next week over that.

'A shame,' Susie had said, staring through the kitchen window thoughtfully as they washed up side by side.

'What's that?' Janet had said, taking a plate from the rack and beginning to dry it.

'Just that first time all holiday you get your hands on a real live John Thomas and you have to put it back in the bag!'

Janet had giggled, but then she'd grown all morose. 'It's easy for ycu. You just have to flutter your lashes, push out your tits, make a joke of it. Me . . . well, I've not got any tits worth mentioning.'

Susie grinned. 'You want me to phone the police, get that young constable in to make a few enquiries?'

'No, ta. Not after you've handled him!'

'Meself, I've always fancied being cuffed and helpless in a cell with a couple of young bobbies. As for that one the other night, a bit of truncheon practice wouldn't go amiss!'

'*Suse*!'

Yet it was that same audacity that finally got Janet a man. Susie had noticed how one of the locals − one of the young surfers, a dark-haired guy named Mike, quieter than the rest − was always watching Janet, looking at her when she didn't know she was being looked at. As for Janet, well, Susie had caught her staring wistfully at Mike on more than one occasion. Susie decided she had to act. She took the trouble to find out a bit more about him from one of the other young blokes, then set about finding a way of not only getting them together, but keeping them together for long enough that they'd hit it off.

It was no good fixing up a quick bit of nookie in the old garage; that wasn't Janet's scene at all. Nor was it any use suggesting they go up to her room, not after the fiasco with the central heating. She'd die of embarrassment if Jack or Ivy heard them. No. What she needed was somewhere private, somewhere Janet would feel safe. Where she needn't fear being interrupted.

The solution came to her that very next night, as she was talking across the bar to one of her regulars: Tom. He had a houseboat, he said, up near Padstow on the River Camel. He was thinking of selling it.

Before he left that night, Susie had everything arranged. She and a guy named Ben — a friend of Mike's — were to go and see the boat that Saturday night. Tom had given her the keys. Did Janet want to come along and look at it with her?

Janet's reaction was predictable. 'What do *you* want a boat for?'

'It's worth a look,' she answered. 'Anyway, it'll be something different, won't it?'

'Oh yeah?' But Janet had agreed to come. Mike had proved more difficult, but by Saturday Ben had persuaded him.

Both Mike and Janet had been surprised to discover themselves alone in the back of Ben's old Rover. Glancing at them in the rear mirror, Susie had wondered whether she hadn't made the mistake of her life, because the two weren't even sitting close. Nor were they looking at each other. As they drove along the dark country lanes, she tried to get a conversation going, but it was a dead loss. Janet's answers were monosyllabic, while Mike's weren't even that. It was like he'd been struck down by laryngitis.

They'd parked in the car park of a pub close to where the boat was moored, then had walked over a narrow footbridge.

The boat was an old canal boat, painted bright red, green and yellow. In the light from the pub across the water, it seemed an idyllic little place.

'Well?' Susie asked, looking to Janet with a satisfied beam. 'What d'you think?'

'How much is he asking for it?'

'Two fifty?'

'Pence, I assume.'

'Nah. Pounds . . .' She nudged her, then handed her the key. 'Open it up. Have a look inside. It's got lights.'

Janet hesitated, then gingerly stepped on board. Susie turned, looking to Mike. 'Go on, then. You next.'

Mike glanced from her to Ben, who nodded his encouragement. Hesitantly, he climbed on after Janet, who had already opened the end door and, ducking inside, switched on the cabin light.

'Mike?'

He turned back, looking to Susie. 'What . . . ?'

She stepped close and handed him the packet of three she'd taken from her purse. 'Go on,' she said, giving him a little shove. 'She's been dying to get you on your own.'

'But . . .' He was staring at the packet as if it were on fire.

'Go on,' Susie insisted. 'Be a man. You've got an hour.'

And with that she turned and, taking Ben by the arm, led him away down the path.

'Well?' she'd asked the next day, standing in the doorway and looking in as Janet tucked in one of the newly made beds. Janet stopped whistling and looked up at her, smiling.

'Well what?'

'Well, did you?'

Janet's grin said it all.

'So are you seeing him again?'

'That'd be telling.'

'Well, tell. There's no secrets, you know. Not between us.'

Janet laughed. 'I guess not. You know, I ought to be angry with you, pulling that stunt last night.'

'Why?'

'Well . . . what if you'd got it wrong? What if . . . well, I could've ended up being raped, couldn't I?'

'But I wasn't wrong, was I? You wanted him and he wanted you. Trouble was, neither of you had the common sense to do something about it. And anyway, me and Ben weren't far away.'

'In the back of the Rover, were you?'

Susie shook her head. 'Against a tree, if you must know. I had to promise him. See – the things I do for you!'

Janet laughed, then came across and hugged her. 'You old slut. You'll get us both in trouble one of these days.'

Susie grinned back at her. 'If we're lucky!'

On their last full day at the Smuggler's, Susie finally put John the barman out of his misery. For all of that long summer the poor sod had looked on while Susie flaunted herself at the bar beside him, his thirst for her unslaked. And now that she was going, he was quieter than ever, as if his world were about to end.

'Look at him, poor sod,' Janet had said a few nights earlier. 'Like an old dog whose Mistress has just died.'

'More like an old dog who wants to give his Mistress a bone,' Susie had answered, nudging Janet in the ribs.

'Well, I think it's sad,' Janet had said. 'There's you, working your way through Newquay like the bubonic plague and old Johnny-boy don't even get a sniff.'

'From what I've seen, he gets more than a sniff down there in that cellar. Every time a barrel runs out he's down there twenty, twenty-five minutes putting a new one on. What d'you reckon he gets up to? Probably 'aving a little booze on the quiet.'

'Either that or he's got a supply of girly mags down there. Or maybe a picture of you he took secretly, and he goes down and has a quiet wank over it.'

Susie laughed. 'Didn't know you 'ad such a dirty mind, Janet Crossley.'

'Yeah, well, it must be catching mustn't it!'

'D'you reckon I should find out?'

'What, you mean go down when he's changing the next barrel?'

Susie nodded. 'Would you cover for me?'

'How d'you mean?'

'You know, stand guard at the top of the stairs. Make sure no one comes down while I'm *checking*.'

Janet looked at her suspiciously. 'What've you got in mind?'

But Susie merely tapped the side of her nose. 'Just stand guard, right?'

And so it was that on their final afternoon at the

Smuggler's, while John was down in the cellar changing the barrel ready for the evening ahead, Susie slipped down and surprised him.

Thirty minutes later she emerged, grinning like the Cheshire Cat and adjusting her top.

'About bleedin' time,' Janet hissed. 'Ol' Jack's been going spare up here!'

Susie laughed, then, putting on a fake Cornish accent, she leaned in and whispered into Janet's ear, 'And Ol' John's been going spare down there!'

Janet stared at her. 'You *didn't*, did you?'

Susie put her hand on an imaginary bible, as if she were in court. 'I tried to defend my honour, honestly, M'Lud, but the rascal had me over a barrel.'

She turned, shouting down into the cellar. 'You all right, John? You want a hand?'

'Not at the moment, thanks, me duck,' he shouted back.

Susie turned back, winking at her friend. 'Call it a going away present. Something to remember me by.'

'There's a whole fucking town going to remember you at this rate.'

'Next summer?' Susie asked, raising an eyebrow.

'Yeah,' Janet said, grinning back at her. 'Why not?'

But they never went back. That winter Janet had got a job with the Building Society, and though Jack and Ivy had written to her, asking if she'd come and work for them again, Susie hadn't fancied going on her own. It wouldn't have been the same.

Some ten years later she'd returned. She had been down in nearby St Austell, on holiday with a friend, and had decided to catch a bus across and look up the old crowd.

Walking down through the town, the memories had all come flooding back, but when she'd got there it was to find the front of the inn boarded up, the building a burned out shell. She had stood there for a time, in shock, as if she'd been told an old friend had died, then had crossed the road and knocked on the door of the Blue Pelican. The owner there had recognised her and let her in, pouring her a drink while he told her what had happened.

It had been a winter's night, out of season, and only Jack and Ivy had been in the Smuggler's when the alarm had been raised. The local fire crew had been out on a call already and so a back-up crew had had to come from Bodmin way. It was only twenty miles, but they'd been too late to save the inn. Jack and Ivy were okay, but they lost everything in the fire. What's more, the building was grossly under-insured. A broken man, Jack had sold the land to a property company and called it a day. He'd gone back to Truro, where he'd originally come from. As for John the barman, and Trev and the rest, he had no word.

It was at that moment, sitting there staring across at the ruined inn, that she finally understood what Time really was. It was like a wind, blowing everything away. Every last thing, making it almost as if they hadn't existed. And when you died, it blew you away too. Until nothing remained. Nothing was remembered.

She had walked back to the bus station in a daze, some small part of her boarded up and burned, alive now only in her recollection of it. Like that moment on the beach when Trev had turned and said he'd loved her.

Sat there on the bench in the waiting room she had cried and cried, as if she'd never stop. On the bus back to St Austell, she had sat at the very back, staring out sightlessly at the passing countryside, remembering it all. So young they'd been. So bloody alive.

And Trev? Where was Trev now? She'd had a mind to look him up in the phonebook and call on him – to see whether she'd been right and he'd married a Cornish girl and had a bunch of Cornish kids – but for once she hadn't found the courage to do it. Or maybe it wasn't courage at all – it was not wanting to know. Not wanting to see him happy and contented when she had wasted all those years.

It had all been a laugh, sure. But you can't keep laughing all your life. Not *all* your life.

Sniffing, she looked up.

Janet tapped her watch pointedly as Susie appeared in the shop doorway, smiling in at her.

'You'd be late for your own bloody funeral, let alone your wedding!'

Susie laughed, remorseless. 'Sorry, Jan. You know what Mandy's like. She insisted on one for the road.'

'Ha! I bet she really had to twist your arm!' she said good naturedly, her face relaxing into an affectionate smile as Susie leaned in to kiss her on the cheek. 'Mind, I don't know how you two could face it after last night. You were both drunk as skunks. My head was killing me this morning.'

'Yeah, well, I'm not surprised!'

'What d'you mean?'

'Well . . . the amount of booze you put away.'

'Me? What about you?'

Susie turned towards the young assistant standing on the other side of the table. The girl was preparing a posy of flowers, the arrangement held in one hand while she deftly enveloped them in cellophane with the other. 'The thing is,' she said, as though divulging a confidence, 'some of us can take it and some of us can't.'

The girl smiled, amused by the friendly banter.

'Yeah, well, some of us have had a lot more practice than others,' Janet replied, gently nudging Susie in the ribs. 'And I guess it helps if you've got hollow legs . . .'

'I dunno. I guess it beats having a pair of pipecleaners hanging from your drawers!'

'Bitch! I don't have to take this you know. I could be at home right now watching *Neighbours*.'

'Your life is *so* exciting,' Susie teased.

'I do all right, don't you worry,' Janet said, releasing her neckscarf and undoing her top button to give her uniform a more casual appearance.

'Phew!' Susie said, putting her carrier bags down against the broad leg of the heavy pine table.

'Well,' she said, watching the florist as she pulled a length of yellow ribbon from the spool hanging from the wall and expertly fashioned it into a bow, 'how's it going?'

'The flowers and fern for the buttonholes are all boxed up, ready for you.' The girl paused, clenching her teeth over one end of the ribbon as she tied it around the posy of flowers. 'And I've put everything for the table decorations in separate boxes. I've given you plenty of oasis so don't worry if you make a few mistakes.' She gave a satisfied smile at the finished bouquet of yellow and orange blooms as she held it at arm's length, then turned to place it with a row of other orders on the floor behind her.

'Now,' she said, turning back to face Susie across the table, 'what time do you want the bouquets delivered tomorrow?'

Susie screwed her face up thoughtfully. 'Well, I've got to leave for the church by two, so let's say flowers by one-thirty?'

'Twelve o'clock absolute latest,' Janet interrupted.

Susie threw her a look as if to say: 'Whose show is this?' but Janet ignored her scowl.

'What if there's a cock-up, Suse? You need to give yourself a bit of time.'

'Yeah, but I don't want them around the house all day. Some idiot'll only come along and sit on them!'

'Look,' the girl interrupted, sensing a developing row, 'I'll tell you what! I'll get them to you by twelve-thirty, eh? That should give you plenty of time. And the place to put them, if you've got room, is in the fridge. It'll keep them nice and fresh.'

'Okay,' Susie sniffed, mollified. 'Twelve-thirty it is. Oh, and don't forget that you're doing the buttonholes for the parents and the ushers.'

'I won't forget. I've got it all written down here,' she said, tapping the order book where she had just written the agreed delivery time. 'Now, if you'll hang on a moment I'll go out the back and get your boxes.'

But before she had taken more than a step the shop door opened, the bell ringing loudly as the wood stroked it at its station above the door frame. A short, stocky man Susie recognised from the newspaper stand a few doors along poked his head and upper body around the door, his hand – encased in a tatty woollen glove, minus fingertips – clutching the edge to give him balance.

He pushed his checked cap back from his blotchy red face. 'Any of you girls got a white Fiesta?'

'Yeah, me. Why?' Janet had raised her hand, as though answering a question in class.

'Well, I'd get out 'ere a bit quick, love. You're about to be booked.'

He pushed the door open wide to make way for her as Janet rushed towards him. 'Oh, shit!' was all they heard as she skated across the shop's quarry tiles and out onto the rain-soaked pavement.

'I hate those bastards!' said the old man, pulling his cap back onto his forehead and following her out onto the street. 'They've got nothin' better to soddin' do than pester decent people all day.'

'Thanks, Alf!' the florist called after him, then turned to Susie, 'That's made his day. There's nothing Alf loves so much as a good argument.'

'Aw, bloody hell,' Susie said, laying her hand apologetically on the girl's arm. 'If there's gonna be a barney, I'd better get out there and smooth things over. I bet I get the blame for this for being late.' And Susie, too, disappeared through the shop doorway.

When she and Janet returned some five minutes later the boxes of flowers were piled up along the wooden table. 'How did you get on?' the assistant called, her face all sympathy as they came through the doorway.

Janet glumly waved the parking ticket in the air. 'He'd already started writing it out.'

'Yeah,' Susie chipped in, 'but when I explained that it wasn't Jan's fault . . .'

'Oh, yeah,' Janet said, smiling in spite of herself, 'this is a cracker. Just listen to this!'

'Well,' Susie began, cocking her head to one side as she recalled what had been said, 'I told him that I was here to pick up the flowers for me mum's funeral, her having passed away last week after a long illness, and that me dad was supposed to meet me here to help but that he'd had a car crash just this morning — a delivery van ran into the back of his Montego — and was laid up in the Homerton. Anyway, I told him that Janet 'ad offered to help, out of the kindness of her heart, and that I'd been late 'cos I'd had to go and see me poor old dad in hospital, you know, make sure he was okay.'

'I didn't know where to look,' Janet said. 'She just opens her mouth and out it all comes. Bloody amazing. You ought to write books, you ought.'

'Did the trick though, didn't it?' Susie grinned, then turned to the shop assistant, who stood there open-mouthed. 'He said he had to issue the ticket 'cos he'd written it out, but that he'd put a note on it explaining the circumstances and that Jan should write in, saying the same. Said he was sure they'd let her off.'

'You really have got the cheek of the devil,' Janet said, pushing the piece of paper into her handbag and removing her keys. 'You could get caught red-handed holding up the Nat West with 'Bank Robber' printed on your t-shirt and you'd still manage to talk your way out of it.'

'It's what's called 'aving a vivid imagination. At least, that's what me dad says.'

'Your poor old dad, you mean?' Janet said, and they all burst out laughing.

*   *   *

'D'you think they'll be all right in your boot?' Susie looked over her shoulder from the passenger seat of Janet's car, then leaned across to nudge the two shallow boxes of yellow roses back against the seat.

''Course they will. We'll only be five minutes. And don't worry about those two — they can't fall off.'

'Cut off down Copenhagen Street,' Susie said, indicating over to the right. 'We'll avoid all those bleedin' speed bumps. And you'd best avoid Highbury Corner this time of day. Cut up through Canonbury and round the back . . .'

Janet glanced at her over the top of her glasses.

'Okay, I'll keep my mouth shut,' Susie said, sitting round in her seat, slumping down and stretching her legs out before her. She glanced at Janet as she concentrated on the road ahead and grinned. 'New glasses, Jan?'

'Yeah,' Janet replied, pushing the large imitation tortoiseshell frames up the bridge of her nose. 'I'm getting as blind as a bat. You know, the other day I stuck me hand out for a taxi before I realised it was a bloody hearse I was hailing.'

Susie was laughing at the comic image. 'Did it stop?'

'Yeah. Cheeky bastard winked at me and offered me a lift.'

'So what did you say?'

'I said he wasn't going anywhere I wanted to go. Not yet, anyway.'

'Sex and death, Jan. Powerful combination that! Wearing glasses . . . it's the first sign your body's packing up on you. You'll be losing your teeth next!'

'Fuck off. It's not funny! I'll be wearing them all the time soon. Steve hates them. Says they make me look like Deirdre out of *Coronation Street*.'

'Well, get yourself some contact lenses.

'Oh, no, I couldn't! I couldn't stick something on me eyeball!'

'Anna wears them.'

'Yeah, well, Anna's more vain than me. No. I'll stick to me glasses thanks very much.'

There was a moment's pause, then Susie spoke again. 'She's looking pretty good, don't you think?'

'Yeah, well, she can afford to. She must've got a pretty big pay-off from that American lot.'

The car screeched to a halt, narrowly avoiding a beaten-up Cortina emerging from the side road. Janet fumbled with the window winder then yelled 'Wanker!' at the driver of the disappearing wreck as it spluttered across the junction.

Susie steadied herself on the dashboard before reaching behind her to check on the boxes. 'Mandy reckons that Anna wants to have a baby,' she said, turning back then leaning forward to wipe her hand across the condensation on the windscreen. 'Reckons she's desperate . . .'

'Aren't we all!'

Susie turned, horrified that she'd made such a gaff. 'Oh, shit, I'm sorry, Jan. I didn't mean . . .'

'No,' Janet said, giving her friend a tolerant smile, 'I know you didn't. It's just that I'm a bit touchy today. It's probably all this business about going for more tests and that. I'm still waiting to hear from the hospital. It does your bloody head in.' She sighed heavily, then pushed the car into second and switched the windscreen wipers onto fast. 'And as if that wasn't bad enough, now Steve's gone all stroppy on me.'

Susie leaned toward her, all sympathy. 'What d'you mean?'

'He's saying that having more tests will just make me even more stressed out, and that maybe we shouldn't go ahead with it.'

'But why? It don't make any sense. You've waited ages to get *this* far!'

Janet pursed her lips momentarily, then answered. 'He says he's worried that if we are offered some treatment and it doesn't work I won't be able to take it. Thinks I'll go doo-lally.' She made her eyes go wide and peered over the rim of her glasses, pulling a funny face as she looked sideways at Susie.

Susie laughed. 'Don't he know you're already bleedin' mental?' But there was little joy in the smile she gave her friend, only sadness.

'What he's worried about,' Janet said, accelerating to avoid a pedestrian who was walking backwards across the road to get a better view of the old Canonbury Tower, 'is that I won't be able to give up. That if it didn't work I'd just want to keep on trying.'

'Well, he's right ain't he? You would, wouldn't you?'

With a deft change of feet, Janet braked for the temporary traffic lights, then sat there, her face set, tapping her fingers on the steering wheel as she stared into the red light.

'Well, whether I wanted to or not, the fact is that we couldn't – we wouldn't be able to afford it, for one thing. But that's not the point. The point is I need him to be with me on this. I've got enough on me plate what with me mother asking me why I'm doing it and going on and on about how we should be happy we've got each other, and what do I want a baby for anyway. I mean, what does she bloody well know about it!'

'Don't be too hard on her, Jan. She's probably just worried for you. Doesn't want to see you hurt.'

Janet turned, looking at Susie as the light changed to green, her eyes moist behind the glasses. 'I couldn't hurt any more than I do already, Suse, so where's the harm in trying, eh?'

'No harm,' Susie answered, laying her hand on her friend's briefly, before they sped away. 'No harm at all.'

On this, her last night as a single woman, Susie was staying at her mum and dad's over in Highbury, instead of at the flat with Joe. As they pulled over to the curb, she wiped a hand across the misted side window and peered through the filmy glass at the small Victorian terraced house, smiling at the familiar sight.

'It'll be all right,' she said, turning round, placing her hand over Janet's once again. 'You'll see. I can feel it in me bones.'

Janet gave a short laugh. 'Oh, that's very reassuri Suse, *very* scientific.'

'Nah. You'll see,' Susie said, squeezing her friend's hand, wanting desperately to do more, to make things all right for her, to somehow make her happy. But she saw in that profile a face wracked by pain, looking older than it should, older than she'd thought possible, and in that moment she was afraid. In that moment she wanted to take them both back, to start again somehow and claim back the promise they'd both lost somewhere along the way.

'Everything'll be fine,' she said, as if she could will it to be so. 'You'll see.'

'Let's hope so,' Janet said, turning to smile at her, composed now that the moment had passed. Then, pushing open her door, she squinted up at the cloud-filled sky before gingerly stepping out into the drizzle.

'Come on then, you old tart. Give us a hand unloading.'

The warmth of the house hit her as Susie walked through the front door, the air thick with the smell of furniture polish. She placed two boxes on the floor in the narrow hallway then went out onto the doorstep to collect the others. Janet's car was just pulling away. Susie gave a shout, then waved, a deep sigh shuddering through her as she watched Janet disappear among the early evening traffic.

'That you, Susie?' The voice came from the floor above.

Susie picked up the boxes and carrier bags then went back inside. 'Yeah, it's me, Mum. Give us a hand will you?'

She could hear her mother's footsteps as she walked across the bedroom floor directly overhead, the sound fading as she went out onto the landing, the thicker pile carpet cushioning her tread. As she appeared on the staircase she beamed down at Susie, her excitement evident.

'I thought you'd got lost!' she said sarcastically. The dark rings under Doreen's eyes exaggerated the already skeletal appearance of her long, thin face; her stained, uneven teeth hidden behind a long-practised smile. Between her bony fingers she held a soft yellow duster, which she pushed into the pocket of her floral apron as she came down the stairs towards Susie.

Doreen nodded at the load in Susie's arms, pushing a

bang of gold-grey hair out of her eyes. Are those for the table decorations or the buttonholes?'

Table.

'Well, take those out into the garden. Put them under the patio table. They'll keep dry there.' She lifted the remaining two boxes from the hall floor and called after her daughter: 'I'll take these into the front room, okay?'

Doreen took a pride in her home. She'd had it hard for most of her married life but they'd scraped by. When the girls were little there were times when she'd held down three cleaning jobs at once, to try to bring a bit of extra cash into the home – sometimes to get them little treats, but more often just to make ends meet. They'd lived in rented rooms back then, using second-hand furniture from her family when they'd first set up home together. Eventually they'd been re-housed by the Council and they had lived in their little house ever since, gradually getting it the way she wanted.

The beige floral wallpaper and carpet gave it a light feel, with the red velour three piece and curtains bringing warmth to the living room. Over the white reproduction fireplace hung a gilt framed print of *The Laughing Cavalier*, looking down with a vague amusement on the row of family photographs lined up along the shelf. In one corner of the room a vast teak cabinet housed the television and video – the latest episode of *Home and Away* showing on the screen with the sound turned down – while in another stood Doreen's pride and joy: a wooden globe cocktail trolley. She'd seen it in a shop window and fallen instantly in love with it, paying it off weekly with a few quid here and there from the housekeeping.

The wooden dining-table at one end of the room stood

in readiness, covered in pages from yesterday's *Sun* and *Mirror*. Doreen carefully placed the boxes of roses on the table, pushing to one side the scissors and rolls of tin foil she had placed there earlier. She was standing there, peering through the cellophane, when Susie appeared at her side.

'What do you think?'

'Well, they're a gorgeous colour, love. But I told you, I ain't done roses before, only carnations . . .'

Susie put an arm round her shoulders. 'It's all right, Mum. There's no difference. The girl in the florist's showed me how to do one the other day. You just bung a bit of fern behind the rose and wrap the foil round both stalks. Listen, I could murder a cup of tea. Let's 'ave that and then get cracking, eh? Babs should be here by then, shouldn't she?'

'You know Babs. Expect her when you see her.'

Susie smiled. Doreen's sister, Barbara, was Susie's favourite relative, perhaps because there were so many similarities between the two of them.

She walked through to the kitchen, following her mum. All the work surfaces were unusually clear and everything looked scrubbed and polished.

'Blimey, you've been busy,' Susie said, pulling out a chair from beneath the table and sinking down into it, relieved to be off her feet momentarily.

'Yes, I have, so don't muck it up. I ain't stopped all bleedin' day long.' Doreen lifted the kettle to check it was full then put it back down and flicked on the switch.

'I don't know why you're killing yourself,' Susie said. 'It's only us that'll see it.'

It was clearly the wrong thing to say. She saw her

mother's lips tighten. 'That's all the thanks I get is it? I break my back trying to make things look nice and . . .'

'But it's not as though the wedding's here, is it?' Susie said, sitting forward. 'All I'm saying is, you don't want to wear yourself out. Save your energy for the do.'

Doreen made a strange little movement of her head. 'I just want things to be done proper, that's all. So just let me do it my way, will you? Just this once.'

'Yeah, okay,' Susie said, smiling at her mother's back as the older woman wiped a dishcloth across the spotless surface. 'There been any calls?'

Doreen looked round. 'Yeah. Bleedin' phone ain't stopped ringing. I've written them down on the pad.'

As Susie walked out into the hall to fetch the piece of paper her mother called after her, 'And don't you be on that phone for hours. There's lots to do.'

'Mother, why don't you pour yourself a gin and calm down,' Susie said, coming back into the kitchen. 'It'll all get done.'

Susie sat down again then put her feet up on the bench, holding up the list of names. She'd call Karen and Anna back later on; they were bound to want to chat.

'What time did Joe phone?'

'About one. But he said you wouldn't be able to get hold of him till tonight 'cos he'd be out most of the afternoon. Oh, and then he was going for a quick drink after work . . . with some of the blokes.'

Susie rolled her eyes. 'Yeah, I know his quick drinks! What did the caterers want?' she said, looking at her watch and realising it was too late to phone them back.

'It's okay, they only wanted to tell you the cake had arrived.'

'Thank Christ for that! And who the hell's Charlie?'

'Charlie?' her mum said, drying her hands on her apron and taking the piece of paper from Susie. 'Oh, that's your Uncle Charlie. That was for your dad, really. Said he had a racing tip.'

'I s'pose *he's* coming tomorrow?' Susie said, screwing up her nose.

''Course he is. They all are.

Susie viewed the prospect with a sense of real foreboding. En masse her relatives were a sight to behold. Her dad's brother, Charles – Charlie Boy, as he was known, despite being the wrong side of fifty – was the area darts champion and as such was afforded minor local celebrity status. He dripped gold from every finger, while rows of heavy chains hung down over the inevitable polo-neck shirt. Chunky identity bracelets clanked together at one wrist, a fake Rolex on the other. His wife, Maureen, was much the same. She swore she'd rather be seen dead than greet the milkman without her earrings on. Those infamous monstrosities dangled like chandeliers from her fleshy lobes, and the gold chains at her neck were displayed across an ample chest that was tanned nut brown, even in the heart of winter. 'Malaga,' she'd say with a fierce pride if you asked. As a pair they made Cannon and Ball seem tasteful.

Susie felt her heart sink at the thought of them being there.

'Well, I hope they bleedin' behave themselves, that's all!'

''Course they will,' Doreen said, sounding far from

convinced as she poured the steaming water into the pot. 'They just like 'aving a good time.'

'Yeah, I know about their good time. They almost wrecked the hall when their Maxine got married. And what about at Lyndsay's wedding, when Charlie did that strip-tease?'

Her mother threw her head back and laughed. 'You know, I'd forgotten about that. What a bleedin' sight! Those lurex pants. And the size of his stomach!'

Even Susie had to laugh, in spite of herself.

'I thought you were gonna say something else there, Ma!'

'Wh-a?' Her mum stared at her, puzzled briefly, then started giggling again. 'Least Maureen didn't join him. Now *that* would have been a sight, all that cellulite shaking about like a cottage cheese cocktail!'

Susie didn't want to contemplate it.

There was a knock at the door. Doreen was still laughing as she went through to answer it. Expecting to see Babs, she was surprised to find Lyndsay there on the doorstep.

'Hello, sweetheart. What a lovely surprise.'

'Oh shit,' Susie murmured to herself, getting up out of her chair.

'I was just passing,' Lyndsay was saying out in the hallway, 'and I realised I'd forgotten to take home the ribbon for Jodie's hair. My mate Sally's coming round first thing tomorrow to do it, so I thought . . .'

'You've got time for a cuppa, ain't you, love?'

Doreen led the way back to the kitchen, where Susie stood pouring the tea. 'Pour one for Lyndsay, will you, Suse.'

She pulled a chair out for her daughter then sat down opposite, exaggerating the relief at being off her feet. 'Where're the kids?'

'Derek's keeping an eye on them, so to speak. They were watching TV when I came out. I left him havin' a kip in the chair.'

'When's he gonna have the operation?' Susie said, turning to hand a mug of tea to her mum and placing another on the table in front of her sister.

'What operation's that?' Lyndsay asked, staring up at Susie blankly.

'To get that armchair removed from his fucking arse!' And Susie laughed out loud, pleased with herself in spite of the disapproving look from her mum.

Lyndsay looked down, sulking, her pursed lips reminiscent of her mother. 'He can't help it. He just gets tired, that's all.'

'Tired! He'd give Sleepy the fuckin' Dwarf a run for his money!'

'Ha ha, very funny.' Lyndsay sipped from her mug, wincing as the hot tea hit the back of her throat.

'Give it a rest you two, will you?' Doreen gripped the edge of the table and levered herself up out of the chair. 'Here, Lynds, come in the other room and have a look at the buttonholes.'

Lyndsay went through, then bent over, staring through the cellophane into the box, one half of her nose and mouth curled upward in a look of disapproval.

'Roses? You having *these* for your buttonholes?'

'Yeah.' Susie felt the muscles of her stomach tighten.

'Not carnations?'

'No.'

254

'Why not?'

''Cos carnations are common.'

'*I* had carnations,' Lyndsay said accusingly.

Susie simply smiled and lifted the mug of tea to her lips.

'Yours were lovely, Lynds,' her mother said hurriedly, trying to smooth things over. 'Lovely pink. But I was saying to Susie, I was, I don't know if I'll be able to do these roses. I've only done carnations before . . .'

'I told you,' Susie said, impatient now, 'they're no different. Look, Babs'll do them. *She* won't make a fuss.'

'I'm *not* making a fuss, I'm just saying I 'ain't done roses before. That's all.' And with that, Doreen walked over to the sideboard and took a pack of cigarettes from the top drawer. Putting one to her mouth she clenched it between her teeth then pushed the packet into her apron pocket. She reached for the disposable, plastic lighter and lit up.

Looking back at her two daughters she realised just why she had never managed to give up her fags. It was true what their father said. They never bleedin' stopped. She drew deeply, savouring the relief as it swam through her veins.

'Well, anyway, I'd shove them somewhere cool tonight or else they won't last,' Lyndsay sniffed loudly as she took a final look into the box before following her mother out into the hallway.

'Get Jodie's ribbon for me will you, Mum. I'll just nip up to the loo before I go,' she added, making for the stairs.

'Use the downstairs,' her mum offered.

'I prefer the upstairs,' Lyndsay said, already halfway up the stairs.

'And keep out of my room!' Susie shouted up after her, following her mother into the kitchen.

'I don't know why you won't show her the dress,' her mother whispered.

Susie laughed. 'Because it annoys her,' she said. 'Besides, she's always got to be in on everything. She wants to know the ins and outs of a cat's arse, that one!'

Her mother shook her head sadly, worn down by the years of endless bickering she had endured from the two girls.

The two of them sat in silence, waiting for Lyndsay to return, Susie listening carefully for sounds from above. The pipes wheezed as Lyndsay flushed the loo. A moment later her footsteps thumped down the stairs.

'Curiosity didn't get the better of you, then?' Susie said, smirking, as Lyndsay came into the room.

'I couldn't give a toss about your stupid dress,' Lyndsay lied. 'All I hope is that you're not gonna make yourself look stupid by having your tits hanging out. It's bad enough you pouring poor Karen into that red satin number.'

'Karen'll look fine, don't you worry!'

Lyndsay sat again, looking at her nails pointedly. 'I don't know why you wanted her as a maid of honour anyway. More like an old maid, if you ask me.'

Susie leaned towards her, her face suddenly hard. 'You're just jealous that I didn't ask *you*!'

Lyndsay glanced at her with affected indifference. 'Me? Jealous! That's rich coming from you! The boot's always been on the other foot and you know it. You were jealous of me when we were kids, and you were jealous when I got married. And *then*, when I had the kids . . .'

Susie sat back, shaking her head, an expression of incredulity on her face. 'You live in cloud cuckoo land, you! If you think I could be jealous of Lord Sleepy of Slumberland, you must be tuppence short of a bleedin' shilling!'

'For Christ's sake, pack it in,' Doreen shouted, standing up and clearing the mugs from the table. 'I'm not 'aving you two spoil this bleedin' wedding!'

'Well, tell her, then,' Susie said, sounding just the way she did when they were children.

'Well, I'm going anyway,' Lyndsay said, taking her leather jacket from the back of the chair and pushing her arms through the sleeves. 'What time d'you want us tomorrow?'

'Not too early,' Susie said, then stood and went to the sink, busying herself rinsing the cups, still angry at her sister.

'What time's Karen coming?'

'About eleven,' Susie answered brusquely. 'But she's gonna be helping me. Anyway, the kids'll get bored if they're hanging round here for hours . . .'

'That's all right,' Doreen interrupted. 'Just bring a couple of videos with you, love.'

Doreen loved the idea of kids' videos, and often wondered aloud how she'd managed to bring up her own kids without a video in the house.

But Lyndsay had her own ideas. 'They won't get bored. They can help you, can't they, Mum?'

Susie turned, glaring at her sister. 'Mummy won't be doing anything other than keeping the old man off the sauce. I don't want the kind of fiasco you had!'

Lyndsay turned to face her, all pretence of indifference

gone. She glowered at her sister. 'My wedding *wasn't* a fiasco! Was it Mum?'

But Susie was in her stride now and before her mother could open her mouth, Susie was off again. 'Come off it! The old man was so pissed he had to have one of you holding him up on either side just to get him up the bleedin' aisle. By time he'd finished breathing all over the vicar the poor sod must 'ave felt like he'd been on a pub crawl to Kingdom Come and back!'

Lyndsay looked down. 'He was feeling a bit emotional, that's all.'

'I bet he bloody well was,' Susie said, smirking now, 'the amount of money he spent on that wedding. Well, at least there's no danger of that happening tomorrow.'

Doreen bristled. 'That's not fair, Susan. You know very well that if your father had the money he would've paid for your wedding.'

Susie slammed a cup down on the drainer, breaking off the handle. 'Well, he soon found the bleedin' money when his precious little princess got married, didn't he?'

Lyndsay gave a smug smile and raised her eyes to the ceiling. 'Here we go again. B-o-r-i-n-g!'

'Too right it's boring. It's boring that I've had to ask Joe to help pay for it instead. I'm only lucky that he don't give a toss about money.' She looked at her sister acidly. 'Besides, the old man probably had to give Derek a fucking dowry when he took you on.'

Doreen stood between the two girls, silently praying that her husband wouldn't walk in at that moment; that really would set the cat among the pigeons.

The ring of the doorbell stopped the girls in their

258

tracks. Doreen looked to Heaven. 'That'll be Babs, so put a sock in it the pair of you.'

'It's all right, I'll let her in,' Lyndsay said, gathering up the hair ribbon. She turned, smiling at Susie as if nothing had happened. 'I'll see you tomorrow. And I hope you're in a better bloody mood by then.'

Susie smiled falsely, then stuck her tongue out at her sister's retreating back and turned to fill the kettle. 'Thank Christ!' she muttered, a shiver running right through her. 'Thank fucking Christ!'

Susie sat at the dining table filing her nails while her mum and aunt sat on either side busying themselves making buttonholes. Babs held the short stem of a yellow rosebud between her thumb and forefinger, measured off a cutting of fern and placed it behind the flower. With her other hand she placed a pre-cut piece of silver tin foil on the table before her and carefully placed the stems at one corner, rolling them across to the opposite corner, firmly encasing them within the shiny shell. Holding it up before her, she smiled her approval before placing it alongside a dozen others, brushing the offcuts from her blue velour tracksuit.

'You wanna hope this bleedin' rain stops before tomorrow,' she said to Susie, nodding towards the window, her pale pink glasses falling down the line of her long, thin nose.

'I know,' Susie said, smiling indulgently. 'I'll listen to the weather forecast later.'

'I'll get a cab tonight, Dor, if it's like this . . .'

'Bobby'll run you home,' Doreen said, looking up.

'If I know Bobby, he'll be in no fit state to zip up his

259

flies, let alone run me home! I don't know why you keep that car of yours, Dor.' Babs chuckled, picked up her glass of stout and drained the last dregs.

'D'you want another one, Babs?' Susie offered, already out of her seat.

Babs winked at her niece and held out her glass. 'Did I tell you about the other week?' she said, as though she'd just remembered something of the utmost importance. She put down the flower she'd been trimming then laughed to herself as she recalled the incident.

'About when I got a taxi back from the bingo?' Babs looked from one to the other and when they shook their heads, continued. 'It was last Wednesday. It was raining cats and dogs when I came out of the bingo – at the old Carlton, as I call it, in Essex Road. I'd had a little win – not much, just a few bob on the four in a row – so I thought I'd treat meself to a mini cab. You can call them from a phone in the hall now. It's usually a fiver. Anyway, I gets home, goes to pay the driver – mind you, he was trying to rip me off for seven fifty – and I can't find me purse. Well, I had that bag inside out on the back seat of the car. Anyway, he's finally cottoned onto what's happening – right miserable bastard, he was, face like a fucking prune – and says if I can't pay he'll 'ave to call the old Bill . . .'

'Bleedin' cheek!' Doreen said sympathetically. 'You should've told him to sod off! Threatening a pensioner. I've warned you about them mini cabs . . .'

Susie placed the refilled glass in Babs' hand then put a finger to her lips, signalling to her mother to be quiet.

'Go on, Babs, what happened then?' Susie urged, smiling encouragement.

Babs scowled at her sister. 'Only just a pensioner, thank you very much! Anyway, so I knocks next door at Doris and Bill's to see if I can borrow the money, forgetting that they go up the Legion on Wednesdays — he's been a member over forty years and she helps raise a bit of money for the disabled. They bought three new artificial legs last year and two arm braces. Bleedin' marvellous they are.'

Babs sniffed then took another sip. 'Anyway, I knew I didn't 'ave any cash knocking around indoors 'cos I'd paid the rent that morning and I get stamps for me 'lectric and gas nowadays. And me telly licence . . .'

'So what *did* you do?' Susie said, trying to steer her back on course.

'You should've called us,' Doreen said, taking a rose and a piece of fern from the box and placing them on the foil. 'Bobby would've popped 'round with the money. Mind, I think he was playing darts that night, so maybe he wouldn't've been here. But you should 'ave, Babs. You know you can always . . .'

'Mu-um?'

Babs smiled, then continued exactly as if her sister hadn't spoken at all. 'Well, I *panicked*. I told him to come in the house and I handed over me toaster — lovely one, it is. My Raymond bought it for me but I can't use it. Me teeth,' she said, pushing up the top row of her dentures, which had a habit of gravitating toward the lower set as she talked. 'The toast's too bleedin' hard, see. But then I thought to meself, what am I giving him a brand new toaster for when I only owe the sour-faced bugger a fiver! But once he'd got it he wouldn't give it back. Said I owed it him for his *inconvenience*! Fuckin' nerve!'

She lifted the glass of stout to her mouth, draining

261

almost half of it in one go. Wiping the creamy froth from her upper lip, she went on, 'So any old how, I locked the front door and dialled 999.'

Susie screeched, enjoying the story, while Doreen sat gobsmacked, slowly shaking her head from side to side.

'You never! And what did the police say?' Susie's smile now stretched from ear to ear.

'They told him to give it back. Then they asked me how much the fare was normally. I told them a fiver, and they told the driver to come back the next afternoon and I'd pay him five pounds. Two lovely young fellers, they were.'

'You're bleedin' mad, you are,' Susie said, grinning. 'What were you gonna give him for a tip, your electric kettle?' She topped up her aunt's glass and gave her an affectionate kiss on the cheek.

'Mad ain't the word,' Doreen said reproachfully. 'I don't know what you were thinking of, inviting him into the bleedin' house, Barbara. He could've been a mass murderer for all you knew. Or one of them rapists. They *do* pensioners these days. No bugger's safe!'

Before her mum could get too far down that particular road, Susie interrupted her. 'So where *did* you lose your purse, Babs?'

Babs smile was beatific. 'Oh, I didn't in the end. A bloke from the bingo phoned next morning to say that the cleaner'd found it on the floor under me seat. Lucky, wasn't I? Oh, and after all that, old sour puss never did collect his money!'

'I'm not surprised!' Susie laughed, pouring herself a vodka and tonic. 'The poor bloke was probably too terrified. Mind, you, Babs, Mum's right . . .'

'Makes a change!' Doreen interrupted.

Susie smiled tolerantly, then carried on. 'You really should be a bit wary of them mini cabs. You never know what the driver's been up to. Some of them are ex-cons. Look, I'll give you the number for the black taxis.'

Babs nodded then concentrated on rolling a flower and fern along a piece of foil, tucking the surplus at the end of the stem back up the line of the stalk before making the final roll. 'By the way,' she said, starting anew, 'did you hear about poor old Rose Sweetman? Lost her Ernie . . .'

'*No*?' Doreen said, surprised. 'I only saw the two of them a couple of weeks ago, in Sainsbury's. He looked as fit as a fiddle.'

'Just goes to show — you can't judge a book . . . He dropped dead, just like that!' Babs snapped her fingers and shook her head slowly from side to side. 'He was driving the cab and had a heart attack. Drove into the back of a milk float. Dead before the ambulance got there. Just shows you, eh? You never can tell. Bloke in the back got whiplash, so I heard.'

'Poor Rose!' Doreen said, shaking her head slowly.

'Poor bloody Ernie, I'd say,' said Susie, unable to stifle a chuckle, ignoring her mother's look. 'And poor bleedin' passenger, too. Must 'ave been a shock. One moment he's quietly readin' his paper on the way to the station, the next thing he knows his driver's a stiff and he's up the arse of a milk float.'

'She'll miss him, will Rose,' Babs said, selecting another bud. 'I s'pose she'll 'ave to go by bus now.'

Susie came back from the kitchen carrying a plate of ham sandwiches in one hand and a large jar of mustard pickle balanced on the three tea plates in the other. She placed the whole lot down in the space Doreen had cleared on the table.

'Here you are, ladies. Waitress service!'

Doreen and Babs finished off the buttonholes they were making then reached across to take one of the thick, white triangles from the large plate of sandwiches, taking turns to spread a layer of chunky yellow pickle across the wafer-thin meat inside.

'You not 'aving one?' Babs pushed the plate a few inches closer to Susie, who shook her head, wrinkling up her nose.

'She never bleedin' eats!' Doreen said, flashing her daughter a chiding look. 'I've told her, she'll make herself bleedin' ill again if she carries on like this. Bleedin' dieting . . .'

'Oh, don't go on, mum. You sound like a soddin' broken record.'

'Well! You *should* eat!' All the arguments had been rehearsed a thousand times; there seemed no point in doing so again. Turning to Babs, Doreen gave a brief cackle as she nodded in Susie's direction. 'Thinks she's fat. *Fat!* I ask you!'

'No, Mum,' Susie corrected her, speaking slowly. 'I don't *think* I'm fat *now*. I *used* to be fat and I don't want to be fat again. All right?'

Doreen put up a hand to fend off the expected attack. 'All right, all right. But there's limits, right? You 'ave to eat.'

Susie glowered. She'd had a weight problem right up to her late twenties, but through the trauma of her break up with Ray Wood – that first time they'd locked him away

264

– she'd lost all will to eat. By the time she was over the worst of it, she had inadvertently slimmed down, and for the first time she could remember, felt good about herself. She could look in the mirror and wasn't appalled by what she saw. Since then she'd kept herself trim, working off her occasional binges, reminding herself just how she'd felt, needing no other motivation.

Shrugging off her mood, she stood, then went across to the cocktail trolley and topped up her drink. She looked across to where her mum and Babs were busy working.

'You two all right down here if I go and do a few odd jobs upstairs?'

'Well, it's not as though you're actually helping us, is it,' Doreen said, smiling.

'I'm supervising!' she said. 'D'you want me to turn the telly on or you gonna sit and run everybody down?'

'Cheeky madam!' Babs said, pushing her empty glass across the table towards Susie. ''Course we're gonna have a bit of a gossip.'

On specific instructions from her mother Susie had given her aunt a small tumbler to drink from in the hope that it would stem the flow of alcohol. It was a lesson learned from years of experience, but a strategy that failed when there was a manned bar nearby. The frequency of her tipples tended to overcome the individual quantity of each.

Doreen looked at Susie and nodded towards the stereo. 'Put on a bit of music, will you, Suse? Some Streisand, or a bit of Julio.'

'Nah, Suse,' Babs said, looking up. 'Put on something with a bit of life to it. A bit of Elvis, or some Tom Jones.'

Babs had been a little raver in her day and Susie recalled many a wedding reception where she'd rock 'n' rolled around the dance floor showing off her stocking tops, to the great amusement of a dozen sniggering nieces and nephews and the eternal embarrassment of her own children.

With Tom's 'It's Not Unusual' playing in her ears, Susie gathered up her drink and make-up bag and made to leave the room. 'Oh, by the way, Janet said to give you both her love.'

'Ah, bless her,' Babs said, pushing her glasses back up her nose as she looked up at Susie. 'How is she?'

'Oh, all right. You know.'

Doreen smiled sympathetically. She herself had tried for years to have another after Susie – trying for the boy she knew her husband had wanted – but nothing had happened. She remembered the sadness, the desperation she had felt at times. 'Not pregnant yet, I s'pose?'

'Nah. But she might be 'aving some treatment.'

'Oh well, fingers crossed,' Doreen said, placing another buttonhole in the box beside her.

'Here Dor, you might be a grandmother again soon,' Babs said, nodding towards Susie. 'I don't s'pose your oven'll stay empty for long, will it, Suse?'

'Thanks Babs!' The very thought of it made Susie feel strange. 'We want to have kids, but . . . well, I don't think we'll rush into it straight away. We want to spend some time together first.'

Susie had already broached the subject with Joe, of course she had, making just the point her aunt had so diplomatically raised, about her advancing age. She had been all for starting a family straight away, but Joe had persuaded her that they should wait a while and enjoy a bit of time alone together before all that business. A bit of 'quality time' as he'd called it. She'd thought that was sweet.

'And you never know,' she added, 'it might be a boy!'

On both occasions when Lyndsay had been pregnant her father had been convinced she was carrying a boy; had wanted to believe that through her his wish would at last be granted. The disappointment had been enormous and he had been unable – or unwilling – to hide it.

Susie laughed, suddenly amused by the thought. 'That would teach the old bastard, wouldn't it? His little princess couldn't give him the thing he wanted, but I could. Yeah, that'd teach the miserable bugger.'

'Don't talk about your father like that,' Doreen called half-heartedly at Susie's retreating back. 'He don't deserve it.'

'Yeah?' Susie said quietly, half to herself as she mounted the stairs. But her mood was soured by her memories of him – of all the times he'd let her down, of his obvious disappointment in her. It could have been so different. It could have been so . . . *nice*. She stopped on the top step, sucking in her breath, trying not to feel so much anger at him, but it was no good.

'Fuck him!' she said, giving the anger expression as she went to her room and shut the door behind her.

Susie stood before the wardrobe, assessing her reflection in the full-length mirror. The clothes she'd been wearing lay in a crumpled heap on the pink shag-pile carpet. Next to them was the plastic carrier bag containing the packet of Dior stockings she had bought specially.

Walking over to the dressing table, she took a lipstick from her make-up bag and, bending in towards the mirror, ran the red block across her pouting lips. Tousling her long blonde hair, she stepped back in front of the tall mirror, pleased with the new effect.

She still had a good body, in spite of her age, and as she ran her hands down her sides, enjoying the feel of the satin fabric beneath her palms, she admired the way it clung to her, silently thanking God for aerobics. There wasn't an ounce of fat on her *and* she'd managed to keep her boobs. Not many her age could say *that*.

The white basque looked anything but virginal. Lace edging lay across the rise of her pale, smooth breasts as the wire cups lifted and separated; the bones fitted down the length of the garment clipping Susie's waist to the size a grown man could completely and effortlessly encircle. From the lace fringe across the bottom of the basque dangled four long, satin suspenders, looking faintly comic as they danced around her naked legs. Beneath it all she wore a white satin thong of such scantiness as to make it negligible.

Turning sideways to see herself in profile, Susie placed a hand beneath each breast and pushed upwards and inwards, producing a cleavage not dissimilar in length and roundness to the one at her rear, so that she stood, an angel's face upon two full, ripe peaches. Pleased with the overall effect, and positive that Joe would be too, she fell onto the bed, a satisfied smile playing on her lips.

She had a drawer full of sexy underwear back at their flat – crotchless, backless, frontless; she'd tried them all. But there were some things she hadn't shown to Joe, things she wasn't ready to share with him yet, if at all;

fearing his judgement of her she supposed, his disapproval. They were remnants from her past, and something in Susie — something deep inside her — forced her to hold onto them, a constant reminder both of her hidden desires and her self-disgust. And of a time in her life when she had indulged both.

She had felt flattered when Ray Wood showed an interest in her: he was good looking with tons of charm and a great line in chat. She, on the other hand, was overweight and unsophisticated. Every time he came into the cake shop where she worked, he would single her out, flattering her, insisting she be the one to serve him, cracking jokes about taking her out.

By their first date she was caught — hook, line and sinker — and it was less than a month before she moved in with him, just before her twenty-fifth birthday. He had taken over his mother's council flat when she'd died; his father had left when he was just a boy and both his brothers were doing time. The place was a hole, but it didn't seem to matter at first — it was exciting. *He* was exciting.

It wasn't long before Susie discovered that she was the real breadwinner. She learned not to ask where his occasional windfalls came from, and in any case, it went as soon as it came — in the bookies, the pub, up the clubs on God knows what. And when he didn't have any money of his own, he'd take hers. She remembered driving herself mad one time hunting high and low for the clock radio she kept by the bed. She couldn't find it anywhere and when she confronted him he admitted selling it up the pub; he'd needed the cash. No remorse, no regrets, no other explanation, just that *he'd* needed the cash.

Often she'd come home from work in the baker's to find him rotting in bed, recovering from the night before, the place untouched since she'd left it that morning. She felt anger; she wanted to show anger, but always he would win her round, would seduce her with his charm and with his other, even more powerful weapon — sex.

Susie had never ever experienced anything like the sex they had together. Their passion was so all-consuming, his domination of her so complete that when they made love he could do with her as he wished. At best she was his compliant partner, at worst his obedient slave. In the beginning it was just that he wanted to be rough with her, to fuck her like an animal. She would dress up for him in the sexy underwear he brought home and he would rip the clothes from her body, biting and scratching her skin, pushing himself into her with such force that she ached inside, her thighs tender with bruising.

But the rougher he was, the more it excited her. She recalled the mornings she had sat on the bus on her way to work, sore from his vicious lovemaking, and in spite of herself she could feel her body becoming aroused at the memory of it, could feel her nipples hardening as she imagined Ray inside her. Placing her bag on her lap, she would close her eyes and fantasise, her hand gently stroking her pubis through her clothes, her fingers pressing down harder and harder as her excitement grew, struggling to contain the gentle shudder of release as she came.

At night — high from cocaine, or something else — he would come back from a club and demand sex. She could be fast asleep and he would wake her, insisting she dress up — the satin and lace giving way to rubber and leather

— so that he could screw her. Or else he would tell her to get in the shower where he would join her, abusing her with a whole assortment of objects — bottles, bars of soap, *anything*. And if she refused, he'd piss on her as she lay in the bed — standing above her and laughing down at her cowering body.

Always there was the verbal abuse, the insults, until, convinced she was as worthless as he said, there seemed no reason not to do as he wanted, and every reason to try to please him.

The only time she ever refused was when he brought two mates home one night and announced that he'd lost at cards and that *she* was going to pay the debt off for him. It wasn't that the idea of fucking someone else appalled her so much as the fact that he didn't seem to care, that he thought he could just use her. She remembered screaming at him, shouting that she wasn't some common prostitute, and afterwards she remembered him beating her black and blue, his face a mask of pure hatred as he stood over her, but he never tried it again. A line, of sorts, was drawn.

When he was arrested — for burglary and 'violently resisting arrest' — she tried unsuccessfully to raise money for his bail. She couldn't ask the girls — she'd had little to do with them since taking up with Ray — and her father turned her down flat. She could still recall the smirk of satisfaction on his face that said; 'You've made your bed, now lie in it!'

Even when he was banged away she would visit him, feeling the same physical attraction for him, the nearness of him unbearable. The enforced separation was like cold turkey but deep inside there remained a seed of sanity that told her this was her release; this was her chance to grab back her life from the clutches of this evil obsession. Painful though it was to acknowledge, it was Lyndsay who had finally helped her get through it, persuading her to give him up, to see him for what he was, to leave.

It hadn't been easy, mind; she hadn't expected it to be. She had stayed with her sister for a couple of days, then moved in with Karen for a bit, while she tried to get her head together. Good old Karen! She hadn't reproached her, nor criticised her. She just listened as Susie exorcised the pain, confessed to the abortions, relieved the guilt — her body convulsing as she cried out in anguish, her face awash with tears over and over again until there was nothing left inside, like a burial urn, the person it once contained now little more than dried up bones.

It wasn't until many months later that she was even aware of Paul Chambers. He worked in the hi-fi shop just along the parade and came in every lunchtime — always the same order; cheese and pickle sandwich and a jam doughnut, day in day out. One day he was talking to one of the other girls and mentioned a particular film — *Amadeus* — that was on at the Screen on the Green. The girl had pulled his leg about wanting to snog someone in the back row and suggested he ask Susie out, seeing as she was footloose and fancy free. She'd been struck by the title of the film because it was the same name as her hairdresser's, on the Essex Road.

He was Susie's age — around twenty-eight — although his boyish, blond looks made him appear younger and there was an air of innocence in his wide, green eyes. It was those eyes that, finally, made her agree to go out with him.

They started seeing one another regularly but he never tried it on with her, never pressurised her. In fact, they had been going out for a couple of months before she felt ready to make love to him. He was gentle, kind, and they became lovers in every sense of the word, Susie revelling in his adoration, basking in his desire to look after her.

The trouble was that pretty soon she began to get bored with it. After a while his consideration began to irritate her, while his gentle lovemaking failed to turn her on. Then, when they'd been seeing one another for almost six months and he began to talk about settling down, about marrying and having babies, alarm bells rang.

She hadn't meant to break Paul's heart. She had loved him — part of her loved him still — but she realised, was forced to realise, that she wasn't *in love* with him.

Walking to the bus stop from work one day she was conscious of somebody walking behind her. It was autumn and the sky was already growing dark. She turned off into a side road to cut up to the main high street, quickening her pace as she heard footsteps close behind her. Suddenly she felt a hand grab her by the shoulder and push her into an alleyway, smashing her back against the cold brick wall. She dropped her bag and made to scream but a hand covered her mouth, forcing her to breathe through her nostrils, the panic she felt causing it to come in quick, heavy bursts. She could feel warm breath on her neck as a face moved closer, her body shaking as he whispered her name; the voice unmistakeable. Ray!

The effect on her was incredible. He stared into her eyes, hypnotising her, so that when he relaxed his grasp she did not move — couldn't move — and when he put his lips over hers, pushing his tongue deep into her mouth so that she thought she would choke, Susie felt powerless to resist. Releasing her arms, he pulled at her clothes, exposing her breasts to the cold night air, roughly moulding the soft flesh in the palm of his hands. Her arms — spread against the cold brick as though she were being crucified — slowly dropped to her sides as his hands possessed her, lifting her skirt and roughly pulling down her tights and panties, all the while whispering in her ear, telling her how much she wanted this, how much she liked it. And when, finally, he was inside her, she clung to him, her nails digging into his buttocks, urging him deeper and deeper . . .

After that she knew things could never work with Paul. It didn't matter that Ray was taken back inside, that she vowed she would never see him again. The damage had been done. She told Paul to find someone else; someone who deserved him. She never explained why it had to end, only that it wasn't his fault. It was hers.

And that was true. It was how she was, deep down beneath all the laughter and the superficial charm. What her father had begun, Ray had finished, destroying whatever self-esteem she'd possessed. Oh, she'd rebuilt herself since then, but deep down it was still there. And that was why she kept those things at the back of the drawer. To remind herself. Just in case she ever forgot.

With a sigh she rolled off the side of the bed, then quickly unclipped the line of hooks and eyes running down the centre of the basque, allowing it to fall from her shoulders onto the floor. For a moment she stared at her naked self in the mirror, wondering what Joe would have made of it had he known, then, scooping up her clothes she quickly dressed, packing away the underclothes in her suitcase, ready for the honeymoon.

*   *   *

Susie flicked over the lid of the suitcase, frowning when it failed to close. Even though she and Joe were going abroad, she knew they couldn't be certain of good weather at this time of year, so she'd packed something to cover every eventuality. No matter if it was hot, cold, windy, rainy or warm, Susie had an outfit that was just right. In fact, she'd bought several new ones from Janet's catalogue and had left the labels on, so that if she didn't need them she could send them back when she got home. It was only sensible, after all.

A case containing the heavier items stood upright, zipped and buckled, by the bedroom door; this one, however, required some rearranging. Susie squatted, pressing her weight down on to the tapestry-effect lid, forcing it down as far as she could, and then in one nifty movement she twisted her body round so that her rump landed full-square in the centre of it, metal clicking against metal as the fastenings came together. Running a hand round the outside of the case she tucked in any stray fabric she could feel, matched up the clip fastenings and locked the case.

Joe will go mad when he sees these, she thought, resting her back against the narrow divan, cushioned by its frilly pink floral duvet. But the smile that curled her lips revealed the seriousness with which she viewed this, knowing full well that he could never stay cross with her for long. She would crack a joke, make him laugh, and he would forgive her.

That was one of the first things that had attracted her to him – his laughter.

She lifted her knees towards her chest – so that her toes gripped the rim of the suitcase – and dropped her chin down onto her folded arms as they rested there. Smiling to herself, she thought about Joe, and the first time they had met.

She had popped into a local wine bar with a girlfriend from the designer boutique where they worked, just for a quick glass after the shop had closed. They hadn't been in there long when she felt a hand on her shoulder, and turning round was surprised to see the face of Simon Paxman, a guy she'd met a few years before; she hadn't known him well – he was a friend of a friend – but she remembered liking him. There had never been any sexual attraction – he was short, with tight, delicate little features that always made her think of him as one of Santa's little helpers – which was perhaps why she'd felt relaxed with him. He asked if he and his friend could join them, and that was when she met Joe.

The attraction was instant, and obviously mutual, so that when – a couple of bottles of wine later – Joe had suggested they all go on somewhere for a meal, and the other two had discreetly made their excuses, they had been quite happy to go on alone, wanting to get to know each other better.

When she thought about it, this was probably the first day in the nine months she had known him that they hadn't seen each other or at least talked on the phone.

She pulled her handbag from beneath the bedside table and rummaged inside, producing her mobile. Moving up onto the bed to get a better signal, she stabbed at numbers on the slim black phone, biting the corner of her lower lip as she awaited the sound of his voice. The call activated the answering machine and Susie smiled to herself as she listened to his deep, warm voice, and the familiar message from the other end. It was like watching a favourite film and mouthing the dialogue. When the speaking tone sounded down the phone, long and shrill, she giggled into it like a naughty schoolgirl.

'It's only me,' she said. 'Where've you been? Here am I, lying on the bed wanting to talk to you, and you're out on the booze with your mates. I've just been trying on a little something I think you might like, something a bit . . . naughty.' She giggled. 'And now I'm lying here, naked, feeling all sexy and wanting to talk . . .' Susie gave a long, languid sigh. 'Ah, well. Call me when you get in. Love you.'

She was just about to switch off the phone when she heard Joe's voice on the other end of the line. 'Susie? Susie, you still there?'

'Have you been sitting there listening to me rabbit on about my underwear you dirty old sod?'

He gave a warm laugh. 'No, I was just getting out of the bath when you rang, but I look forward to playing back the message later. Your underwear, eh?'

Susie giggled. 'How was your drink with the boys?'

'Very restrained, you'll be pleased to hear. We ended up going over to the Slug and Lettuce for a couple of bottles of wine. In fact, I ended up drinking Perrier.'

'Perrier! Bleedin' hell, you all right?'

'I'm just completely knackered. I don't think I've recovered from the stag night yet, and I had a heavy workload to get through today on top of everything else.'

'Ah, poor baby,' Susie cooed seductively into the phone.

'I don't suppose you want to nip over and give me a quick massage, do you, Suse?'

'You suppose right, matey,' she said, laughing. 'Besides, I'm saving myself for when we're married.'

'Ha! I'm glad you've only just thought of that,' he said, amused. 'Anyway, not long now.'

'No,' she said, the thought both exciting and comforting, 'not long now.'

'Nervous?'

'Nah. You?'

There was a moment's hesitation before he spoke. 'A bit.'

'Well you'd better not be thinking of jilting me at the church,' she warned light-heartedly, steering the conversation away from eleventh hour heart to hearts, ''cos I tell you now, I'd flog me frock and take out a contract on you.'

He roared with laughter at the other end, only half convinced that she was joking. 'Well in that case I'd better get to bed, just in case I oversleep.'

'What time's Simon getting round to you,' she said, her tone suddenly business-like. 'And did you remember to double-check the booking for the cars. And what about . . .'

'Don't worry,' he said reassuringly. 'It's all taken care of. I called Simon and gave him a list of jobs. You know how he loves fussing about. He was in his element.'

'But what . . .'

'Susie! I told you, it'll all be fine. No, it won't be fine. It'll be a brilliant day. Just so long as you're there, that is.'

She felt her eyes fill with tears and sniffed loudly.

He laughed affectionately down the phone. 'You daft thing,' he said, imagining her at the other end.

'I'd better let you go,' she said.

'Yeah, better had. I need my beauty sleep, even if you don't.'

But she didn't want to let him go, not yet. 'I love you,' she said quietly. She'd told him so a hundred times before, but this time the words seemed to convey so much more.

'I love you too, Suse. Don't you ever doubt that.'

She shook her head, without speaking.

'Night darling,' he said.

'Night.'

She clicked the phone off then lay back, reminiscing . . .

They had sex on that first night. He was confident but not pushy and it seemed the natural thing to do. The next morning they were at ease with each other. There was no awkwardness, no embarrassment, no excuses made, just smiles of pleasure, affection, and lots of laughter. From the first she felt right about it, and when he asked her to come back to bed, she phoned in sick, then joined him.

So it began.

Now, less than a year later, it was the eve of their wedding. She knew that traditionally this was the time when all brides experienced those niggling little doubts, had second thoughts, hankered after past loves. But not Susie. This was all she had ever wanted. *He* was all she had ever wanted.

Joe said that he felt the same; that meeting Susie had tamed him, satisfied him, made him feel complete. But sometimes she would be doing something – washing up, ironing – and she'd glance up to see him looking at her, staring at her, a strange contemplative expression on his face. She had worried about those looks, those doubting moments when she had felt herself under scrutiny and been found wanting. She felt that at any time she would be found out and the dream shattered.

Susie walked over to the window, pressing her nose to the smooth, icy pane as she watched the rain falling, its fine spray caught like angel's dust in the orange glow of the street lamp. She gave a brief sigh, her shoulders drooping with disappointment and annoyance at the continued bad weather, then turned her cheek to the cold glass, her face in profile against the blackness of the sky beyond, the faint sound of traffic rising up from the street. Briefly she closed her eyes.

In her mind she conjured up an image of Joe's face and the semblance of a smile played upon her lips, as she remembered once again that first kiss. *No*, she told herself, *I don't have the tiniest little doubt that I'm doing the right thing*.

Raising her hand to the glass she drew a heart in the condensation, her fingernail skating across the damp surface as she etched *Susie Loves Joe* within its shape.

From the room below came squeals of laughter, the voices of the two sisters almost indistinguishable as they flowed together in easy conversation, her mother's finally rising above the other as she called up the stairs to Susie.

Susie let out a long breath. From tomorrow everything would be different. From tomorrow she would be somebody's wife. Joe's wife.

The two shallow boxes of finished buttonholes had been placed on the sideboard and her aunt and mother were unpacking an assortment of flowers and foliage onto the table from the larger boxes they had brought in from the garden, laying them out on the news-paper.

'Well, what do you think?' Doreen said, looking up at her daughter as she came into the room.

Susie peered through the cellophane loosely draped across the top of each box. 'They look great! See, told you you could do it, you clever old cow, you.'

'Here, what about me?' cried Babs.

'You as well,' Susie said, smiling across at the two women.

'Right!' Doreen said, laying down the scissors she was holding. 'I think we'll have a nice cup of tea, then get cracking on the table arrangements. I'll just go and put the kettle on.'

'Don't do one for me,' Babs shouted after her as Doreen disappeared down the hallway. She turned back, winking at her niece as she pushed her empty glass across the table towards her. 'Pour us a small stout, will you, Suse?' she whispered conspiratorially. 'I can't abide your mother's tea. Tastes like gnat's piss.'

Susie gave a throaty laugh as she walked over to the cocktail globe and took a fresh bottle of beer from the polished semi-dome. Levering off the cap she placed the stout on the table in front of her aunt, the white creamy froth fizzing up through the neck of the dark bottle.

'I don't think she ever got over rationing,' Susie said, referring to her mother's insistence on making a whole pot of tea from just one teabag.

'I don't think she ever got over the war, full stop!' Babs said, tilting the glass as she carefully poured the thick, black liquid, straightening it at just the right moment to produce a half-inch head at the top of the glass.

281

Susie pulled out a chair and sat across from her aunt. 'What d'you mean?' she asked, leaning forward, placing her elbows on the table and resting her chin on her hands.

'Well . . . you know,' Babs said, sounding uncharacteristically coy.

'*What*?' Susie insisted. She had no idea what her aunt was talking about and couldn't prevent herself from giggling at her apparent reticence.

'You know,' Babs said, lowering her voice and leaning toward Susie conspiratorially. 'The Yanks. The soldier boys. I think it was the only time in her life she really enjoyed herself. She wasn't bad looking in them days, your mum.'

'I know,' Susie said, leaning back in her chair and smiling. 'I've seen the pictures. So she was a bit of a one, was she?'

'We both were,' Babs said, laughing at the recollection. 'No point being any other way in them days. Every night you went to sleep you didn't know if the bleedin' Germans'd bomb you in your bed, so you 'ad a good time, made the most of it.'

'I bet you've got a few stories to tell about bunk-ups in the blackout eh, Babs!' Susie teased.

'Oi, miss! Show a bit of respect. It's your bleedin' auntie you're talking to!' Babs reached for her glass, her lips curling into a smile as she raised it to her lips and took a mouthful of stout.

'Mind you,' she went on, 'I did 'ave me moments!'

'I bet you did,' Susie said encouragingly, playing with the stem of a small pink rose, holding it beneath her nostrils and breathing in its faint and disappointing scent.

'I remember one time when I sat through three showings of the same film, tucked up on the back row of the old Adelphi with a gorgeous yank. Bud his name was.' She paused at the memory of him and gave a gentle sigh. '*To Have and Have Not . . .*'

'What?' Susie said, confused.

'*To Have and Have Not*. That was the name of the film. It had Bogart and Bacall in it. Beautiful film, that was . . .'

'I've just put Bobby's dinner in the oven,' Doreen announced, walking into the living room and catching the end of the conversation. 'What was a beautiful film?'

'*To Have and Have Not*.'

'Ooh, yeah. They don't make them like that any more,' Doreen said agreeably, sitting down at the table, a hand resting on each thigh as she sat back in her chair.

'I don't know what you two are going on about "beautiful film" for. Sounds to me like you only went to the pictures to get your leg over.' Susie looked across the table at the older women, trying not to laugh, amused by the way they were sitting there like two naughty little girls.

'Cheeky little cow! What's she been saying?' Doreen looked accusingly to Babs, who had her head tilted back, draining the last drops from her glass.

'I was just telling her about the war. About the yanks,' she said, wiping a hand across her mouth. 'Here, do you remember that sergeant you went out with? The one Mum liked . . .'

Doreen smiled, relaxing back in her chair.

Of course she remembered him, Susie thought as she looked across at her, thinking how different she seemed suddenly.

'What was his name?' she asked, intrigued by this revelation.

'Jeff . . . Jeff MacNamara.'

'That's right,' Babs said. 'They used to call him Mac, didn't they?'

Doreen nodded. 'Lovely fella, he was. Good looking bloke, too!'

'Where did he come from?' Susie was fascinated. This was like discovering a previously unknown relative.

'Palatine, Chicago,' Babs answered for her sister. 'He was in the Marines.'

'Nice uniforms them yanks had . . .' Doreen remarked wistfully. 'Really smart! Clean looking!'

'He must've been nice if Nan liked him,' Susie said. 'She don't like no-one usually!'

Her grandmother, Elsie was a formidable woman. Built like a battleship, woe betide anyone who got on the wrong side of *her*. She'd been known to wallop both men and women who dared cross her and Susie's long-suffering grandad bore testimony to the power of her left hook.

'Yeah, well, he used to bring her stuff. You know, cakes, bananas, eggs, even the odd bit of meat. D'you remember, Babs, how she used to show off to the neighbours?' Doreen said, turning to her sister. 'She'd leave a bit of fruit in a bowl in the middle of the table so's they'd see it, or go on about making her Albert a nice meat pie for his dinner when she was nagging on the doorstep.'

'Yeah,' said Babs, nodding, 'nothing she liked better than to lord it over people . . .'

'So what happened to him? You know, to this Mac fella?' Susie asked, getting up out of her seat and walking over to the sideboard.

'He went home in '45,' Doreen said tonelessly, reaching into the pocket of her apron to take out the cigarette packet. Shaking one from the box she put it between her thin lips.

'Just like that?' Susie asked, turning back to look across the room at her mother.

'They all did. Well, what else were they gonna do? Most of them 'ad wives or sweethearts back in America and our boys would be coming home 'cos the war had ended.' Doreen lit her cigarette then drew deeply on it.

'Did *he* have a wife or sweetheart?'

Susie loved the idea of her mother being involved in a romantic liaison.

'No,' Babs answered for her. 'Least, he said he didn't!'

Susie looked to her mother, intrigued now. 'So why didn't you keep in touch?'

Doreen sniffed. 'Didn't see much point. Chicago was too far away.'

'So when did you meet the old man, then?' Susie said, picking up a frame from the back of the sideboard. It was a photograph of her parents on their wedding day. It was hard to believe that the young woman in the picture — beautiful in her lace and satin bridal gown, her face full of hope — was the same one that sat across from her now.

Babs extended her hand towards Susie. 'Let's 'ave a butchers,' she said, taking the frame and holding it up before her, pushing her glasses back up the bridge of her nose. She laughed. 'You know, I'd forgotten what Bobby looked like when he 'ad hair!'

'Well, Mum?' Susie persisted. 'When *did* you meet Dad?'

285

'Oh!' Doreen said suddenly, as if coming to. 'Just after he was demobbed, in '46. We got married three months later.'

'You didn't waste much bleedin' time!' Susie exclaimed, surprised by her mother's impulsive behaviour. 'Why did you do that?'

''Cos he asked, I s'pose,' Doreen replied dully, as if the thought had never occurred to her before. She took the frame from Babs and looked at the photograph. Drawing hard on her cigarette, she blew smoke from the corner of her mouth, staring at it a moment longer before laying it down on the table.

''Cos he asked!' Susie sat back, indignant at the thought of it. 'He might have bleedin' well asked, but you didn't 'ave to say yes, did you?'

'Things was different in them days,' Babs explained. 'Take me! It was my Harry's mate that I fancied, but it was Harry who asked me out. We started courtin' and before I knew what was what, Bob's your uncle and I'm up the aisle.'

'Yeah, and look how that ended up!' Susie said, reaching across to take back the photograph. 'It's just a wonder you two didn't get divorced an' all!'

'You gotta expect ups and downs when you're married,' Doreen said defensively. 'You're gonna have to learn that, my lady. It can't all be a bed of roses.'

'Especially when your husband's a prick!' Susie said beneath her breath.

Doreen avoided her daughter's eye and remained silent, while Babs looked reproachfully at Susie over the rim of her glasses.

'That kettle must've boiled by now,' Doreen said,

stubbing out her cigarette and pulling herself up out of her seat.

'Don't do me one,' Babs called after her as Doreen once more made her way down the hallway and into the kitchen.

There was the sound of a key turning in the front door.

'Doreen?' her father's voice called from the doorway. 'My tea ready?'

'I don't know why you couldn't eat in the kitchen,' Susie said irritably as she cleared a space on the living room table, moving the remaining flowers then brushing aside stray leaves and fern spines.

'It's my house and I'll eat where I bloody well like,' her father replied belligerently, nudging her aside and sitting himself down at the head of the table.

Bob Fuller was seventy years old and no longer the imposing, intimidating figure Susie remembered from her childhood. The physical strength he'd once displayed had turned to fat now, his angularity to roundness, so that his jowly grey face appeared to rest directly upon his chest even when he stood upright. The thick, black wavy hair that Babs had so admired had thinned, rendering him partially bald, the little that remained completely grey and imaginatively distributed across his shiny pate.

Although he'd retired from his job as a car salesman more than five years back, he still went in every Friday, so that the boss could get away for a long weekend. Susie's dad didn't like his boss and often referred to him as a 'bit of a ponce', but he was grateful for the pocket money, and glad of an excuse to get out of the house.

Doreen brought a set of cutlery and a place mat from the kitchen and laid them before her husband on the table, working around him like an anxious waitress serving her first customer.

'Got you a nice bit of fish for your tea, Bob. Nice bit of haddock. Your favourite.'

Her dad made no reply; nor did her mother expect one. So used to each other were they after all these years that had Doreen by some miracle said 'bollock' instead of 'haddock' he'd probably never have noticed. And when she returned to the living room with his 'favourite meal', a tea towel draped over her hand as she held the hot plate, there was no thanks either.

Picking up his knife and fork, Bob looked down at his plate and then across the table, exaggerating the movement of his head from side to side as he surveyed it.

'Salt an' vinegar!' he said flatly, attacking the fish, peas spraying across the table like ball bearings from an exploding cluster bomb. 'Where's the bleedin' salt an' vinegar?'

'Ooh, blimey!' Doreen said, realising her mistake. 'Sorry, Bob, I'll run and get them for you.'

Susie opened her mouth to reproach her mother, to tell her to let the lazy bastard get them himself, but she knew there was no point. She wouldn't get her to change now, even supposing her mother wanted to. No, long ago Susie had come to recognise that the world was made up of givers and takers and that her mother was the former, while her father was most definitely the latter. Her only sadness was that they both so readily and whole-heartedly fulfilled their role. Mind, there was a whole generation out there just like them: men and women who didn't know any better; who, frankly, would have thought it odd to behave any other way.

Not that Susie was a women's libber. It was just that things had changed, and watching her mum and dad was like watching a pair of dinosaurs.

'Want another drink, Babs?' Susie asked, walking over to the cocktail globe.

'Course she does,' Bob answered for her. 'Give her a nice port and lemon,' he ordered, his mouth full of food as he called to his daughter over his shoulder.

Ignoring him, Susie poured a fresh glass of stout and placed it on the table in front of Babs. 'D'you want one?' she asked him begrudgingly, moving across to pour the beer even before he replied.

'And get one for your mother,' he said, swallowing the large lump of food in his mouth.

'It's all right, Bob,' Doreen said, placing the salt and vinegar at his elbow, 'I've just made a nice pot of tea.'

He glanced up at her askance, then looked back at his plate, the knife and fork busy in his hands.

'Oh, all right,' Doreen acquiesced. 'Go on, then, Suse, just a little one. I'll 'ave a Dubonnet and lemonade.'

Susie placed a pint glass and a can of lager on the table in front of her dad. 'If you want a cup of tea then 'ave a cup of tea,' she said to her mother.

'No, no, your father's right. After all, it's a special occasion, ain't it?'

Susie raised her eyes skywards and shook her head, exasperated. She poured her mother the smallest of drinks and herself a large vodka and tonic. It saddened her to think that she had probably inherited her liking of alcohol from her father; it certainly wasn't from Doreen.

289

Babs had once confided that the reason her sister didn't drink was due to an over indulgence on one particular occasion when they were teenagers. Doreen apparently remembered very little, other than waking up on her gran's front doorstep with the most almighty of hangovers, a dead chicken under one arm and an empty bottle of gin under the other. Where she'd got the chicken they'd never quite worked out, but it hadn't drunk itself to death, that was for sure: Doreen hadn't given it a chance!

'You sure you don't want a bit of dinner, Babs?' Doreen asked, raising the glass to her lips and taking a sip. 'I can easy do you somethin'.'

Babs shook her head and took another mouthful of stout.

'No good asking you,' she said accusingly to Susie. 'Well, I tell you what, miss, you better make sure you 'ave something in the morning, else you'll flake out in that bleedin' church.'

'I don't know what you think you look like,' her father joined in, pushing away his plate and resting back in his chair. 'Here, I'll tell you what you look like, shall I? A soddin' advert for Belsen, that's what!' He guffawed, then grabbed at her wrist as she walked past him to fetch some ice from the kitchen, holding up the bony limb like a trophy. 'See?'

'Oh, piss off!' Susie said angrily, pulling away. 'Anyway, it's better than looking like Mr Blobby, you fat git!'

'Don't talk to your father like that, Susan!' Doreen said half-heartedly.

'Well, look at him! He's got a bleedin' nerve criticising the way I look when he's sitting there like a tub of fuckin' lard!'

'I like a man with a bit of meat on him,' Babs chipped in, her speech beginning to sound slurred. 'Something to get hold of. I tell you who I love. That Robbie Coltrane. Now he's a big man . . .'

Bob turned in his seat, staring at Babs, annoyed now. 'What *are* you goin' on about, woman? Robbie bleedin' Coltrane!'

In spite of her annoyance, Susie couldn't help smiling, but Doreen sat straight-faced, unable to see the joke in what Babs had said.

Bob cleared his throat noisily, then picked at his decayed and stained teeth with his fingernail, inspecting a piece of fish on the end of his forefinger before wiping it on the edge of the dinner plate. 'All I 'ope,' he said, running his tongue across his top row of teeth before looking pointedly at Susie, 'is that you don't show yourself up tomorrow, that's all!'

'*Me*?' Susie said incredulously. 'I wasn't the one who made a total prat of meself at Lyndsay's bleedin' wedding, was I? It wasn't me who couldn't walk up the fuckin' aisle I was so rat-arsed! I wasn't the one who nearly crippled those two old biddies fallin' on them!'. And I certainly wasn't the one who thought I was Billy bleedin' Epstein . . .'

'Frank Sinatra!' Babs corrected her.

'Does it *matter*?' Susie said. 'Whoever he tries to take off he still sounds like some pissed old fart!'

'Nothing wrong with Lyndsay's wedding,' he said defensively. 'You didn't hear *her* complaining!'

'She couldn't *afford* to complain, could she? You were paying for *her* soddin' wedding!'

'Ah, so that's what it all boils down to is it?' he said,

a triumphant gleam in his eyes. 'Well, I'll tell you this for nothing, madam, even if I'd 'ad the money I'd have begrudged laying it out on *this* wedding. 'Cos knowing you it ain't gonna last more than five bleedin' minutes!'

'Oh, bollocks!' Susie shouted back over her shoulder as she stomped out to the kitchen. 'You'd 'ave 'ad the bleedin' money if you hadn't pissed it away down the bookies all those years! Or in the pub!'

'You can bleedin' talk!' he said, a colour in his face now. 'The way you knock it back, I bet you were hawkin' your guts up the other night after being out on the piss with your cronies.'

Susie bridled, made to answer, then, with a dismissive sneer at her father, vanished into the kitchen.

Doreen shifted nervously in her seat and reached for her glass, taking a mouthful of the mildly fizzy liquid. Ever since Susie had been a teenager and discovered that answering her father back no longer resulted in a beating – that she was finally physically too big for him to get away with it – Doreen had found herself the perpetual mediator in a conflict at times so ferocious that a light blue UN helmet wouldn't have been out of place. If it wasn't Susie and Bob it was Susie and Lyndsay. Always Susie and somebody.

Susie came back and stood in the living room doorway, glass in hand, gently rotating the heavy tumbler, letting the cubes of ice tinkle against it, chilling the clear liquid. Looking up, she watched her mother as she sat on the edge of her chair, preparing the base for a flower arrangement, the row with her father momentarily forgotten.

Her father glanced at her over the top of his newspaper

as Susie walked across to the table, his gaze dismissive, ever-critical.

'The florist said to put a load of fern around the bottom here,' Susie said, ignoring him and indicating an area on the lump of oasis where it now rested in its tray. 'Then you build up the flowers, the longer ones at the bottom and in the centre.'

'What d'you reckon?' said Doreen after a few minutes, sitting back in her chair to better assess the fern-skirted lump of oasis on the table before her.

Susie tilted her head to the side, taking a couple of steps back from the table to gain a different perspective. 'I'd put another layer on top, Mum, before you start with the flowers. Don't you think, Babs?'

'Could do,' her aunt agreed. 'Anyhow, best do one, Dor, and see how you go. You can always take them out again if it's a balls up.'

Susie looked at her watch. 'Well, you better get cracking, you two, it's eight o'clock already . . .'

Her father's voice rose from behind the newspaper. 'Here! Don't stand there giving your bleedin' orders, madam! Get your bum on a chair and do some soddin' work yourself for a change, instead of expecting your mother to do it all!'

'Talk about the pot calling the kettle black!' Susie said, amazed at his cheek. 'She does everything for you bar wipe your fuckin' arse, so don't start on me. Anyway, mummy offered, didn't you, Mum?'

'It won't take long, Bob,' Doreen said soothingly, her smile saccharine sweet. 'And I *did* offer. The florist was so expensive . . .'

'Yeah, well, I know how she takes you on,' he said,

293

ignoring her explanation, folding the paper and laying it to one side on the table.

Susie bridled. 'Take her on! *How* do I take her on?'

'Don't start, Susie. Please . . .' Doreen pleaded, seeing how Bob was sitting there, simply spoiling to continue the fight.

Susie leaned in toward him, her hands planted firmly on her hips, her expression one of purest scorn. 'You've got no fucking idea, 'ave you? My mum and my aunt are helping me with the flower arrangements for my wedding. I don't call that taking anybody on. I call that bleedin' normal. Just 'cos *you* wouldn't give me the drippings off your fucking nose!'

'Drippings off me nose! Drippings off me nose! I've worked hard for you all my bleedin' life, my girl, and don't you forget it!' he bellowed, picking up the newspaper and throwing it to the floor like an infant in a tantrum. 'I sweated blood for you lot!'

'Brown ale, more like!' Susie countered, facing him like a cock bantam in a fight ring.

'Why, you . . .' He rose abruptly, tipping his chair back on its hind legs. It fell to the ground with a thump. 'You've got too fuckin' much of it, you 'ave,' he growled, wagging his finger in front of her face.

Instinctively, Susie took a step back. 'You just don't like the truth, that's your trouble,' she said, eyeing him coldly.

'Ungrateful little cow!' he said, glaring at his daughter before turning away.

'Bob?' Doreen called out. 'Bobby!' But he wasn't to be placated. Susie was standing closer to her mother now, watching him silently as he stepped over the piece of upturned furniture and out into the hallway.

'Bobby?' Doreen called forlornly, going to the door.

'If anyone wants me I'm up the Drayton,' he yelled back, the front door slamming in his wake.

'And good riddance!' Susie called after him, but it was half-hearted now. She looked to her mother and saw the misery in her face. She wanted to go across and hug her, but she knew it would be no good. 'He'll be all right,' she said. 'You know how he is.'

'Yeah,' her mum said resignedly. 'Yeah.' Then, returning to the table, she began to clear away his plate, her thin lips pinched.

Susie sat back against the headboard, the mobile pressed to her ear, then swung her legs up onto the bed. As the ringing stopped, she leaned forward slightly, taking a breath, then held it as Anna's answer machine switched in at the other end of the line. She listened to the message, smiling to herself all the while. Very la-di-da it was. They were always pulling Anna's leg about the posh voice she put on, giving each other knowing looks as it steadily reverted during the course of one of their drunken evenings out together. She may have gone to America, but she was still Islington through and through. Some things you couldn't change.

'Hi!' she said, as the message ended and the machine beeped. 'Where are you? Havin' fun, I hope! Anyway, it's only me, the bride to be! Give me a tinkle when you're back in. All right? Byee!'

Cutting contact, she tried Karen's number. Frustrated by the engaged signal, she tossed the phone down onto the end of the bed.

'Bleedin' typical!'

Susie huffed, then sat back again, listening as the gentle, syrupy voice of Jim Reeves drifted up from the living room. She didn't share her mother's taste in music, but for once she found it strangely comforting as she stared up at the window, out into the blackness, as she'd done so many hundreds of times before.

This had always been her room. When they'd first moved in Lyndsay had nabbed the biggest room; no discussion — she wanted it, she got it. But Susie hadn't argued anyway. She was just grateful that they no longer had to share; that, finally, she had somewhere she could be alone; somewhere she could escape to.

Susie shivered, then stretched her arms up above her, bringing her hands to rest on the top of her head, the fingers interlaced.

When she looked back at her childhood — that is, when she thought about it at all — it seemed to be a long succession of disappointments. She was pretty sure it wasn't all like that, that there *had* been some good times, but she couldn't recall them — not in the way she could recall the bad.

Like the time the miserable old bastard had stopped her going to see *Dr Zhivago*. She could laugh about it now, but at the time it had felt as though her world had come to an end.

She had been nine years old at the time, and every day for weeks, on the way in to school, she had passed the billboard with that poster on it — the one with Julie Christie and Omar Sharif in the sleigh. She could recall even now how she had felt, standing there looking up at it, fascinated by the glamorous image. She had imagined herself, grown up and swathed in expensive furs, being whisked away through the snow by some handsome doctor. Not that it would happen, of course. No. Because she was fat. Every time she looked in the mirror, every time she went out into the playground at school, she would be reminded of it.

'Fatty Fuller,' some of the boys called her — if not always to her face, then certainly behind her back. Or just plain 'Fatso', like it was her name. She tried to ignore it, but it was hard, especially when little pricks like Eric Slater started whispering it in the row behind her at assembly.

It was on just one of those days — a miserable rainy Monday, when the name-calling had almost got too much for her — when, on arriving home for tea, her mum had announced that their dad had had a bit of good fortune on the horses that weekend and that they were all going to go 'Up West' the following Saturday to see a movie.

Such trips, back then, had been a rare treat. Though they wouldn't admit it now, Bob and Doreen Fuller had had a hard time making ends meet, especially with the old man's drinking habits, so a trip up to the West End, to the bright lights of Leicester Square happened once, maybe twice a year at most.

'Can we see *Dr Zhivago*, Mum?' Susie had asked excitedly, pronouncing the 'Z' as if it were in zither. 'Please, Mum. *Please* . . .'

'I'll ask your father when he gets home,' her mum had answered, smiling at her affectionately, the sudden mood of euphoria in the house like something infectious.

'Yeah, Mum,' Lyndsay had chipped in unexpectedly. 'Can we? They say it's really 'trif.'

'Yeah,' Susie had said, feeling genuine affection for her sister at that moment. 'Can we?'

To their astonishment, their dad had said yes. Pushing back his plate, he had belched, wiped his mouth with the back of his hand, then nodded vigorously. 'Why not?' he'd said. 'Why the bleedin' 'ell not?'

For the rest of that week Susie had walked about in a haze of excitement, unable to concentrate on anything but the thought of going to see the film. Now, when she passed the hoarding, it was with the thrill of knowing it was only days before she would see that image for herself, brought alive on the big screen in front of her.

Slowly the days had passed — far too slowly it had seemed at the time — until it was Friday and the unexpected treat was but a day away . . . a matter of hours. It was then it had happened.

She couldn't remember now just how it had started. Maybe she was coming out of the girls' lavatories and they'd been waiting for her, or maybe she'd just walked into the group of them by chance, but one moment she was daydreaming, the next she had her back against the wall, a crowd of braying schoolmates — girls as well as boys — surrounding her. And there, right in the centre of that braying crowd, was Eric Slater, his crew-cutted head jerking toward her aggressively as he led the chant.

'Fatso Fuller, Fatso Fuller,
Drops her knickers so the boys can pull 'er!'

She remembered putting her hands over her ears and crouching down, as if she were fending off punches, gritting her teeth and praying that they'd get fed up and leave her alone, but the chant went on and on, getting louder and louder, more and more aggressive with each repetition.

> '*Fat*-so Fuller, *Fat*-so Fuller,
> *Drops* her knickers so the *boys* can pull 'er!'

For a moment longer she held on, crouched there with her back to the cold brick wall, oblivious of the water seeping into the hem of her little gingham dress. Close to tears, her cheeks burned with shame, and finally she snapped. Like a coiled spring releasing, she threw herself at the ringleader and, with a punch that Cassius Clay himself would have been proud of, knocked her crew-cutted tormentor off his feet.

She stood over him in the silence that followed, her chest rising and falling heavily, her clenched fist ready to strike again, her long blonde plaits dangling comically above his head. But Eric Slater wasn't having any of it. With a whimper he crawled away, his eyes filled with disbelief, blood pouring down his face from his broken nose.

Again, it seemed, the haze had descended, for she hadn't noticed the crowd about her disappear, nor had she seen Mr Hughes, the duty teacher, appear as if from nowhere to grab her by the arm and frogmarch her back inside and up the stairs to the headmaster's study. The next thing she remembered was her mother standing there across from her, cringing with apology as Old Stoney, as they called him, ranted on about how disgraceful her behaviour had been; what a little savage she was and how he wouldn't tolerate it.

She had gone home early, walking along in total silence beside her startled mother. Back indoors she'd gone straight up to her room, to wait for what had seemed more like days than hours for her father to come home from work.

That had been awful. The waiting. And when finally she heard the door downstairs slam and his footsteps in the linoed hallway, the sudden panic she felt was unbelievable. She was for it now.

She had gone to the door and opened it a crack, listening, trying to make out what was being said. At first there was nothing but her mother's voice, too low to make out, then — as if to confirm her worst fears — her father had shouted:

'*What*? She did what?'

She tensed, then heard him bellow up at her from the foot of the stairs.

'Su-san! Get your arse down 'ere at once!'

She swallowed drily, then stepped out onto the landing. 'It wasn't my fault,' she'd rehearsed beneath her breath. 'They teased me.' But one look at him told her she wasn't going to get a hearing.

'You little cow!' he said, his hand catching her squarely on the backside and sending her sprawling down the passage. 'You spiteful little mare! Who the hell do you think you are, eh, goin' round breakin' a kid's nose?'

Susie had turned her head, looking up at him, the tears falling freely now. She'd tried to speak, to offer some kind of defence of what she'd done, but she was too choked to say a word. All she could see was his red and angry face, staring back at her, full of disgust, full of anger and disappointment.

It wasn't my fault, she kept saying to herself. *It wasn't my fault!*

'Get up!' he yelled at her. 'Come on, you little cow, get up . . . Let's see how *you* like it!'

'Bob . . .' her mum had said, taking his arm and holding it before he could take another swipe at her. 'No, Bob, please. You'll hurt her!'

'Hurt her? Bleedin' little bugger deserves to be hurt! Showin' us up like that! Who the *fuck* does she think she is?'

She could see it even now. How he leaned back a little, full of himself, as if he'd just walloped someone his own size. But bad as that was, it hadn't been the worst of it. No. The worst of it was what had happened next.

She closed her eyes, seeing it again: seeing how his anger had changed slowly to a smirk as the idea occurred to him — as he saw how he could — *really* punish her.

'Well,' he'd said, staring down at her with disdain. 'Don't think you're gettin' away with it, Miss. 'Cos I'll tell you what. You're gonna stay here.'

She remembered frowning at him, not understanding

'Yeah,' he'd said, his smirk triumphant now. 'Auntie Babs can look after you. Serves you right, eh? And maybe you'll think twice next time before lashing out. 'Cos I tell you, young Madam, you don't learn to curb your temper, you're gonna find yourself in *big* trouble one of these days!'

Even then she hadn't understood. Even then. In fact, it had taken Lyndsay to bring home to her exactly what he'd meant. It had been dark by then and she had been lying on her bed for hours, cried out, it seemed, the darkness inside as well as out.

'Suse?' Lyndsay had whispered from the shadowed doorway.

'Go away,' she'd said, afraid her sister would try and comfort her.

But Lyndsay wasn't going to go away. 'I'm sorry,' she'd said, coming across to stand beside the bed. 'I'll tell you all about it, eh?'

She had turned, looking up at Lyndsay, but it was impossible to make out her face in the darkness. 'Tell me all about what?'

'The film. Dad says you can't go now. He says . . .'

But she'd not heard any more. Groaning, she'd buried her face in the damp pillow once again, her world collapsed about her.

They'd gone, of course. The three of them had gone, just as if nothing had happened, Mum and Dad walking off down the road with Lyndsay in between, holding their hands, while she had stayed at home with Babs.

Standing, Susie let a shuddering sigh escape her. Nothing had changed. Long years had passed, yet still she felt the hurt. It made her realise that it was true what the experts on the telly said: everything that was significant in your life – everything that was going to shape you in future years – happened to you while you were still a child. The rest . . . well, the rest was just trying to make sense of it. Yeah, and trying to repair the damage.

She went to the window and stood there, her finger-tips pressed to the cold pane as she looked out at the empty street.

There were two appendices to her tale. Years later, when she'd first started living with Ray, they had shown

Dr Zhivago on the box. Ray had been out, clubbing it, so she had watched it on her own, sitting there in the darkness of their tiny living room, a bottle of vodka in one hand, a box of tissues beside the other. It was the first time she had seen it – the first time, to tell the truth, that she'd been able to face seeing it – and she had wept buckets. But afterwards it wasn't the film she'd thought of, but that day at school, and afterwards at home. That day, when her father had finally destroyed the last tiny fragment of love and trust she'd had for him.

Two nights later, sitting in Bailey's after hours, a bloke had come up to her, not knowing she was with Ray, and begun to chat her up. There'd been a fight. Ray had almost put the guy's eye out with a glass. Things had been smoothed over, just, until the bloke found out who she was.

She remembered how he'd broken away from his mates and come across, as if he was about to start things up again. Ray had turned to face him, but it was her he'd pointed at.

'You!' he'd said, sneering at her. 'I know you! Susie Fuller!'

She had stared back at him, recognition suddenly dawning on her. She should have known, if only by the broken nose. Eric Slater. She'd stood, suddenly angry, suddenly, inexplicably back *there*!

'You bastard!' she'd said, pointing at him accusingly. 'You made me miss that film!'

He'd stared at her, wide-eyed and open-mouthed. '*What*?'

'The film! You made me miss the bloody film!'

And then, just as suddenly, she saw how absurd it was.

All these years she'd blamed him. All these years she'd held a grudge. But it hadn't been him she was really angry at. Looking at him – at his prematurely receding hairline and at his fledgling beer gut – she had wondered what it had all been about. All that cruelty. All that name-calling. Why, the little bugger had been every bit as insecure – every bit as afraid – as her.

She laughed, then turned to Ray and nudged him. 'Apologise.'

'What?' Ray stared at her as if she was mad.

'Apologise!'

He'd laughed, impressed, it seemed, then, humouring her, had looked to her one-time tormentor and held out his hand.

'Sorry, mate.'

'Good.' But even as she said it – even as the circle was closed, the episode buried – she had known that some things could never be resolved.

'You should have loved me,' she said, drawing an invisible heart on the cold, clear surface of the window pane, saying it finally, accusing her father. 'You should have listened to me. You should have . . .' She shuddered, the tears beginning to flow again, then said it softly, the words whispered to the darkness. 'You should have *understood*.'

Susie heard the phone ringing downstairs in the hallway. When, finally, it stopped, she went to the door, listening, then heard her mother's voice calling up the stairs.

'Suse? It's for you!'

She went down and took the receiver from her mum, smiling, expecting to hear Anna, or maybe Joe on the other end, but she was totally unprepared for the voice that greeted her. As it spoke her name, she felt her stomach turn, an overwhelming nausea rising up, threatening to choke her.

'Susie? Are you still there?' it persisted. The clipped, coldness of that voice was unmistakeable. It was Max.

'What d'you want?' Susie said, with more self-assurance than she felt at that moment.

'That's no way to talk to an old friend, now is it?' he said, giving a little chuckle.

'You're no fucking friend of mine,' she said through clenched teeth, only wishing that at that moment he was standing there in front of her. She used to day-dream about Max Daniels. In her dream she was a brawny rugby player scoring with a conversion kick that sent the ball flying up over the stand and out of the stadium, only realising when it was in mid-air that it wasn't a rugby ball she'd kicked but Max's shrivelled bollocks. 'Why are you calling?'

'I just phoned to congratulate you on the happy and, might I say, *unexpected* news,' he said sarcastically. 'He's a *very* lucky man. But then I'm sure he already knows that.'

'How did you . . .'

'My old friend, Simon. Who'd you think? He's terribly chuffed to be the best man. He even asked me what he should put in his speech.' The roar of laughter was sickening and for a moment Susie held the handset to her chest, unable to bear it.

'You'll be pleased to hear I was *very* restrained, Susie my love,' he added after a moment. '*Terribly* well behaved. Not *one* of your dark little secrets passed my lips.'

'What d'you want, Max?'

'I don't *want* anything, sweetheart. I'm just phoning to offer you some work, that's all.' His tone was suddenly serious, more businesslike.

'What kind of work?' Susie reached behind her and pulled closed the living room door.

'Modelling. You know, the kind you're good at!'

'Not interested.'

'There's some decent money it for you . . .'

'I said I'm not interested, you arsehole!' she shouted down the phone. Doreen tentatively opened the living room door but Susie reached across and yanked it shut again.

'You know, you really shouldn't be so hasty, darling,' Max's tone had changed, the laughter gone from his voice now. 'Girls like you should recognise what they're good at and stick to it.'

'Just listen to me you fucking slimeball, you lump of steaming dog shit. I wouldn't come near you again if I was dying of thirst and you were pissing Perrier from that tiny little dick of yours! So in future don't phone me. Don't even *think* of me! All right?' And with that Susie slammed the phone into its cradle with such force that it jumped out again and landed on the floor.

Almost immediately the living room door opened and Doreen and Babs stood there looking out at Susie as she bent down to pick up the handset, her hand shaking as she placed it back on the phone.

'What the hell was all that about?' Doreen said, concerned.

'Leave it will you, Mum?' Susie said quietly, replaying the conversation in her mind.

'Well, who was it?'

'I said, leave it will you?' she said, raising her voice. 'It's none of your business.'

'What goes on in my house *is* my business, Miss!' Doreen said, a feigned sternness in her voice.

Susie gave Doreen a dismissive look, recognising one of her father's phrases and hating the sound of it on her mother's lips. 'Yeah, well, I'm not gonna be in your house much longer, am I?' she said angrily, feeling as though she would explode as wave upon wave of mixed emotions washed over her; wanting desperately to be alone to think.

'It was nobody,' she said, more calmly. 'Nobody to worry about.' And with that she reached out for the end of the bannister, pulling herself round to the foot of the stairs, her feet trailing like lumps of lead as she slowly climbed towards her bedroom.

Closing the door behind her, she leaned her full weight back against it and slid to the floor, burying her head in her hands. She hadn't heard from Max in over a year.

'Why now? Why does he have to spoil things now?' she asked herself, images of that last, shameful meeting flashing through her mind like some horrific slide-show . . .

Susie pushed the compact mirror back into her handbag. Throwing her head forward she tousled her blonde mane, scrunching hair in each hand, and when she threw her head back she looked like a wild animal. Her sparkling green eyes, ready, waiting, like a lion's, shone out through blonde wisps. She ran her moist pink tongue over her lips, leaving them glistening invitingly, took a deep breath and knocked at the door.

Max opened it almost immediately and stood in the doorway looking out at her. 'What a bitch,' he thought to himself, 'she knows exactly what she's doing.' And seeing her, and knowing that there would be just the two of them in that room, made his penis go hard, forcing itself up against his tight jeans.

'Come in beautiful,' he said. 'I'm glad you decided to come.'

'Did you think I wouldn't?' she teased.

'I thought you might have had second thoughts.'

'Why? You're not dangerous, are you?' she answered, laughing, goading him.

'All men are a little dangerous,' he said lightly.

'You're right there,' she said, looking him in the eyes.

'Anyway, come and sit down and let me get you a drink. What would you like?' he asked, leading her over to a leather Chesterfield, its antique hide scratched and cracked with age.

'Oh, umm . . .' She hesitated, looking around to see whether he meant tea, coffee or alcohol, unsure of herself suddenly in this alien environment.

Sensing her uncertainty Max suggested a gin and tonic and wandered off into the adjoining room to fix it. Susie looked around the studio. It was a large room and looked as though it could do with a fresh coat of white paint, its high ceiling and walls converging in a grey haze. The odd tasteful piece was dotted around the place – oil paintings, a few items of furniture like the sofa, the beautiful Chinese silk rug with the hole in it – but in general the place had a slightly shabby air to it, a sort of underlying decay.

'Here we are,' said Max, offering her a tall, heavy glass. 'Lots of ice and a slice of lemon. Hope it's okay.' And before sinking next to her on the sofa, he went over to the light switch and turned the dimmer round.

'I do hate bright lights, don't you?'

It was not a question that required a response.

They were sitting an arm's length apart on the long sofa, Max turned sideways to look at her. She guessed that his jeans and t-shirt were standard uniform for photographers, a sort of understated, casually trendy look, and there was a certain attractiveness in the simplicity of it. His arm lay across the back of the sofa, his fingertips almost touching her neck.

'Now tell me, my beautiful Susie, what are we going to do with you?'

'Well, I thought the idea was to test me out in front of the camera,' she said, her voice suddenly small, her confidence lost. She wasn't used to this kind of situation, but this man had a way of making her feel like a little girl again.

'Then that's what we'll do!' he said, jumping to his feet, already, it seemed, halfway across the studio. 'Take your shoes off,' he called back at her, 'then go and stand in front of that white backdrop.'

Standing there in her bare feet she looked across at Max as he stood behind the camera. There was an assuredness and swiftness of movement as he organised himself, a single-minded attention to the job in hand that suddenly made him very attractive to her. Yes, there was something incredibly sexy about watching a man do the thing he does better than anything else in the world – to see him display the self-confidence that comes with knowing he is in complete control of what he's doing and enjoying the power he has from knowing that you understand nothing of his expertise. It was like Susie was seeing him for the first time.

'Okay, sweetheart, we're ready to shoot. Now just relax, because I know you're going to be incredible!'

Susie felt as stiff as a snowman's scarf after a blizzard and about as wet, but with Max's encouragement, which rang of something from a sixties movie — 'Great, baby, you're looking groovy . . .'; 'Fab, doll, *really* fab.' — she tried to loosen up and make some of the moves and poses she'd seen in magazines.

'Okay, relax a minute, sweetie,' Max said. 'I need to change the film.'

Susie stood there looking at him, watching his hands as he worked.

And then he was walking towards her. Slowly he lifted his arms until he had one hand resting on each of her shoulders, their faces almost level. And gently he started to massage her shoulders and her neck.

'You need to loosen up a little. You look stunning through that lens, you know. It's just a question of allowing your body to bend, to move.'

His fingers worked into her skin, kneading the muscles, the pressure pushing through her body. She closed her eyes, moving her head in small circular movements, almost unconscious of the fact that his hands had slid down her shoulders and were rearranging her t-shirt so that it fell to one side, revealing a bare shoulder.

'Okay, honey, let's go again,' he said softly, releasing her but holding her with his eyes.

This time it was much better. She moved with a

fluidity that filled every frame with graceful beauty and she took pleasure in giving herself up to the camera, abandoning herself to this man, enjoying his power over her and his enjoyment of her. It was like a fantasy world where she and the camera were dancing around each other, teasing each other, waiting to fuck.

'Okay, beautiful, take five.'

As Max reloaded the camera, behind the tripod, away from the lights, Susie heard his voice.

'Have you ever thought about doing topless? You should, you know. You've a great body.'

She couldn't see his face. She wanted to see his eyes.

'No. I've never really thought about it.'

'Do you want to try it?'

'Maybe. Sometime,' she said uncertainly.

'No. I mean, do you want to try it *now*. I think you're ready.'

'What do you mean, *ready*?'

It was like a tennis match, the ball being beaten over the net from the baseline, each player's stroke cautious but firm.

'It's like this. I look at you through this lens and I can see your face, your body, the way you're using it, and I know you're ready . . .'

Susie could feel it too. She could feel her body moving as though she were not in control of it any longer; had no control over the way she looked into the camera and said; 'Okay, you bastard, fuck me if you dare!'

She could see him now, see his eyes as they emerged from the shadows.

'Okay,' she said, finally, her voice barely audible, and, turning her back on him, she pulled her t-shirt up over her head and threw it to the side. When she turned to face him, the sight of her stirred him to the point where he just wanted to grab hold of her there and then and make love to her until she cried out for him to stop. She could see it in his eyes. Her golden skin, glistening with a sheen of perspiration under the lights, begged to be touched. Looking at her, her breasts struck him as the most perfect things he had ever seen, her nipples like two soft, brown mushroom caps.

He took a swig from his glass and slowly moved across to where she was standing. Looking into her eyes he reached up to his mouth with one hand and removed an ice cube.

'A trick of the trade,' he whispered, his eyes smiling, and gently moved the cube over her breasts, first one nipple and then the other, until they stood up like stalks, hard and erect. Instinctively she pushed out her chest, the desire to be touched almost overwhelming her.

Slowly he bent his head and with a feather-light touch his tongue caught the melted ice as it fell like tears from the ends of her breasts. Taking one nipple into his mouth he teased it between his teeth, making her groan with pleasure as she reached up to hold him against her.

'Oh, yes,' she moaned softly. 'Harder, do it harder.'

But he was already moving to the other breast, nibbling it, licking it, while his fingers pulled and teased at the one he'd left. He was on his knees now and as he kissed her stomach, his moist tongue playing across her skin, her desire for him to be inside her became almost unbearable. She felt that if he were to touch her clitoris right then she would explode in one amazing orgasm . . . and it was as if he knew it. Running his tongue along the band of her jeans, he looked up at her as he slowly unzipped them, confirming what he already knew — that she was his to do with as he pleased.

She reached down to push her jeans and panties over her hips, but he held on to her hands and pushed them away. And then, with painful slowness, he slid them down to her ankles. Obediently she stepped out of them, and then he did the same with her panties, until she stood there naked before him.

He ran his fingertips up the inside of her thighs. It felt like a butterfly against her skin, sending a shiver racing through her body. Then they were standing face to face, his lips on hers.

'Now it's your turn,' he whispered into her ear, and with a gentle pressure on her shoulders, she dropped to her knees.

He removed his t-shirt in one swift movement, revealing a tanned, muscled chest covered in dark, curly hair, and as Susie unbuttoned his jeans she could feel the bursting stiffness of his penis against her fingers. She pushed his jeans down past his knees, then freed his shorts, releasing his swollen member.

Max reached down and ran his fingers through her hair, strands of it touching his skin in a whisper, the feel of it heightening his desire, as gently he guided her face towards his penis.

Susie knew what he wanted and she wanted to please him. She took his penis deep into her mouth, rolling her tongue about it, moving backward and forward along the length of the shaft, excited by it, aware of the hot moistness filling her body.

Max released a pained groan as he came, his hands

clenched around handfuls of her hair as he pushed into her. Then, very slowly, he released her, his body slumping as the tension drained out of him. But Susie knelt there, her nipples still hard, her body aching with desire.

Max pulled up his jeans then reached down, lifting Susie to her feet. He kissed her gently on her moistened lips and ran his hands over her body, but it was like agony to her: she wanted to feel his hard penis pushing up inside her, to feel his nails digging into her back, his teeth biting at her skin.

'Okay, baby, let's try another roll,' Max whispered, then moved back behind the camera.

Susie just stood there.

Max looked through the lens at her. 'God, you look so beautiful now,' he said. 'Just look into the camera and make me want to fuck you all over again.'

Susie felt like an animal. She wanted to walk away but the need to be satisfied, to have him release her from this torment, rooted her there. Just one touch and she knew she would explode – she was on the edge of ecstasy and it felt like hell. She moved her hands over her breasts, her nipples tingling as she took them in her hands, pinching them between her fingertips.

'Brilliant! That's it, baby! You've really got it now! I'm as horny as hell.' The camera whirred.

Susie lightly moved her hands down over her stomach and onto her thighs. The ache in her body overwhelmed her and, closing her eyes, she moved her hands down over the mound of hair, gently teasing the tight curls between her fingers, and then she found her clitoris, the excitement almost unbearable now.

The camera whirred as Max snapped.

With one hand at her breast, pulling on her nipple, the other hand moved backward and forward inside her, first one finger and then two, feeling the juices of her desire, until her face contorted as agony met ecstasy and she was consumed by the orgasm she'd needed.

As she lay there in a heap on the floor, consumed by a confusion of emotions, Max knelt beside her. She could smell the perspiration on him and as he grabbed at her breast she could feel his excitement. He tugged at her nipples, but this time she felt nothing but pain. His mouth was over hers and as she felt his hot breath over her face she wanted to cry out, wanted to go back and do it differently, but it was too late now. He had won.

And as he rolled her onto her stomach, pressing her cheek against the hard, white floor, she felt it was inevitable that it should be like this. As he pushed into her from behind, she raised her hips to accommodate him, feeling nothing, wanting nothing from this now other than for it to be over.

Susie woke and looked about her. The room was in darkness, the ticking of her travelling clock the only sound.

She stretched, for a moment not knowing where she was, then she remembered. After a long chat with Karen on the mobile, she had lain there thinking before finally dozing off. She was still fully clothed beneath the thick woollen blanket, and realised that her mother must have come in and covered her over. Pushing the heavy cloth away from her face, she stroked the spot on her cheek where the scratchy fabric had irritated her skin.

The light from the landing could be seen beneath the edge of the door. Yawning, Susie turned onto her side to look at the clock. Eleven forty-five. Outside, the occasional car could be heard splashing along the rain-soaked road, the distant rumblings of the railway, the noise strangely comforting as she lay there cocooned beneath the warmth of the blanket.

She looked about her for her glass, then remembered that she'd meant to go down and get something before phoning Karen but had forgotten. She made a chewing motion to create some moisture in her parched mouth, her lips dry and crisp as she rolled them in on one another, then sat up, knowing she'd have to go downstairs.

Outside, on the landing, she could hear loud snoring coming from her parents' room — the all-too-familiar grunt and whistle her dad made when he'd had a few jars too many. Through the crack where their door rested ajar, she saw the glow from a bedside lamp and imagined her mother sitting up in bed reading the papers. God knew how she ever got any sleep with that racket going on!

Downstairs it was pitch black. Making her way quietly down the stairs, Susie flicked on the hall light then made her way into the kitchen. Switching on the fluorescent, she went to the fridge and, in the harsh, flickering light, poured herself a glass of orange juice, draining it in one go, relishing its cold sweetness, then refilled it. She turned, looking round her, conscious at that moment that here, in her mother's kitchen, she was still a child, the daughter of the house, and that tomorrow all that would change. Tomorrow, at last, she would be free of all this — be her own woman.

In the centre of the kitchen table stood a cream, glazed

vase of flowers left over from the buttonholes, and as Susie sat cupping the cold glass of juice, she marvelled at their delicate beauty. So strange they seemed, here among all these mundane household objects.

The ticking of the wall clock echoed loudly in the stillness of the room as the seconds passed, its hands moving slowly, inexorably towards the twelve. Susie looked up, watching it, mesmerized by its movement, by the slow transition into her wedding day. She felt herself lulled by it, hypnotised, until the sudden rattle of the front door broke her concentration. She went to the kitchen window, looking out on the garden, at the trees and bushes as they bristled and swayed in the wind.

At least the rain has stopped, she thought, noting how the surfaces of the puddles along the path were still like tiny mirrors.

Switching off the kitchen light she went out into the hallway once more. Poking her head round the living-room door she could see the mass of flower arrangements on the table and smiled to herself, excited by the thought of the day ahead. Her day.

Turning away, her eye was caught by a scrap of bright yellow paper tucked beneath the corner of the telephone, her mother's spidery handwriting scrawled across it. Carefully pulling it out, so as not to make a noise, she held it up before her to better decipher Doreen's erratic hand, muttering the words under her breath as she read each one.

Anna — lots to tell you. See you tomorrow.

Susie raised her eyebrows, intrigued, and made a mental note to give her friend a quick buzz in the morning. Then, as her eyes scanned the next line, a smile spread across her face. She mouthed the words, imagining him saying them:

Joe — says don't be late.

Susie bit her lip to stop herself from getting all emotional and soppy, sniffing loudly as she rubbed an index finger backwards and forwards across her nostrils. And, finally, the name that made her heart sink, the one that had come back to haunt her: *Max*. No message; simply *Max*.

'The bastard!' she whispered quietly under her breath, screwing the paper into a tight ball and squeezing it in her clenched fist, focusing all her hatred for the man into that note; crushing it until her long fingernails dug painfully into her palms.

She thought of those photographs, imagined Joe seeing them, and felt sick to her stomach. But Joe wasn't going to see them. No. She wasn't going to let Max to hurt her again, to ruin everything for her now that she was about to be happy at last. She wouldn't allow it.

Pushing the ball of paper into the pocket of her skirt, Susie turned to mount the stairs, her thoughts racing, jumping like a firecracker from one thing to another, so that she almost walked past the white envelope that lay face down on the doormat. Stopping to pick it up, she turned it over in her hand, staring at her name, written across the front in a neat, familiar hand. Instinctively she looked up through the glass-panelled front door, as if for a shape, a silhouette, but all was darkness. Frowning, she went across and sat on the bottom stair, holding the corner of the envelope between thumb and forefinger.

For more than a minute she stared at it, torn between wanting to hide it somewhere — afraid of what it

318

might hold — and wanting to read it, to satisfy her curiosity.

But the temptation was irresistible. Carefully she prised back the gummed flap. Inside was a single sheet of white notepaper. Opening it out, her eyes were drawn first to the signature, confirming what she already knew, a sigh welling up from deep inside her as she read Paul's name.

The note was short and typically sweet:

Darling Susie,

I can't come to the church — but then you probably guessed I wouldn't. It would be too much to bear. But you know I'll be thinking of you and that I'll always love you. And if you ever need me . . .

Yours forever,
Paul

Susie stared at the note, reading it over and over again, her vision blurred, tears rolling down her nose and dripping onto the paper, disfiguring the words even as she committed them to memory.

From the living room she could hear the distant chime of the mantel clock as midnight struck.

She stood, wiping her hand across her face, then turned and began to climb the stairs. Today was her wedding day.

– *Janet* –

Pushing her legs down the length of the mattress, Janet rolled to the other side of the large pine bed, stretching out, relishing the space, loving the feel of the warm sheet upon her skin. Turning onto her back she lay spread-eagled beneath the white cotton duvet, luxuriating in this Saturday morning ritual.

Through half-closed eyes she looked across to the window, still covered by its white cotton blind, the blue and white striped curtains neatly tied back on either side. Light filled the room in spite of the blind, the thick material filtering the morning sunlight like a screen. She imagined it beating down upon the rain-soaked streets and gardens, drinking up yesterday's downpour, drying them out, and was glad that Susie's big day wasn't going to be spoiled by the weather.

Through the open door she could hear Steve a little way off in the kitchen, preparing tea and toast, and smiled to herself, thanking her lucky stars that she had such a good man. She knew from talking to friends that some men didn't think they ought to lift a finger in the home; they reckoned that if they went out to work it absolved them from knowing how to work a can opener or switch on a kettle. A girl at work had once told her a story about the time she'd been rushed to hospital with appendicitis. They had kept her in for a few days after they operated and when she did arrive home she almost had a relapse: there was nearly a week's washing-up piled in the sink, rubbish scattered over the kitchen floor where the cat had attacked the overflowing rubbish bin, the bathroom floor was awash with wet towels and the washing-machine hadn't so much as been looked at let alone used. Worst of all, the silly woman had cleared it all up without a word! *More fool her!* Janet thought indignantly.

The sound of the radio drifted in from the other room. Closing her eyes again, Janet curled herself foetally, listening to the music – the new Eurovision song, 'Love City Groove' – and imagined Steve bopping around the kitchen, as he often did. She gave a satisfied sigh, feeling for the first time in a long while that things really were going to be all right. That was what the sunshine meant. It was like a sign to her.

Uncurling her limbs she lay flat in the bed, then, pushing her Snoopy nightshirt up about her waist, she placed the palm of her hand across her naked abdomen. Beneath its touch she could feel no pain, none of the usual achiness that dragged her womb when her period came, sucking the life from her body. She allowed herself a brief smile of hope, as if to say, so far so good.

She had been due to come on two days ago. Normally she was as regular as clockwork: every twenty-eight days around lunchtime. It was a regular source of regret, but it also had its positive side. At least the agony of wondering whether or not she had conceived that month wasn't unnecessarily prolonged; she knew exactly when to expect her period if it were going to come, as it inevitably did, and the process of mourning the passing of yet another 'lost' child was at least short-lived. Not only that, but it meant she could begin to prepare herself for the month ahead: could slowly raise her hopes again. Endlessly again, it seemed.

Hope. She had lived on hope these past few years, like a beggar living on credit.

For the past two days, however, she had walked around on tenterhooks. Every little twinge took on significance, every sensation monitored and analysed so that she became preoccupied with her every movement, willing her body to hold onto that blood, to stem its flow, to allow a baby to grow inside her. She had told Steve nothing of this, of course. She hadn't dared allow herself to utter even the *possibility* that she could be pregnant, as if articulating it would curse her and break the fragile spell.

Almost unconsciously Janet held her breath as she slowly moved a hand down between her legs, squeezing her eyes shut as she forced her fingers to feel for the dampness of blood through the thin cotton of her panties. Relieved but disbelieving she brought her hand up above the covers, opening her eyes to inspect her fingers for any trace of that which, she'd come to realise, she dreaded above all else; but there was no sign of blood upon them and a heavy sigh of relief escaped from Janet's mouth as she raised them to her lips, kissing them lightly as if in thanks.

Maybe this time, she thought, afraid of the excitement she felt. *Maybe* this *time*.

* * *

Steve had had a calming influence on Janet, he'd made her less neurotic, so that, on occasions, even she would admit that she'd been anally retentive before she'd met him — obsessed with housework and tidiness, the order of things. There was a time when she would have been aggravated beyond belief by having toast crumbs over the bedcover, let alone reams of grubby newspapers spread across her precious white linen, but now this Saturday morning ritual was an important part of her life with Steve — something she positively looked forward to. She didn't have to rush off to work at the building society; he didn't have to go off to the sports shop he part-owned with his brother. They could just hang out and do nothing. Relax together.

Propped up on a mountain of soft white pillows, Janet popped the last bite-size piece of butter-soaked toast between her lips, closing her eyes as she sucked the tips of her fingers and thumb before resting them upon the duvet. At her elbow a newspaper and magazine lay discarded. At her feet Steve lay across the width of the bed, his chin resting on her shrouded toes as they stretched up through the cover, his eyes scanning the paper spread before him as he flipped over the pages. There was a casual neatness about Steve, so that even when he was relaxing, slouching on the bed in t-shirt and boxer shorts, he looked almost ready for work. His straight brown hair always looked immaculate — the short, feather style requiring the minimum of attention — and wearing the faintest shadow of a beard meant he never suffered from morning stubble.

On the bedside table two half-filled mugs of tea sat

side by side, upon beer mats advertising Steve's favourite brew, Fuller's ESB, and as he swivelled round and reached across for his, so Janet leaned towards the table and lifted hers also, the china mugs clinking against each other in mid-air.

'Cheers!' Steve said, laughing as he cupped his other hand below the mug so as to catch the drips of coffee spilling down its side. Draining the last of the lukewarm liquid, he replaced the cup and leaned towards her, kissing her on the cheek.

'So, what's the plan of action?' he said, rolling onto his back so that his head rested in her lap, his eyes turned, smiling, to look at her.

Even through the duvet she could feel the hard boniness of his head as it lay over her pubis, his cheek resting against the gentle swell of her abdomen, and part of her ached to tell him about her hopes for their baby. She wanted to be able to tell him that, finally, she had been able to give him the child she knew he longed for – *they* longed for; she wanted to feel the thrill of achievement, to feel whole, to *appear* whole in his eyes, but she knew she must wait.

Janet rested a hand on the side of his head, playing with his hair, gently twisting strands around her finger. 'Aren't you going out for a run this morning?' she asked, her thumb moving down to stroke his beard, the coarse hair bristling against her skin.

'Yeah, I thought I'd do a quick two-miler,' he said, breathing in deeply through his nose and then pushing out his chest as it escaped through his mouth. Rolling on to his stomach, he reached up to play with the buttons on her nightshirt. 'Unless you want me to come back to bed, of course.' Having undone the top button he had moved down to the next.

Janet tapped his hand playfully. 'I think you'd better go for a run. You could do with the exercise,' she said, reaching down to pinch the skin at his waist between her thumb and forefinger.

'I thought we might both get some exercise,' he said, pretending to fight his way back beneath the cover, before Janet gently pushed him and he dramatically fell off the edge of the bed to lay flat on his back across the floor.

'Idiot!' she said, laughing, and threw a pillow down at him, watching it land full in his face. Leaning back on the bed she pulled the duvet up around her neck like a maiden defending her honour, grinning, waiting for him to get up. It was so easy for her to love Steve.

'So, what time do we need to leave?' he asked, the voice rising up from the floor where he still lay, the pillow now resting beside his head.

'The wedding's at two-thirty,' Janet said, leaning toward the side of the bed, resting on one elbow. 'It'll only take a quarter of an hour to get to the church. Mind, I promised Susie I'd get there early just to make sure everything's okay, so I s'pose we'd better leave here about quarter to two.'

'What's this bloke of Susie's like?' he asked, turning over and showing off with a couple of quick press-ups.

'Dunno, really. Karen's met him. Says he's *all right*, but you can never tell with her. She never goes overboard on any of the men she meets. Except you, of course. She adores *you*.'

'The girl's got taste,' he said, rolling onto his back like a basset hound and smiling up at her.

'She's the matron of honour, you know,' Janet said, shaking her head. 'I don't know why she let Susie talk her into it.'

'Why? What's wrong with that?'

'Well, you know what Susie's like! Poor old Karen'll look like mutton dressed up as lamb. She'll pour her into some skimpy number with her boobs hanging out . . .'

'Can't wait!' Steve said, licking his lips.

Janet lashed out in mock annoyance, missing him as he rolled to the side, laughing.

'You know what I mean! Karen hasn't exactly got the figure for it, has she.'

Conscious that he shouldn't say the wrong thing here, Steve simply said: 'She'll be fine. Don't worry.'

'D'you think I should give Mandy a ring? See if she wants to come with us?' Janet said after a moment's thought.

'What about Mr Personality?'

'You know what they're like! She wasn't sure at the hen night if Pete was going to the church or not. She might feel a bit funny going on her own.'

'I don't see why. Anna will be on her own, won't she?'

'Yeah, but Anna's not married, she's used to going places on her own.'

'I wouldn't have said that Mandy strikes you as particularly shy,' Steve observed.

Janet burst out laughing, suddenly recalling her friend two days before, limbo dancing under the legs of the black male stripper. She certainly hadn't appeared shy then, Janet had to admit. Steve gave her a questioning look and in between giggling fits she told him all about

Mandy's little performance, still marvelling at the display of new-found confidence.

She had fed him snippets about the evening when she'd arrived home in the early hours of Friday morning, leaving out some of the more embarrassing little details, like when one of the strippers – Cowboy Joe – had dropped his kit right in front of them, his fringed leather chaps falling to the floor at the pull of a single string, revealing a spray of small, bright green feathers covering his flaccid willy. Predictably Susie had shouted out some comment about tickling his fancy so that he had turned back to face her and, urged on by the riotous audience, had encouraged her to pluck away the feathers one by one. By the end of it his penis was anything but flaccid and when Susie removed the final feather and placed it on the tip of the erect member, it looked so comical they had clung to each other in hysterics.

'I'll give Mand a ring a bit later on, then, just to check,' Janet said, then, as an afterthought, added: 'Oh, and if Pete does come along, for Christ's sake talk to him won't you.'

'What about?' Steve laughed. 'The man's a moron! There are small rodents from Bolivia with more brain power than him!'

'Well, talk about anything. I don't know. Football!'

'I would except he's a Spurs supporter. It's like I said, brain-dead!'

Janet couldn't stop herself from laughing but threw another pillow onto Steve's upturned face. Poor Pete! He really was a pathetic specimen. In all the time she'd known him – and it was as long as Mandy had, because they'd met him on that infamous holiday at Butlin's –

she'd never managed to have a proper conversation with him. She wasn't sure who to feel sorry for most: him for being him or Mandy for having married him.

'Did I ever tell you about *their* wedding? asked Janet.

'No,' he said, putting on a fake camp accent, as if he were the world's worst gossip and was utterly *anxious* to hear.

Janet laughed. 'Well,' she went on, 'we should've known the marriage was doomed right from the start. I remember we were standing in the gardens at the back of the church — they got married at St Mary's on the Upper Street — and the photographer was poncing around organising everyone. Anyway, he lines up a lovey-dovey shot of Mandy and Pete under this tree — all covered in blossom it was — when all of a sudden a bird flies across and shits all over Pete's head. And not a dainty one, either! That was one bird that'd had a curry the night before!'

Steve roared and Janet could barely breathe she was laughing so much.

'You should have seen his mum,' she wheezed, 'fussing about him with a hanky trying to wipe it off, but making it ten times worse, smearing it all over his hair.'

She took a calming breath. 'Not only that, but at the ceremony Pete got the stammers so bad that it took him all of five minutes to say his name. His face got redder and redder until the whole congregation was a mass of heaving shoulders as everyone struggled not to laugh.'

'Nah,' Steve said, 'really?'

Janet nodded, then broke into a fit of giggles again.

'Yeah, and then at the reception Susie was sick in Pete's mum's handbag. She didn't find out for three days! Can you imagine it . . . there she was with a full trolley in Tesco's!'

Steve roared again and beat the floor with his palms.

She knew that he loved hearing about her and the girls when they were younger, before he'd met her. He always said how he wished he'd known her back then, delighting in her stories of their wild antics. He said he'd never been lucky enough to come across a group of girls like them. *Rude girls*, he called them.

She'd never thought of herself as rude; most of what they got up to was just harmless fun. She hadn't even lost her virginity until she was eighteen, for God's sake! She'd been working away in Cornwall for the summer, just her and Susie, and finally did it on a boat with a guy she'd fancied. She wasn't on the pill then, so they'd had to use a condom. She remembered feeling a bit like a tart when he got the packet out of his pocket, knowing then that he'd expected her to have sex with him. Even now she could vividly recall the rubbery smell of it as they'd fumbled in the darkness.

Steve hauled himself up from the floor and sat next to her on the edge of the bed, smiling. 'Well, my peach, let's just hope there's no shit flying around at *this* wedding!'

'I wouldn't count on it. Not with Susie's family. The whole lot of them are bloody loony. Even the ones that seem normal. Get a drink inside them and it's like something off *One Flew Over the Cuckoo's Nest*, complete with seven-foot Indian!'

She laughed strangely. 'D'you know, I remember staying with Susie once when we were kids — about fourteen, we were. We were sleeping in Lyndsay's room at the back, 'cos it was bigger, and Susie woke me up from a dead sleep, shaking me and whispering to me to come over to the window. When I looked out I thought I was still dreaming. There was her old man, completely starkers, beer gut wobbling in the wind, trying not to catch his wedding tackle on the wire fence as he climbed over into next door's garden. I remember there was a full moon and it was like he was under the floodlights at a football match as he sprinted across the grass and into the neighbour's wendy-house. A minute of two later the woman next door stumbled up her garden path, bare legs poking out from under her leather coat and falling off the sides of her stiletto heels as they sank into the mud. And as she bends down to get inside the little house, her bare arse smiles up at us.'

Steve sat there with his mouth open, uncomprehending, as though she were talking in an alien tongue. 'Bloody hell! What happened?'

'What d'you think happened?'

'No, what happened when he came out?'

'I don't know. We heard Susie's mum moving about in the room next door and jumped back into bed.'

'D'you think she knew?'

''Course she knew. The racket he made getting back over the fence I'd say the whole of the bloody street knew! We got under the blankets and pulled them up over our heads. It was really weird seeing your mate's dad in his birthday suit, though . . .'

Steve shook his head in disbelief. 'Perhaps I should ask May if she fancies paying me a visit in the potting shed?' he said, smirking. May was their next-door neighbour and only just on the right side of eighty.

'Not if you want to keep *your* wedding tackle in one

piece, mate,' she said, gently pushing him in the chest. It was this kind of thing that showed how far they had come together. A couple of years ago if he'd made a crack about having an affair with somebody — even if it was in fun — she'd have hit the roof; sulked for days, maybe even weeks afterwards. Her ex-husband's betrayal — his infidelity, the way he had left — had left her emotions so raw that the merest reminder brought untold misery. Steve was a real diamond to have put up with her.

'So,' Steve said, moving over to the chest of drawers and pulling out a pair of tracksuit bottoms, 'Anna hasn't found herself a bloke, then?'

'Nah. Susie reckons she broke up with the American because she wanted have a baby and he didn't.' There was a moment's pause before she suddenly said, 'P'raps I should offer your services. That'd solve her problem!'

Janet had never quite been able to forget a harmless remark Steve once made about Anna being the friend he found most fanciable. In his mind it wasn't the same as saying he fancied Anna, simply that she was the most attractive, but in Janet's it was tantamount to confessing that he wanted to sleep with Anna because she was both beautiful and fertile.

Steve tied the drawstring at his waist, knowing from past experience that it was best not to rise to Janet's bait. He bent down, reaching under the bed for his trainers, then sat back down on the edge of the mattress. 'I can't see her wanting a kid, myself,' he said, pushing his foot inside the grubby leather shoe then tying his lace into a bow and then a double knot. 'She enjoys her career too much, that one!'

'Hmm. Maybe,' Janet said, not so convinced. 'Anyway, that's what Susie said.'

'Yeah, well, maybe it's Susie who wants the kids and she's indulging in a bit of projection,' he said, bending over to tie the lace of the other shoe.

'What d'you mean, *projection*?' she said, impressed. That was one of the things she liked about Steve. He seemed to know all kinds of things.

'You know, saying that somebody else wants something when it's really *you* who wants it. Projecting your own hopes, wishes, fears or whatever onto another person as though they were theirs. Parents do it all the time.'

'Mmm, s'pose so,' she said, considering the possibility. She'd never really imagined Susie having her own kids. Oh, Susie liked them well enough, and they always seemed to like her, but Janet had never thought of her as, well, *responsible* enough to raise kids. She barely seemed able to take care of herself.

Kneeling up, she leaned across towards Steve, resting her hands on his shoulders and nuzzling into the back of his neck.

'I love it when you talk intellectual to me,' she whispered in her huskiest voice, nibbling around the edge of his ear.

'I bet that's what Einstein's wife used to say when she wanted a bit nooky,' he said, laughing and leaning back into her. 'But don't start what you're not prepared to finish,' he said, twisting his head round to meet her lips.

Looking down into his face she felt an overwhelming love for him. It would have been so easy to fall back into bed with him right then. So often in the past their lovemaking had been clinical, orchestrated, to maximise the possibility of her falling pregnant, moments like these, moments of spontaneous passion, had been few and far between. But she didn't want to spoil things now; she didn't want to take any risks.

She gently pulled away, falling back against the pillows.

'You'd better get going,' she said, smiling across at him. 'Or else we won't make it to this wedding.'

'I'll have to make it a three-miler,' he said, standing up from the bed. 'I've got a bit more energy to burn off now!' He nodded down, indicating his all-too-obvious erection.

Janet burst out laughing although, secretly, she delighted in knowing that Steve still desired her. She wouldn't have blamed him if his feelings had worn a bit thin in that area, having endured a sex life cluttered with thermometers, cushions and calendars. Not to speak of the baggy boxer shorts and the lukewarm baths she'd insisted he take.

'You wanna watch you don't get any birds landing on that,' she joked, 'feathered or otherwise. Now go on. On your way, mate!' she added, nodding toward the door.

He bent down to kiss her on the cheek, his hands cupped over his erection. 'Ah, you're a terrible woman!'

As he disappeared down the hallway she called after him: 'And don't you go inviting May over to look at your seedlings in that condition!' smiling to herself as his laughter drifted through, until the front door slammed behind him.

'And I love you . . .' she said wistfully, speaking the words into the sudden silence.

Janet curled up beneath the duvet, allowing herself a few

more minutes before she got up and prepared herself for the big event. A few days back it had seemed to loom before her, but now, if she was honest about it, Susie's wedding had faded almost into insignificance. What, only a few days ago, had been the biggest event in her social calendar, was now merely something to be endured. Now she just wanted the day to pass, and the next and the next, until she could be sure that the pregnancy she wanted above all else was a reality, that the infertility that had come to dominate and scar her life was at an end.

Rolling onto her back she lay a hand on her abdomen, concentrating, wishing away any threatening ache or pain, determined to deny them. Pushing herself further up the bed, she pulled her hands up, under her nightshirt, cupping her naked breasts, each one easily contained in her slim hands. Even so she was convinced of their sudden fullness, imagining them swollen as her body prepared itself. Her nipples lay flat upon the gentle rise of her breast, inert and unfeeling, though she was convinced of their soreness. Taking each one between thumb and finger, she allowed herself to imagine a baby suckling from them, its soft cheek against her breast as they comforted each other with their closeness. Laying her head back against the wooden bedstead she closed her eyes, planting the seed of thought, willing it to take root in her consciousness, until it became not just a possibility but a certainty. *Pregnant* . . .

Without conscious effort her thumbs moved gently, rhythmically, against the smooth curve of her breasts. Janet smiled as she felt the warm moistness in the corner of each eye as the tears ran down her cheeks onto her neck – tears not of despair, but of hope.

The letterbox clattered as it sprang shut. Pushing back the duvet, Janet slowly swung her legs round, onto the carpet. For a moment she sat there, hands resting on her knees, wondering if it was nausea she felt, telling herself it must be. She smiled.

On the way to the bathroom she made a detour to the front door, stooping to gather the assortment of envelopes spread over the doormat, sorting them into two piles as she squatted there. Pushing Steve's pile away from the door, she picked up the three letters addressed to her and went into the bathroom, placing them on the side of the bath as she sat down on the loo.

Her pink bikini briefs stretched across from knee to knee as she sat with them wide apart. With one hand she pulled at the front and with the other, the back so as to reveal the thin cotton fabric of the crotch, obsessively looking for spots of blood. Nothing! The relief flowed through her. Pulling a strip of paper from the toilet roll, she carefully folded the squares back on one another to form a pad. Holding it in her hand, she stared at it, seeing in it another test, another hurdle; willing it to retain its purity, its essential *whiteness*.

With an intake of breath she pushed the paper down between her legs, pressing the pad against her soft, moist vulva, holding it there for the count of ten, her growing confidence allowing her to tweak her nose at fate. Yet as she brought the paper out again, she could barely bring herself to look, caution forcing her to acknowledge that the body had a habit of playing nasty tricks. Confidence gave way to doubt in the split second it took her to half-open her eyes, so that she scanned the surface through two narrow slits expecting to see a pad of blood-soaked paper laying limply across her fingers. But there was no blood.

Janet shuddered, checking it again. There *was* no blood. She wrapped her arms round her belly, as if to thank her baby, her shoulders slumping with relief. She closed her eyes briefly, then opened them again, staring at the silk white gloss surface of the loo door.

Remembering the letters she reached out and took them from the side of the bath. Shuffling through, she put the white envelopes containing her bank statement and Marks & Spencer account back on the side unopened. Holding the long buff envelope up in front of her she read the words printed in red in the top right-hand corner, the inefficiency of the franking block rendering them barely legible. The M--dl-sex Hos--tal.

Taking out the single sheet of white notepaper, she read it through quickly, her chest rising and falling rapidly, her mouth suddenly dry. She had been given an appointment at the hospital's fertility clinic in two months' time.

Every day for the past three months – ever since her GP had finally agreed to refer her – she had eagerly awaited the arrival of this letter. In her desperation she had reached out for it as a lifeline. But now . . .

Janet smiled at the irony that it should arrive on this day. Folding it back into its envelope she put it with the others, reaching past them to drop the plug into the bath before turning on the taps.

Maybe this time.

Almost without her noticing it, the bath water had cooled around her. Lifting her leg she stretched her toes towards the hot tap, operating it with the practised skill of a safe cracker, manipulating the chrome knob to achieve a gentle flow of fresh water. Enjoying the warmth as it spread towards her, she nestled into the inflatable headrest suctioned to the inside of the bath. An air-filled breast protruded beside each of her ears, the flesh-coloured plastic overprinted with a tasteless black and red brassiere. She'd bought the blow-up bosoms for Steve last Christmas as a joke, attaching a little note saying something about how she knew he'd always wanted to get his head between a pair of thirty-eight double Ds!

With vague interest she looked at her watch, realising that she had been laying there for nearly half an hour, thinking back over her years of infertility.

It seemed to her that for the past two years she had thought of little else, that the passing of time had been little more than a mechanism to get her from one disappointment to another as her body failed to live up to her expectations. Obsessively she had searched for the reason, had foraged through her past for something she might have done to cause it, convinced that she had to be guilty of bringing this curse down on herself.

Like most women she had always assumed that she would have children, that she would decide how many she wanted and when she wanted them. When she was married to Mike, she had got pregnant without any problem, and as painful as that memory was, it had also proved strangely comforting at times. And even if it had happened nearly a decade ago at least it gave her hope.

She marvelled at people's insensitivity, at the way they dealt with it as though she had toothache or indigestion, telling her to relax, to stop thinking about it, as though she were in control, as though she could genuinely prevent it from dominating her life. Not that she had ever really been able to talk to anyone about her anguish. How could she? They wouldn't understand. Nobody but a barren woman could possibly *imagine* the pain she suffered, the resentment she felt every time she saw a pregnant woman, the jealousy as she watched them walking down the street. It was unbearable at times, their swollen bellies taunting her, mocking her own useless body.

Janet sank down in the bath, the water lapping around her chin. Through pouting lips she blew across the surface of the water, mesmerized by the patterns as they rippled away from her and disappeared. Reaching forward she pulled the bath rack closer and grabbed the soap. Bringing her foot up to rest on the side of the rack, her toes clinging monkey-fashion to the thin chrome bar at the top, she rubbed the soap into her leg until it formed a rich, creamy lather. Then, taking up the orange and white Bic, she gently pulled it up her leg, drawing the soap toward her as the razor glided from ankle to knee, over her shin and round behind, over her calf. She worked methodically, strip by strip, like a gardener mowing the lawn, until her legs were smooth and hairless.

Satisfied, she sank back against the cushioning breasts, studying the hairs floating on the surface, noting how they clung to the tiny soap suds as they drifted to the water's edge.

Her hand was now resting on her belly, the feel of it strange beneath her wrinkled fingertips. Gently she moved her outstretched palm from side to side. Looking down at her breasts as they stared up at her from just below the water line, she felt convinced of their altered shape and gave a self-satisfied smile.

Closing her eyes, she allowed herself to daydream about the possibility that she might, just *might*, be pregnant. She imagined herself telling Steve, and saw him beam with pride. She had seen that look on other men – that unique look of pride in having created another human being; the unfathomable joy of knowing that a part of your essential self would live on after one's death. She knew just how well that look would sit upon Steve's face and longed to place it there, for no matter how many times he had reassured her that it didn't matter if they never had kids or told her that he loved her and wouldn't change her for anything, she knew what he really felt. She knew how deep his disappointment ran; knew he thought she had failed him. She *knew*.

His parents hadn't helped either. They wanted grand-children. Of course they did, she understood that, but their constant pressure had been unforgivable, not to say insensitive. They had gone on and on about Steve's sister and how easy she had found it to conceive until one day Janet had made some comment about how the silly cow could probably get herself up the duff just looking at a banana. She knew it wasn't really his sister's fault, even so she couldn't bring herself to visit after that, to punish herself even more with the acute jealousy she knew she'd feel.

The water had cooled to tepid and, looking at her watch, Janet realised suddenly that Steve would be back any moment.

Grabbing the thick white bath towel from the rail, she swiftly wrapped it around her shoulders, enjoying the feel

342

of the soft, warm cotton against her skin. Dabbing her arms she pulled the towel around, over her bust, fastening it like a sarong. Bending at the waist, she threw her wet hair forward, wrapping it in a small hand towel so that it stood like a turban upon her head.

Reaching into the cabinet beneath the hand basin, she took out a large, plastic bottle of baby lotion. Squeezing some of the bright pink cream into the palm of her hand, she began to massage it into her shoulder and down the length of her outstretched arm. Heavy with moisture, the bath towel fell to the floor, leaving her naked. She wiped her other hand across the mirror above the basin and turned sideways to view herself in profile, running a hand down the contour of her body from breast to thigh. Bending to pick up the towel she dabbed at her legs before standing up to dry the rest of her body.

Dropping the towel on the cork-topped stool beside her, she turned back to the basin and, taking her toothbrush from the enamel cup, began to clean her teeth. It wasn't until she reached for the towel again and held it to her face that she saw it.

For a moment she stared in disbelief.

The bright red mark was like a scar against the towel's whiteness, the long thin streak of blood like a knife slash. Her heart skipped a beat. She actually felt it stop. And at that same moment her head filled with blood, throbbing at her temples as though trying to escape the mounting turmoil inside her. She rubbed at the stain with the side of her fist, trying to deny it, to obliterate it, but the stain spread steadily, as if it wouldn't stop until it filled the whole of the deep cotton pile.

Lifting up her foot to rest on the stool Janet frantically

ran her hands over her leg, searching for the razor cut she knew had to be there. She did the same with the other leg, repeatedly running her hands over the smooth skin, willing the blood to seep through her fingertips, to run down her shin. She made a silent vow that if only that could happen she would never ask for anything ever again. For that brief moment she prayed to a God she wasn't even sure existed, promising undying devotion if it could only be so.

But she knew. She *knew*.

Finally, with a heavy reluctance, she dropped her leg onto the floor and stood there, paralysed with fear, as nausea threatened to overwhelm her. Her arm felt as heavy as a tree trunk as she raised her hand and laid it over her stomach, even now fearful of the effects of the sickness on the unborn child she yet carried inside her.

The towel lay in a crumpled heap at her feet. Reaching down she pulled it up, lifting it to her face and kissing it lightly. Staring straight ahead and clutching a handful of towelling tightly in her fist, she reached down and pushed it between her legs, pressing it up against her vagina. She held it there for a minute of more, before finally relaxing her hand. Holding the bloodied towel out before her, her body convulsed just once before she collapsed to the floor clutching her stomach, trying to prevent her baby from leaving her body, the sound that escaped her lips barely human.

No . . . Oh, God Almighty, no . . .

She could remember every moment of her pregnancy, every moment of the pure, unadulterated joy of knowing that she was soon to be a mother. From the moment she did the first pregnancy test, sitting on the side of the bath watching the indicator turn pink, she had thought of nothing else but the baby, walking around in a haze of complete happiness.

Once they had made the decision to try for one it was as though her relationship with Mike moved into another phase, a different kind of closeness developing out of their shared desire to create this new life, this shared part of them. And when she'd told him that they had really done it she had felt, maybe for the first and only time, that he loved her. *Really* loved her.

She couldn't wait to tell people, to hear their congratulations, the warmth in their voices and even, she had to admit, their envy. And almost immediately she had worn maternity clothes even though it wasn't necessary; she felt special and she wanted everyone she met to know the reason why. Nothing she had ever experienced could compare to the feelings she had at that time.

There was a babywear shop that she passed on her way home from work and every evening she would stop to look in the window, grinning inanely as she admired each tiny garment, struck for the first time by their smallness. There was a beautiful hand-smocked dress in the centre of the display, pure white with pale pink stitching, its little cuffs designed for wrists no bigger than a fifty pence piece. One evening the shop was still open as she stopped and, unable to resist temptation, she had gone inside and bought the dress. Even now she had it, wrapped in white tissue paper at the bottom of her dressing table drawer.

She was at work when the first alarm bells had rung. Feeling tired she had gone into the Ladies to grab a moment's peace, and was sitting there on the loo, daydreaming, when a colleague opened the outer door and shouted that the manager was looking for her. It wasn't until she leaned forward to get up that she saw the blood in the bowl; just two red spots, mesmerizing her as they gently glided down the white porcelain and into the water.

The doctor had told her not to worry, that it sometimes happened, and to get herself along for a scan. She'd phoned Mike straight away and had told him what the doctor had said, but she could hear the concern in his voice as he agreed to meet her at the hospital.

She didn't have to wait for the doctor to tell her there was no heartbeat, she could see the distress on his face as he pushed the sensor back and forth across her abdomen. He swallowed hard – a sound that seemed to fill the air and echo around the room – before simply saying, 'I'm sorry'. There was no need to say more: they all knew the baby was dead. Mike collapsed over her as she lay there, burying his face in her pubis, his tears soaking into the dark hair, and she had reached down to stroke his head, to comfort him.

She had felt numb and the tears refused to come. Out in the street life was carrying on as normal, the crowds that passed her by oblivious to her pain and the dead child she carried inside her. How could anything be normal ever again. She wanted to scream at them, to wipe away each smile and choke each sound of laughter.

Back home she had been close to collapse. Mike had carried her across the threshold and into the bedroom. Laying her on the bed he had undressed her, her body looking so small suddenly as she curled herself into a ball

346

and crept beneath the cover. Waking from sleep, for a split second she had convinced herself that it had all been a bad dream, but the reality of her loss could be felt on her face, the skin tight with the streaks of dried tears, and in her eyes which were sore from silent crying. Through the thin wall she could hear Mike on the telephone in the living room, breaking the news to family and friends. It made her want to hide away, to avoid his admission of their failure. How could she face anyone ever again?

It had taken days for nature to run its course and for the life her body could not sustain to be expelled from her womb. The pain had been appalling. She had thought it would be quick and had not been prepared for the prolonged agony, as though, even in death her baby would not let her forget its brief existence.

Four days and nights were spent in the same clothes, unchanged, unwashed, until, finally, she decided she must take a bath. It wasn't until she stood to get out that she spotted a strange little thing floating on the water, and as she reached for it it slipped through her fingers, sliding back across the water. Finally she had it on the end of her finger, this tiny little thing that in her mind had been a baby with arms and legs and a face. For several minutes she had stood there looking down at it as it clung to her fingertip. Then, turning on the cold tap, she held it beneath the running water, washing it away.

There was no single act in the whole of her life that she regretted more than that one. For years afterwards she had endured nightmares about that moment when she had washed away her baby; horrible, terrifying dreams, imagining it ever after fighting to get back up the drainpipe to her, helpless, alone, abandoned. In some dreams — and these were the worst — it even called to her plaintively, 'Ma-ma . . . Ma-ma . . .', the haunting sound of its distress breaking her heart.

But life went on. By returning to its former state, her body finally told her it was time to put all that behind her. Her breasts were no longer swollen, her stomach — which had grown hard — was soft once more. Her body was no longer preparing for the birth of a child: it was back to 'normal'. But she did not feel normal, she felt suicidal, and part of her wanted to wallow in her grief. About a week after the miscarriage Mike returned to work. Every day during the week that followed she walked to the nearby park, sitting on a seat by the playground, watching the children on the swings and slides, their high-pitched voices full of joy. All she could think about was her own dead child, telling herself over and over again that it just wasn't fair, and asking an unhearing God why it had had to be her.

Friends had tried to help, had offered sympathy. Embarrassed, not knowing what to say, they had listened as she relived the chain of events, obsessively recounting every minute detail of the miscarriage as she desperately clung to the memory. When Mike's patience had finally worn thin, when at last he'd tired of consoling and reassuring her, it was Karen who had sat and listened. For hours at a time she had sat with Janet, holding her hand and stroking her face as the tears flowed again and again, until they had both felt drained of emotion. The others had all been there for her, but it was Karen who seemed to understand her loss. Only with Mandy had Janet felt reluctant to unburden her pain, envious of her friend's children and the unfairness of it all.

It was many weeks before she and Mike had made love again, finally hopeful for the future. Their baby had been a part of them but, finally, they were able to accept that it was not meant to be. They knew they must move forward, move on. Janet knew she must try again.

But that was it. She had never again experienced the joy of 'motherhood'; and she and Mike had never shared in the wonder of creating a life. And now, of course, they never would.

T he sound of the key turning in the lock, of the front door slamming, roused her and she wondered how long she had been sitting there. Her face rested against the top edge of the bath and as she slowly lifted her head, a long red ridge marked her cheek. She rubbed it absent-mindedly with the tips of her fingers.

Rocking forward onto her knees she leaned towards the bathroom door and slipped the lock across, slumping down to rest her back against the cold painted wood. She listened to Steve's footsteps as he walked up the hallway to the bedroom and then back down again, stopping at the living room and then the kitchen before finally reaching the bathroom. The door rattled, as he turned the handle.

'Jan?'

She closed her eyes. Once more tears squeezed from below the lids, silently trickling down her blotched face.

'Jan? You okay?' The door rattled again as he shook it on its hinges. They never locked the bathroom door! 'Janet! Answer me!'

She grabbed the towel and held it to her face, trying

to muffle the sound as she sniffed into its thick folds. Taking a deep breath she spoke in a voice that was not hers, reassuring him.

'I'm fine. I'll be out in a minute.'

'Why the bloody hell have you locked it?' he shouted through the door, a mixture of relief and exasperation in his voice as he stomped off up the hallway without awaiting an answer.

'Because . . . ' she said silently, wiping her hands across her face, then slowly getting to her feet. *Because.*

'Did you phone Mandy?' Steve asked, turning the key in the ignition.

Janet shook her head.

'Was that a yes or a no?' he asked sarcastically as he tipped the indicator, looked over his shoulder and pulled away from the curb.

'No.'

'Why not?'

'I forgot!' she lied, staring straight ahead.

'Well, d'you want me to stop up the road and give her a bell?'

'It's too late now,' she said flatly. 'She's probably already on her way.'

'Up to you. She's your friend,' he said pointedly.

They had barely exchanged a civil word since he'd returned from his run. He had put his arm around her, trying to recapture their earlier closeness, unaware of the cause of her unhappiness, but she hadn't wanted him to comfort her, nor pity her. She had pushed him away, despising him for still wanting her, for still desiring this body which, in her heart, she felt had failed them both.

350

As she sat on the edge of the bed, he had stood over her, gently asking her what was wrong. He'd bent down to kiss her, but she had turned her head, leaving it all unspoken, still hanging in the air between them.

'Are you going to keep this up all day?' he said, breaking the silence.

'Keep what up?'

'Don't give me that shit! You know very well what. This cold shoulder crap!'

Janet shrugged and turned her head to look out of the side window, her eyes glazing over as they stared unseeing past the bustling crowds of Saturday shoppers, mothers pushing buggies and herding children through the throng heading towards the busy market, old ladies steering shopping trollies round passers-by.

'What is it I'm supposed to have done?' he said, pulling up at the traffic lights just past the Angel, the tone quieter now as he drew on his final reserves of patience.

'Nothing!'

'Well, if you don't tell me, I can't make things right, can I?' he coaxed, pushing the gearstick into first and slowly pulling away, coasting round the corner, off the main road.

'No,' she scowled, 'you can't make things *right*, can you.'

He glanced at her, hurt by the sharpness of her tone. 'I don't understand. Just tell me what's upset you.'

'Just leave me alone, will you.'

Steve huffed, exasperated now. 'Great bloody wedding this is going to be if you're going to be in this stinking mood all day!'

'If you don't like it you know what you can do!' she snarled.

'Don't tempt me!' he said, slowing to let a pedestrian cross with a trolley-load of shopping from the supermarket.

'Oh, just piss off,' she said, under her breath but loud enough for him to hear.

'What the fuck's your problem?' he yelled, his anger rising now. 'You pre-menstrual or something?' As they pulled away abruptly, Janet was thrown forward in her seat.

She felt as though he had slapped her across the face, and in a split second her cheeks turned red as her head filled with blood.

'You bastard!' she spat.

'What?'

'Let me out of this fucking car!' she said, releasing her seat belt and reaching for the door lever.

'Don't be a stupid cow!' he shouted, keeping one hand on the steering wheel while stretching across her, making a grab for the door handle.

'I want to get out!' she screeched, like a child having a tantrum. She made another grab for the handle and as Steve stretched across to stop her, the car swerved to the left smashing into the side of a battered old van travelling up the inside lane.

There was a scream, a yell and then silence; it was all over in a flash. Then Janet was conscious of people standing around the car, of someone opening Steve's door to see if they were all right, and of the angry red face of the other driver as he stood in front of the two vehicles assessing the damage. He was big and fat and down his bare, hairy arms were displayed an array of tattoos declaring his love of Michelle, his mum and Chelsea Football Club.

'What the fucking 'ell d'you think you're playing at, eh pal?' he yelled, making his way round to the driver's door, his flabby jowls playing like a concertina as he walked towards them.

'I'm sorry mate. I didn't see you. I . . .' Steve apologised, remaining firmly in his seat.

'Didn't see me! Didn't see me! I ain't exactly a fucking midget am I, you dozy bastard,' he spat as he leaned into the car, spraying saliva across Steve's face. 'Look at me van!'

Steve looked across at the dent in the front wing, relieved by what seemed to be pretty superficial damage. 'Doesn't look too bad to me,' he ventured.

'Don't look too bad! Don't look too bad!' he repeated incredulously, his face growing redder and more threatening by the minute, his thick tongue – appearing too large for his not inconsiderable mouth – turning and twisting over his lips.

'You a fucking parrot or what?' Janet had turned in her seat to face him, refusing to catch the look on Steve's face that said 'For Christ's sake keep your mouth shut'. 'Listen, you arsehole, he's said he's sorry, so just write down the name of your insurance company and we can all get moving. Anyway,' she said, looking disdainfully out the window, 'another dent in that pile of scrap won't make much difference.'

'Pile of scrap! I'll give you pile of scrap, you cheeky little bitch. That van cost me two K.'

'Yeah well, they saw you coming didn't they?' she said. Then, looking him up and down, she added; 'Mind, they couldn't very well miss you, could they?'

'Jan, there's no need to get upset,' Steve said, placing a hand gently on her arm, trying to calm her.

'And you can bugger off out of it, and all!' she said, pulling her arm away. 'If you'd been concentrating on what you were bloody well doing we wouldn't have hit his mobile fucking trash can, would we?'

Suddenly the two men, their faces cheek by jowl, were united as this woman's common enemy as she glared back at them through the netting veil dropping down from her smart cream pillbox hat.

Steve sat gripping the steering wheel, the picture of controlled neatness in his smart navy suit, white shirt and carefully knotted silk tie, and beside him the fat driver looked ridiculously incongruous as he glared menacingly across at her. His face was smooth and rounded like a sweaty pork sausage, and the stale smell of him invaded the Fiesta despite the little traffic-light air freshener hanging from the rear-view mirror, so that he looked as out of place as a rag and bone man at a Deb's coming-out ball.

He straightened up, resting a hand on the Fiesta's bonnet, addressing the crowd that had gathered round the scene, many in red and white scarves on their way to the Arsenal game, ranting about the damage to his precious van and the two bleedin' wankers who had caused it.

'Well, don't just sit there!' she said, giving Steve a poke.

Steve wearily lifted his head from the steering wheel and looked at her a moment as though deciding whether or not this was the final straw, his self restraint evident as he spoke. 'Right! Fine!' he said, unfastening his safety belt. 'I'll just go and sort out the bloody gorilla shall I?

Quite handy we're on our way to the church – you can arrange my funeral at the same time. Okay?' And with that he stepped gingerly out onto the road, watched by the quietening crowd, like a prayer-weary Christian entering the lion's den.

Inevitably an argument rapidly ensued as the other driver tried it on, attempting to convince Steve that another, obviously older, battle scar on his van's wing had been caused in this latest collision, offering to settle it there and then without involving the insurers – the phrase 'two hundred sods should see to it!' being repeated in his best parrot fashion. As the discussion got more heated, so the two men edged further and further towards the middle of the road, a line of traffic building up behind them, as much out of curiosity and a lusting after some fisticuffs as through any difficulty in manoeuvring around them.

Janet watched them a moment, then decided she'd better go and sort things out. Taking off her hat and laying it on the back seat, she slid across to the driver's side, holding onto the hem of her brown knee-length skirt as she stepped out of the car.

'Listen!' she said, interrupting their flow. 'Let's just cut the crap shall we? We're not paying for you to get that shitheap put to rights. We've admitted the accident was his fault,' she nodded toward Steve, 'but that little dent is all we're paying for. Now, do you understand that or shall I say it again using only three-letter words?'

'Leave this to me, Jan,' Steve said, clearly afraid that he was going to pay physically for her loose tongue.

Her look was dismissive, but when she opened her mouth to speak again, Steve grabbed hold of her arm.

355

'Look! I said leave it to me. You had no bloody problem keeping your mouth shut earlier, did you?'

'Take your bleedin' hands off me,' she yelled, making a great show of shrugging him off. 'In fact, you can keep your hands off me full stop!'

'What the hell's the matter with you?' he said. 'You sound like a bloody nutter!'

'You're telling me, mate,' the driver chipped in, laughing.

'And you can mind your own fucking business, you cretin!' she spat out, a look of total disdain on her face. 'Mind you, just as well you are really,' she added, smirking now, ''cos if you had even half a brain you'd be dangerous!'

But it was water off a duck's back as the ape-man got into his stride.

''Ere pal, you sure you wasn't trying to bump her off when you smashed into me? With a gob like her's it'd be the only way to shut 'er up, I reckon — unless there's something else she likes you to shove in 'er mouth . . .' And again, he enjoyed a great wobbly belly laugh.

Before anyone had a chance to speak, another thought occurred to him and great folds of flesh rippled over his stomach as he enjoyed the joke.

'Mind you,' he said, relishing the moment, 'her tongue's so bloody sharp I'd be worried she'd slice the fucker off!'

The crowd had swelled, and many of them laughed as the confrontation moved into new, more interesting, territory.

'Let me tell you, you bollocky bastard . . .'

'Jan, leave it,' Steve whispered in her ear, trying unsuccessfully to manoeuvre her back inside the car.

'Let me tell you,' she went on, shrugging him off, 'the only way you'd get *your* dick in anyone's mouth was if they were handcuffed, blindfolded and drugged!'

Steve's groan was audible as he laid a hand more firmly on Janet's arm, fearing the retribution he felt was inevitable now.

Several women in the crowd tittered and shouted encouragement from the sidelines.

She had obviously hit a nerve and if looks could kill she would've been ten feet under. 'You wanna keep that mouth of yours shut, you poker-faced old bitch,' the fat man spat, shaking a finger threateningly in her face, 'before I shut it for you!' He hoisted up his baggy jeans so that they rested over his beer gut.

'Oh, yeah, you and whose army, you gormless great lump of lard.'

'Jan, that's *enough*!' Steve said, grabbing hold of her wrist and pulling her back towards the car door.

'Aw, piss off, you!' she screeched, summoning all her strength to pull away from him. 'Just bugger off and leave me alone. I know that's what you wanna do anyway, so why don't you have the balls to do it. Go on, just go!'

'Janet?' he began, unable to hide the bewilderment he felt. 'Jan? What's the matter?'

'I can't bear it any more,' she wailed, pummelling his chest with her fists. 'I can't bear *you* anymore. Just go away and leave me in peace!'

Horns started blaring from somewhere up the line of vehicles, and then someone announced that the police were on their way. In an instant the ape-man had squeezed himself back into his battered van, his tyres screeching as he roared round the corner, down the hill and out of sight.

Back in the car Janet and Steve sat in silence waiting for the line of traffic to pass. Janet's eye was caught by two black limousines speeding by. She looked at her watch and realised that they were late for the wedding.

She sat back, her eyes closed, feeling suddenly exhausted. Steve covered her hand with his, and this time she didn't pull away but let it rest there, warm and comforting.

'I'm sorry,' he said quietly.

Tears burned at the back of her eyes and she fought to contain them, taking a deep shuddering breath before daring to draw back the lids.

'You've nothing to be sorry for. It's me,' she said, giving him the briefest of smiles.

'I had a letter this morning,' she said after a moment's silence, 'from the hospital.'

'And?'

'They've offered us more tests.' She glanced across trying to judge his reaction.

He was watching her closely. 'So? What do you want to do?'

'I want us to have them.'

He smiled. 'If that's what you want, then that's what we'll do.'

'You don't mind?'

Turning round in his seat he took her face between his hands, refusing to allow her to avert her eyes as he spoke. 'I love you, Janet Crossley, and all I want is to make you happy. If that's what you want to do, then we'll do it.'

Her face broke into a smile as she brought her hands up

to rest over his. 'Even if it means reading dirty magazines and wanking into a bottle?'

He hesitated, then shrugged. 'So what's new?'

Closing the heavy wooden door behind them, they moved out of the warm sunshine into the cool, gloomy interior of the church. The ceremony had begun and the noise of Janet's heels clicking on the stone floor made her wince, the sound echoing loudly in that solemn stillness. Pushing herself up onto tip toes, she gingerly made her way through to the main body of the church, only relaxing when she reached the sanctuary of the red carpet that ran the length of the central aisle. Steve followed her closely, smiling with amusement at her attempt to slip in unnoticed.

A row of huge stone pillars joined by a series of little arches ran down either side of the church, the space behind them cast into deep shadow, while a line of small windows high up the walls threw light down into the nave. Running parallel to the pillars were rows of deep mahogany pews, endless prayer cushions, lovingly decorated in needlepoint, stowed away beneath the seats. Red hymn books lay open on the narrow shelf along each of the backrests. Directly ahead, above the altar, shafts of sunlight beamed down through the stained-glass window where the Madonna sat nursing her child. That same light beat down upon the bride and groom as they stood at the foot of the three stone steps that led up to the chancel.

Screwing up her eyes, Janet peered around the congregation for familiar faces, quickly recognising Susie's family and many of her friends sitting over on the left-hand side.

At the very front sat Susie's mum, Doreen. Dressed in an uncharacteristically bold peacock blue, she somehow managed to look both proud and wistful as she sat staring up at her daughter and her husband as they stood side by side at the altar. By the look of them, the occasion had forced a temporary truce between the two, bringing an unusual calm to their often explosive relationship. Babs – good old Babs – looked radiant in bright pink, while dotted among the first half-dozen pews were a delicious array of hard-faced women in outfits that would brighten the gloomiest morning, and with delightfully flamboyant hats that would have graced Ladies' Day at Ascot. Orange and yellow, blue and lilac, red and green – the palette of colours brought life to that dim, almost subterranean place, lifting the women above the drabness of their surroundings, above the comparative dullness of their besuited spouses.

Halfway along the pews Janet recognised Anna as she turned in profile to glance across the aisle. She looked for Mandy but couldn't see her, and wished now she had called her as she'd planned.

The pews towards the back were filled with friends of Susie and her parents. The younger generation were done up to the nines, many of the girls looking as though they had stepped out of the pages of a glossy magazine. Their suits and dresses were obviously expensive and their designer accessories – the Gucci belt, the Chanel bag, the Japanese fake Rolex watch – were there to make a statement; to make them appear, Janet thought unkindly, quite other than what they were. She considered them fools for being impressed by such things. After all, what could a Rolex do that a Swatch couldn't, apart from decimate your bank account? And what kind of person would want to wear an imitation—gold C-shaped earring, just to show she could afford to buy from Chanel? Janet smiled to herself, thinking that maybe the C wasn't so inappropriate after all!

Several of the older people, mainly women, were there just because they liked a good wedding and had nipped in on their way to Chapel Market do their shopping. Making no concession to the special occasion, they had just wandered in off the street, dressed as they were in drab everyday coats and jackets, their hair sadly lacking the lacquered, coiffured appearance of those in the pews nearer the front.

Pushing Steve ahead of her, Janet made a few strides up the cushioned floor of the aisle and nudged him into an empty pew at the back.

'I wonder where they're up to?' she whispered in Steve's ear. 'I can't hear a soddin' thing!'

Craning her neck to see past the old lady in front of her, Janet looked over towards the altar. Even from the back Susie looked wonderful, and the sight of her brought a lump to Janet's throat. The dress was cream silk and of stunning simplicity. There were no frills, nor flounces nor bows; it fitted her like a sheath, showing every curve as it ran the full length of her body down to her toes. Cut away across her bust and the tops of her arms to reveal silky, smooth shoulders, she managed to achieve a look that was at once serene and sexy. Her hair had been pulled back and a delicate crown of tiny cream roses held in place a short veil of sheer ivory lace.

Karen stood just behind her, putting her weight first on one foot and then the other. The full-length red satin

361

dress she wore had a surprisingly slimming effect. Again, the design was simple as it followed the shape of her body, the top plunging gently into a sweetheart neckline. A ring of small, multi-coloured flowers capped her short, dark bob and as she turned slightly Janet could see that they matched the posy of flowers in her hand, the long, red satin gloves she wore reaching up above her elbows. She felt a tinge of envy that she had not been asked to be maid of honour; not that she would admit it to anyone.

Beside her two small bridesmaids – Lyndsay's daughter and a niece of Joe's – fidgeted restlessly and, bored by the proceedings, whispered to one another, giggling all the while. Their red and white floral dresses were straight out of Alice in Wonderland, gathered at the waist so that the skirts, with their multi-layered netted petticoats, ballooned out and hung, bell-shaped, to their ankles. On their feet they wore tiny satin ballet pumps, while in their hands each held a small basket of flowers to match Karen's, with the same delicate flowers twisted and threaded through their fine blonde hair.

Janet gave a deep sigh. What was it about weddings that made people feel so sentimental? Perhaps it was the look of innocence about young bridesmaids, or perhaps it was the open declaration of two people in love, or maybe – just maybe – it was the endearing naivety of those same two people believing that their marriage would really last forever.

Her mouth forming a bitter smile, she was incredulous now at how stupid she had been all those years ago when she and Mike had married. Certainly she had believed it would be forever, that they would make old bones together, and marriage had reinforced that certainty.

Now, as she looked up the aisle towards where Susie stood beside her husband-to-be – standing at the same altar where Janet had stood with Mike – she felt a sense of sadness and foreboding. Of course she was pleased for Susie; pleased that she'd at last found someone and that she was having such a lovely day to celebrate that. But she hoped her friend didn't expect more from marriage than it was able to deliver; that she didn't believe that marriage in itself would bring her the happiness she clearly longed for.

Up at the altar, the vicar was asking the best man for the rings. Janet craned her neck the other way to see him reach inside his jacket, into the tiny pocket of his jaunty paisley waistcoat, before placing the rings on a small tray the vicar held out towards him. Turning to face Susie and Joe and, smiling kindly down at them, the vicar began the formal wedding service, asking them each in turn to repeat their marriage vows.

Janet strained to hear Susie's voice as she promised to love, honour and obey, and to Joe's quiet pledge to cherish her for as long as they both should live. Listening to them as they repeated each line, she wondered whether either of them had really considered the implications, had really thought about what they were saying, what they were committing themselves to. Closing her eyes she was back there, on her own wedding day, looking up into Mike's face, smiling at him as he looked into her eyes and made his vows. At the thought of it a small sound left her lips and they curled into a twisted smile as she remembered just how hollow those promises had turned out to be . . .

The strangest thing about the whole affair was that Janet had had her suspicions only a week or so before. Going through a pile of washing one afternoon, she had found a note in his jeans. It was nothing much, only a telephone number, but the handwriting was curiously ornate and seemed . . . well, *feminine*.

By itself it wouldn't have alerted her. Normally she'd have set it aside for him, propped it up behind the clock on the mantelpiece, assuming it was some customer wanting Mike to do a private job, perhaps; sort out their electrics for cash and nothing through the firm's books. But there had been other things too, little things that got her instincts twitching. It wasn't just the sex – or lack of it! No, it was just that he was out a lot more often these days. He stayed longer at the pub after work, or spent more time over at his friend Rick's, helping him with the car. And there were other things. When he came in now he went straight into the shower. That wasn't like him. The old Mike used to slob around for a good few hours, drinking tea and reading the evening paper, before he'd even go near water. Not only that, but he was dressing much more smartly these days. He'd even bought new clothes. Susie had commented on it when they'd last been out together.

'He's looking a bit tasty, your Mike. I'd watch he ain't got a bit on the side if I was you, Jan,' Susie had teased. And though Janet had laughed and made a joke of it, the comment had disturbed her. And then the note.

All that afternoon she walked about on tenterhooks, wondering what to do – whether to phone the number and see who answered, or whether to confront Mike when he got in and ask him directly if it was what she feared it

364

was. But in the end she did neither. In the end she threw it in the bin and said nothing.

But that wasn't the end of it. Three days later Janet found herself staring out the kitchen window in a trance, seeing that handwriting in the air before her, the telephone number imprinted so clearly in her memory it was as if she had the piece of paper right there in front of her.

She had to do something. Had to find out one way or the other or she'd burst. But how? How should she go about it?

One thing was certain. She didn't want Mike to know about her suspicions, because if she was wrong . . .

No, she didn't even want to contemplate that. She knew how angry he'd got in the past over her jealousy and mistrust. They'd rowed often enough in their early years for her to know that she'd have to have proof positive before she had it out with him, else he'd make her life a misery.

That was, if he *was* cheating on her.

She'd thought about asking one of her friends what to do — Karen, perhaps, or Susie — but decided against. They'd help, sure, but deep down they'd pity her, and she didn't want that. No. Whatever she did, she'd have to do it alone. So what, then? Should she follow him about and see where he went, or hire a private investigator?

The very thought of it frightened her. Janet couldn't imagine herself doing it. She wasn't sure she had the nerve. Besides, it seemed so . . . disloyal. So sneaky. Strangely, she felt ashamed even for thinking about it.

Another day went by. An awful, uncertain, empty day. She realised she had to do something. Had to, or she'd go stark staring mad. She kept seeing that bloody telephone number. And now she was beginning to look at every woman she passed, in the streets or in the supermarket, and wonder to herself: 'Is it her? Or maybe she's the one?'

Five days after she'd first found the note she summoned up the courage and dialled the number. She let it ring, ten, eleven, twelve times, and was about to put it down when a voice answered. A male voice.

'Mace's Electrical Supplies . . . can I help you?'

She put the phone down.

'Stupid,' she said, staring at herself in the wall mirror beside the phone, a surge of relief washing through her body. 'How could I have been so stupid. It's work. Of course it's work.'

She shook her head, unable to believe she'd worked herself up into such a state over nothing. After all, this was Mike she was talking about. Sure, she loved him, but even she had to admit that he wasn't exactly a perstud. She laughed, then, almost lightheaded now, she went out to the kitchen and put the kettle on.

'Stupid,' she said again, shaking her head, realising that her eyes were moist as she gave way to the relief. 'That'll teach me!' she told herself.

That night she cooked him steak and chips, his favourite, then poured him a lager and put it by his elbow as he sat down at the dinner table.

'What's this for?' he'd asked, looking up at her suspiciously. 'Ain't our anniversary, is it?'

'No,' she said, smiling. 'I just felt like it.' Janet turned away, busying herself about the kitchen, happy, suddenly, inexplicably happy that everything was so normal. 'You fancy an early night?' she asked, glancing at him as she wiped down the top of the cooker.

'Can't tonight,' he said, his mouth half full. 'Got to see someone about a job. Give them an estimate. I promised weeks back. They phoned today. It's over Eltham way. I won't be back 'til gone eleven.'

'Ah . . .' She kept the disappointment from her voice. 'Never mind. It's good that you're getting so much work. We could do with the money.'

'Yeah . . .' he said noncommittally.

She looked at him, saw how he worked his way steadily through his meal, never looking up, and sighed inwardly.

'I'll stay up, if you like? *Cell Block H* is on late. I can watch that . . .'

'Suit yourself,' he said, giving her the barest glance. 'But if I was you, I'd get some kip. Besides, I've 'ad a hard day already. Don't wanna disappoint you now, do I?'

That attempt at familiarity reassured her. For a moment she'd begun to think . . .

Janet crossed the kitchen, touching his shoulder as she went to the kettle and filled it at the tap. 'I'll do you a flask, love. I know how you get thirsty.'

He grunted and pushed his empty plate away. 'If you like.'

She smiled at her reflection in the glass. 'You thought any more about holidays this summer?'

'Holidays?'

'Yeah.' She plugged in the kettle and flicked the switch. 'We ought to book soon if we're gonna get somewhere decent. Mandy said her and Pete might go to Torremolinos this year.'

367

Mike sniffed. 'Well, they're fuckin' welcome to it. Bleedin' shit-hole that place.'

She turned, surprised. 'I thought you liked it.'

'Nah,' he said, stretching, then standing up. 'Anyway. Better get me skates on. I'm late already.'

Janet went to say something. She made a gesture toward the kettle, but he was gone. She heard the door slam. A moment later his van started up and accelerated away.

She went through and stood at the living room window, looking out from the darkness of the room into the empty, bright-lit street, then sighed.

'Ah well,' she said, turning away, speaking to herself. 'I s'pose I should be grateful he works so hard.'

She had waited up for him, but her programme ended, midnight came and went and still he wasn't home. Exhausted, she had finally succumbed to sleep, waking only when the alarm clock rang the next morning.

Reaching across, she fumbled over the bedside table until she found the familiar square shape of the clock. Smothering it with her palm, its shrill ringing cut out abruptly. She leaned forward and peered at it through the slits of her eyes, falling back on her pillow to relish the ten minutes' lie-in she allowed herself before getting up for work.

She had started in the building society just before she and Mike had met, twelve years ago, and had never once thought of leaving. She loved the work, the responsibility; and then there was the social side. They were a great bunch of girls, always having a laugh and a joke.

Sometimes she even felt guilty for being paid to enjoy herself so much.

Pulling the duvet up about her ears she rolled over, snuggling into the warmth of Mike's back, her face tickled by tendrils of his curly hair as she nuzzled into his neck. His skin felt clammy in the heat of the bed, a faint odour of perspiration rising up to fill her nostrils. She breathed in deeply, enjoying this closeness, turned on by the pure animal attraction of his naked body. Dropping her arm around his waist she slowly moved her hand across his stomach, the muscles tensing beneath her touch as she teased the hairs between her fingers. Unfurling her hand she lay it over his penis, disappointed by its softness as it lay there flaccid and unresponsive. He reached down and gently uncurled her fingers, leaving her arm hanging uselessly over the rise of his rump.

'I need to go for a pee,' he said flatly, but made no effort to move.

'Yeah, fine,' she said huffily, rolling onto her back and lacing her fingers behind her head as she stared up at the ceiling, annoyed with herself for offering him the opportunity to reject her once again. She couldn't remember the last time they had made love. Lately Mike always seemed to be too tired, or not feeling well, or needing to rush off somewhere; there was always some excuse. She'd thought seriously about suggesting he go to see their doctor, just in case there really was something wrong, but didn't hold out much hope that he would. He wasn't the type to admit that he wasn't hammering away at it at every opportunity; that he wasn't a *real* man.

She lay there a while longer, the silence broken only by the sound of an occasional passing car, then pushed back the duvet and swung her legs down onto the carpet. Going over to the built-in pine wardrobe, she pulled open the louvre doors and reached inside, grabbing a couple of garments from their hangers and draping them over the crook of her arm. Pulling out some underclothes and tights from the top drawer of the dressing table, she made for the door.

'I'm 'aving a bath!' she called as she went out into the hallway.

She quickly bathed, then dressed in the neat, ultra-sensible clothes her job demanded. The finished effect was one of dull conformity. Not that she cared. If anything, she rather liked it.

Walking into the kitchen she flicked on the kettle and switched on the portable TV. Selina Scott's face filled the screen, making Janet lament her botched attempt to copy the breakfast superstar's neat hairdo. Pushing her damp hair back from her face, she turned down the volume, even as the Rick Astley video of 'Never Gonna Give You Up' began to play. Two mugs, two cereal bowls, two spoons, two knives and two plates were quickly gathered from various cupboards and drawers and efficiently laid out on the small pine table; cornflakes, butter, jam and milk followed.

The kettle clicked off as it came to the boil. Dropping a teabag into each mug she poured the water, leaving the bags to float on the surface. Squeezing each against the side of the mug with a spoon, forcing out the last of the liquid, she swung the teaspoon from mug to bin in one easy, expert movement.

'Mike!' she called along the hallway. 'You getting up? I've made the tea!'

As she stood in the doorway, the sound of the letterbox clanking shut made her turn. She looked down at the newspaper laying open on the doormat. Gathering it up, she went back in the kitchen and sat down to her breakfast.

She flicked through the paper disinterestedly. In her opinion the news was far too depressing to be consumed on a daily basis, like a dose of bran. Most people she knew had enough problems of their own without being asked to worry about what was going on in the rest of the world. It wasn't that she didn't care, she just felt that ignorance was bliss, and what she didn't know couldn't harm her.

Looking up at the clock, she checked the time against her watch, drained the last of the tea from her mug, then walked over to the door.

'Mike?' she yelled. 'You're gonna be late if you don't get up! It's half eight!'

Pouring cornflakes into the bowl she'd set aside for him, Janet put away the box, then placing her own dirty dishes in the sink, she turned on the hot tap to rinse them under the running water. Suddenly, she was aware of him out of the corner of her eye and turned to see him standing in the doorway.

'What you dressed like that for?' she said, looking him up and down as he stood there wearing the casual jeans and sweatshirt which, out of necessity, were reserved for weekends. The firm of electricians Mike worked for insisted their employees wore overalls printed with their emblem, with just a white t-shirt underneath.

'What's the matter,' she said, handing him the mug of lukewarm tea. 'Don't you feel well?'

'Nah, not really,' he said quietly, looking down at the

skin that had formed across the surface of the tea, gently rotating the cup so that it dislodged itself from the sides.

'What's the matter with you?'

'Dunno really.'

'Well, what you gonna do? Go to the doctor's or what?'

He shrugged, still peering down into the mug. She reached across and took it from him, throwing the contents into the sink.

'I'll make you a fresh one,' she said, switching on the kettle.

'No . . .'

'It's no trouble,' she said brightly. 'I've got a couple of minutes before I 'ave to go. How'd it go last night? You get the job?'

'Jan, I . . .'

'What?' she said, dropping another teabag into the mug. Receiving no response she looked over her shoulder at him. His face seemed pale and drawn.

'You don't look well,' she said sympathetically. 'I think you ought to go and see the doctor, and don't let that snotty bird at reception fob you off. Tell her it's an emergency.'

She poured the boiling water into the mug. Having removed the bag, she stirred in the milk and set the mug down on the table.

'There!' she said, nodding towards the chair. 'Sit down a bit. Maybe you'd feel better if you had something to eat?'

Obediently he sat on the chair, resting his elbows on the table and rubbing his hands up and down his face, over and over again. Janet came to stand beside him and gently laying a hand on his head, she ran her fingers through his hair.

'I'd better go,' she said after a moment, glancing up at the clock.

'No, wait!' he responded, reaching up to grab hold of her wrist. 'Sit down. I need to talk to you.' He kicked at the legs of the chair opposite, pushing it back from the table, then guided her round into it so that they sat facing each other across the divide.

'What?' she said, laughing. 'What is it?'

He sat there a moment staring into her smiling face. But no words came.

'Come on, Mike, stop playin' silly buggers! I'll be late. What is it?'

He gave a little shrug. 'I've got to go to hospital. It's Louise . . .'

'Hospital? You all right?' Then she took in what he'd actually said. 'Louise? Who's Louise?'

'She started, you see. Last night. Every fifteen minutes, like. We had to get the ambulance.'

It was like he was talking a different language. She shook her head, as if to clear it. 'What do you mean?'

'Oh, it was okay as it turned out. A false alarm. But they've kept her in. Just in case. That's where I've got to go. Now.'

She sat back, staring at him. 'Louise? Who the . . .'

'Yeah,' he said, as if he hadn't heard her. 'The baby should be here any time now and I said I'd be with her when it came. I've got to go, Jan. I . . .'

Mike stopped, wiping his hand across his face. He was sweating suddenly.

'Oh,' she said, the sound very small. She stared at

him a moment, trying to take it all in, trying to pierce the numbness that had descended on her, but it was impossible. It was as if a door had suddenly opened in the house of her being — a door that led through into a room she'd never been in before; had never thought existed.

Louise. She was called Louise.

'I'll pack your bag,' she said, a frightening calmness in her voice suddenly.

'Nah, it's okay.' Again he wiped his hand across his face, as if to remove something. He gave a little shudder. 'You understand then, Jan?'

Janet stared back at him, mouth open. Then, stirring herself, she stood. 'I've gotta go,' she said. 'I'll be late otherwise.'

She picked up her keys and went out into the hallway. Taking her jacket from the peg, she bent down and picked up her handbag, then opened the door.

Out in the fresh air, she breathed deeply, looked at her watch, then set off for work at a brisk pace.

Louise. Her name was Louise and she was having Mike's baby.

She gave a little shiver, then hurried on. If she didn't hurry she'd be late, and she didn't like being late.

There was an audible, collective sigh of relief from Susie's side of the church as the vicar pronounced the couple man and wife.

In the front pew, in a moment of unguarded, unrestrained gusto Doreen blew her nose into a crumpled ball of damp tissue, the sound of it echoing round the church as it bounced off the grey stone walls. The ring of tiny feathers encircling the brim of her peacock blue sombrero danced around her head like a halo of cotton wool, two of them finally breaking free, floating up and away, caught on the gust of warm air.

Lyndsay nudged her mother in the ribs and made a grab for the feathers, clutching at thin air as they rose and fell with each movement of her arm, stretching further and further in her determination to recapture them as though performing an impromptu aerobics exercise. As they floated up beyond her reach, she lifted her foot onto the seat of the pew, the tight skirt of her lilac linen suit rising up over her thigh as she made to lever herself onto the wooden seat. Waking suddenly from his nap, her husband restrained her with a sharp tug on her elbow, turning pink with embarrassment as their toddler giggled loudly in the seat beside him.

From the pew behind, Babs offered fresh supplies of multi-coloured tissues, keeping back a couple of pink ones – to match her outfit – to dab at the tears gathering at the corners of her eyes. Pushing the empty packet back into the handbag resting on the seat beside her, she sat like Mary Poppins pulling one thing after another out of the neat, black holdall. First was the box of confetti, in readiness for when they moved outside for the photographs, followed by a large silver horseshoe dangling from a length of white satin ribbon, gathered at the top with a tiny posy of artificial forget-me-nots. Next came her trusty instamatic camera, and as she rummaged around for her compact and lipstick, the gentle tinkling of two miniature brandy bottles could be heard as they tumbled together inside the torn lining.

'Christ Almighty, Babs!' Lyndsay whispered, looking

over her padded shoulder at the contents of her aunt's lap. 'You've got everything in there bar the bleedin' kitchen sink!'

'Don't swear!' Doreen hissed from the corner of her mouth, her smile strained, her eyes remaining firmly fixed on the bride and groom as they stood at the altar.

Lyndsay crossed herself, then sat round in her seat.

From the back of the church Janet watched the groom lift Susie's veil from her face, pushing it back over her head to reveal a radiant smile. She wiped a tissue over her tear-streaked cheek. Feeling Steve's eyes on her she averted her face, looking across the aisle to the rows of pews where Joe's family and friends sat watching the couple embrace. There was certainly no mistaking which group of guests belonged to which newly-wed as they sat there quietly, conservatively dressed and displaying not quite as much obvious pleasure in this union as Susie's side. She scanned the rows for a familiar face, but there were none, and it struck her suddenly that this was the first wedding she had been to where she only actually knew one half of the couple getting hitched.

From halfway up the aisle Anna looked back at her and smiled, her face perfectly framed beneath her wide-brimmed black straw hat, the starkness of her black Versace suit relieved only by the whiteness of her skin and the heavy gold chain around her neck. *Trust Anna to get it right*, she thought, looking up to glance at Steve and regretting the impulse purchase sitting on her own head. She lifted her hand a fraction and gave a brief wave with her fingers.

As the bride and groom were led away to sign the register, low murmurings replaced the silence as neighbours aired their views on the dresses, the flowers, the service. Janet turned to Steve and was commenting on the strange way Susie's dad was standing when she felt someone prod her shoulder.

'Shove over!' Mandy said, bending down to whisper in her ear, nudging her along the pew. ''Ave I missed it?'

'Yeah, they're off signing the register,' Janet said as she nudged Steve to move along the seat and Mandy slid into the space beside her. 'Where've you been?' she said, reaching across Steve for a copy of the wedding service to give her.

'To hell and back! Oh, shit I shouldn't say that in here should I,' she said, clasping her hand over her mouth. 'Oh, bugger, I shouldn't say that either, should I. Oh, sod it!'

Janet couldn't help giggling as Mandy became more and more flustered. 'Just calm down,' she said, placing a hand on her arm and looking up a moment to give one of her best 'Up Yours' looks to those who had turned to scowl at them. 'So what happened?'

Mandy took a deep breath, then let it all out again, deciding in that split second that this was not the time to give a potted history of her affair with Jonathan and to go into last night's fiasco with that bastard, Barry. 'Luke was rushed to hospital with appendicitis . . .'

'Oh, no! Is he all right?' Janet nudged Steve, who leaned in to hear what was being said.

'He is now, thank God,' Mandy answered, looking skywards to the painted ceiling of the church.

'When did this happen?'

'Late last night. Pete phoned from the hospital. We've been there all this time.' Mandy looked at her watch.

'Poor little sod!' Janet sympathised, squeezing her friend's hand.

'Yeah, he did look rough, I must say. But the doctors reckon he'll be out in a couple of days and he'll be as right as rain in no time.'

'Where's Pete now?'

'I left him at home in bed. He was knackered. I just ran in, did a quick change,' Mandy held out her arms, indicating that Janet should approve the smart navy and cream suit she wore, 'and dashed round 'ere. Didn't even 'ave time to put me war paint on.' She reached inside her bag and pulled out a small mirror and a lipstick. Pulling a look of distaste at herself in the mirror she quickly applied a coat of the deep pink lipstick. 'Christ! I look like a bleedin' animal! What's Susie look like?' she said, pushing them back inside the bag.

'Ahh, she looks really lovely, doesn't she Steve?' Janet said, prodding him. 'The dress is beautiful. Just right,' and she made a circle shape with her thumb and middle finger.

'And what about Karen?'

'Not too bad considering,' Janet said, confident that Mandy would understand exactly what that meant. *Considering: Karen was a little overweight; scarlet satin wasn't the most subtle choice in the circumstances; considering she never normally wore dresses* and *Susie wouldn't want to be upstaged.*

'I thought it was gonna look a right dog's dinner when Susie described it,' she went on, 'but actually she looks quite glamorous. Quite feminine for a change.'

'And what about the groom?' Mandy said, suddenly

remembering the unknown element in all this. 'What d'you reckon?'

Janet glanced at Steve, who was sitting forward talking to someone in the pew in front, then leaned in towards her, whispering into her ear. 'I've only seen him in profile but he looks pretty dishy, actually. I can see why she got him up the aisle a bit quick. It can't be easy landing someone who's available *and* straight when you get to our age.'

'Especially one who don't 'ave to put an elastic band round his wodger to do the business!' Mandy said seriously.

Janet burst out laughing, clasping a hand over her mouth to stifle the noise. Realising what she had said, Mandy, too, dissolved into helpless laughter.

'How d'you know he doesn't?'

'Good point,' Mandy conceded. 'It don't always follow that hunks are top notch in the dick department. You didn't see how big his feet are, did you?'

Steve raised his eyes skywards as the two of them sat there giggling like schoolgirls, and seeing him they got even worse, oblivious of the disapproving looks being thrown their way from all around the church.

'Anyway, how do you know about things like that, respectable married woman like you?' Janet strained to keep the volume down as the words squeaked out.

Mandy raised a hand to wave at Anna, who was smiling at them from her seat near the front of the church.

'Who's that next to Anna?' she said.

Janet craned her neck round but couldn't get a look at his face and shrugged her shoulders.

Suddenly, realising that all other close family and friends were up there in the front pews, Mandy said,

'Why are you sitting back 'ere instead of up there with Anna and the others?'

Janet turned to look at Steve and they both smiled as she turned back to Mandy. 'Tell you later,' she whispered.

Mandy was just about to open her mouth when the music started and the congregation rose to their feet.

As Susie emerged by the altar there was no other word for her but stunning. Janet could see her properly for the first time and was touched by her innocent beauty, the fact that she had decided to get married in church seeming somehow fitting and appropriate, despite what some people thought. Smiling broadly, she held onto Joe's arm, obviously delighting in the novelty of her new role.

At the top of the steps the newly-weds stood side by side, waiting for bridesmaids and best man to assume their positions. Karen stood immediately behind Susie, self-consciously fiddling with her neckline as it plunged down to reveal rather too much of her impressive cleav-age. Next to her the best man leaned in and whispered something in her ear, making her smile and drop her hands to her sides.

'I think Karen's scored!' Janet said, their faces coming into focus as she placed her glasses on her nose.

'Who with?' Mandy asked quickly, rummaging in her handbag.

'The best man.'

'Shit!' she hissed.

'What's the matter?' Janet said, stretching sideways to see past the extravagant hat in front of her.

'I've left me glasses in the car!' Mandy said, dropping her bag onto the seat behind her. 'What's he like?'

380

'Looks like a bit of all right from here.'

'Don't mind me,' Steve said good naturedly.

Janet stood on tip toes to kiss him affectionately on the cheek. 'We won't!' she said.

'Good on her, I say,' Mandy laughed. 'Anyway, it's tradition ain't it, the bridesmaid and the best man. D'you remember my wedding?' Once again the two of them burst out laughing at the shared memory, but this time the noise was drowned out by the sound of organ music as it vibrated around the church.

Steve smiled down indulgently, waiting to be drawn into this intimacy, to become privy to the joke.

Janet glanced up at him. 'Well,' she began slowly, 'we were all Mandy's bridesmaids — me, Anna, Karen and Susie — and Pete's brother, Barry, was Best Man. He couldn't keep his hands off Susie all day long, followed her round like a dog sniffing a bitch on heat, with his tongue dragging across the floor. Come the evening he was slobbering all over her on the dance floor, but it wasn't till everyone went out to the car park . . .'

'Pitch black it was,' Mandy added. 'We were just going off on our honeymoon . . .'

'Yeah, well, we all went out there and Mandy and Pete ran off to their car as the rest of us chased them with rice and confetti. Mandy jumps in the front as Pete opens the back door to chuck in a bag or something . . .'

'My little vanity case . . .'

'And who should be on the back seat with her frock tucked up under her armpits and her knickers round her ankles?'

'Oh, no!' Steve groaned.

'Yep!' Janet beamed. 'And who should be squatting

down between her legs with his trousers round his knees . . . ?'

Steve slowly shook his head from side to side while the two friends leaned in to one another, relishing the memory of that moment.

'I'll never forget your face!' Janet giggled helplessly.

'I'll never forget me mother's face!' Mandy said, serious suddenly. 'It took me an hour to explain what it was they was doing!'

All three of them burst out laughing, calming slowly as they waited for the wedding party to file down the church, taking them out into the bright sunshine. Assembled finally, they set off, carefully negotiating the three narrow stone steps down onto the red carpet that ran the length of the aisle and almost up to the large wooden doors at the front of the church. Slowly they began to make their way along the aisle and as they passed through the church, family and friends reached out to the newly-weds to squeeze their arms and pat their shoulders in congratulation. Susie beamed at the gathering, turning her head from side to side as she passed each pew, delighting in the attention, savouring her big moment.

As they passed by, guests would file out and join the congregation so that by the time they were halfway down the aisle, the shuffling numbers had swollen to almost eighty people.

A few paces ahead of the party the photographer pigeon-stepped backwards, shooting pictures as he moved with sure-footed confidence towards the doors. His slight, wiry frame weaved with agility despite the plethora of equipment it bore. His camera hung from a leather strap around his neck, while another dangled from his shoulder on brightly-coloured striped webbing. From the other shoulder a blue canvas equipment bag swung backwards and forwards as he moved, knocking against the upturned pocket flap of his scruffy tweed jacket. Every few steps he would push a lock of greasy black hair back from his forehead.

As he neared the doors the ushers pulled them open, inviting a fresh breeze to invade the church. It blew straight up the aisle and through the approaching congregation, causing fabric to rustle and flimsy hats to wobble precariously on coiffured heads.

'What you doing?' Janet said, glancing down to see Mandy frantically pushing her hand around the inside of her voluminous handbag.

'Looking for me camera. I'm sure I put it in 'ere somewhere.'

As Susie and the rest of them got closer, Janet raised her hand to wave and gave the bride a warm, genuinely affectionate smile. She was glad that things were finally going right for her; that she had finally found someone who was better than the wham-bam-and-thank-you-ma'am merchants she'd grown accustomed to.

'See what I mean?' she whispered in Mandy's ear, her eyes fixed on the groom. 'He's a bit of all right, don't you think? I reckon they make a lovely couple, don't you, Mand?'

There was no response, and as Janet turned her face to look at Mandy, she was shocked by the transformation in her friend's face. With the colour and stillness of a stone statue, Mandy stood motionless, her eyes staring straight ahead, unblinking. Her mouth sat open as though she had been paralysed in mid-sentence.

'Mand?' Janet said quietly, placing a hand on her arm and shaking her gently. 'Mandy, what's the matter? You all right?'

But there was no response. It was as though she had drifted into a trance.

The next few moments seemed to Janet to move in slow motion.

Glancing up she caught Susie's eye as the bride walked towards her, less than ten feet off. In that split second Mandy pulled away from her, falling into the aisle, where she produced a spasm of projectile vomiting of such impressive proportions that the groom's footwear was dramatically transformed from shiny black to slimy puce before Mandy collapsed on top of them without decorum, her body slumped across the width of the bright red carpet.

Pandemonium ensued as the wedding guests, trapped now behind the bride and groom, strained to see what was going on, pushing forward and threatening to tumble in a heap amidst the contents of Mandy's stomach.

Janet stepped out, bending down beside Mandy and cradling her head in her lap, brushing the matted hair away from her face. She looked up for Steve. 'Can you get her a glass of water from somewhere.'

'Where?' he shrugged, looking about him.

'I don't know!' she shouted impatiently. 'Get someone to perform a bloody miracle!'

'Mandy? Mand, it's me,' she said softly, stroking her friend's face gently.

There was no response. 'Mandy! Mand, wake up!' she said a little louder now, her voice edged with panic now as she slapped her friend across the cheek.

Slowly Mandy opened her eyes, for a moment uncertain of her whereabouts, her eyes scanning the bizarre panorama above her as celestial cherubs threatened to fly down from the gilded ceiling and shoot her through the heart with their little bows and arrows. As she gradually took in the faces of those gathered around her, the full horror of what had happened hit her. Her head shot round sharply and she stared up into Susie's face.

The bride towered over her, a mixture of sympathy and annoyance playing across her features, as she hitched up her dress to prevent it from trailing in the spreading vomit. Pushing back against the press of bodies like a policewoman on crowd control, her eyes jumped from the vicar, silhouetted beneath the arch of the open doorway, his hands clasped together in silent prayer, to the photographer, standing on the seat of the pew, a broad grin on his face as he clicked away with his camera, to Mandy laying prostrate across the aisle in a pool of sick.

Pushing her arm through to link it with Joe's, she turned to look imploringly at her new husband but the bridegroom was staring down at Mandy in a state of shock. There was a look of complete terror on his face, taking on a ghostliness as the colour completely drained from it.

'You bastard!' Mandy said quietly, struggling to her feet, then falling to her knees as the soles of her shoes slid on the vomit. 'You *bastard*!' she repeated, loudly this time, a look of pure hatred in her eyes as she glared up at the startled groom.

'Mandy!' Janet rebuked her, reaching down and grabbing hold of her arm, hauling Mandy back to her feet.

'Don't Mandy me!' she hissed, pulling away from her, her face contorted with agony. 'I'm gonna kill 'im!' she screeched, pushing herself up from her position on all fours. 'I'm gonna smash his fuckin' face in!'

Janet glanced over her shoulder at the vicar and smiled apologetically. Bewildered, she turned back and took hold of Mandy by the shoulders, not really knowing what her friend planned to do next, but feeling this was probably the appropriate course of action. As she looked up, it was like they were two players on a stage as a sea of faces stared back at them, the first three rows in the stalls, as it were, with those at the back elevated to the dress circle as they stood on the pews.

Steve suddenly entered stage left, carrying a glass of water. 'Here, Mand, drink this,' he said soothingly, offering it up to her, unaware of the recent outburst.

Reaching out for it, Mandy grabbed hold of the plastic tumbler and in one swift movement swung it through the air, its contents splashing across the bridegroom's face as he stood open-mouthed, water dripping from his dark hair and the ends of his sagging bow tie.

The whole congregation stood paralysed with disbelief until Karen pushed past Susie, grabbed hold of Mandy by the shoulders and swiftly turned her about, pushing her in the direction of the doors.

'Quick! Help me get her out of here,' she whispered to Janet, and meeting no resistance, the two of them, one on either side, frog-marched Mandy's limp body along the aisle and onto the church steps, leaving a stunned silence in their wake.

Mandy stared straight ahead, across the narrow road

to the park opposite. 'I can't believe it!' was all she said, over and over again. 'I can't fuckin' believe it!'

'We'd better get her out of sight,' Karen said quickly, speaking over her head. 'What about the park?'

Janet nodded. 'I'll see to her. You get back to Susie. She'll want you in the photos.'

'Just a minute ladies,' came a treacly voice from beside a climbing rose bush off to the side. 'Just a couple more.' The photographer moved round in front of the gate to better his angle.

Janet stepped in front of Mandy blocking his view. 'If you don't piss off you little lump of dog turd I'll ram that fucking camera where the sun don't shine!' she spat down at him, her eyes narrowing with a look of pure venom. And as he turned tail, briskly moving round to the side of the church and out of sight, she shouted, 'Arsehole!' at his retreating back.

'Okay,' she said, turning to Karen. 'What's goin' on? D'you know what all this is about?'

'You're not going to believe it!' Karen said, shaking her head, not sure she believed it herself.

'What? What is it?'

Karen took a deep breath, squeezed Mandy's arm, and said quietly, 'I reckon Susie's just married Mandy's lover!'

Despite the clear blue sky, there was a chill in the air. The two women sat together on an old wooden bench at the far end of the park so that if they looked up they could see the elegant spire of the church rising above the tree tops. That part of the square was empty with most other adults gathered at the other end, watching their children as they ran noisily around the playground or indulged their imagination as they climbed amongst the cluster of trees and bushes covering the grassy mound beyond.

The sound of bells filled the silence as they sat holding hands, each reliving in their mind the fiasco of moments before.

'D'you want to talk about it?' Janet asked finally, gently squeezing Mandy's hand as it lay, limp and cold, inside her own.

Mandy sat with her head bowed, defeated. She made no response.

'Is it true what Karen said? About you and Joe?'

'Jonathan . . .'

'What?'

'His name's Jonathan,' Mandy said, lifting her head. 'Or should I say Lying Bastard!'

Janet shook her head, unable to take it all in. 'But didn't you *know*?' she said incredulously.

Mandy flashed her a look of contempt.

'Sorry,' Janet apologised. 'But the whole thing really does seem pretty incredible.'

'*You* think it's incredible!' she said reproachfully. 'How d'you think *I* feel?'

'I know, I know,' Janet soothed, squeezing her hand once more.

'How could he do it to me? Marrying my best mate!'

'Presumably he didn't *know* she was your best mate, unless he's really thick. Otherwise he'd have realised there'd be a scene. Unless he's got a death wish, of course.'

The memory of Mandy grossing up all over his feet flashed into Janet's mind and she bit her lip to prevent herself from giggling. 'Bloody hell, Mand,' she added, as though the thought had only just occurred, 'what's Susie gonna say?'

Judging by the look on Mandy's face, this was the first thought she'd given her friend, and suddenly she was struck by the full horror of the situation.

The church bells rang relentlessly.

'Shit! What am I gonna say to her? How am I gonna explain?'

'You don't!' Janet said emphatically.

A mongrel wandered in through the gate and sauntered over to them, pawing at Janet's leg. 'Piss off!' she growled irritably, kicking it away before turning back to Mandy. 'You can't say nothing because it's her bloody wedding day, for Christ's sake, and she won't take kindly to being told her old man's been having some pre-nuptial rumpy-pumpy with her best mate!'

Mandy looked at her imploringly. 'It wasn't *like* that!'

'It might not have been like that for you, but he's just walked up the aisle with someone else, Mand. No, take it from me, he wasn't after the full service, he just wanted a quick oil change!'

Mandy held her face in her hands, her shoulders shaking as she cried.

'I'm sorry, love,' Janet said, more quietly now, conscious that she'd said the wrong thing yet again. 'Look, Mand, it wasn't your fault. You didn't know Jonathan was Joe, did you? You're not the one who did the dirty on Susie. *He* did. He was the one doing the cheating, he was the one playing away from home.'

'Oh, my God!' Mandy gasped, dropping her hands and grabbing hold of Janet's arm. 'Pete!'

'Oh, shit!'

'Oh, fuck, Jan. What am I gonna do? It's bound to come out and then the shit'll well and truly hit the fan!'

Janet rolled her eyes to heaven. 'Now, let's just calm down,' she said, turning to face Mandy and taking a hand in each of hers. 'Let's just sit and think a minute.'

The two women sat holding hands, staring into one another's face, the wheels and cogs almost visibly turning as they struggled for inspiration. Out of the corner of her eye Janet was conscious of a young boy approaching on a bicycle. 'Lesbos!' he called out as he passed them, pushing hard on the pedals to speed his escape. 'Titty-lickers!'

'Mouthy little bastard!' Janet said under her breath, looking over her shoulder to see him disappear through the bottom gate and out onto the road.

Turning her attention back to a forlorn-looking Mandy she nodded decisively. 'Right,' she said, 'this is what we'll do! We'll explain about you having been up all night 'cos of Luke being in the hospital, an' all that, and we'll say that 'cos you were so knackered they gave you some stuff to take . . .'

'Stuff?' Mandy stared back at her like a codfish. 'What d'you mean? *Stuff*.'

'You know, some kind of drug or something to perk you up. Anyway, we'll say you took this drug and felt fine but then when you were in the church you came over all funny. You felt really sick and then you started hallucinating . . .'

'Hallucinating?'

'Yeah, you know, thought you were seeing things.'

'I know what it bloody well means. But you really think anyone'll believe us?'

'Yeah, 'course they will!' Janet assured her, feeling pleased with herself. 'Anyway, you got any better suggestions?'

Mandy shook her head. She still looked as though she wished the ground would swallow her up.

'Right! So, we say you started hallucinating and you thought Joe . . .'

'Jonathan!'

'Joe, Jonathan, whatever his fucking name is, you mistook him for a bloke you thought had attacked you. No, I know! You thought he'd raped you, and you wanted to kill him.' Janet smiled expectantly at Mandy, who stared back at her, a look of utter dismay on her face.

'Sounds a pile of unbelievable crap to me . . .'

'Well, I think it's a bloody brilliant idea,' Janet said, disappointed by her friend's lack of enthusiasm or appreciation.

'But they might know by now,' she said quietly, tears gathering along the rim of her eyes. 'He might 'ave told them.'

'No, no, no,' Janet reassured her. 'Karen'll have smoothed it over. Listen! You sit here a minute while I nip over and see if I can see Steve. I'll get him to drive you back to our place in your car and you can 'ave a shower and change – just rummage through my wardrobe – and I'll get off to the reception and sort things out.'

'But how can I face him?'

'Steve won't take any notice.'

'No, not Steve, you div! Jonathan. How can I face Jonathan?'

'How can *you* face *him*?' Janet bristled, suddenly indignant on her friend's behalf. '*He* should be the one worrying about facing *you*! The words *stringing* and *balls* are probably at the forefront of his tiny little mind at the moment. Yeah,' she said, nodding her head with satisfaction, 'I bet his underpants are pretty full, and I don't mean with his wedding tackle!'

Mandy held a hand to her mouth, smiling in spite of herself.

'Trust me!' Mandy sighed, leaning back against the bench and looking up at the sky despairingly. 'First time I stray from the straight and narrow and he turns out to be an utter shit!'

'What did you expect? A knight in shining armour!'

Mandy sighed, silent a moment, then: 'I really thought he loved me, you know, Jan?' she said, shaking her head at her own naivety. 'Can you believe that?'

Touched by her vulnerability, Janet's eyes moistened, her love for Mandy at that moment as strong as it had ever been. 'It's easy to mistake lust for love when that's what we want to believe.'

'I've been a right silly cow, ain't I?' Mandy said, sitting up, a deep sigh passing through her.

'Haven't we all at one time or another!' Janet replied, with feeling. 'Now, listen, I'm gonna go and find Steve. You wait here and I'll send him over. Then I'll go and have a word with Susie.'

'Poor Susie,' Mandy whimpered, threatening to burst into tears again.

'Yeah, poor Susie!'

Groups of wedding guests were huddled together in the gardens behind the church, and there was only one subject being discussed. Janet looked around for Karen

392

and spotted her sitting on a bench at the far end deep in conversation with the best man, Jonathan's old friend, Simon Paxman.

Seeing her approach them, Simon nodded in Janet's direction and Karen turned round, saw her and jumped to her feet, hitching her skirt as she ran up the path towards her.

'Where is she?' she said, her face full of concern.

'Over there,' Janet said solemnly, nodding towards the park. 'I'm gonna get Steve to take her back to my place so she can get cleaned up, then he'll bring her on to the do.'

Simon had joined them and he and Karen exchanged looks.

'D'you think that's a good idea?' Karen asked doubtfully.

'What d'you mean?'

'Well, in view of what's happened. D'you think it's a good idea for Mandy to turn up. Things are pretty tense already,' Karen added, laughing ironically at the gross understatement. 'Christ knows what'll happen once Susie gets a minute alone with Joe.'

'Jonathan.'

'What?'

'Oh, never mind!' Janet said, waving her hand dismissively. 'Look, the thing is . . .' She stopped in mid-sentence and looked at Simon.

'It's okay,' Karen reassured her. 'Simon knows everything. He knew Joe was having an affair and put two and two together.'

'You knew!' she said, the accusation slapping him across the face.

'It's not *my* fault!' Simon said, putting his hands up defensively. 'How could I stop him?'

'Men! You're all the bloody same. You just can't keep the sodding thing inside your pants, can you? The first whiff of a bit of available crumpet and you're off like a badger up a drainpipe!'

'Hey, hang on! *I* haven't done anything.'

'I thought you liked Susie,' she persisted.

'I did. I do. This was nothing to do with Susie,' he stumbled. 'It was just a last-ditch fling. A quick . . .'

'Shag! Yes, well, I'm sure my friend who's sitting over in the park crying her eyes out will be very comforted to hear that. It'll make her feel a *lot* better.'

'I didn't mean . . .'

'Look!' Karen interceded. 'This is getting us nowhere. What are we going to tell everyone?'

'Well, as it so happens,' Janet said, scowling at Simon, 'I've had an idea.'

Susie and Joe stood beneath the drooping boughs of an ancient ash tree. She was gazing up into his face, the fixed smile on her lips revealing neither warmth nor happiness, as he looked down upon her with a mixture of dread and apprehension.

The photographer did his best to cajole them, to encourage them to relax and enjoy this, the happiest day of their lives, but somehow his words fell on deaf ears and, exhausted from the strain of it all, he decided to work swiftly through his portfolio of practised shots in an attempt at damage limitation.

'*Okay, Mr President*,' he murmured beneath his breath, focusing again, '*now smile towards the grassy*

394

knoll . . .' With most of the guests gathered either side of the pathway leading to the tall, iron gates, Janet stood alone against the church wall watching the bride and groom ready themselves to run the gauntlet of hollow congratulations. The photographer was issuing his final set of instructions when Susie looked across and saw her there, and was still talking as she walked away, over to where Janet stood.

'You look lovely,' Janet said, smiling at her before leaning across to kiss her on the cheek.

Susie gave a brief smile. 'How is she?'

'She'll be fine. It was the drugs they gave her.'

'Yeah, so Karen said.'

'They must've been too strong for her . . .'

'I'm not completely stupid, Jan,' Susie said quietly.

Janet dropped her eyes, staring at her feet as she stood fidgeting, grinding stones into the damp earth with the toe of her shoe.

'I'm so sorry, Suse,' she said looking up into her friend's face, a lump rising in her throat. 'Mandy didn't know, you know.'

'Yeah, I know,' she said, nodding. 'It's not her fault.' She threw a glance at Joe who stood nervously playing with his tie as he watched them talking.

'I don't think it meant anything. To Joe, I mean. I don't think it meant anything to him.'

Susie looked across at him again and gave a deep sigh. 'No,' she said wearily, turning back to Janet, 'I don't s'pose it did.'

'So what are you gonna do now?'

Susie looked up at the sky, the sun obliterated now by the gathering storm clouds. 'Right now I'm gonna get into the car before it pisses down, then I'm gonna get as drunk as a skunk.' She looked across to Joe who smiled tentatively.

'He looks as though he'll try and make amends,' Janet said, looking across to where he stood, amused by his obvious discomfort.

'Yeah, well he ain't gonna get away with this one so easy,' she said, looking away disdainfully as he tried to coax a smile from her. 'All I wanted was a nice, normal wedding to the man of my dreams. And what do I get? A fucking farce where the husband from hell's been knocking off me best mate! All I'm waiting for is an ex-wife in a french maid's outfit to turn up and me old man to drop his trousers! Am I unlucky or what?'

Janet stood there shaking her head. 'Oh, Suse,' she said, biting her bottom lip before a small snort of laughter escaped her. 'All that puke!'

'I know,' Susie said, a look of distaste on her face. 'It's all in his shoes, you know,' she nodded in Joe's direction. 'He wanted to go and change but I wouldn't let him. Serves him right, the cheating bastard!'

'What did the vicar say?'

'He was quite good really. Says it happens a lot.'

'What? People throwing up all over the church?'

'Yeah. Nerves an' all that. Anyway, your Steve's in there helping to clear it up, bless him.'

The photographer was beckoning her from his position near the gate.

Susie leaned toward Janet. 'If I get any more grief from that slitty-eyed little git he'll get that camera shoved up his arse, wide-angled lens an' all!' she said under her breath. She looked up and gave him a cloyingly sweet smile, then nodded to indicate that she understood what he wanted. 'I'd better go,' she said, turning to Janet. 'I'll see you at the hall.'

Janet ran a hand down Susie's back affectionately, then watched as she hitched up her dress and made off along the path. After a couple of steps Susie stopped and turned back. 'Thanks, Jan . . . you know, for trying to help an' all that,' she said, a look of quiet resignation on her face.

'S'all right,' Janet said quietly, smiling sadly as Susie walked away, silently wishing her all the luck in the world.

It looked as though she was going to need it.

Behind the two Rollers carrying the bride and groom, the bridesmaids and best man, a motley assortment of cars and vans tagged along in a bizarre cavalcade.

Janet walked across to the railings surrounding the park, peering through the bars to check that Mandy was all right. She could see her, there where she'd left her, sitting on the bench at the far end of the Square, her head hung backwards over the top of the backrest as she stared up at the darkening sky.

Turning round, Janet leaned against the black iron railings, looking out across the narrow road towards the church. Steve saw her the moment he walked out onto the steps, quickly skipping down them and across the road as cars began to draw up carrying the guests for the next wedding.

He was a couple of strides away when he began slowly shaking his head.

'I might've known it wouldn't be a straightforward

little wedding. Not where your mates are involved,' he said, smiling.

'Oh, God, I know! Was there a lot of mess?'

'Well, what with Mandy spreading her load over the red Axminster and some of the more moronic guests trampling it in with their size tens – yes! You could say there was!'

Janet laughed and went to give him a hug. 'Christ, you stink!' she said, drawing back. 'It must be on your shoes or something.'

'Shit! I s'pose I'd better go home and change,' he said, checking the soles of his shoes.

'Oh, good,' she said, 'then you won't mind taking Mandy with you, will you?' and nodded into the Square.

'What for?'

'So she can change. What d'you think? At the moment she looks like she's been pebble-dashed. Sit her on a couple of carrier bags or something.'

Steve looked into the park, staring off into the distance, nothing in his look indicating whether or not he had located Mandy.

Janet stood behind him so that her body rested slightly into his back.

'That's nice,' he said, pushing his body against hers before attempting to turn round to face her.

But she leaned against him, preventing him from moving. 'I do love you,' she whispered.

He dropped a hand down to his side and reached back, stroking her thigh through the thin fabric of her skirt.

'I love you, too,' he said, resting his hand over the cheek of her bum.

They stood there a moment, moulded as one, until the first drops of rain began to fall.

'Jan?' Steve said seriously.

'Yes?' she replied quietly, nuzzling into his neck.

'I don't s'pose you fancy a quick one in the back of the car before we go?'

Rain beat down relentlessly upon all sides of the Fiesta, the water flowing freely down every window, obscuring Janet's view out onto the deserted street. As the heavens opened people had scurried for cover, like a wave of ants, sheltering beneath the umbrella of trees at one end of the park. She had shouted across to Mandy to get to her car and Steve would join her there, but for the moment he was here, beside her.

'We can't,' she protested faintly.

'Why not?' Steve said, negotiating the gearstick to lean across and nuzzle into the warm softness of her neck.

'I'm on. It'd be too messy.'

'We don't have to go all the way,' he said, nibbling the delicate shell of her ear.

'Huh! I've heard that one before. Besides, someone might see us.'

'Go on with you, there's no-one about.'

She giggled as he reached up inside her jacket and gently squeezed her breast.

'And anyway, my skirt's too tight.'

'Poor excuse. Take it off,' he murmured, pulling aside the silky fabric of her bra, feeling the small, hard nipple between his fingertips.

'Steve!'

'Take it off,' he said, more urgently now, and moved his hand down her bare skin to the zip at her waist, easing it down over the curve of her hip as she lifted herself from the seat, allowing him to push the skirt to the floor.

He looked down at her legs, the sight of the pale band of skin above her grey stocking tops exciting him further. He reached across for her hand and placed it over his erect penis.

Janet gave a self-satisfied smile and increased the pressure, pushing down on the swollen member, its hardness unrelenting, responding to her touch, straining to be released.

As Steve's fingers fumbled urgently with the buttons of her jacket, she reached across with both hands and unzipped his fly, delicately reaching inside with just two cool, slim fingers, to draw his penis out to meet her lips as she leaned forward invitingly. As her warm, moist mouth played over the tip of his swollen member, Steve groaned gently, the sound heightening Janet's own pleasure, increasing her own desire.

Slowly she lifted her head, knowing she had brought him to the edge of orgasm, and leaning back against the seat, she allowed him to unclip the front fastening on her bra, pushing his face inside her open jacket to take her nipple into his mouth, his teeth delicately pulling at the darkened stalk as it rose provocatively from her small, unspoilt breasts.

His hand moved down over the top of her scanty, silky briefs, and with painful slowness his fingers played upon her skin until she pushed his hand away, wanting him inside her.

'Make love to me.'

'But I thought you said . . .'

'Forget what I said. Fuck the upholstery!'

Sliding across into the passenger seat, Steve watched her as she moved above him, deftly preparing herself for him. Gently, he eased her down on to him, her eyes closing as a wave of pleasure washed through her body, exposing every nerve end with each delicious thrust of his body, oblivious of the discomfort as her head and shoulders bashed against the windscreen with quickening regularity, until explosively, simultaneously, they came.

A few seconds later a clap of thunder sounded overhead and as they both laughed, Steve's penis was suddenly expelled, soft and damp, upon the dark, curly hair around his groin, causing them both to giggle.

'Christ Al-bloody-mighty,' Janet complained, trying to launch herself into the driver's seat, her butt almost inside the glove compartment, 'it's not so much a case of who's going to lie in the wet patch, but who's gonna get the bloody brake handle up their bum!'

Steve remained slumped in the seat, his eyes closed, his breathing heavy.

'Here, don't bloody conk out on me,' Janet said, nudging him. 'I don't fancy being plastered over the Islington Gazette — "Stiff Found In Car".' There was a moment's pause, then. 'D'you get it, Steve?' she said, laughing suddenly; '"*Stiff* Found In Car".'

Steve opened one eye, looked across at her, closed it again and blindly reached down below his knees to retrieve his trousers.

Outside the rain was beginning to ease and, directly

above them, the sun was emerging, bright and warm, from behind a cluster of huge, dark clouds.

'Look!' Janet said, pointing up, through the window. 'The sun's coming out. There's going to be a rainbow!'

~ Karen ~

As the limousine pulled onto the housing estate where the reception was to be held, Karen lifted Lyndsay's daughter, Jodie, onto her knee to give her a better view out of the window. Heads turned as the car made its slow way along the driveway, negotiating the speed bumps and avoiding the odd toddler that strayed into its path. Along the balconies overlooking the narrow, tarmac road, a number of women stood with their arms folded, resting on the rough brickwork, their faces smiling down on the group as it headed toward the community hall. They loved a good wedding.

Moments earlier they had looked down on the bride and groom as they stepped from their car, hurriedly making their way into the low, brick-built block to avoid the rain.

As Karen's car pulled up outside the main doors the driver of the other car was pulling away. Leaning out of his window, he shouted across to her driver, his eyes following a group of young lads who were walking aimlessly around the courtyard.

'Watch those little bastards,' he warned, nodding his

head in their direction. 'I 'ad me silver lady 'alf-inched last time I was 'ere.'

'Cheers!' Karen's driver replied, scowling across at them and winding up his window as the other car sped away.

Stepping out onto the path Karen ran her hands down her sides, smoothing the clinging satin dress down the length of her body, thankful that she wouldn't have to wear it for much longer. Simon made a great show of helping the two young bridesmaids out of the limo, swinging each of them high up into the air before delivering them, giggling, next to Karen on the narrow pavement.

'Thanks very much,' Simon said, turning to the driver who was closing the door behind him. 'You got time for a drink?'

The man lifted his grey driver's cap from his head, smoothed back his hair and replaced it. 'Better not,' he said, nodding towards the group of boys who were now sitting along the low wall in front of the flats, eyeing their prey like a clutch of vultures. 'In the time it'd take to down half a lager they'd 'ave me bleedin' wheels off! No, ta. I'll be away, if it's all the same to you.'

As he walked round the front of the Rolls Royce to get to the driver's seat, he pulled a large white handkerchief from his trouser pocket, scrunched it into a pad and rubbed it over the already highly polished silver statuette, flashing a self-satisfied smile at the group of boys as they looked on from across the yard. As the car purred away Karen placed a hand over her mouth to hide her amusement, and wondered whether he'd heard the boys' taunt of 'Wanker!' as they chased after the car, seeing it off their territory.

Ushering the two young bridesmaids inside the building, Karen and Simon stepped through into the brightly-lit lobby area, its fluorescent strips glaring down relentlessly, highlighting each crack and blemish on the smoke-scarred walls and ceiling. Off to one side stood four tubular coat racks, their empty metal hangers still dancing on the incoming breeze. Along another wall were two doors leading to the toilets. The two girls ran off, giggling, into the Ladies, the door slamming shut behind them.

Karen and Simon exchanged a smile. In the short time they had known each other, and through the unfortunate events of the past hour, they had formed a kind of bond; had become allies in the battle to suppress the truth. At *all* costs.

In front of them, a pair of double doors, the upper panels made up of frosted glass, led into the hall where the reception would be held. Above them a banner of silver, pink and white foil printed with the words 'Congratulations Susie & Joe' rustled gently. Taking a deep breath, preparing herself for the charade to follow, Karen took no more than two steps towards it then stopped dead. The most Almighty racket had started up on the other side of the doors. With one hand gripping the door handle and her ear pressed to the glass she stood listening to the battle being fought, the opponents clearly unmatched as Susie's tirades rang out in a clear screech that filled and echoed around the hall like chalk scraping a blackboard, completely overwhelming Joe's pathetic attempts to plead his innocence.

Simon gripped the handle of the other door and pressed

his car to its glass panel, his face looking into Karen's as he winced at his friend's feeble attempts to defend himself.

'What are you doing?'

Karen looked round to see the two little bridesmaids, standing side by side like Tweedledee and Tweedledum, staring up at Simon and her, quizzical looks on their faces.

'Nothing,' Karen whispered back.

'Yes you are,' Jodie persisted. 'What are you doing?'

'Sshh!' Karen hissed, pressing a finger to her lips. 'Go and play.'

'Where?'

Karen looked around the small lobby. 'Well, go and sit down over there,' she said, nodding towards a couple of stacking chairs beside the coat racks. 'That's what bridesmaids do.'

'Well, why ain't you doin' it?'

Karen rounded on her tormentor. 'Because I'm the *chief* bridesmaid.'

It seemed to do the trick. Pouting, the girls walked across and slumped down on the hard chairs, covering their mouths as they whispered into their small, cupped hands.

'We're thirsty,' they sang in unison, smiling at one another as they mouthed the words.

'Shut up, munchkins,' Simon growled, straining to catch what was being said on the other side of the door. The girls were so taken aback by his changed tone they burst into tears.

'Oh, shit!' Simon said under his breath, pressing his ear back against the glass.

Inside, voices rose and fell like a bad radio transmission,

as Susie and Joe moved around the hall, she throwing accusations and abuse across the abyss while he ducked and dived to avoid them.

'Do you think we should go in?' Karen whispered doubtfully. 'Before she makes herself a widow!'

'Oh I don't know,' Simon replied thoughtfully, 'seeing as how the shit's hit the fan, we might as well let her give him hell now rather than have it carry on through the reception. The last thing we want is this spraying round the room like pellets from a bunny's bottom!'

Karen nudged him in the ribs, laughing in spite of herself, and looked over to where the girls sat. They scowled back. Jodie poked out her tongue.

At the sound of car doors slamming and the sudden murmurings from outside, Karen turned, spotting several familiar faces through the clear glass panel of the main door.

'Shit! They're here!' she said, relinquishing the handle as though it were red hot. 'What'll we do?'

'Stall them,' Simon suggested, straightening himself and tightening the knot on his tie. 'And *smile* '

Seeing her mother approach, Jodie became brave, imbued with a sudden confidence. 'I'm gonna tell my mum about you two!' she threatened.

But Jodie was small fry compared with Karen's other worries and Karen dismissed her with a look she'd used many times before on any number of her misbehaving pupils — a look that told them they crossed her at their peril.

Before they could work out just how exactly they were going to forestall the descending hoards, the front doors swung open, a wave of noise sweeping into the small lobby, drowning out the argument raging in the hall beyond. Karen and Simon stood before the doors, barring the way as the lobby filled with guests.

At first people just stood around, expecting something to happen, anticipating some formal opening of the reception ceremony, content for the most part to stand and chat. The bridesmaids had been chucked off their chairs to make way for Susie's nan and grandad, who then sat like honoured royalty holding court. Predictably, it was Susie's dad who started the first rumblings of dissatisfaction at being kept waiting.

'What're we buggerin' about out 'ere for?' Bob Fuller asked tactlessly.

'Budge up a bit, will yer,' came a disgruntled voice from the back. 'It's pissing down out 'ere and we're getting soaked!'

The crowd shifted forward, pressing in on Karen and Simon as they spread their bodies across the double doors, their voices rising with the stirrings of discontent.

'Well, come on. Let's get inside then,' said Susie's dad, pushing his way to the front to challenge them.

'Sorry, Mr Fuller. There's a bit of a hold up.'

'Hold up! What kind of bleedin' hold up?'

'It's the caterers,' Karen said quickly. 'They had an accident. Yeah, they, er . . . dropped a trifle right in front of the doors.' She nodded behind her.

'Yes,' Simon joined in, breathing a sigh of relief, 'they're clearing it up right now. I mean, you don't want to tread it through the hall, do you? Could be a bit dangerous if someone were to slip on it,' and he gave a look of concern towards Susie's elderly relatives before forcing himself to meet Susie's dad eyeball to eyeball.

'Grandad?' Jodie called up through the quietened throng.

'Yes, sweetheart?'

'Susie's been having a row with her boyfriend,' the little treasure announced, smirking up at Karen.

On cue, the row on the other side rose to new heights as silence descended upon the lobby.

'Who's that?' Doreen Fuller said, looking a little confused.

'Use your bleedin' loaf, woman. Who d'you think it is?' her husband said, turning on her. 'Nobody else 'as got a trap on 'er like your bleedin' daughter. Just listen to 'er!'

Karen cringed as obscenity after obscenity rang out in Susie's unmistakeable voice, rising to a crescendo and culminating in a loud crash before silence fell. Lifting her cheek from the door she faced the gathering, a mixture of dread and relief washing over her.

'I'll just nip in and see if they've cleared it up yet,' Karen announced, smiling up at them, knowing she was fooling no-one.

'There's a good girl,' Doreen said quietly, patting Karen's arm.

'Tell them to get a bloody move on, will you?' Bob Fuller demanded, 'before we all die of bleedin' thirst out 'ere.'

There was a general murmur of agreement from the assembled guests, who shifted uncomfortably in the claustrophobic surroundings.

'Maybe they're consummating the wedding,' a voice rang out from the other side of the lobby and was greeted with raucous laughter and general approval.

'Go on, my son!' Charlie Fuller shouted encouragingly to the groom on the other side of the door.

'Give it a rest, will you, Charlie,' Doreen pleaded, catching the disapproving looks from Susie's new in-laws.

'What's the matter with you, you miserable cow,' he responded affably. 'It's only a bit of fun.'

'And we all know *your* idea of fun, don't we Charlie Boy,' Babs said, coming to her sister's aid. 'Just 'cos you drop your trousers at the drop of a hat . . .'

'Yeah, get 'em off, Charlie!' a voice called out, and cheers rang out around the room, with a couple of voices joining together to sing the stripper's anthem.

Charlie loved an audience and started to ham it up for all he was worth, undoing his tie and then the buttons of his shirt.

'Watch out girls,' Susie's cousin shouted from further back. 'He'll knock your eyes out, will Charlie. He's hung like a tin of Vim!'

'Oi! Watch your mouth!' Lyndsay yelled back. 'There are kids here you know,' and she pulled Jodie protectively towards her, covering her ears as she pressed the other one against her side.

Karen turned about and tentatively opened the door, just wide enough for her to ease through, closing it quickly behind her. Across the other side of the hall, with his legs dangling over the edge of the stage, Joe sat with his head in his hands. On the floor beside him Susie stood with her arms folded, her face set in a determined grimace. On seeing Karen her shoulders drooped with relief and she even managed a smile as she walked across the hall to greet her.

'You all right?' Karen asked, taking hold of her hands.

Susie nodded. 'What's happening?' she said, nodding towards the doors at the crowd she knew must be waiting beyond them.

'Don't worry about them. What's happening in here?'

'You don't 'ave to pretend, Karen. I know.'

Karen gave her a puzzled look.

'About him and Mandy,' Susie said, flicking her head in Joe's direction. 'I know everything.'

'I'm so sorry, Suse,' Karen said, moving closer and hugging her. Then, leaning back to look her in the eye she added: 'I don't think it was serious, you know.'

'No, so he says.'

'It was probably just nerves, you know — tying the knot, losing his freedom and all that. Men are just big kids, you should know that.'

'Yeah, I know,' Susie said wearily, glancing across at Joe who remained sitting there, slumped forward, like he'd just been in a major road accident and was in shock.

'I walloped him, you know,' she said, turning back to face Karen. She lowered her voice. 'I think I've given him a shiner!'

Karen brought her hand up over her mouth as she imagined Joe fending off Susie's formidable left hook.

Susie couldn't stop herself from smiling and the two of them looked over to Joe.

'Come on,' Karen said, assuming control. 'Let's get him sorted out. I don't think I can keep the pigs from the trough for much longer.'

'Talking of pigs, I s'pose me old man's out there?'

Karen laughed. 'Yeah. Mouthy as ever.'

Susie nodded. 'Well, keep an eye on him, okay? He was

hitting the bottle even before we got to the church. Christ knows what he'll be like later on.'

Karen smiled and squeezed her friend's shoulder. 'I'll keep an eye out,' she said. Then, leaning forward, she pecked Susie's cheek. 'And it'll be okay. I know it will.'

'You reckon?' Susie said, then smiling weakly: 'Come on. Let's get them in here, before they break down the doors!'

Karen sat down on the hard wooden chair, relieved to be off her feet at last. Along the hall, by the double doors — now propped open by a couple of cigarette packets wedged underneath them — the bride and groom stood side by side, greeting their guests and offering them a glass of dry sherry to celebrate the occasion of their union. She shook her head at the hypocrisy of it all and drained the narrow glass in one go.

By the time they had welcomed the final guest, Joe's eye had turned from pinky-red to purple and the degree of sight through the puffy lid from partial to non-existent. The three of them had agreed on a story to explain away the injury — involving a waitress, a trifle, Joe's slippery shoes from the earlier unfortunate incident, and a crash to the ground — and although Karen had her doubts about how many people would be fooled by it, it provided everybody with an explanation they could feel comfortable with.

On entering the hall people quickly made their way to the tables dotted around the walls, settling themselves in for the duration, those in prime positions near the bar, the food table — as yet uncovered — and the stage being the first to be seized, with Susie's and Joe's relations automatically gravitating to opposite sides of the room.

Each of the unsightly wooden tables was covered with a white paper cloth printed with silver horseshoes and in its centre stood one of the flower arrangements Babs and Doreen had laboured over the night before. On each table were two circular glass ashtrays, inside which the caterers had placed books of matches, their white covers overprinted in silver with the words 'Susie & Joe' entwined in a delicate script.

At one end of the room, beneath the stage, two tables had been pushed together to accommodate the main wedding party, silver horseshoes pinned to each corner and dominated by a huge floral display. Around the walls hung clusters of pink and white balloons, dangling on lengths of white satin ribbon and draped with pink and grey streamers. Two bundles had already been pulled to the ground and were being kicked around the centre of the hall by a group of over-dressed youngsters.

Doreen Fuller slowly made her way to the table where Karen was sitting peacefully observing the scene. Beside Doreen, one hand gripping a wooden walking stick, the other bent at the elbow and supported by her daughter, waddled the substantial figure of Susie's nan, Elsie. Behind them, Babs supported the frail, wiry frame of Elsie's long-suffering husband, Albert.

'Karen, love,' Doreen said, her thin lips curling into a smile as she guided her mother's quite considerable buttocks over the seat of the chair before dropping them down onto their target. 'D'you mind if Mum and Dad sit here, only it's not so far for them to go to the loo.' The final three words mouthed silently.

''Course not,' Karen answered, standing up. 'I should be over there anyway,' and she nodded towards the top table.

'You remember Karen, don't you, Mum?' Doreen shouted in the old lady's ear. 'Susie's friend from school.'

Elsie looked her up and down. 'Yes, I remember you,' she said, pausing a moment while she wiped a huge white handkerchief across her watery eye. 'Put on a bit of weight since I last saw you, though,' she added, with the total disregard for social graces that is only tolerated in the very young and the elderly.

'Take no notice of her, Karen,' Doreen said, throwing her mother a look. 'You look lovely. Don't she Babs?'

'Lovely!' Babs puffed, as she manoeuvred her father into the seat beside his wife, then eased into the one beside him.

'Here, give us me bag up will you, Doreen,' Elsie demanded. 'I'll 'ave to put me slippers on. That corn of mine's killing me!'

Doreen dutifully pulled a pair of plaid, fur-lined slippers from her mother's handbag and to the old lady's obvious relief placed them on her broad, disfigured feet.

'You all right now?' Doreen said, straightening up.

'I could do with a drink,' Albert said.

'You've got your sherry there,' Doreen nodded down at the untouched glass on the table. 'That's a decent sherry, that is. Cost our Susie over four pounds a bottle, so it's not that cheap rubbish.'

'I don't care how much it cost, I can't drink the stuff,' he replied, wrinkling up his nose in distaste. 'Anyway, it's a bleedin' woman's drink! Give us a nice drop of brown ale any day!'

Doreen shook her head, exasperated.

'It's okay, Doreen,' Karen said, tapping the older woman's arm, 'I'll get your dad a beer from the bar.'

'If you're going up, I'll 'ave a snowball,' Elsie said, pushing her barely touched glass of sherry to one side. 'And I don't want a cherry in it. Can't eat 'em,' she explained, grinning up at Karen to reveal a dark shrunken mouth bereft of teeth.

Karen nodded that she understood the problem, trying to keep herself from laughing. She looked towards Babs who was lifting a pair of soft, vinyl slipperettes out of her bag which she then proceeded to swap for the pointed pink stilettoes on her feet.

'Oooh, that's better,' she said, wriggling her toes inside the new footwear. 'If there's one thing I can't abide it's uncomfortable shoes.'

'Drink, Babs?'

'Yes, please, Karen, love. I'll 'ave a stout. That's if you can manage.'

'Yeah, don't worry. I'll get a tray. How about you Doreen?'

'No, I'll finish these off,' she said pointedly, picking up the first of the glasses of sherry. 'Can't let them go to waste.'

'You want to watch it if you're on a mission, Doreen,' Karen laughed, waving her hand round the room to draw attention to the endless glasses of untouched sherry that littered the tables or had been surreptitiously placed on the floor beneath chairs. 'You'll be under the table if you attempt to drink your way through that lot!'

Doreen tutted her annoyance at this wanton disregard for etiquette and the sheer wastefulness. Meanwhile,

Karen made her way towards the bar where a crowd of thirsty guests were already standing four-deep as they fought to get a decent drink.

Leaning against the door leading out to the lobby, Karen stepped out of her shoes, savouring the feel of the cold linoed floor against the soles of her feet. Around the hall groups of people stood or sat talking, relaxed now that the formalities of the day were all but at an end. There were only the speeches to go and then they could really start enjoying themselves.

Many of the chairbacks were draped with suit jackets as men stood about in their shirtsleeves, the ties at their necks loosened into a lazy schoolboy knot. Bobby Fuller had been handing round cigars and their foul smoke filled the hall, hanging over them like a cloud as the men blew extravagantly into the warm air.

Women gathered round the tables, catching up on news, gossiping and discussing the do. Even though many of them were related, their main source of contact was the exchange of Christmas cards. They only ever got to see one another at weddings and funerals, and as the last wedding had been Charlie Boy's Maxine four years before, and the last funeral Bob Fuller's mum the year after that, there was a good deal to catch up on.

Sitting at another table was a group of women; a couple Karen thought she recognised from the shop where Susie worked and others she knew from her schooldays, immediately recognisable in spite of the passing years; girls who'd been on the periphery of her little group, who'd never quite penetrated the inner circle of the five friends, but who Susie kept in touch with anyway. Beneath the changed hairstyles and the make-up, within the folds of their fleshy bodies, remained the essence of their girlhood features, and Karen smiled to herself as she remembered them as they were back then, in their green and red uniforms, unsophisticated and carefree. Each one now had a story to tell and as she observed them she mused over what those stories might be.

Watching them, their pleasant, smiling faces obviously delighting in one another's company, it struck her — not for the first time — how much more appealing women were than men.

At a corner table Anna sat engrossed with James, the young waiter she had met on the hen night, their elbows resting on the table, their heads almost touching as they laughed and talked. She had been surprised when she'd seen them together in the church, but it was good to see Anna enjoying herself again. Karen recalled the weeks of torment her friend had endured after the break up with Callum and her own feeling of inadequacy as she had listened to her crying down the phone, unable to do more than offer sympathy with the width of an ocean between them. But of all of them Anna remained the success story — she was bright, beautiful, had a career and now, finally, she had decided what it was she really wanted out of life. Karen wondered whether she would ever have the courage to do that.

A rush of cold air filled the lobby, causing her to shiver as it wafted over her bare shoulders and arms. Turning round she saw Steve and Mandy standing in the doorway. Pushing her feet back into her pointed, red satin shoes she walked over to them, her arms outstretched, and gave Mandy a hug.

'I'll just nip off and find Jan,' Steve said, squeezing Mandy's arm.

'Thanks, Steve,' Mandy said quietly, as the two women parted, standing there holding hands.

'No problem!' he smiled, winking at her before making his way into the smoke-filled hall.

'You okay?' Karen said, leading her towards the two empty chairs by the coat racks.

'As well as can be expected,' she replied, forcing a smile. 'How's Susie?'

'As well as can be expected!'

They both laughed. 'What a pair!' Mandy said, sighing loudly. 'D'you think she knows?'

'She guessed.'

'Oh, shit!' Mandy squeaked, threatening to burst into tears again.

'Hey, it's all right,' Karen said, calming her. 'Susie's handling it pretty well under the circumstances.'

'What about Jonathan?'

'Well, you've ruined his shoes!' Karen nudged Mandy in the ribs, forcing her to laugh. 'And Susie's given him one hell of a shiner.'

Mandy held her hand over her mouth, her eyes widening, unsure whether to laugh or cry.

'Oh, Kar, what 'ave I done!'

'*You* haven't done anything. You didn't know he was Susie's bloke, *did* you?'

Mandy shook her head solemnly.

'No, so there you are. It's not your fault.' Karen squeezed Mandy's hand, signalling the end to any further argument she might have to this pronouncement. 'Now, the next thing is for us to get you a drink. You could probably do with one.'

'Steve gave me a brandy at the flat. He's one in a million, that one.'

Karen looked into the hall and saw him standing by the bar with Janet, his hand caressing her neck as they cuddled up to one another, and she had to admit that Steve was one of the few men she really was fond of.

'Well, start as you mean to go on! Brandy it is then,' and pulling Mandy to her feet she led her into the fray.

'Wait here,' Karen said as they reached the press of bodies waiting to be served. 'Bridesmaids get preferential treatment!' and she made her way round the side of the crowd, quickly catching the eye of the barman.

Mandy stood there feeling awkward, staring at the floor in order to avoid the unpleasant looks she had convinced herself were being hurled in her direction. When Janet came up and placed an arm around her shoulder she felt like bursting into tears out of sheer gratitude, and when Anna, too, came over and squeezed her hand, she felt a surge of love for these women as her confidence gradually resurfaced.

'I knew there had to be some compensation for agreeing to wear this dress,' Karen said handing Mandy a tumbler half full with brandy. 'Well, cheers everyone!' and she held her glass aloft as the others joined in the toast, their glasses clinking together as they raised them in the air.

'You're a crafty cow, you are,' Janet said, turning to Anna and nodding her head towards where James sat talking to Simon Paxman. 'When did all this happen?'

Anna laughed to hide her embarrassment.

'Well?' Janet persisted.

'I went back to his place the other night. For a nightcap.'

The other three girls burst out laughing.

'It's what they call a euphemism,' said Karen.

'It's what they call being bleedin' lucky, if you ask me,' said Mandy solemnly, and this time the other three roared with laughter.

'Well I have to admit,' Janet said, looking across to the young waiter, 'he is seriously cute. And, er, how *was* the nightcap?'

Anna raised her eyes.

'What did you 'ave, Anna,' Mandy asked. 'A Long Slow Screw?'

'No,' Karen joined in, 'it must've been a Wallbanger!'

'Ha ha ha, very funny,' Anna laughed good naturedly.

'Whatever it was they probably started off with Between the Sheets!' Janet giggled.

All four of them laughed now, at ease with one another and with little regard for the looks they received from others.

'C'mon then,' Janet urged, 'don't be shy. Tell us all about it.'

'I'm going to have to have a word with that Steve of yours. You're obviously not getting enough sex to be so interested in what I get up to,' Anna teased. 'Anyway,' she said, faking a yawn, 'we just had a quiet drink and then I went home to bed.'

The others laughed raucously.

'Yeah, and my mum's married to the Pope!' Janet said. 'Go on, tell us. Where does he live, for a start?'

'Actually, he lives quite near me, in Barnsbury. Coincidence, eh?'

'Must be fate,' Karen observed and they exchanged a brief smile.

'And you went back there after the strippers?' Janet said, pulling the story back on course.

'Yes, I went back there after the strippers,' Anna replied, mimicking her tone. 'It was seeing all that sweaty naked flesh! Actually,' she added, her mood more serious suddenly, 'I didn't really find those strippers that sexy when we were there – they looked a bit silly really – but when I thought about them in the cab on the way home I got really turned on . . .'

'So you thought you'd stop off for a quick knee trembler with our little friend over there.'

'Janet! Is there no romance in your soul?' Karen laughed.

'Nah, I leave all that kind of thing to Steve.'

And as the banter continued the noise got louder, the gestures more extravagant as they fell against one another like a gang of giggling schoolgirls discussing their first french kiss.

'Okay, you lot. So what's the joke?'

At the sound of Susie's voice the laughter stopped abruptly and there was a moment's awkward silence before Karen spoke.

'Anna was just telling us about her night of passion with her toy boy.'

'Shhh,' Anna said, glancing across at James. 'And anyway, he's not *that* much younger than me!'

'In your dreams, Anna,' Janet said. 'Karen teaches *kids* that are older than him!'

Anna dug her in the ribs as they all enjoyed the joke. Only Mandy remained silent, looking down at her feet.

'Well, good luck to you, babe,' Susie said to Anna. 'Get it while you can, that's what I say.'

Karen and Anna caught one another's eye and made some excuse to move away and circulate, quickly followed by Janet who went off in search of Steve, leaving Mandy and Susie standing there together.

'How you feeling?' Susie said gently.

'I'm fine, thanks,' Mandy replied, still unable to meet her friend's eyes.

The sound of Susie taking a deep breath through her nose and then exhaling it through her mouth filled the silence that hung between them.

'I know it wasn't your fault, Mand,' she said finally.

Looking up, tears clinging to her lashes, she spoke so quietly the words could barely be heard above the general hubbub. 'I'm so sorry, Susie. I . . .'

Before she could go on, Susie took hold of her hands – the empty glass now cupped between the two of them – cutting short the apology.

'It wasn't your fault!'

Mandy slowly shook her head, refusing to deflect responsibility.

'It wasn't your fault!' Susie said again, more slowly this time, as though that would make it sink in. 'I'm only sorry he used you like that.'

Mandy winced as what she knew to be the truth was finally vocalised, her mind swirling in a storm of tortured emotions as she struggled to suppress the anger that threatened to overwhelm her. She felt anger toward Jonathan, certainly; but anger toward Susie too, for forcing her to face up to the situation and for having what she had thought, up until a few hours ago, was hers. But most of all she felt anger at herself, for being so gullible, so stupid.

She gave a brief smile. 'You don't have to apologise for him, Susie. And certainly not to me. You're the innocent party in all this.'

'Yeah, ironic, ain't it? When I think of all the times the boot's been on the other foot. You know, when *I've* been the bit on the side.'

'The only difference is,' Mandy said, wiping a hand across her nose, 'I never thought of myself as a bit on the side 'cos I never knew he had a bit anywhere else!' She reached into her pocket for a tissue, held it to her nose and blew into it loudly.

'I s'pose not,' Susie said thoughtfully. 'In fact I s'pose if anything Joe was the bit on the side, what with you being married an' that.'

Every time she was forced to consider Pete's role as the injured husband in this shambolic affair, Mandy experienced a resurgence of nausea.

'You don't think Pete'll find out, do you?' she asked apprehensively.

'Well, *I'm* not gonna tell him,' Susie reassured her, squeezing her hand. 'And I don't s'pose *he* will,' she added, looking over to where Joe sat nervously fiddling with his tie as he watched the two women. 'Not unless he's looking for a matching pair of black eyes!'

They both laughed, but there was no happiness there.

'C'mon,' Susie said, taking hold of the empty glass before dropping Mandy's hands. 'Let's get a drink. I

425

don't know about you, but I plan to get well and truly plastered!'

'Yeah,' Mandy said uncertainly. Then, with something of the old sparkle: 'Yeah, let's go for it, why not!'

'Karen! . . . Karen!'

The urgent whisper made Karen turn from where she was repairing her make-up at the mirror in the ladies' loos and stare. Mandy was standing in the doorway, a look of panic in her face. Putting her make-up back in her handbag, Karen hurried across, taking Mandy's hands.

'Hey . . . What is it now?'

'It's *them*,' Mandy said. 'They're here!'

'Who . . . ?' she began, then understood. 'Pete, you mean.'

'Yeah . . . and Barry, too. They turned up together.' She swallowed, then bit her bottom lip with her teeth anxiously. 'You don't think he's told him, do you?'

'Who, Barry?' Karen shook her head, then answered her friend, her voice exuding far more confidence than she felt. 'No. He's gutless that one. If he told Pete about Jonathan, he'd have to tell him everything, and I don't think he's ready for that, do you?'

Mandy hesitated, then shook her head, but it was clear she wasn't convinced.

'Besides,' Karen went on. 'Pete'd never believe him, would he? He'd think Barry was pulling his plonker. I mean, his wife going out with Susie's new hubby. Not very likely is it?'

Mandy's lip quivered dangerously a moment, then she shook her head again. 'So what should I do?'

Karen squeezed her hands. 'You do nothing. Go and

have a drink. I'll have a chat with Pinky and Perky for you!'

Mandy laughed. 'It's true, ain't it?'

Karen narrowed her eyes. 'What?'

'About men. They're more bleedin' trouble than they're worth, the lot of them!'

It was Karen's turn to laugh. 'Not all of them. Not Steve, for instance. And then there's your boys . . .'

But the mention of her boys only panicked Mandy again. Her voice rose in a wail. 'But what if he finds out, Kar! What'll the boys think? Oh shit! Oh, fuck and damn and shit!'

'Mandy . . .' Karen softened her voice, as if she were speaking to a troubled pupil. 'It'll be all right. I promise it will. Now go and have that drink and leave it all to me. What you did . . . well, it wasn't a bad thing, okay? In fact, for you it was probably a good thing. It was . . . *natural*. And you're not to blame for Susie's problem. If only our parents had warned us about this kind of thing, eh?'

Mandy smiled at that. 'Yeah, and about marrying the first dickhead that came along, eh?'

'Yeah,' Karen grinned and hugged her friend. 'That's right. Now go. I'll join you in a mo.'

Karen waited until Mandy had gone, then took a long, deep breath. *Here goes*, she thought. As things were turning out, her role was a bit like that of a chef in a busy kitchen, keeping everything simmering nicely without bubbling over or burning to a cinder.

She saw them almost immediately, there by the bar, getting in their first beers of the evening. As she watched, Pete reached across to take the two straight pint glasses, then turned to hand one to his brother. Gritting her teeth, Karen made a bee-line directly for them. She was only two or three paces from Pete when he turned and looked at her, his vacant stare changing into a half-smile of recognition. Pete didn't like her, she knew. Like a lot of men of his type, he sensed her hostility towards him almost instinctively.

'How's Luke?' she asked, before he could say anything. 'Mandy said he had a tough time of it.'

'Silly little bugger,' Pete said, with genuine sympathy. 'He'd 'ad the pain days and thought it was cramp.' Pete shook his head, staring away thoughtfully a moment before he took a sip of his beer. 'Damn near fuckin' killed him, didn't it?'

'I'm sorry,' she said, conscious of Barry just behind him, watching her, his deep-set eyes giving her a surreptitious up-and-down then dwelling on her boobs. *Creep*, she thought, remembering what Mandy'd told her. Then, to Pete: 'I'm glad he's going to be all right. You okay?'

'Me?' He looked up at her, surprised by her concern. 'Yeah.' He lifted his pint. 'A few more of these and I'll be sound as a bell.'

'Good,' she said, meaning to move on and socialise elsewhere, confident that Pete knew nothing. Yet even as she made to step away, she heard a couple of the men at the bar discussing Mandy's performance at the church and saw that Barry had turned, listening.

Shit, she thought, seeing a tiny wondering glint appear in Barry's eyes. Watching him, she saw how his brow furrowed as he concentrated on what they were saying.

'Hey, Bal . . .' Pete said, Karen forgotten. 'Let's go see your ex and her new hubby. Give them our best.'

Barry turned back, leering at his brother. 'I've already given her *my* best, remember!'

Pete snorted. 'You and half of Islington! Mum ain't forgiven you for that, you know? She didn't know where to put her face!'

Barry grinned obscenely. 'Well, thank God Susie knew where to put *hers*!'

Karen watched them go across, filled with a fresh loathing for the two of them and wondering not for the first time how Mandy had put up with it all these years, married to that half-man. No wonder she'd felt the need to break out from it. But what bad luck! What awful, bloody luck!

She watched Pete and Barry swagger across, beers in hand, and felt the urge to follow — that same urge that makes people leave their houses to go and stare at road accidents and burning houses.

Susie was talking to one of her aunts, Joe tagging along like a pet dog at her elbow, silent, obedient, on his best behaviour. When Pete approached she saw how Susie barely glanced at him, then did a double-take, realising who it was.

'Pete . . .' she said, a momentary uncertainty in her face. 'Er . . . how's Luke?'

'Fine,' he said, as if the subject tired him already. 'So where is the poor bastard? I can't wait to meet him!'

Karen saw the muscles flicker at the corner of Susie's eyes and admired her friend's self-control. Personally she'd have given the cheeky bugger a back-hander. But after that moment's uncertainty, Susie grasped the opportunity to get back at Joe with both hands.

'Pete, this is my husband, Joe. And Joe . . .' She looked

at Joe with a tight smile, 'this is Pete . . . Mandy's husband.'

'Oh, shit!' Joe said, and flinched.

'What?' Pete said, staring back at him dumb-founded. 'I didn't quite catch that, pal.'

Susie leaned toward Pete. 'He said shit. Guess he knows you well, eh?'

Pete's mouth fell open like a cod's with surprise. But beside him, Barry was staring at Joe as if he knew him but couldn't quite place him.

'Don't I . . . ?'

Karen stepped up and took Barry's arm, leading him away politely but firmly.

'I think we ought to have a word,' she said to his ear. 'Before you open your big gob and shove your club foot right in it!'

'Me?' Barry said, stopping and pulling his hand away. He stood back from her, his eyes narrowed. 'Why? What do I know?'

She leaned in to him again. 'You know fucking well what you know, you nasty little shit. Your own brother's wife. How could you?'

He bridled at that. 'You don't know what you're talkin' about, you!' Then, smiling nastily. 'Anyway, what if I *do* know something?'

Karen poked him hard in the chest. 'You got off lightly the other day, mate! If I'd have been Mandy I'd have cut it off with a bread knife. So keep it shut, right?'

Barry stared back at her, the mixture of fear and amazement in his face almost comic. 'All right,' he said quietly, resentfully. 'But you better watch it, teacher. You're too fuckin' mouthy.'

She simply laughed, then turned her back on him and walked away. *Sticks and stones might break my bones, but names . . .*

Karen gave a little shudder then made her way across to where Anna was standing, looking on with amusement at Simon's attempts at chatting up her young waiter.

'You think Simon knows that James is with you?' Karen asked, nudging her friend gently.

'No,' Anna said, smiling broadly, enjoying James's patent discomfort, 'and I'm not going to tell him . . . yet.' She eyed the two men a moment longer. 'Did you know he was gay?'

Karen gave a brief smile. 'What made *you* think he was?'

'You forget I've worked in New York!' Anna laughed.

'Well, you'd better break the bad news to Simon soon. The speeches are due any moment.'

'Ah, it's a shame, don't you think? They make such a nice couple . . .'

The two girls stood there giggling until Karen turned, looking into her old friend's face. 'I'm really pleased for you, Anna. You deserve a bit of good luck. And he looks nice.'

Anna nodded. 'He is. Lovely hands he's got.'

'Tell me,' Karen said, grinning.

'Later,' Anna said. 'Right now I'd better break those two lovebirds up.'

'Well gently does it, eh?'

Anna brushed her arm as she walked across. 'I will . . .'

The waitresses had been round the tables with trays of filled champagne glasses, handing them out to the guests ready for the toasts. Now the hall fell silent as Simon stood and looking about him with a smile, began his best man's speech, a small pile of handwritten notes beside his glass. He seemed relaxed, urbane, and in his beautifully cut suit would have looked like a visitor from the local Manor House descended among the local peasantry. It was something he was clearly conscious of as he cleared his throat and looked about him at the staring faces.

'When Joe asked me to be his best man,' Simon began, 'the first thing that sprang to mind was . . . how much?'

There was laughter at that, muted and polite. No one was quite sure of this one just yet.

'Well,' he continued, 'when we'd settled how much I was paying Joe for the honour, the next thing I had to sort out was my speech. Should it be funny . . . anecdotal . . . *dirty*?'

A cheer went up. Beer mugs were raised in salute. Simon clearly had their measure. Even Bobby Fuller was smiling now. Only Doreen looked down into her lap, fearing the worst, conscious of Joe's parents sitting po-faced along the line of the table.

'Anyway, there I was ruminating . . .'

There was a roar of laughter.

'*Ruminating*, I said, about Joe's bachelor days, and straight away I thought of a holiday he and I once had in the Algarve . . .'

At the mention of the Algarve, Joe put his head in his hands and groaned. 'Christ, Simon,' he murmured, 'aren't I in enough trouble already?'

But Simon seemed not to hear; or if he did, he wasn't going to let his friend's discomfort spoil a good story.

'We'd booked at the last moment, you understand. One

of those cheap deals where you have to take what comes. Well, it wasn't until we got there that we realised we'd booked in to a hotel that faced onto a nudist beach.'

A raucous cheer went up at that.

Simon gave a nod to them. 'I see you know the place . . .'

More laughter.

'Anyway, I can remember that first day vividly. Being the sophisticated man of the world that I am, I felt quite at ease from the word go. But poor Joe . . .' Simon looked round at his friend, who was blushing a deep red at the recollection, and shook his head. 'Poor, poor Joe was *very* embarrassed. All day he walked around with his hands over his jewels until he instinctively reached up to catch a beach ball – then it was well and truly a case of privates on parade, and I can tell you they were not only standing to attention but saluting as well.'

There was a loud roar of appreciative laughter from around the hall.

'Well, as you can imagine, he won quite a few admirers that day. Which, I guess, is as good a way as any of saying just how lucky a woman our dear Susie is.'

Simon looked to the bride with a smile, noted how she sat there stony-faced, then, with a tiny shrug, carried on, glancing down at his notes.

'But just as Susie's a lucky woman, so Joe's a very lucky man. Or so I'm told.'

Simon turned and, bending down, picked up the thick folder he had got from his car earlier, and plonked it down on the table in front of him. He looked up and, placing one hand on top of the file, grinned. 'I have here a few signed affidavits . . .'

There was another roar of laughter.

'Cheeky bastard,' Susie muttered, smiling despite herself.

'Affidavits,' Simon continued, winking down at Susie, 'in testimony of Susie's own amorous capabilities . . .'

'Amorous *what*?' someone shouted.

'Shagging certificates,' someone else chipped in. 'They're like swimming certificates, only you get one for every length!'

And they were off again, the guffaws of laughter filling the hall. After a moment Simon raised his hand for silence.

'As I was saying, I have ample evidence of Susie's capacity to make Joe the happiest man on earth.'

Simon cleared his throat, then, dropping the file onto the floor behind him once more, he smiled broadly. 'But the past is the past. At weddings we look forward, into the future. The shared future of two people very much in love.'

At the mention of the word love, Susie glowered. Joe lifted his head briefly to glance at her, swallowing deeply when he saw the expression on her face.

'And it is traditional at such times as this to celebrate not merely with a feast, but with gifts . . . gifts which express our hope for that future.'

Simon stopped and looked about him, nodding once more, seemingly serious for a moment.

'It's difficult, isn't it, deciding what to buy two people who've got everything? I mean, it's not like buying for a teenage couple, after all. Susie and Joe have got two toasters, two TV sets, two microwaves . . .'

'Two-timing,' Susie murmured, looking daggers at her groom.

434

'Two of everything, in fact,' Simon continued, oblivious. 'In the circumstances, I got to thinking that anything I was likely to buy them in the household department would probably end up in a car boot sale!'

This time the laughter was mainly from the women. The men were clearly getting restless. It had been almost thirty seconds now without a joke or dirty innuendo.

'So after scratching my head for a bit, I decided I'd get them some clothes, but after searching about for a bit I changed my mind. Besides, I didn't think Joe would look that good in the leather mask . . . Anyway, while I was at the zoo watching the monkeys . . .'

There was laughter again. One or two of the men got up and scratched their buttocks exaggeratedly.

'Well, you do, don't you?' Simon continued. 'And while I was there I came up with the idea of buying Susie a bird. A rare Indonesian parrot, maybe, with brightly coloured plumage, or perhaps a South American cockatoo. But then Karen told me that Susie had had a cockatoo . . .'

'Yeah,' someone shouted, amidst the raucous laughter, 'or three, or four!'

Simon smiled and raised a hand for silence once more. 'Birds . . . well, my good friend Joe has kept a few birds in his time. Ruffled a few feathers, too. But I never thought he'd be the one to end up caged . . . metaphorically speaking, of course, and in such a delightful, gilded cage.' Simon smiled down at Susie. 'For a long time I thought that Joe would end up the world's oldest bachelor . . .'

'If I'd known he *would* have,' Susie murmured loud enough to cause a titter from around the hall.

'. . . but that sad fate has evaded him.'

Simon turned the page, then looked up again, smiling

steadily. 'Weddings . . . well, as we all know, weddings are an occasion for meeting old friends and distant relatives, for sharing a drink and . . .'

'Get on with it!' Bobby Fuller shouted, ignoring his daughter's scowl. 'I'm bleedin' parched.'

There were ironic cheers at that. Simon looked about him, raising an eyebrow, then threw aside his notes: 'You want *jokes*, right?'

A cheer went up.

'All right. But first a true story. I was travelling home the other night in a black cab and, completely out of the blue, the driver says to me, "You know what, mate?" "What?" I said. "My wife's having an affair." "An affair?" I say. "Yeah," he says. "I came 'ome the other night and she was sittin' there. Just sittin' there. An' I knew." "Knew?" I asked, wondering just how he'd known. And what. "Yeah," he says. "I could tell. The back door was open and there were two warm tea mugs on the kitchen table." "Ah," I says, intrigued now. "Yeah," he says. "I even know who it is." So I wait, expecting him to go on, but he's silent, brooding over the wheel as he drives me through the night. After a while my curiosity gets the better of me. "So?" I say. "What are you going to do?" "Do?" he says, pulling up at a red light and turning to look at me through the glass. "When I catch up with that bastard, I'm gonna shove his white cane right up his guide dog's arse!"'

There was pandemonium. Glasses were raised.

'To the bride and groom,' Simon said, knowing that he ought to quit while he was ahead. 'And thanks to the wonderful bridesmaids, to our delightful maid of honour, Karen, and to Doreen and Babs for doing the flowers.

Oh, and to Englebert Humperdink, for giving us the *Last Waltz* and making the DJ's job so easy! Cheers, everyone!'

Glasses were drained. A half dozen or so of the more desperate drinkers took the opportunity to creep across to the bar to refill their pint glasses. Simon stood a little while longer, waiting for things to calm down, then spoke again.

'And now can I ask the father of the bride, Mr Robert Fuller, to make a short speech . . .'

As the applause died and Bobby Fuller got to his feet, Karen looked about her at the crowded hall, her eyes falling on a few of the men who sat there, their hair neatly styled, their paunchy figures stuffed into tight-fitting dark suits for the occasion. Normally they'd be in neat slacks and v-necked sporting jumpers — a bland, casual look that was their uniform, that placed them immediately as members of a specific social group, Islington Man. It amazed her, that compulsion towards conformity that they displayed; the overwhelming fear they had of being thought different; the need that was in them to surround themselves with mirrors — mirrors that reflected back their own dullness.

When she thought of the men she'd known, it was with a sense of disappointment and dismay. There had been nothing original about any of them, nothing unique. They were just like the eggs you cooked for breakfast, only eggs were innocuous. Eat a bad egg and you'd be ill for a day or two, but these . . . these *men*, could fuck up your entire life. It was just as she'd said to Mandy earlier: nobody had warned them; nobody had prepared them for the world. No, they'd had to learn all of the important stuff themselves, by making mistakes.

For a moment Karen looked inward, remembering. It hadn't always been so. As a child it had been different. The world, then, had seemed exciting and full of promise. She'd grown up in a council flat on the third floor of a block of flats on the Barnsbury Estate, sharing it with her mum and dad and her elder brother, Gary. She'd been a tomboy in her adolescence; had gone to the Arsenal with her brother and his mates, enjoying being a 'boy' among boys. But then puberty had switched in and all the confusion it brought with it. Things had changed. Suddenly it was no longer possible to be mates with her brother's friends.

Karen shivered then looked across to where Mandy's Pete sat beside his brother, like two great slabs of meat carved into some vaguely human form, and for a moment she wondered – as she often did – if the world were some kind of practical joke played on them by a malicious deity; an endless joke that no one could ever see the point of.

Not that the women were that much better. There were her friends, of course, they at least had a spark of individuality, but there was something about this lifestyle that destroyed any chance they had to be themselves – that tripped them up even before the race had properly begun.

She switched her attention from the men, looking briefly to her friends – to Susie, Mandy, Janet, Anna – realising as she did that it wasn't prettiness she admired in a woman, it was strength, the inner spirit that some women had. She'd learned how to recognise it, knew it at a glance now. It came from being a misfit in this world of couples.

As Susie's dad sat down, Karen turned, looking to Simon, and raised her glass.

Nice speech, she mouthed.

Thanks, he mouthed back, then stood, clearing his throat before he called for order once again.

'And now may I call upon the groom to give the final speech.'

There were cheers and catcalls as Joe got to his feet, then murmurs from all round as attention was drawn to his swollen eye. It was almost closed now.

Joe stood there a moment, staring down at the table, composing himself, then he turned, looking at Susie thoughtfully through one eye and a slit, and began.

'I just want to say how lucky I am . . .'

'Yeah . . . with luck like yours I wouldn't walk under too many ladders, mate!' someone called out, to the amusement of all. Joe ran his tongue over his lips, then carried on.

'Lucky to have as my darling wife my sweet and adorable Susie . . .'

'Arsehole!' Susie muttered beneath her breath.

'Bastard!' Mandy murmured at the same time.

Karen looked down, stifling a laugh.

'. . . and I want her to know that I'll do my best, my very best to make her as happy as she deserves.'

'Cheating little git,' Susie muttered, refusing to meet his pleading look.

'Ahh . . .' Babs said, dabbing her eyes and looking to Karen. 'What a lovely speech.'

Joe pressed on regardless. 'I want to thank Susie's mum and dad for having her.'

'Yeah, and the rest!' the same wag called from the back of the hall, causing a fresh bout of laughter.

'And finally,' Joe said, scowling at the heckler, 'I want you to raise your glasses and toast the landlord of The Crown for letting us have the beer at cost!'

There were cheers and nods of admiration for Joe's spirit in the face of what was — all agreed — the deepest shit a man could get himself into on his wedding day without getting spliced in a sewer!

As people began to get up from the tables and make their way to the bar, Karen sat back, feeling morose, the thought of her friend Susie being stuck with yet another man she couldn't trust suddenly oppressing her. Arseholes . . . why were men always such arseholes? Why couldn't they let their brains lead them for once and not their dicks?

No, and women weren't like that, not even Susie, for all her adventures. When they found what they were looking for they stuck with it. But not men. No. Those useless fuckers couldn't help themselves, could they? One whiff of a woman's scent and they were off again, club in hand, playing the great hunter.

She sighed heavily, then looked up. Susie was watching her.

'What's up?' Susie asked. 'You look as peed off as a panda with piles!'

Karen giggled. 'Well . . . look about you, Suse. I mean, did we really deserve it?'

Susie stared at her, puzzled. 'What d'you mean?'

Karen opened her mouth, about to respond, then shook her head. 'Never mind. Let's go and mingle.'

The disco was now well and truly under way. Under instructions from Susie, the DJ placed another Tamla Motown record on the turntable, the opening bars of 'Heard It Through The Grapevine' were greeted with cheers of approval as people filed onto the dance floor, the singing from the audience almost as loud as Marvin Gaye's voice blasting through the speakers as they joined together in the familiar refrain.

'Takes you back, doesn't it?' Karen said, smiling down at Anna as she sat down next to her at the corner table.

Anna grinned, recalling the times they'd danced to this, dominating the floor at the Tottenham Royal as they moved in perfect synchronicity, performing the group dance they'd perfected after hours of practice in the school playground. 'Yeah,' she sighed. 'I love this song.'

'Who is it?' James asked innocently. 'I don't think I've heard it before.'

Anna and Karen exchanged a look of utter disbelief.

'I'm James, by the way,' he said, extending a hand across Anna towards Karen. 'We haven't been formally introduced.'

'No. Hi. I'm Karen. The blushing bridesmaid, as you can see.'

'I can't believe you don't know this song,' Anna said, still shaking her head. '*Everyone* knows this song!'

James shrugged. 'I'm sorry,' he said, smiling amiably, 'it was probably before my . . .' Realising what he was about to say he cut himself off short.

'Yes,' Anna said, her face serious suddenly. 'Silly me! Of *course* it was before your time.'

There was a moment of awkward silence and Karen wondered whether she should leave them to it. She wasn't sure she could take another argument!

'I'll just get us some drinks, shall I?' James said, standing up and gathering together the empty glasses. 'What would you like, Karen?'

'A gin and tonic, please,' she said, smiling up at him.

'It's not his fault,' she said to Anna once he was out of ear shot. 'He can't help being younger than you.'

'I know,' Anna replied, annoyed with herself for being so sensitive. 'It's just that, well, I dunno. It doesn't *feel right* somehow.'

'It felt right the other night by all accounts,' Karen giggled as she nudged Anna in the ribs.

'Don't *you* start!' Anna said, her face showing the semblance of a smile. 'Oh, I don't know, Kar,' she went on, a weariness in her voice, 'maybe it's okay if it's just sex, but don't you think the age difference is too great for a proper relationship?' She glanced across to the bar where James stood talking to one of Susie's young cousins, the two of them laughing at some shared joke.

'It's what *you* think that matters. Bugger everybody else!'

'I'll leave that to the best man,' she said flippantly, her eyes still on James. 'I'm sorry, I'm sorry,' she quickly apologised, cross with herself, 'that was a cheap joke. He's a nice guy, Simon.'

'Never mind Simon, we're talking about you. Listen, it doesn't have to be heavy, you know. You and James.

442

You could just have a fling. Enjoy yourself for a bit. You *should*.'

Anna gave a deep sigh, her shoulders drooping as she sank lower in her seat, a sudden despondency washing over her.

'Christ!' Karen said, laying a hand over hers. 'I'm sorry I came over. You've been looking so happy all day.'

'Oh ... it's not you,' Anna said, turning to face her.

'What then?'

Anna shook her head, biting the corner of her mouth as though she were trying to prevent the words from passing her lips.

'Is it Callum?' Karen said gently, and beneath her palm she could feel Anna's hand tense up. Then, suddenly, the tears came.

'Hey, come on,' Karen said sympathetically, helping Anna up and ushering her across the hall. 'Let's go and have a chat.'

In the Ladies Karen leaned against the roller towel while Anna splashed water over her mascara-streaked face, sniffing loudly to clear her blocked-up nose.

'Christ!' she said, a hand resting on each tap as she leaned forward and peered into the mirror. 'I look like shit!'

'Serves you right! For you it's temporary. The rest of us have to live with it on a permanent basis!'

Anna smiled gratefully at her friend's reflection and, unable to stop herself, began to sob again. Karen stepped across and hugged her. Yet even as she did, they could hear Doreen Fuller's voice outside announcing that she was just nipping into the loo. Unable to face the inevitable cross-examination, the two friends rushed into one of the two empty cubicles and closed the door.

They stood there, listening to Doreen in the next cubicle, humming to herself gaily as she peed, their hands over each other's mouth so that they didn't burst out laughing, especially as it seemed to go on and on for ever. Finally, hearing the outer door creak shut as Doreen rejoined the party, the two friends sighed with relief. Karen closed the lid to the toilet and sat down; Anna sat sideways on her lap, her hand on Karen's shoulder to balance her.

'He phoned me,' Anna said simply.

'Callum?'

'Yes. When we were out on the hen night. He left a message on the machine.'

'From America?'

'No. He's over here.'

'Blimey! Have you *seen* him?'

Anna shook her head emphatically. 'I can't,' she said, her face looking suddenly ugly as it contorted to stop herself from bursting into tears again. 'He phoned again this morning.'

'What did he say?'

'I couldn't speak to him,' she said, sniffing loudly and tearing a strip of paper tissue from the roll hanging in front of her. She folded it into a square and blew her nose loudly. 'I left the answering machine on.'

'Well. Did he leave a message, or what?'

Anna nodded, wiping the tissue across her nostrils. 'Said he was going back to the States on Monday and needs to see me.'

'So what's your problem? See him!'

'I can't, Karen. I just can't face him.'

'Why?' Karen said, shrugging as she fought to understand Anna's reasoning. 'Look! You love him, you *know* you do. You've told me you do. You've moped around ever since you split up. And now he wants to see you. I don't understand. What's the bloody matter with you?'

Anna dabbed at her eyes with the damp ball of tissue.

'Anna?'

'I had an abortion.'

'What?' Karen asked, not sure she'd heard correctly, so tiny was Anna's voice.

'I killed Callum's baby,' Anna said, turning to face her friend, meeting her eyes, expecting her condemnation. 'That's why I can't face him. You see, I love him so much, Karen. Oh, I've tried hating him — for not understanding, for making me go through it all on my own — but I know now that he was right.' She shook her head in despair, the tears falling freely onto her stockinged thighs, soaking into the thin silk. 'I feel so ashamed,' she whispered.

Karen reached up, hugging Anna tightly as she rested her face against Karen's head, comforting her until, finally, she was all cried out. A guest came into the loo, rattled the door, went into the cubicle next door, had a pee and left.

'You know you have to see him, don't you?' she said once the crying had stopped. 'You'll regret it for the rest of your life if you don't.'

Anna shook her head.

'Listen! It's taken me a long time to realise that you have to grab whatever chance of happiness you get in this world. You live a bit and then you die. We're not immortal, not any of us. We get one chance and

if we blow it we end up bitter and sad . . . and alone.'
She laughed suddenly. 'You know what? It's cost me a
fortune in therapy to understand that and I'm giving you
the advice for free, so be grateful!'

Anna laughed then wiped a hand across her cheek.
'I didn't know *you* went to therapy,' she said quietly,
sniffing. 'You seem too . . . well, *balanced*.'

'Yeah, well, there's quite a bit you don't know about
me,' she said, giving a strange laugh.

Anna turned to face her, curious. 'Like what?'

Karen averted her eyes, unable to meet Anna's gaze.

'Like *what*?' she persisted, nudging her friend. 'Come
on . . .'

'We're not talking about me, we're talking about
you.'

'Wrong! We've finished talking about me.'

'You're going to call him then?' Karen said, smiling
up at her.

Anna nodded.

'Good girl!' Karen laughed and patted Anna's knee.
'Now for Christ's sake get up before I completely lose
all feeling in my legs.'

The two of them were just coming out of the cubicle
when one of Susie's friends opened the outer door into the
Ladies, stopping in her tracks when she saw them, Anna
looking dishevelled and Karen limping as she regained the
feeling in her lower limbs.

'Oops, sorry!' she said, a startled look on her face as
she made an embarrassed about-turn and left the door to
swing shut behind her.

Anna fell against Karen, grabbing hold of her shoulder
as she laughed.

446

'Did you see the look on her face?' Anna cried.

Karen nodded.

'I think she thought we were going to ravish her. It'll probably all be round the hall by time we get out that we were having some hanky-panky in the bog!'

'Oh, Christ!' Karen said, a worried expression on her face. 'You don't think it will, do you?'

'Your face!' Anna said, pointing at her friend's reflection as she peered into the mirror, dabbing at the black smudges under her eyes. 'Who gives a shit in any case. Anyway, no-one'll take it seriously.'

'Chris might,' Karen said quietly, more to herself more than to Anna.

'Chris? Oh, *your* Chris,' she said, suddenly remembering that Karen's new boyfriend was supposed to be showing up. 'When's he supposed to be arriving?'

Karen looked down at the delicate gold watch she was wearing over her long satin glove. 'Should be here by now, actually.'

'Great! Give us a mo and you can introduce me. I'm dying to meet him.'

'Anna?'

'Uh huh?' she said, pushing her fingers through her hair.

Karen paused a moment, biting her lip. 'Oh, nothing.'

'What?' Anna laughed, catching her eye as she looked into the mirror. 'What is it?'

'Well, it's just that . . . well, you see, Chris . . .'

'Yeah?'

'It's just that, well, Chris might not be quite how you imagined.'

Anna turned to face her, resting her back against the

447

washbasin. 'What do you mean, not how I've imagined?' she said, giving her a quizzical look. 'I haven't imagined anything.'

'I'm sure you have.'

'I haven't, I tell you,' Anna giggled, bemused by Karen's concern. 'Anyway,' she said, turning back to take one last look in the mirror, 'what does it matter what I think, or what anyone thinks, as long as you're happy.'

'It's not as simple as that.'

''Course it is. You said so yourself.' Karen gave her a questioning look. 'You said we have to grab what chance of happiness we can. So there, you see, as long as you're happy what does it matter what anybody else thinks?'

'It sounds straightforward but . . .'

'No buts,' Anna said, turning round and gently pushing Karen towards the door. 'Let's go and meet this Chris of yours.'

Karen quickly turned around, pressing her back against the door, barring Anna's way. 'It's *not* that simple,' she said, her voice raised now. 'You have to let me explain!'

'Explain what?' Anna said, taken aback.

Karen took a deep breath then spoke, her voice much quieter. 'When I said that Chris might not be how you imagined, I know I was right.'

Anna opened her mouth to speak but Karen held up her hand.

'You see, what I know for a fact is that . . .' she paused a moment, averting her eyes. 'Is that you think Chris is a fella . . .'

The few moments that passed before the penny dropped seemed like an eternity.

'And he isn't?'

'No! Chris is short for Christine.'

'And she's a friend of yours?'

'No. She's more than a friend.'

Anna raised her eyebrows. 'Ah . . . I see.'

'Don't do that!' Karen snapped.

'Do what?'

'Say "I see" like that.'

'Like what?'

'Like you've made a judgement on us.'

'Isn't that what you want me to do?'

'No! I want you to accept that I'm not *like* you — or the others. That I don't want to sleep with men . . .'

'But you do want to sleep with this Chris?'

'Yes! Yes I do!'

'How long have you known?' Anna said quietly, this time it was she who looked away.

'I'm not sure,' Karen answered, looking up at the ceiling. 'I s'pose part of me has always known.'

'Why didn't you say something?'

Karen gave a sardonic laugh.

'And you think you're in love with this woman?'

'I don't think. I *know* I am.'

Anna took a deep breath, her shoulders sagging as she exhaled. She took a step towards Karen and reached down to take her hands in between her own. 'I can't pretend I understand all this. Christ, I should,' she laughed, 'the number of articles I've run on gay women over the years. But it's different when it's someone you know.'

Karen smiled back.

'And you never know, you might get over it.'

Karen laughed out loud. 'It's not a dose of chicken pox, Anna. I don't think I want to *get over it*. I actually think

I'm quite happy about it. In fact, I don't think I've ever been happier.'

Anna looked at her friend at last, her voice suddenly softer. 'Listen, if you're in love, then I'm happy for you.' She wrapped her arms around Karen's neck as her friend slowly lifted her arms about Anna's waist and they stood there hugging, the tears and the laughter flowing together as Karen felt the relief wash over her.

'Christ Almighty!' Anna said finally, leaning back to look into Karen's face, 'I don't think I could take any more surprises today. Let me go and "powder my nose", then you can take me out and introduce me to this Christine.' She laughed softly. 'After that, I think I'll just sit quietly in a corner.'

Karen smiled, wiping her damp eyes and her nose on the sleeve of her glove. 'Okay,' she said, leaning across to kiss Anna's cheek. 'I know you're going to get on like a house on fire.'

She stood back, watching her friend go back inside the cubicle and shut the door behind her, then turned to look at herself in the mirror, remembering the day her life had changed . . .

She had left for the weekend course straight after school had finished on that early summer Friday afternoon. After travelling for more than a couple of hours Karen glanced down anxiously at the clock on the dashboard and accelerated off the slip road onto the dual carriageway. A crash on the motorway had caused a hold-up and it now looked like she would be late arriving at the training centre, her only comfort being that she probably wouldn't be the only one.

There was nothing more frustrating than sitting in the middle of a traffic jam, feeling completely impotent. She'd tried some breathing exercises but as she moved her head from side to side she could hear her neck click and feel the tension in her shoulders. She took in little of the lush green countryside as she sped along at a steady sixty. The vast expanse of corn fields on either side of the road appeared to change from gold to brown in the time it took to blink as fast-moving low clouds skated across the face of the sun, blocking out the brilliant light. A moment later it re-emerged, lifting the colours back into vivid life. In the fields beyond, bright yellow rape ran like a band of gold across the horizon, while on the other side, distant hills folded in on one another in a smudge of greens and browns.

As she passed the large white road sign, Karen looked down at the instructions laid out on the front passenger seat beside her, relieved that she was nearly there. She looked at the clock again. She was fifteen minutes late already, and she hated being late!

The long tarmac driveway leading up to Beaumont Manor gave way to gravel as she drove into the shadow of the stately mansion which, thirty years ago, had been turned into a conference centre. Following the signs and arrows she slowly made her way into the car park at the side of the impressive stone building, sandwiched between the house itself and a line of single-storey concrete residential blocks, circa 1960.

Slumping back in her seat, she put the handbrake on, then reached across for the instructions and itinerary, conscious now that she needed to get a move on if she wasn't to make an embarrassing late entrance once the course started at two. She hadn't been at all keen to go on it, but her school needed to appoint a new teacher governor and she had drawn the short straw. That's how it felt anyway. In reality, the Head, recognising her great mediating qualities — the way she always made an effort to listen to other people's points of view and to work through problems — had asked her if she would be interested in taking up the post. This weekend away was the 'reward', and with a social life resembling that of an introverted nun, it wasn't something to turn her nose up at.

Leaving her holdall in the boot, she made her way round to the front of the house and up the grey stone steps leading into the main building. The entrance hall was cool and dark, its oak-panelled walls giving the place a rich texture, the whole area dominated by a huge marble fireplace rising almost ten feet up the far wall.

As she stood there, looking up at the ornate, sculpted ceiling, Karen felt a hand placed gently on her shoulder.

'Excuse me, dear, are you with COHSE?'

'Sorry?' Karen said, turning to see a kindly, grey-haired lady standing beside her, clipboard in hand.

'Are you with the COHSE group from Cleethorpes, dear?'

'The cosy group of what?' Karen said, completely baffled.

The old lady gave a genteel titter. 'You're not a nurse, are you, my dear,' she said, reprimanding herself as though just by looking at her that much should have been obvious.

'No, sorry. Teacher,' she said, apologetically.

'Oh, well, never mind,' the old lady sighed, taking her glasses from her nose and allowing them to dangle across her chest on a long silver chain, and catching sight of another young woman making her way up the steps, she gave Karen a brief smile of dismissal and set off to find her missing angels of mercy.

By the time Karen made contact with her group organiser there was just enough time to grab a quick sandwich and a glass of juice before she had to make her way to the opening session of the three-day course. The beautiful book-lined room on the first floor of the house was flooded with light as the sun shone in through the full-length windows, their heavy brocade drapes pulled aside and tied back with extravagant silk tassles.

The dozen or so fellow teachers who made up her group filed into the room, a gentle chatter flowing around them as they introduced themselves, falling into easy conversation in the way that people do when there is established common ground. Finding her name card on the polished oval table running the length of the room, Karen took her designated seat, observing those around her, trying to get their measure.

Standing behind her, a man's voice dominated the conversation as he stood talking with three female delegates, his tone uncompromisingly dogmatic as he held forth his views on how he saw the role of the teacher governor. Ignoring the tutor's polite cough, signalling that she was ready to begin the session, his voice continued to boom out, oblivious of everything else around him.

When the second cough fell on deaf ears, Karen turned

round in her seat. 'Excuse me,' she said politely, 'but I think we're ready to start,' and she nodded towards the tutor who smiled sweetly across at him.

With neither acknowledgment nor apology he made his way round to his seat opposite Karen and placed his brief-case noisily upon the table, taking several more minutes to unpack various pads, pens and other paraphernalia.

The three-hour session was almost halfway through when the heavy wooden door opened and in walked a woman — about Karen's age, she guessed — wearing a broad, open smile. Apologising to the tutor for her late arrival, Karen was immediately struck by the confidence she exuded walking into an unnerving situation like that; it wasn't that she was unaware of those about her, more that she felt at ease among them. The tutor asked her to tell everyone her name and Karen glanced down at the name card next to her own, signalling to the newcomer that her place was there, beside her.

When they broke briefly for coffee a few minutes later, the two introduced themselves properly. Christine Brooks — she said to call her Chris — worked at a London comprehensive, teaching English and Drama, and Karen immediately judged that she was great at what she did; she was so in control. She was slim, with pale skin and lovely bone-structure — enhanced by the elfin cut of her straight, aubergine-coloured hair — and her clothes had that air of peculiar individuality that said to all around her that she was someone special.

Sitting beside her Karen felt decidedly dull. Over her black leggings and dark denim shirt she wore a black pin-stripe waistcoat, her original intention to appear both casual and business-like. Now she fervently wished she had introduced some colour — a bright scarf or a piece of jewellery — to make her look more interesting, more daring.

At the end of the day's session, Chris leaned in to her as she was pushing her papers into a neat pile in front of her, speaking quietly between clenched teeth. 'Is that guy real?' she said, nodding towards the obnoxious fellow opposite.

Karen feigned a bout of coughing to disguise her amusement.

'I tell you what,' Chris went on, sweetly smiling across at him as his voice boomed out above the general hubbub of conversation, 'I reckon his colleagues must've clubbed together to send him here just to get a bit of peace and quiet in the staffroom.'

'Maybe he's got a hearing problem,' Karen suggested.

'Well if *he* hasn't, the rest of us will have by the time he's finished with us. I've never known anyone who liked the sound of his own voice so much!'

'Lucky old you. I've known quite a few, I'm afraid.'

'All men, I bet.'

Karen considered a moment. 'Yeah, I guess they were,' she confirmed. 'Most of them anyway.'

'I hope they didn't spout as much crap as he does! Talk about verbal diarrhoea!'

Karen giggled as she pushed back her chair then coughed into her hand as the group opposite looked across at the two of them. She caught Chris's eye which set her off again and they hurriedly collected together their possessions making ready to leave.

'Excuse me ladies,' he shouted across at them as they were about to escape.

Turning back like naughty schoolgirls caught bunking off, they looked sheepishly over their shoulders at the object of their ridicule.

'We are meeting up for an aperitif before dinner, and wondered if you would like to join us?' he looked around benignly on his gathered flock.

'Well, um . . .' Karen faltered.

'It's very kind of you,' Chris announced confidently, 'but we thought we'd go over some of these notes before dinner,' and she waved the sheaf of papers in the air. 'As I missed the early part, Karen's kindly offered to go through everything with me.' She glanced sideways at her comrade in crime as Karen stood smiling inanely.

'But let us know where you'll be so we can find you if we finish early,' Chris suggested brightly.

'Well, now we know where to avoid,' she whispered to Karen as they made their way from the room, quickening their step as they heard the dreaded voice booming up at the rear.

Karen was in the process of tying an orange and purple chiffon scarf around her hair when the knock came at the door. 'Just a mo',' she called, pulling it into a bow and tilting her head to one side to assess the effect in the mirror.

'Sorry,' she apologised to Chris as she opened the door.

'That's okay. Ready?'

Karen nodded. Grabbing her shoulder bag from the chair beside her, she quickly scanned the room, switched off the light and closed the door behind them. 'Where shall we go? We can't let the others see us.'

'All taken care of,' Chris grinned, holding up a brochure on the training centre. 'According to this there's another bar on the second floor. C'mon, I'll buy you a drink.'

They hadn't actually noticed other drinkers leave the bar. It was only when Karen threw her head back, laughing noisily at something Chris had said, that she looked about her to see that they were the only two left in the room. They giggled helplessly knowing that they would be late for dinner and could still be heard as they ran from the bar and down the wide staircase.

The talk had been mainly about work; about the thankless but ultimately rewarding career to which they both appeared dedicated. Chris spoke about her school in London, her colleagues and some of the more eccentric or problematic pupils, the two of them swapping stories about difficult parents and the stresses involved in the job. What always amazed Karen was the way a mother, who could barely control her one child, could have the nerve to complain about the way her class was being run when she as a teacher had thirty to contend with.

After dinner they sneaked away from the rest of the group and headed back to their bar.

'This is the life!' Chris said, handing Karen her brandy and slumping into the red leather armchair opposite. 'Cheers, m'dear!'

Karen raised her glass and smiled across at her. 'Cheers!'

'So, where do you live, Karen? Near the school?'

'Not too far. The school's in Bloomsbury, so it's a couple of stops on the tube.'

'On your own or d'you share?'

'On my own. How about you?'

'Same. With the occasional lodger.'

Karen gave a brief laugh as though she understood the hidden meaning in what Chris had said, though she would have been hard pushed to articulate it. And as the evening drew to a close they delved further into each other's lives, lifting stones along the path and uncovering tiny details, small intimacies. So that, when they finally parted in the early hours of the morning outside Karen's door, there was already a close bond of friendship existing between them.

Propped up on a pile of pillows, Karen stared into the darkness of her small room, her eyes fixed straight ahead on the haze of light from the car park outside as it fought to penetrate the rough, hessian curtains. Every so often it would flicker until finally it settled into a pattern and Karen anticipated its movements, mesmerized by the predictability of it. Gradually, heavy from the effects of the drink, her eyes closed and as she drifted into sleep, a smile played on her lips.

Karen's face broke into a broad grin when Chris knocked on her door the following morning, collecting her on her way to the dining room for breakfast. And all through the day there was a shared light-heartedness as the two continued to enjoy one another's company, Karen delighting in the infectious vitality of her new-found friend. So that by the time she found herself sitting on the end of her bed, pulling on her black opaque tights as she dressed for dinner that evening, she was really quite glad she had come to Beaumont Manor and was only sorry that this was her last night.

Busying herself while she awaited Chris's arrival,

Karen suddenly felt slightly silly; a little nervous, a little anxious, excited, like a teenager going out on a big date. She laughed dismissively and forced herself to sit down on the padded stool in front of the minimalist dressing table. Leaning forward on her elbows she stared at her reflection in the mirror, stretching the skin at her temple in a futile attempt to smooth away the lines around her eyes. Released from her hand, the skin sprang back into place, leaving a red mark where the pressure had been placed. With a look of resignation she reached into her tiny make-up bag and lifted out a lipstick, removing the lid and rolling the deep pink stick over her full lips. When the knock at the door finally came, she jumped up, grabbing at a sheet of tissue paper to dab away the excess lipstick before opening the door.

Avoiding the others, they went to 'their' bar and sat at 'their' table, comfortable in the shared intimacy of the moment, content with each other's company. From her armchair, Karen watched Chris as she walked to the bar, her stride long and gangly, making no concession to the elegant surroundings. Over her black leggings she wore a flowing silk blouse in a delicate shade of lavender, the colour accentuated by the ornate earrings dropping almost to her shoulders, studded with purple and lavender semi-precious stones. As she moved, the fine silk billowed about her, catching the contours of her slender body as it swam around it.

They talked and laughed all evening, even achieving a degree of civility towards the man they'd nicknamed Boomer, exchanging smiles and knowing looks as they chatted to the rest of the group throughout dinner. But when Chris placed her cool, slender hand over Karen's, she had felt a compulsion to pull away. It was an innocent gesture and had not been done surreptitiously, but openly, on the table top littered with the remnants of an enjoyable evening. Karen's fingers twitched beneath her touch and sensing her discomfort Chris pulled away, dropping her own hand into her lap, while continuing to laugh and joke with others, her feelings apparently unhurt, her confidence seemingly unshaken.

Confused by her embarrassment, Karen found it hard to enjoy the rest of the meal and when the others invited her along to the bar for a nightcap, she made some excuse about a headache and made her way back to her room alone.

Wearing her baggy t-shirt and slouch socks, she lay stretched out on her stomach across the bed, propped up on her elbows, a book open before her. No page was turned as she stared blankly at the words which seemed to float separately before her. Over and over again her eyes scanned the same paragraph with no understanding of its content or meaning. Finally, she dropped it over the side onto the floor and turned over onto her back, staring up at the ceiling.

All she could think about was that touch; the feel of Chris's hand over hers, and the split second of panic she had felt wondering if she knew, if they *all* knew. The thrill it had sent shooting through her body had been like an electric shock, attacking her nerve ends as it pulsed through to her fingertips. She had never experienced anything like it. Many times she had hugged and kissed girl friends, but it was never like this. This was different.

She closed her eyes and conjured up Chris's image in her

mind, the mere thought of her sending a shiver through Karen so that the hairs at the back of her neck stood on end. When a knock came at the door, she froze, the sound of her breathing suddenly amplified as it filled the silence. It seemed like an age before the second knock came, more insistent this time.

'Karen! Karen, it's me. Chris!'

Taking a deep breath she forced herself to stand up, breathing out slowly before taking the few steps to the door.

'I didn't wake you, did I?' Chris asked, looking her up and down.

Karen shook her head. 'I was reading.'

From behind her back Chris produced a half-bottle of brandy. 'Thought you might like a nightcap.'

'Well, er . . .'

'Come on, live dangerously! Anyway, it's our last night . . .' She grinned in at Karen. 'Yes?'

Karen pulled the door wide open, stepping aside to make room for her to pass. 'You're incorrigible!'

'I know,' she said, flashing a smile over her shoulder as she made her way over to the tray of tea things and picked up two cups. Turning round she passed them to Karen while she unscrewed the lid of the bottle.

'Very classy,' Karen laughed, taking a handle in each hand.

'Beggars can't be choosers!' Chris announced loftily, half-filling each cup. Setting down the bottle on the side she took one from Karen. 'Right! I propose a toast!'

'To what?'

Lifting up the cup in front of her she stood facing Karen, their eyes perfectly aligned. 'To . . .new friends.'

'New friends,' Karen repeated, as she raised her cup to the toast.

'And new experiences,' Chris added, holding Karen's eyes.

Karen gave a brief, uncertain smile as she clinked her cup against Chris's, averting her eyes as she brought it to her lips. As the brandy hit the back of her throat she spluttered into the cup, the amber liquid dribbling from the side of her mouth and down her chin.

Chris laughed and, lifting her hand, she caught a droplet of brandy on her finger as it fell from Karen's face. Slowly, deliberately, she took it into her mouth, allowing the moist tip to play upon her tongue, savouring the taste of the brandy as it swam to the back of her throat. Taking hold of Karen's hand as it limply held the empty cup, Chris tipped half of her own brandy into it.

'Here,' she said, looking into Karen's eyes, challenging her to pull her hand away. And when she didn't move, Chris leaned into her, her tongue delicately licking at the remaining drop of liquid at the side of her mouth, before kissing Karen gently on the lips.

A storm of emotions raged inside her as she fought to overcome the growing excitement that was taking over her body. Even as her mind told her she shouldn't be enjoying this – that this was a woman she was kissing, for Christ's sake! – her body responded as she became aroused, exhilarated by how good it felt to be near this other woman, wanting, no, *aching* for her touch.

Taking the cup from her hand, Chris reached across and placed both of them on the tray. Moving back across she sat on the end of the bed, reaching up towards Karen with outstretched arms. As she looked down at Chris, as she saw her arms reach up towards her, to draw her in, Karen felt as though she were standing on the parapet of a bridge, shivering in the cold. If she were to jump into the water she would get warm, but it was a long way to fall and she was scared.

Patiently, Chris's arms reached out for her, her lips curling into a knowing smile of encouragement. With painful slowness, Karen lifted her arms, grasping Chris's hands as though they were a lifeline, tightly clasping her fingers lest she drown as the dark, deep water swirled about her head.

Karen allowed herself to be guided down onto the bed, to sit nervously on its edge, her face turned away, avoiding Chris's gaze. Reaching up, Chris ran a cool, slender finger down Karen's cheek, looping a curl of hair behind her ear, the delicacy of the touch, the intimacy of the gesture sending a thrill through her body. Even now she fought to deny it, struggled against this longing that threatened to overwhelm her.

Eventually she looked up. Chris's fine features were softened by the lamplight and Karen found herself wanting to trace the line of mouth and nose and eyes. It was akin to the feeling she had when she saw an exquisite piece of sculpture in a museum, and she felt equally hesitant about touching.

Chris stretched out on the bed, her shoes kicked off, her feet, encased inside thin black socks, pressed into each other like small sleeping animals.

'Lie with me?' she asked, patting the space beside her. 'Here, curl up close. Come on . . . Don't be afraid. I don't bite.'

Karen settled in beside her, this woman who suddenly

seemed so much older, more worldly than she, allowing her to put an arm about her neck and back. Chris was soft and warm against her and for a moment Karen felt drowsy. Her friend stroked her shoulder and then half turned, placing her other arm about her, holding her. For a time they rested there like that, relaxed. Slowly, Karen brought her arm up to hold Chris to her. She felt the other woman stir, a deep, shuddering breath drawn from her.

'Can I stay the night?' she whispered, moving gently against Karen as she spoke. Her leg slid across and settled between Karen's own, her hips slightly raised so that she lay half upon her. It felt comfortable. More than comfortable. It felt *right*. Something in Karen responded to the movement and she let her hand slide down and rest lightly upon Chris's thigh.

'All right,' she said finally, and felt something slip away from her as she uttered the single, innocuous word.

Again there was a moment when neither spoke nor moved. Then Chris lifted her head slightly, her neck stretching into the light from the lamp, her soft lips coming close.

They kissed.

It was a long, slow kiss, gentle and almost chaste at first, but then more passionate. Chris let her mouth fall open and her tongue traced the shape of Karen's lips, coaxing the other to respond. Karen felt a strange shudder of desire ripple through her and pushed her own tongue into Chris's mouth, the tip of it playing gently upon the other's. All the while, Chris's fingers caressed her skin, tracing a line down her bare arm, stroking her waist, moving slowly round, pressing through the cloth. Karen shivered and let her own hand move downward, cupping the other's smoothly rounded cheek, before reaching across, her fingers busy at the buttons of Chris's blouse.

Chris was lifting the folds of Karen's t-shirt now and she shifted slightly to help her, feeling a sudden urgency in herself. Then, abruptly, she pushed Chris's hands away and sat up. Chris watched her, puzzled, suddenly disappointed. But then Karen pulled the t-shirt up and over her head, letting it drop to the floor. Chris smiled, drinking in the sight of her naked breasts.

'Help me,' she said, looking down to the buttons on her blouse, her fingers closing over one then another, then she, too, shrugged off her top, letting its pretty print fall in a heap on top of the t-shirt. Karen couldn't take her eyes from the other woman's small, perfect breasts, the skin as pale and delicate as the finest porcelain, and so attractive in comparison with her own, she felt.

They embraced closer now, pressed tight against each other, kissing deeply, urgently, the warmth and smell of their bodies merging, became as one. Chris ran a finger along the top of Karen's panties then, bending over her, kissed her inner thighs, her fingers trailing lines of pleasure down the insides of her legs. Karen caressed her neck and moaned softly to herself, almost rhythmically. Then, when Chris had done she pulled her close again and raised a finger to Karen's lips, looking deeply into her eyes.

'Are you okay?'

Karen smiled up at her.

'You feel so good,' Chris said, unable to keep her hands still; kneading and caressing Karen's flesh, working in towards the warm, moist sex of her, her fingers curling into a soft delicious knot within her. She watched as Karen's face changed and became a mask of urgency, of desperation almost, her breathing deep and erratic, her eyes closed.

Karen leaned forward kissing the other's breasts, raising her mouth to suck at the hard, jutting nipples. Chris was moaning uncontrollably now, a breathless, hoarse sound that inflamed Karen, urging her on. Karen was tugging at her leggings, trying to ease them down.

'Oh God,' she said, barely audible, 'take them off!' She let Karen work them loose then draw them down her legs, before kneeling to face her, slowly easing her own small panties seductively over her hips.

Naked, aroused, they paused to look at each other, facing each other on the bed. A dark rich growth surrounded Karen's sex, contrasted against the vivid auburn of Chris's.

'You're beautiful,' Karen said, looking into Chris's eyes. 'I never imagined it would be like this.' She reached out to touch one of the small, firm breasts and let out a tiny, shuddering sigh.

Chris watched her, delighting in her touch, then lay down on her back, looking up at her. 'Come,' she said. 'Come down here to me.'

Slowly, as though she were savouring the moment, Karen lowered herself beside her, consumed by a fine, exquisite pleasure as their flesh touched and then rubbed softly against each other's. Chris put her arms about her and kissed her face and neck, as Karen's legs moved apart to let her lay there, as a man might lay there. But this was different. *So* different. She felt so safe, so perfectly loved. For once, it seemed, her desire was perfectly mirrored.

Their movements grew more urgent, each holding and caressing the other as their bodies slapped together, sweat-filmed and anxious. Karen felt the wet warmth of Chris press down against her own moist sex and wanted to cry out. They gasped and panted with pleasure, moaning and rocking against one another. After a moment Karen closed her eyes and felt the muscles tighten and begin to spasm, a blood-red wave of pleasure robbing her of thought, making her grunt and moan like an animal. And from afar she could hear Chris's voice, distorted and almost pained, making low, disgusting noises of ecstasy as she came.

Afterwards they lay there in the lamplight, barely touching on the small bed, facing each other, their eyes watching one another.

'Scared?' Chris said quietly, reaching up to push hair from Karen's damp cheek.

Karen gave the briefest nod.

'Don't be. The hardest bit's behind you now. I know. I've been there,' and she laughed, a warm, rich laugh that made Karen smile. But inside her mind was a mass of confusion as she fought to come to terms with what had happened. A part of her knew that it had been inevitable, but still she battled to deny herself, to deny what had happened here, in this room.

Karen reached over and turned off the lamp, her arm falling across Chris's body, and she cupped her breast, the bud of the nipple soft beneath her palm. For a moment or two she watched Chris as her eyes slowly closed in half sleep then Karen, too, turned onto her back and lay there, staring up at the ceiling. Finally! Finally it had happened. Part of her still refused to believe it even as she felt Chris's warm naked flesh beside her, but there was a part of her that felt relief, relieved that now she knew . . .for sure.

Karen reached down and lazily scratched at herself, feeling slightly tender, then let her hand rest there, like a tiny bird, and closed her eyes, remembering, feeling herself aroused by the memory of it. She turned on her side, facing into Chris and reached out to take her in her arms again.

They met in the darkness, and kissed.

K aren smiled, remembering that night, recalling all the changes it had made in her. In truth she had never surfaced. Nor did she want to. She looked at Anna now and felt a flood of warmth for her.

'Come on,' she said. 'Let's go out and join the others.'

Crossing the threshold into the hall the two girls were aware of the party having moved into a new phase. The disco had given way to a slightly out of tune piano and up on stage accompanying it stood a swaying, sweating Bob Fuller, a glass of beer in one hand and the DJ's mike in the other. Karen nudged Anna and they giggled, leaning into one another until Karen self-consciously pulled away, turning to join the applause as the final notes of the song faded away.

Watching her, Anna made to speak. She wanted to say that it was all right, that nothing had changed between them, but the words would not come.

'James'll think you've done a runner,' Karen said, turning back to her. She looked over to the empty seats where they had been sitting earlier. 'Where is he anyway?'

The two of them scanned the hall until, finally, Anna spotted him propping up the bar, looking down into the admiring doe eyes of Susie's cousin, Kimberley. 'Doesn't look like he's been missing me too much!' she said, nodding her head in their direction.

'Christ!' Karen exclaimed, following her gaze. 'Last time I saw her she was into My Little Pony!'

'Yeah, well, now it looks like the only *little* thing she's into has got *two* legs and a cute arse!'

'I remember when she used to wear this ruddy great brace on her teeth! She's turned into quite a pretty young girl.'

'Well, thanks a bunch, Karen! You're a real bloody comfort!'

Karen laughed. 'Sorry,' she apologised. 'Anyway, it's probably harmless enough. Come and help me find Chris. She should be here by now.'

The music had started up again and Susie's dad was giving his idiosyncratic rendition of 'A-Won't A-You Come 'ome A-Bill Bailey?'. As Karen glanced up at him — eyes closed, belting it out for all he was worth — she felt a sneaking admiration for his total disregard for what other people thought of him. As she looked around the hall, many of the older men and women sat mouthing the words to the song, dragging them up from the depths of their memory, delighting in the shared moment as the passing years were briefly pushed aside. As the song came to an end, his appreciative audience applauded enthusiastically. Ignoring the hecklers amongst the youngsters keen to get back to 'some *real* music — music from *this* century!', he was well into his stride. Reaching down to take a fresh glass of beer from Charlie Boy standing at the foot of the stage, he spoke a few uncharacteristically touching words into the microphone, dedicating the next song to his beloved wife, Doreen. There were aahhs of appreciation from many of the women as they looked scathingly at their own beer-swigging husbands, followed by hoots of laughter from those same men as he launched into the opening bars of the old Englebert Humperdink favourite, 'Please release me, let me go . . .'

Karen spotted Doreen on the other side of the hall and felt her humiliation as the woman tilted back on her heels, downing a glass of sherry in one go. Babs leaned against her sister's back, to prevent her from falling onto their table, as she arrived with plates of food for Elsie and Albert, a mountain of ham, chicken drumsticks, cocktail sausages, and an assortment of salads – topped off with pickled onions – filling each one. Reaching down into her handbag, Elsie brought out a set of sparkling false teeth. Dusting them with her handkerchief, Karen watched, mesmerized, as the old lady pushed them into her shrunken mouth, adeptly rearranging her gums around them with a quick movement of the jaw, before parting her lips to reveal an impressive set of gnashers with which to enjoy the supper laid out before her.

The buffet had been uncovered over on the far side, and elderly, poker-faced waitresses in black skirts and tops and crisp white aprons, tidied, cleared and refilled the fare, slipping backwards and forwards to the tiny kitchen behind the bar.

To the strangled strains of Bobby Fuller, couples smooched around the dance floor – older men and women enjoying a reprise from the pulsating discotheque, women dancing with women, in the absence of any willing male partner, and grown ups with children desperate to appear older than their years. At the edge of the dance floor a group of Joe's mates, cans of lager in one hand and cigars in the other, draped their arms around each other's shoulders and swayed from side to side to the music, yelling the odd refrain. Karen shook her head at the sad sight.

As she scanned the room once again she felt a hand on her shoulder and before she could turn round she felt a warm whisper of breath on her neck.

'Looking for someone?'

Karen's face lit up as she turned to face Chris.

'Sorry I'm late.'

'You're not,' Karen smiled, leaning across to kiss her on the cheek.

'Wow! You look . . . amazing!' Chris exclaimed, stepping back to get a good look at Karen, and they both burst out laughing. Then, leaning over, she whispered; 'Would've looked better in lavender.'

Karen nudged her gently in the ribs, smiling with her mouth while attempting to give a reproving look with her eyes.

'Come and meet Anna,' she said, reaching down to squeeze her hand reassuringly.

Aware of her presence, Anna had turned away from the two women slightly, confused by her emotions; wanting to do and say the right thing. It wasn't until Karen said her name that she turned to face them.

'This is Chris. Chris, this is my very old friend, Anna.'

'Hey, not so much of the old if you don't mind,' she joked, extending her hand. 'Nice to meet you, Chris.'

'You too. I've heard a lot about you.'

Anna smiled politely and there was a moment of awkward silence.

'How was the wedding?' Chris asked, making conversation.

Anna and Karen burst out laughing and Chris looked on bemused as the two of them fell against each other, helpless with laughter.

'What?' Chris asked bewildered. 'What did I say?'

'It's not you,' Karen said, patting her arm. 'It's just that asking "How was the wedding?" was a bit like asking Nelson "How was the Battle of Trafalgar?"'

Chris gave a quizzical look.

'I'll tell you all about it when we get home,' she said, smiling at her affectionately. 'Now, let me go and get you a drink. Do you want one, Anna?'

'I'll get them,' Anna volunteered, but Karen laid a hand on her shoulder. 'No, you stay here and chat to Chris. Besides,' she added, tilting her nose into the air, 'I get preferential treatment.'

As she waited for the drinks to be poured Karen looked across to the two women as they stood talking. She felt a great sense of relief that she had finally told someone about her and Chris, and that that someone had been Anna. She felt that Anna would be the most accepting, that she wouldn't reject her or be repelled by her. It had been hard enough admitting to herself that she was a lesbian; she hadn't wanted to believe it, hadn't wanted to face it. Oh, she knew she was different from her friends long before Chris came on the scene, of course; had felt desire for other women. But there was always the hope that if she did nothing about it, it meant she wasn't gay;

472

always the fear that if she acted out her fantasy, someone would find out. Fascinated by the idea of loving another woman, at the same time she had been turned off by what she thought lesbians were supposed to be like. She didn't want to look like or be a man. Chris changed all that.

Looking across at this woman – her lover – she felt an overwhelming love and a deep gratitude, for leading her gently to where she was now; the happiest she had ever been. It was still difficult for them to be open about how they felt, about what they were, because of their jobs, they feared they would be victimised. But having finally admitted it to herself she had taken the first step, and now Anna knew . . .

Karen turned to collect the three drinks from the bar and as she turned back, ready to make her way across the hall once more, she saw Susie making a bee-line for Anna and Chris and her heart skipped a beat. She'd known that by bringing Chris along she would have to explain – indeed, she'd *wanted* to explain – but now, faced with the prospect of telling Susie, she felt vulnerable, exposed.

As she approached she heard Anna making the introductions: 'Susie, this is Karen's friend, Chris. Chris, this, of course, is the blushing bride.'

'Blushing ain't the word!' Susie said, slurring slightly. 'After what's gone on today it's a wonder me head ain't on fucking fire! Anyway,' she added, looking at Chris, 'pleased to meet you.'

Chris held out her hand and Anna was struck by how slender it was, noting the elaborate, heavy silver rings she wore.

'I'm a dopey cow,' Susie said, turning to Karen as she arrived with the drinks; 'when you said you was

173

bringing Chris to the wedding I thought you meant your boyfriend,' and she tittered into her empty glass.

The other three women looked to each other and with an eerie degree of synchronicity took a swig from their glasses.

'You a teacher, an' all, Chris?' Susie asked, reaching across and taking Anna's glass from her hand before taking a mouthful of the clear, cool liquid.

'That's right.'

'At the same school?'

'No,' Karen interjected. 'We met on a course,' and she and her lover exchanged a look of such intimacy that even in her inebriated condition Susie picked up on it. She looked from Karen to Chris, but it wasn't until she looked back at Karen and met her eyes that it clicked, the cogs almost visibly turning as she ingested each piece of information, sorting the pieces as the jigsaw finally came together.

'Oh,' was all she could manage to say, taking another mouthful of Anna's drink before passing it back to her. 'I need a drink,' she said.

'I'll get you one,' Karen offered, making to leave.

'No!' Susie said, rather too loudly, too quickly. 'You stay with, er, Chris. Anna, come and get a drink with me,' and avoiding Karen's eyes this time she scurried off towards the bar, dragging Anna beside her and whispering to her as soon as they were out of Karen's earshot.

Karen left it until Anna had gone to sit back at the table before going over to Susie.

'Did she tell you?' she said, slipping in beside her, her elbow resting on the bar.

'Tell me what?' Susie said, staring out into the hall.

'Don't play games. This is important to me, Susie.'

'Why didn't you tell us?' Susie said after a moment.

'I couldn't.'

'Couldn't? Why not. We're supposed to be your mates, ain't we?'

'I didn't . . . I wasn't sure how you'd react.'

'Well, what did you expect us to do?'

'Oh, I don't know,' she said, sighing. 'I s'pose I was worried you might think I fancied you, or something. I thought you might think we couldn't be friends anymore.'

Susie gave a deep sigh. 'Look, Karen,' she said. 'Look around this hall. I tell you,' she said, surveying the men there, 'if it wasn't for the sex, I'd just as soon live with a woman. I could talk to a woman. I mean *really* talk. This lot,' and she gestured out towards some of the more drunken specimens, her voice rising, 'they're just a bunch of daft buggers, the lot of them!'

Karen gently squeezed her arm in an attempt to quieten her.

'No,' Susie said, more calmly now. 'If you're happy, then it's sweet,' and she turned, wrapping her arms around Karen's neck, clearing a row of drinks from the bar as they fell against it.

~ *Real Women* ~

Anna sat back at the table, the empty chair beside her a clear reminder that James was still at the bar, apparently engrossed in his conversation with Susie's cousin. With a polite smile to her neighbour — an elderly lady who continually smiled and nodded at whoever would glance her way — Anna looked down. At times like this she began to wish she smoked. It would at least have been something to do with her hands. As it was her champagne glass had been taken, and until James returned from the bar, she was forced by convention to sit and wait.

Anna huffed, exasperated, forcing herself not to look toward the bar, then, controlled by some instinct stronger than herself, she turned and stared. There was no doubting it: the closeness of their bodies, the way they looked at each other, never breaking eye contact, their smiles, yes, and that laughter. Anna looked down, hurt by the thought, but there was no denying it. She was jealous. Jealous of some seventeen-year-old bimbo with pert little tits inside a low-cut dress. Sucking in her lips, she cursed that the years had provided no answers to that. However old she got, she had never cured herself of her jealousy.

Right now she felt as if she were fifteen again and at her first party.

Shit! she said inwardly, getting up, determined not to succumb to the mood that had descended on her. *I'll be damned if I'll wait 'til he's good and ready. Besides*, she added to herself, looking across at him, her eyes narrowed now, *I'm a grown woman. I can get my own bloody drink!*

Yes, and if he thinks he can piss me about . . .

She marched up to him and tapped his shoulder.

'Friend of yours?' she asked, as he turned his head, clearly surprised to see her.

'Er . . . this is . . .'

'I thought you were getting me a drink,' she said, not wanting to be introduced. 'You've taken your bloody time, haven't you?'

He turned to face her. 'Well, you just disappeared. I thought . . .'

'You thought you could come over and chat up some brainless little bimbo . . .'

'Here!' the girl behind him protested. 'Who you callin' a fuckin' bimbo!'

Anna leaned past James. 'You! Now piss off!'

Shocked, the girl swallowed, then turned and left, clearly unhappy.

Anna looked back at James. He had a sour expression on his face now. Slowly he shook his head. 'I was just talking, that's all. There was no need.'

'No?' Anna laughed in disbelief, then spoke again, her voice almost inaudible beneath the pounding music. 'I thought you were different, James. You know that? I really thought that you weren't like the rest. I thought . . .'

She stopped, looking down, suddenly bitter, disappointed with him.

He reached out, touching her arm. 'Look, I'm sorry. She was just . . .'

Anna looked up. 'No. It's me who ought to be sorry. Sorry for phoning you that night. For taking you up on your offer. It wouldn't have worked, would it? I mean, look at you.' She laughed sourly, then shook her head. 'You could be my son.'

'Oedipus,' he said, smiling, trying to coax an answer from her. His hand still lay on her arm, warm, linking them physically.

'No,' she answered, reaching up to cover his hand briefly, gently squeezing it before she removed it. 'It was nice but . . .' She swallowed, then met his eyes again, steeling herself to be as honest as she could. 'I saw it just now. How it would be, I mean. Every time you looked at another woman I'd be jealous. I'd wonder . . . well, I'd be wondering if you were staying with me out of pity. Or because I was a good screw . . .'

He winced at that. 'Hey . . .'

Anna smiled. 'Oh, I know I'm a good screw. But love's something more than that, isn't it? Love's about what happens once that passion's faded. It's about . . . well, it's about growing old together. And I've a head start on you there.'

James looked down, sighing. 'So you don't want to see me any more, is that it?'

Anna reached out, her hand touching his neck, the firm line of his jaw, remembering how sweet it had been, and gave a little shudder. 'Yes,' she said after a moment. 'I guess that's what I'm saying.'

He looked up at her, his eyes full of hurt now 'And me?'

She smiled again. 'Oh, you'll be all right. You have a gift, James. You could charm Mary Whitehouse into bed.'

He laughed. 'You think I've this thing on older women, then?'

Anna sighed, then shook her head. 'No. You'd be better off with someone your own age. Someone like your friend . . .'

He turned, glancing across at Susie's cousin where she now stood with several of her mates in a huddle, then looked back at Anna. 'Like her, you mean?'

'You could do worse.'

'I thought you said she was a bimbo.'

'Female rivalry. I got my shots in first, before she had time to call me an old bag.'

He laughed. 'You know, you're really quite remarkable, Anna. I'm glad I met you. It was . . . memorable.'

She grinned. 'Yeah, I know . . . and any time I want to repeat the experience . . .'

He grinned back at her lasciviously. 'Mind reader, too, huh? But seriously. It doesn't have to be heavy.'

Anna considered a moment, then shook her head. 'Maybe not for you, but for me . . .' Smiling, she put out her hand. 'Well, goodbye, James. And good luck. Oh, and send me a wedding invite.'

His smile — that smile she'd come to like so much — danced briefly in his eyes again. 'You could have a long wait.'

'And good luck with your plan to become an architect. Don't let go of that. You'll regret it if you do.'

'I won't,' he said. 'Oh, and here.'

He handed her a drink.

She stared at it. 'What is it?'

'A double brandy. I thought I'd get you drunk.'

She smiled, realising suddenly that she had purged herself of what she had been feeling earlier; that what she felt now was much kinder, much healthier. She liked James, she realised, but he wasn't a solution. He wasn't what she'd been looking for. Even so, she wished him all the best with whatever fate dealt him.

'You're a wicked man, James Holland.' She handed him back the drink. 'Here, give it to the bimbo.' She winked. 'Not that she'd need it, I reckon.'

'You reckon?'

Anna nodded, and leaning in to kiss his cheek, hurried away before the moment was spoiled.

There, she thought, looking about her, trying to locate one of her friends among the mass of milling bodies. *A clean break*. But part of her felt awful. Part of her wanted to turn around and get drunk — hideously drunk — and then sleep with him again.

No, she told herself, spying Janet standing with Susie's Lyndsay in the corner. *It's done. Now leave it be*.

Even so, she couldn't help herself; couldn't prevent herself from turning to watch James take the glass across and hand it to her; couldn't stop the sharp pain of jealousy and loneliness she felt seeing the girl's face light up.

Damn, she thought, feeling all of her strength go from her. *Why did I do that? Why the bloody hell did I have to look back?*

Mandy set down the well-gnawed chicken bone, pushed

her plate aside, then sat back, wiping her mouth with one of the specially printed napkins, Susie's name linked to Joe's inside a silver heart in one corner of the crinkly white paper. Glancing across at the top table, she saw that Joe was watching her again, making what he thought were secretive attempts to gain her attention.

No, she told herself, pointedly ignoring him. *The bastard can stew in his own juices.*

Turning back, she looked across the table to where her husband, Pete sat, deep in conversation with one of Susie's numerous uncles. Beside him sat his brother, Barry. Barry the bastard. Barry the blackmailer. Mandy glared at him, her eyes shooting arrows of pure hatred at him. She had noticed earlier how awkwardly he was sitting; now she commented on it.

'Need a cushion, Bal? Old war wound playing you up?'

'Sarky cow,' he muttered under his breath, then, nudging Pete, he leaned across and pointed toward where Karen stood with a short-haired woman Mandy didn't know.

'Here, get a load of that, Pete!' Barry said, a nastily salacious grin forming. 'Oughtn't to be allowed. Mind you, they reckon all them teachers are lessies. Probably 'cos they're all too fuckin' ugly,' and he laughed into his glass as he raised it to his lips.

'What?' Pete turned and stared at his brother, not understanding a word.

'You know — lessies. They're all like men, ain't they.'

'Let's fuckin' well hope not!' Mandy said under her breath.

'Nah, what they need is a good seeing to!'

'You know what, Barry?' Mandy began, leaning across

484

the table. 'You wanna stick a microphone up your arse so everyone can hear you. I've never heard such a load of old crap in all my life. That's my friend you're talking about.'

'So?' Barry leaned toward her, leering now. 'I know your mates. They're a load of old slags, the lot of them. Yeah, 'specially that really good friend of yours, the bride.'

Mandy felt herself go cold with anger. 'I don't know what you mean?'

But Barry didn't heed the warning in her voice; he went on regardless. 'You know what I fuckin' means. Susie'd shag anyone, given the chance. And I should know. Nah, she's nothin' but an old slapper. I only came to this do to get a look at the poor bastard who'd been stupid enough to marry her.'

Something snapped in her. Standing up, Mandy reached across and, snatching Pete's beer from his hand, tipped it over Barry's head.

Barry made a spluttering, inarticulate noise of surprise and half stood, pushing his chair back so that it fell over. He was soaked, his shirt front sticking to his chest, his suit jacket dark with moisture, his hair slick and dripping.

'You bitch!' he spluttered. 'You mad fuckin' cow!'

Pete had sat back, staring at the scene in disbelief.

Mandy glared at her husband. 'Well, he deserved it. Who the fuck does he think he is?'

'*Me?*' Barry snarled at her, enraged. 'Don't you play high and mighty with me, you little tart! It wasn't me screwin' around with the groom, was it?'

Pete stared at his brother a moment, taking in what he'd just said, then jerked round, looking at Mandy.

'Mand?'

Mandy gave a dismissive shrug. Seeing it, Pete looked to his brother again, his face hard.

'You're right out of order, Barry. You'd better fuckin' explain yourself.'

'You heard me,' Barry said belligerently, staring fixedly at Mandy, his eyes two tiny points of hate in his over fleshed face. 'Ask her. Go on, fuckin' ask her!'

But to Mandy's surprise, Pete didn't ask her. Instead he stood and took a swing at Barry, landing a punch full in his brother's face. At once a number of the other male guests, drawn by the raised voices, stepped in and pulled him back.

'Cool it, you two,' someone said. 'This is a fuckin' weddin'!'

But Barry wasn't finished. Dabbing at his split lip tenderly, he gestured towards Mandy. 'Ask her,' he said again. 'Go on, ask her. She's been on more fuckin' floors than a carpet layer! Talk about treadin' the boards! It's a fuckin' wonder she ain't got an arse full of splinters!'

Now Pete did stare at her, his eyes wide with disbelief, his mouth open. 'Mand?'

Mandy felt all of the fight go from her. She felt suddenly tired – tired of this charade and of the years she'd kept it up.

'Mand! Tell me it ain't true.'

But she knew she couldn't do that. And she couldn't explain. It would have taken too long. Besides, all she felt now was hurt. Hurt at being betrayed. Hurt at all those wasted years she'd spent with Pete. Hurt that some retard like Barry could just come along and blow her life away.

with a few words. Standing there, facing them across the table, she began to cry.

Pete stood there a moment, staring at her, trying to come to terms with it all, forcing himself to take it all in. Then, with a brief nod to those holding him back, he shrugged off their restraining hands and, urgently pushing through the press of bodies, made directly for Jonathan, muttering to himself as he went.

'I'm gonna fuckin' kill him!'

He almost made it, but other hands grabbed and restrained him before he could hurl himself across the table at the startled groom.

'You cunt!' he yelled, loud enough to make the dancers out in the centre of the floor jerk their heads round, surprised. 'You fuckin' prick! That was my wife, you bastard! My fuckin' wife!'

At the first sign of trouble, Susie had left Karen and made her way across. Now, as two of the men dragged Pete from the hall, Susie went around the table and stood, hands on hips, confronting Jonathan. As she did, the music from the speakers died. The hall fell silent.

'See what you've done?' she said, glaring at him. Then, raising her voice: 'See what you've fuckin' well done?'

'I'm sorry,' Joe began, aware of his parents staring at them from the far end of the table. Standing up, he took a step toward her. 'I didn't mean . . .'

The last word became an anguished howl as Susie reached out and grabbed a handful of his hair, pulling him fiercely toward her. Then, with an almost savage glee, she tugged his head forward and down, smack bang into the top layer of the three-tier wedding cake. He ploughed into it like an airplane nose-diving into a hill, his hands going out and back.

A great cheer went up. Susie turned and, with a broad smile, bowed to the watching crowd.

As Joe struggled to extricate himself from the cake, Susie walked across to where Mandy stood, blowing her nose, her mascara smeared once more. As she did the music started up again. 'Band of Gold' by Freda Payne.

'I'm sorry,' Mandy began, but Susie shook her head and reached out to hug her.

'Don't apologise to me, sweetheart. It wasn't your fault. But you'd better go and sort things out with Pete, eh?'

Mandy looked into her friend's open face and returned the briefest of smiles. 'I guess so.'

'How d'you feel?'

'Pretty awful.'

'Ah well, could 'ave been worse, eh?'

Mandy stared at her. 'How?'

Susie thought a moment, then shrugged, the gesture making both of them fall into a fit of the giggles.

'Shit!' Susie said, as they sobered up again. 'I didn't read about any of this in *Brides* magazine!'

'Yeah well,' Mandy answered, 'marriage *is* a bit like childbirth. Everyone tells you how lovely it is and nobody tells you it's more painful than shitting a three-piece suite. But then at least having a baby's over in a few hours . . .'

Susie grinned. 'Maybe I should've asked for some gas and air on me wedding list.'

The two women were silent a moment, looking at each other, smiling.

'Did I tell you I bumped into Nick the other day? You

know, Nick who used to go out with me?' Mandy said suddenly.

'The brainy one?'

Mandy nodded.

'No . . . really?'

With a little sigh, Mandy leaned across and kissed Susie's cheek. 'Thanks, Suse, but I'd better go now. Got a life to sort out.'

Susie nodded then kissed her back. 'Good luck.'

Mandy grinned. 'It can only get better . . . can't it?'

Susie watched her friend walk slowly away across the crowded hall, then turned, looking back to where Joe's mother was helping him remove bits of cake from his hair, fussing about him like an old hen.

'Yeah, and you can keep him,' she said quietly, a sudden bitterness creeping back into her mood. Then, taking a deep breath, she began to make her way back across. But she had only got halfway when an all too familiar voice made her stop in her tracks.

'. . . a right fuckin' fiasco, if you ask me. Ink's not even dry on the wedding s'tificate and she's already ballsed it up!'

Susie turned, furiously angry, spotting her father at once, but before she could say a word, before she could even take a step towards him, she saw her mother stand and, with an uncharacteristic savagery, poke her father full in the chest.

'Why don't you put a bleedin' cork in it and give that fuckin' mouth of yours a rest for once, Bob Fuller!'

Susie gasped, then, seeing the collection of empty sherry glasses at her mother's elbow, understood.

'I was only sayin'...' her father began again, but he got no further. Again, Doreen Fuller poked him hard in the chest.

'That's your bleedin' trouble, ain't it? Always got something to say, but the trouble is it's never worth bleedin' hearing! An' I 'ave to put up with it, night after bleedin' night. On and bleedin' on. And you know what? I'm soddin' glad you spend most of your time down that pub. I thank bleedin' God for it, I do!'

'Go on, Ma,' Susie said quietly, delighted that after all these years the worm had turned.

'Mum?'

Susie turned, then groaned. Lyndsay, hearing the commotion, had come across and was about to throw her three penneth into the argument.

Doreen turned to her eldest daughter and smiled. 'What d'you want, love?'

Lyndsay gave a disappointed frown, as if she were suddenly the mother. 'Language, Mum. Besides...'

'Besides what?' Doreen said, bristling now. 'It's about time someone told the old git what he was.'

You tell her, Mum, Susie said, grinning now, but not daring to get involved.

'Mu-um,' Lyndsay admonished.

'Oh, bugger off!' Doreen said finally, turning and beckoning to one of the waitresses. 'Here, love, bring us a drink, will you?'

Lyndsay stared a moment longer, then, with a move of disgust, turned on her heel and walked away.

Bob Fuller, meanwhile, had sat back, flabbergasted both by the unexpectedness and the savagery of his wife's attack on him. For once he had nothing to say.

Leaning forward in her chair, Susie's gran, Elsie now chirped up. 'Lovely dress, Susie. You look really nice in it.'

'Thanks, Nan, I got it in Harrods,' Susie replied, going round and planting a kiss on her gran's cheek. Then, out of sheer love of her, she moved across and bent down to kiss her mother.

'I'll pay for it in the morning, won't I?' Doreen whispered.

'Yeah,' Susie whispered back. 'But I bet it was worth it. I don't s'pose you've 'ad as much fun in years!'

Doreen grinned. 'Yeah. I've waited nearly fifty years to get that off me chest,' and she reached up to take the drink from the waitress who'd appeared at her elbow. 'I sure told the old sod, didn't I?'

Susie hugged her, then straightened up again. 'Gotta mix,' she said, smiling tightly at her father before turning away.

And for the first time Susie could remember, Bob Fuller made no parting remark to her back.

'Hey, are you okay, Anna?'

Anna looked up at Karen and smiled bleakly. 'I guess so,' she said, then, at her friend's questioning glance, she shrugged. 'To be honest, I feel awful.'

'Your toy boy ran off with the barbie doll, right?'

Anna laughed, then grew serious again. 'No. I dumped him. I . . . told him it wouldn't work out.'

'Ah . . .' Karen pulled out the seat beside Anna and sat. 'You want to talk about it?'

Anna smiled. 'Just like old times, huh?'

'Uhuh . . .' Karen took her hand. 'You don't mind?'

Anna looked down at where Karen's hand held her own and shook her head. 'No. And I don't think you're going to try to seduce me.'

Karen grinned. 'Good. Anyway . . . I don't fancy you.'

Anna gave her a playful push.

'So?' Karen asked. 'What happened?'

Anna sighed. 'Oh, I don't know . . . I was just looking at the two of them and . . .'

'And?'

'I'm just too old for this, Kar. I ought to have been married a long time ago. I ought to have had kids by now. My life . . . well, shit, Kar, my life's a bloody mess.'

Karen leaned in to her, her voice soft, soothing. 'No it isn't. Your life's fine. The non-emotional side of it, anyway. As for the rest, that'll come.'

'Yeah?' Anna looked down, then shrugged. 'But when? I don't know anymore, Kar. It ought to get easier, but it doesn't. I mean, just now . . . I got so jealous, looking at him. At the way he was looking at her. But when I thought about it I realised it wasn't them, together, I was jealous of, it was her. I'm jealous of how much time she's got to get it right.'

Karen squeezed her hand. 'Go on . . .'

Anna looked up. 'I realised it wasn't him I wanted. I realised . . .'

She stopped, staring past Karen's shoulder, as if she'd just seen a ghost.

'What?' Karen frowned, trying to gain her attention back, then turned, following her gaze. Through the crowd of bodies on the dance floor she could see that the main doors were open. Someone stood there.

Looking back at Anna, she was surprised to see her smiling. A strange, apprehensive smile.

'Callum?' she asked.

Anna nodded, then slowly got to her feet. As Karen watched, she walked between the guests and revellers, making her way towards the door, and as she did the figure there began to make his way toward her. They met in the middle of the dance floor.

Before she could make out the details of his face, she knew it was him. Her breath caught and she forgot at once what she had been saying, her eyes taking in the sight she'd never thought she'd ever see again.

Callum, she thought, wondering in the same instant how he'd found out where she was. She was conscious that Karen had said something; had asked her a question, but she wasn't really listening. She nodded and stood, beginning to make her way toward him, her fear changing into a strange, almost frightening hope as she saw him begin to make his way to her, his face a mirror of her own.

At the centre of the dance floor, in a space that seemed abandoned by the other dancers, they met, their hands linking without a word being spoken. For a moment they just stared at each other, a mixture of hope and fear written in both their faces. Squeezing her hands gently, he released them, and taking her shoulders, drew her in to him, the warmth and smell of him like something in a dream. For a moment she closed her eyes, content just to let him hold her, there in the centre of it all, the music, the press of bodies somehow outside of the magic circle in which they stood. And then he spoke.

'I've missed you, you know.'

She moved back slightly, looking at him, drinking in the sight of him, of those lovely eyes of his.

'And I've missed you.'

'Yeah?' That soft American accent of his sent a ripple of delight through her. 'And there's something else . . . I love you, Anna.'

'Yes?' Her voice was so small it was a wonder he heard her.

'And I want to marry you.'

She closed her eyes, her top teeth biting into her lip, then put her mouth to his ear. 'I love you, Callum.'

He turned his face slowly and kissed her softly. It was the barest brushing together of their lips, even so, it made her shiver with desire for him. 'And?' he said, drawing his face back only enough so that he could see her.

'And yes,' she said. 'I will marry you. And have your babies and . . .'

He put his finger to her lips. 'I didn't say . . .'

'No,' she said. 'It's what I want. I was wrong. I . . . I got it all wrong. I . . .' And suddenly she burst into tears.

'What is it?' he asked, holding her, bewildered now, his hands stroking her back. 'What have I said?'

'It's nothing,' she said, looking up at him through misted eyes. 'It's just that I'm happy. And I never thought I'd be happy . . . ever again.'

'Then that's good,' he said, and kissed her again – this time letting his mouth linger over hers, their bodies pressing close, moulding together like the old times.

Janet stood in the far corner of the room, away from the bar, listening as Lyndsay told her the latest gossip. Yet after the last few days' events Janet was only vaguely aware of what she was saying. Instead her mind kept going back, to the hen night dinner, to the club they'd gone on to afterwards, to meeting Susie in the flower shop, and, still prominent in her memory, to that morning and her own disappointment. *Life's strange*, she thought. *I used to think it was so cut and dried, but now . . . well, now I know nothing.*

'. . . so, anyway,' Lyndsay said, 'it wasn't until they got back that they realised the bugger had ripped them off. Four hundred quid it cost, and all they got was the case!'

Janet laughed, then realised that she shouldn't have laughed and quickly covered her gaff. 'That's a shame,' she said, watching as Lyndsay's Jodie came across and began to tug at her mother's skirt.

'Well, when they went back there, he was gone. Naturally.'

Again Jodie tugged at her mother's skirt. 'Mum, Mum . . . will you dance with me?'

Lyndsay half turned and made a shooing motion. 'Go an' ask your dad. He's doin' nothing.'

Janet saw the disappointment in the young girl's face. Saw how she turned and began to make her way back toward the dance floor, her shoulders sagging, when suddenly someone moved past her and, taking Jodie's hand, pulled her gently round then knelt beside her.

It was her Steve.

She watched, mesmerised, Lyndsay's voice a distant murmuring, as Jodie's face lit up in a broad beam of delight. She nodded, then, as Steve got to his feet, did a full curtsey before taking his hand again and walking out onto the dance floor.

She watched, a lump rising in her throat, as Steve gently twirled the little girl round the dance floor, then lifted her, so that her head was on his level, their arms outstretched in a kind of mock-waltz. Steve was smiling broadly and Jodie was giggling now. Slowly they turned, dreamlike in the glare of the flashing disco lights, and as they did, Janet felt an overwhelming love for him, knowing in that instant that, whatever happened, everything would be all right.

I love you, she said silently, then, on impulse, blew him a kiss. He saw and blew one back, and Jodie, seeing it, put a hand out to draw his face round so that he was looking at her.

Janet laughed, then let out a long, contented sigh of happiness. It was going to be all right. As long as they had each other, it was all going to be all right.

Walking slowly through the entrance lobby Mandy leaned against the door leading into the hall, facing inward but seeing nothing. She felt detached from her surroundings, as though her body were part of this unreality while the rest of her were elsewhere. As the music pulsed through her head, she tried to think back, to go over the conversation she had just had, to comprehend the consequences of it.

When she had emerged from the hall Pete had been sitting on the low wall opposite, his head in his hands. Sensing her there, he had looked up and there had been such sorrow in his eyes Mandy heard herself whimper as she made to speak, as she tried to explain.

She had been surprised by his lack of anger – she had expected it, and part of her would have welcomed it – but it seemed that for both of them her revelation brought relief as well as misery. And she hated herself for resenting that he should feel that relief too, that he didn't, even in some small way, still love her; yes, and despised herself for wanting it all.

They both knew it was over. It wasn't the affair, they both acknowledged that. If it was just the sex they could probably have dealt with it, could have patched things up. But no. It was something irreparable. There was simply no love between them any longer; not even any real affection. Nothing. They were just a habit for each other, and one that Mandy knew she had to break. Her only regret was that she hadn't done it earlier.

The outside doors had been propped open to let in some air and as the cool night breeze washed over her, she imagined it blowing away the wasted years of despair, cleansing her, preparing her for a new phase of her life.

A dog wandered in and Mandy watched it as it meandered through the hall, pulling scraps of food from discarded plates before finally stopping to piss up the leg of the top table, creating havoc as children chased it around the room. The faces of her sons kept flashing into her mind and she felt a tear trickle down the side of her nose. Above all she kept hearing Luke's voice and a current favourite phrase. 'Get a life!' he'd say. 'Get a life!'. Well, he hadn't aimed it at her, but Mandy felt that in the end they would both see that she had no option; if she was going to survive, she would have to leave home. To set up somewhere else.

Reaching down she unclipped the flap of her shoulder

bag and pushing her hand inside she searched around the pockets. Feeling the slip of paper between her fingers she smiled weakly before replacing it; she had no need to look for Nick's number, it had already been committed to memory.

Up on stage Simon Paxman spoke softly into the DJ's microphone, announcing that it was last orders at the bar and that there would be just two more records before the bride's father saw the celebrations out with a song. The announcement was greeted with good-natured jeering as the floor emptied and the crowd moved like a wave towards the bar. Hobbling along at the rear was Bob Fuller, empty glass in hand.

'What's the matter with your dad, Suse?' Karen called to Susie, who was standing a little way off, watching her father cross the room.

Susie screeched, suddenly remembering that with all that had gone on she'd forgotten to tell everyone.

'Oh, God, it was *so* funny,' she said, eager now to get it out. 'It 'appened this morning. The silly old sod moaned about 'aving to wear a new shirt – said it'd rub his neck. Said he wanted me mum to iron his best white one. 'Course, good as gold, she gets out the board and she's standing there, in a world of her own, when he,' she nodded towards her father who was now standing at the bar, 'comes up on her like creeping fuckin' Jesus and stands there at the end of the ironing board. She's running the iron up the length of the shirt when she suddenly sees him there. Frightened the fuckin' life out of her! Anyway, she pushes the iron right off the end of the board and . . . guess what it lands on?'

Karen shook her head and Chris sat there open-mouthed, fascinated.

'His willy!' she shrieked. 'The dozy bastard was standing there in the altogether and the fuckin' iron landed on his dick!'

'Oh my God!' Karen exclaimed, clamping her hand over her mouth. 'Your poor old dad.'

'Yeah, poor old dad,' Susie said quietly and as she caught Karen's eye the two of them burst out laughing.

'Who told you, your mum?' Karen said, wiping a tear from the corner of her eye, leaning in towards Chris.

Susie nodded. 'Well, he wouldn't, would he?'

'What did you say?'

'I asked her if she managed to get all the creases out?' This time all three women clung together, convulsed with laughter.

'What's the joke?' Mandy asked, bending down and poking her head in between those of her friends.

'Aw, it's a good one, Mand. I'll tell you later,' Susie said, and she reached up to squeeze her hand. 'Here, I meant to say, 'ave you 'ad a look at the photos? They're over on the top table with that slimy little what's-his-name?'

'Photographer,' Karen suggested helpfully, giggling.

'Yeah, photographer. There's some crackers of you, Mand,' Susie said, trying to keep a straight face.

'In technicolour,' Karen added.

'Aw, piss off the pair of you,' Mandy said, playfully pushing their heads together, and the three of them laughed while Chris looked on, an outsider.

Suddenly conscious that she might be feeling excluded, Karen quickly turned to her. 'Sorry. You two haven't really been introduced have you? Chris, this is

Mandy. Mandy, Chris,' and she looked from one to the other.

The two women smiled at each other across the table, Mandy stopping herself just in time from committing the *faux pas* of saying she thought Chris was a man. She'd obviously got it wrong.

'Have you seen Anna?' Karen said to fill the awkward moment of silence, tipping her head in the direction of the dance floor.

'Blimey! He's a bit of all right!' Susie leered, looking over her shoulder at Callum as he and Anna clung together in the middle of the hall beyond a row of forty-somethings looking faintly absurd as they thrust their pelvises and shook their butts to Wigfield's 'Saturday night'. 'But he's not the bloke she came with, is he?' she asked, confused now.

Karen smiled as she shook her head, prolonging the revelation.

'He's pretty bloody gorgeous, whoever he is,' Mandy observed wistfully. 'I wonder if he's got a brother?'

They laughed together, watching the couple as they barely moved to the music.

'Go on, Kar, who is he?'

Karen waited a moment. 'Callum!'

'*No!*' Mandy and Susie said in unison, their eyes wide with disbelief. But before they could ask for an explanation Janet rushed over, leaning down to invade the circle.

'Okay, you lot, shake a leg!'

'What?' Karen said, looking baffled.

'Get yourselves on to the dance floor. He's putting on the last record and I've made a request.'

'What've you asked for?' Mandy asked, straightening up.

'You'll see,' Janet said, grinning down at them. 'Now, shift yourselves!'

'I can't dance in this,' Karen protested, pulling at the skirt of her dress.

'Don't be a silly cow,' Susie said, pushing back her chair. 'If I can, so can you.'

Karen looked imploringly to Chris, who simply nudged her, saying, 'Go on, you dance with your friends.'

'You sure?'

''Course I'm sure,' and they exchanged such a tender smile that the others looked away in embarrassment.

'Right!' Susie said, unpinning her veil and throwing it onto the seat; 'I'm ready!'

'I'll grab Anna,' Janet said, marching onto the dance floor beneath the amused gaze of her friends. They all smiled across at Callum as Anna pointed them out and, tipping an imaginary hat, he obligingly made his way to the edge of the floor.

Before half a dozen notes had left the speakers, there was a howl of recognition from the five as they rushed, grinning, into the middle of the floor, the Four Tops' 'Reach Out I'll Be There' blasting out, filling the hall with its unforgettable tune. In an instant the years were swept aside as they sang the familiar words, and danced the steps they'd committed to memory long ago; only now the song held a special poignancy for each of them. And as the music rang out, all of them mouthing the words across the circle, there was an unspoken bond between the five of them. They knew that, no matter what, they would always be there for each other.

As the DJ signed off and the lights stopped flashing, Bob Fuller struggled up onto the stage. Most people stayed on the dance floor, motionless as they awaited the final song. Susie felt a hand on her shoulder but before she could turn she felt Joe's face on her neck.

'Susie, I'm so sorry,' he said quietly.

She didn't reply.

'I just panicked,' he said shakily. 'It was just a fling. I promise. Nothing more.'

Still she maintained her silence.

'I do love you, you know,' he whispered, pushing himself against her back.

Susie shivered, feeling the tears begin to burn at the back of her eyes she fought to contain them – yes, as she'd done throughout the day. Her big day. Slowly she turned to face him.

'I wanted it to be so special,' she said simply, a deep hurt replacing the anger in her eyes.

Joe hung his head, the full weight of his shame bearing down on him.

Susie sighed. 'I just thought that this time things would be different. I thought *you* were different.'

'It was a mistake, Susie,' he said, his eyes moist now. 'A big mistake. Marriage, the wedding and everything . . . it all happened so fast . . .'

'Regretting it already are you?'

He shook his head. 'The only thing I regret is hurting you. If I could turn the clock back . . .'

'Great wedding,' Simon slurred, bumping into them. 'Before I forget, I've left the telemessages on the top table with the photos and the horseshoes and so on.' He made to stumble away again but turned back. 'Oh,

I meant to say, Susie. Max called last night and said to wish you all the best. Said he was sorry he couldn't be here. He also said something about not sending the present he'd promised because he thought you deserved something better. That's Max for you — a real softee!'

Susie smiled weakly then turned back to Joe, lifting her face towards her husband's, their lips meeting, their passion for each other undeniable despite all that had happened.

As they broke from the kiss she drew her face back, scowling at him. 'If you ever, *ever*, do anything like that again, it's over. D'you understand that?'

He gave a brief nod, like a chastised schoolboy in front of the head teacher, then kissed her again.

Karen beckoned Chris over and they stood side by side, their shoulders and arms touching, as they waited for the song. Beside them Janet and Steve held hands and as Mandy made to leave the floor Janet grabbed hold of her arm and pulled her back.

'Oh, no you don't,' she said as they each put an arm around her shoulders. 'You're staying with us tonight.'

As Mandy looked up at them she was on the verge of tears, knowing that the unreality of the day was almost at an end. Even so, she managed a smile.

'Did I tell you I bumped into Nick Laker yesterday?' she said. 'As I was going to catch the bus . . .'

'Yeah?' Janet said, meaning to ask her about it, but before she could the piano struck up. Bob Fuller cleared his throat, and, his legs held awkwardly apart, leaned in to the microphone and warbled the opening bars of his favourite song.

'Who's sorry now . . . Who's sorry now . . .'

POCKET BOOKS

A SELECTED LIST OF TITLES AVAILABLE FROM POCKET BOOKS

THE PRICES SHOWN BELOW WERE CORRECT AT THE TIME OF GOING TO PRESS. HOWEVER POCKET BOOKS RESERVE THE RIGHT TO SHOW NEW RETAIL PRICES ON COVERS WHICH MAY DIFFER FROM THOSE PREVIOUSLY ADVERTISED IN THE TEXT OR ELSEWHERE.

All Pocket Books titles are available by post from:

Book Service By Post, P.O. Box 29, Douglas, Isle of Man IM99 1BQ

Credit cards accepted. Please telephone 01624 675137, fax 01624 670923, Internet http://www.bookpost.co.uk or e-mail: bookshop@enterprise.net for details.

Free postage and packing in the UK. Overseas customers allow £1 per book (paperbacks) and £3 per book (hardbacks).